Turn our Eyes Away

By

Zoe Zorka

W & B Publishers
USA

Turn Our Eyes Away © 2014 All rights reserved
by Zoe Zorka

W & B Publishers

For information:
W & B Publishers
Post Office Box 193
Colfax, NC 27235
www.a-argusbooks.com

ISBN: 978-0-6922583-9-2
ISBN: 0-6922583-9-6

Book Cover designed by Sophia Olson

Printed in the United States of America

Part I

I'm a broken soul, I'm an open book.
With many torn out pages.
And I walk through fire, but I thirst
for truth.
For what I've never tasted.
And it calls to me again.
The comfort of the sin.

I got a war inside, with a flag in
hand.
I'll wait to cry surrender.
While the pride in me, is fighting
who I am.
Why is it that I linger?
I guess every man decides to take or
save a life.

Turn our eyes away, turn our eyes
away.
From this path we've taken, washing
clean our faces.
Turn our eyes away, turn our eyes
away.
Leaning on the hope that, one day,
even we,
One day even we will be saved.

-Trent Dabbs, Turn Our Eyes Away

Detroit, MI- A Detroit area woman was found dead this morning in her home after a 911 call reported finding the body. The woman, whose name has not yet been released, but appears to be in her late twenties, was pronounced dead at the scene. Investigators are questioning "persons of interest" in the case, but have not yet named any official suspects or ruled whether it was suicide or homicide. More details to follow.

\

DETROIT POLICE DEPARTMENT Case 07013091911

█████████████

911 CALL, DECEMBER 20, 21:34 EST

911 Operator: 911, what's your emergency?

Caller: Oh my god, oh my god….she's
                  dead. Oh my god, there's blood
                  everywhere…I can't [inaudible
                  00:00:08]

911 Operator: Ma'm, you'll have to slow down.
                  Has someone been hurt?

Caller: I think she's dead. [sobbing]
                  Yeah, she's definitely [expletive]
                  dead. [Expletive] I can't believe
                  this!

911 Operator: Can you give me your location?

911 CALL, DECEMBER 20, 21:34 EST

Caller: ████████ ....it's just right by [inaudible 00:00:50] crossroad is [inaudible 00:00:52] Oh my God, it's all my fault...I did this...

911 Operator: Ma'am, help is on the way. What did you do?

Caller: I didn't mean for this [inaudible 00:00:59]. I didn't...realize it was [inaudible 00:01:01]

911 Operator: OK, just calm down. Help is on the way. Is there anyone else in the house? Ma'am? Are you still with me?

Caller: I don't think anyone's here

911 Operator: The police should be arriving any minute now.

Caller: I think I'm gonna be sick. I've
                   never seen a dead body.
                   [inaudible 00:01:17]

911 Operator: Ma'am, I want you to remain as
                   calm as possible and don't touch
                   anything. I want you to remain
                   there and wait for law
                   enforcement to arrive.

Caller: I think the cops are here. The
                   door's open. I'm gonna go meet
                   them outside.

911 Operator: Stay calm and keep your hands
                   where the police can see them

[inaudible voices 00:05:17]

DETROIT POLICE DEPARTMENT INTERNAL TRANSCRIPT

Case 07013091

December 21

CP – Captain Dinesh Patel

SG – Sgt. Lisa Giles

SG – Sgt. Amanda Davis

SG – Sgt. Michael Polchenski

DP – Detective Carmine Polizzi

PA – Patrolman Muhammed Aminosharie

PA – Patrolman Wesley Bryant

SG: The date right now is December 21 and the time is 0015 hours. We have Captain Dinesh Patel, Sgt. Lisa Giles, Sgt. Amanda Davis, Sgt. Michael Polchenski, Detective Carmine Polizzi, and Patrolman Muhammed Aminosharie, and Patrolman Wesley Bryant who were the arresting officers on the scene. The suspect is in, um,

4

custody, and we are debriefing before Detective
Polizzi holds the interview.

[inaudible background voices and noises]

CP: Can someone tell me what the hell's going on?
Who called this in?

[sounds of papers and typing]

SG: The suspect, sir. The 911 call came from her cell
phone at-

DP: Wait, *she* called it in? And she, you say she
confessed?

CP: The suspect is female?

PA: Yes, sir. Sergeant Davis has already-

CP: Witnesses?

[inaudible voices]

CP: Dammit. And she's waived a lawyer?

SG: Yeah, apparently so. [Phone ringing] Look, there's
already people- I don't know, family, friends,

outside. She must have called someone else because-

CP: Goddamnit. Where's her cell phone? Didn't you take it before you booked her?

SD: Sir, she could have texted while on the 911 call. Most smartphones let you-

CP: Where's her smartphone now? We need to do this by the book or else she walks. Does everyone understand?

[inaudible voices 00:03:15]

PA: Her phone and possessions were entered into evidence immediately after her arrest. She had her phone, an iPad, a wallet with several credit cards, ID's, and $56 cash. She also had what appears to be makeup and a hair thing-

CP: Jesus Christ, ask fucking Davis what that is-

SD: It's a-

PA: And the 9 mm handgun with ah, I believe, a full round in the clip.

6

CP: Where'd she get that? Was it fired?

SG: It's apparently registered to a family member. She does appear to have a C and C permit but not for that particular weapon, so we *might* be able to hold her on that. The gun is being processed as we-

[Sound of knocking]

Female: Sir, I have two individuals claiming to be the suspect's lawyers and demanding to speak with her. I also have several self-described friends and one very angry-

CP: Well, get them in fucking interview rooms before we have another homicide tonight! Christ, why couldn't this have landed in St. Clair Shores? Is the gun a federal offense?

SG: I don't know.

CP: Find out. The last thing we need is the Feds and their [inaudible 00:06:13]

[CP's phone ringing]

CP: Polizzi, start interviewing our girl. Make sure you get the waiver signed *before* you begin.

DP: Yes sir.

CP: Drugs? Alcohol? Bath salts?

PA: Waiting on blood test. Initial Breathalyzer report at scene showed .001. No drugs or paraphernalia were found on her person.

CP: No priors? [inaudible 00:06:56] Giles and Polenchski- start interviewing the friends.

SG: All of them?

CP: As many as you can. And Polizzi- after you get that signed, I want you to get her passcodes for her phone, iPad, and whatever other electronic devices these kids have today. Let's make it *very* clear to her that it's in her best interest to provide her passcodes unless she wants to add obstruction charges to her growing resume.

DP: Yes sir.

CP: I need Davis start working with crime lab to process all electronic evidence from suspect and victim. I want their texts, tweets, updates, photos, snaps, documents- anything and everything relevant to the case. Check for apps that are really hidden folders.

Look through the history on *all* browsers. That's how they missed nailing Casey Anthony.

SD: Sir, that may take some-

CP: I'll approve the overtime for tech. Then I want the *victim's* computer, phone, iPad, iWatch, Google glasses whatever the kids now have- all brought down and processed immediately as well. Is that understood?

[inaudible 00:07:15]

CP: I don't think I need to remind everyone about the sensitive nature of this case. We have a crime involving two white females who apparently knew each other. Am I right on that?

SG: It appears so based on initial reports of um, the arresting officers.

CP: I need those reports completed within the hour.

PA: Yes sir.

CP: *No one* talks to the press. You know how it is with this thing- those damn vultures will be circling any minute now for the fucking morning news. Holiday

shopping rush and homicide on Detroit's East side.
A white woman is dead, which means that
Christmas came early for at least one of these
jackass pseudo-journalists.

[muffled laughter]

CP: Giles and Polenchski- I want you to *encourage* any
      of the friends you interview to share their texts with
      the victim or suspect as well.

SG: What should we tell the friends?

CP: Nothing. I want them knowing as little as possible.
      You don't know anything as far as they're
      concerned.

SG: Play dumb, copy that.

CP: I'm serious. We need to handle this with kid
      gloves. I want SITREPs within the hour from
      everyone. I'm going to personally observe
      Detective Polizzi's interview.

[Phone ringing]

DETROIT POLICE DEPARTMENT INTERVIEW WITH
██████████ Case 07013091

██████████ interview December 21, 0115 EST

Detective Polizzi: For the record, you have been read your Miranda rights and you've waived a lawyer, is that correct?

██████████:   Yeah

DP: I'm going to need you to sign this for me. You can take some time to look it over.

[Suspect signs]

DP: Let it be noted that the suspect waived her right to a lawyer at 0217 Eastern Standard Time. Can I get you anything? Water? Soda?

██:   No

DP: So what can you tell me about tonight? (Extended pause) Look, you're gonna have to give me something. Did you kill ████████████?

██:   [suspect shakes head]

DP: Now you know we have the 911 tapes. Is this your voice?

[DP Plays clip of tape]

DP: I need a yes or no. A headshake isn't gonna cut it. I need a verbal yes or no.

██:   [inaudible 00:01:18]

DP: I can't hear you.

██:   Yes

DP: So just to be clear, you can confirm this was you on the tape saying it was your fault?

██:   I said it was my fault, yeah, I guess it is...sorta....[suspect puts head on table]

DP: The weapon found in your purse- is that yours?

██:   Yes

DP: Did you intend to use it when you drove to ████ ██████'s house tonight?

██:   [shakes head]

DP: Yes or no.

█:   No

DP: So why did you go over there?

█:   I just wanted to talk to her.

DP: And you knew the victim because she was-

█:   No, no. [Suspect begins crying] I knew her from a long [inaudible 00:02:13]

[Knock on door]

DP: Hold on one second.

[Muffled voices]

DP: Your iPad and iPhone are both locked with passcodes. You can save us some trouble and give us those codes or we can have our techs unlock them. It would be in your best interest to cooperate.

█:   0604

DP: Both?

[Suspect nods]

DP: You realize that any electronic evidence can be used against you the same as physical evidence, correct?

█:   Yeah, I know

Case Number

07013091

Item Number

314

Pouch Number

3 of 81

Evidence Room Location # 19C

Description of Evidence

Electronic Journal of Oda Mizra retrieved from cloud drive
on iPad (item number 28)

	Date Recovered
Detroit Police Department	21 December

Page 1 of 174

October 10

"Do you think one word can change someone's life?"

I paused, stopped applying my lip liner, and turned away
from the mirror to face Marissa, who was lying on her
stomach on my bed reading the latest issue of some
women's magazine.

Electronic Journal of Oda Mizra

File Name: MPJ-701_Reflection Journal

"Why are you reading that?" I admonished her, taking a sip of my Vernors before returning to my reflection in the mirror and applying Mac's latest gloss color with surgical precision.

Without missing a beat, I continued.

"You realize those magazines are targeted at the lowest common denominator of society? The average American woman reads at a grade eight reading level, and now you are too. Those magazines are retarded, therefore I refuse to buy into the false, over-blown, misaligned, self-confidence delusion they propagate."

"Um, OK, apparently someone's been reading a thesaurus," she replied, pronouncing it *the-sir-us*, tearing out a page of shoes.

I started to correct it, but realized it would be useless. Marissa is sweet, but just slightly smarter than the brightest *Jersey Shore* cast mate.

"You know who reads those magazines? The pathetic lonely women of America as they eat their *Lean Cuisine for One* and pin ideas to a Pinterest wedding board for a wedding that will only happen in their imagination," I continued, turning to the side and grabbing a loose handful of stomach fat. Disgusting.

"You made fun of me for Pinterest! Let me have that dream wedding to Ryan Gosling!" she mock cried.

"Didn't he have a kid with Eva Longoria?" I asked, running the flatiron through my hair. "And I have Pinterest. I'm

@oliviamizra. You should add me. I don't have any friends yet.

"It's Eva *Mendes*. Did you do it to make a wedding board for your and Ashley's wedding? Because there 's these shoes that I could wear with my bridesmaid dress."

"Oh, give me that," I snapped, yanking it from her hand. "What's *this* bullshit? Those shoes are not only ugly, but also $950. Please enlighten me about your new sugar daddy or your escort occupation. Plus, you're a nurse. If you showed up to work looking like the model in the 'career' section, and yes, I can't say 'career' and the name of this magazine together with a straight face, your male co-workers would think someone hired you for a bachelor party."

I paused for dramatic effect before lighting up again.

"Wait! Are you also doing bachelorette parties as "Naughty Nurse"? Oh, *please, please*, let me come!"

"Bitch," she giggled, throwing a pillow at me.

"Don't bump into me while I'm doing this. I don't want to have to redo it all."

I pinched my stomach and inspected it closer. My stomach definitely looks like that of a 60-year-old woman- flabby and crepey. Absolutely heinous.

I turned sideways in the mirror, grabbing more of my olive-skinned flesh between my hands. I sighed. I definitely got my dad's Middle Eastern genes, which weren't always a bad thing. Despite towering over most other girls at 5'8," my waist to hip ratio was nice, although I would have preferred it if my ample rear end were possibly a little bit smaller. My long black hair, which came almost to my rib cage, had never once been dyed and my dark lashes negated any need for mascara. I had dark brown eyes, but I always wished for blue ones like my mom and brother. I tried the color contacts once, but they didn't really work. My eyes ended up looking a dull shade of gray. I peered closer into the mirror and obsessively tweezed a stray hair between my eyebrows. Lifting my right eyebrow with my left hand, I looked for any more stray hairs that the lady at the salon may have missed.

"Yeah, it's like *you're* performing open heart surgery over there. Can I have my magazine back?" she asked.

I turned the page, comparing my elbow skin to the model's on the page. "Oh look here, it says, and I quote, '*all* women are beautiful.' Come on, that's just lying. There are many heinous females in this world. They should be *told* they're heinous. It builds character."

I rolled my eyes, tossed the magazine back at her, returned to the mirror, this time painstakingly sectioning off and flat ironing my hair- again. Despite highly cognitive task, I was still able to multitask, so I continued.

"Is your hair naturally that black?" Marissa asked.

"No, you twit. I'm a ginger," I replied sarcastically.

"Then you have no soul. Which may be true."

I shushed her and picked up my lip liner. "Look, if I don't get this lip thing perfect, then I have kitten ass. Do you know what that is?"

"No, enlighten me."

"When old ladies put on dark lipstick, and it gets into the old lady wrinkles around their lips, it looks like the wrong end of a cat."

She shook her head in pure disbelief.

"You're not old-"

I shushed her. "Shhhh. I'm closer to 30 than 20 and that is enough reason to be depressed. Plus, I gained half a pound this week."

"So that makes you what- 95.5 pounds?"

"One fifteen," I replied with a tone of disgust. "If I keep gaining a pound a week at this rate, I'll be celebrating my 30th birthday on a motorized scooter."

"You wouldn't have to worry about falling down drunk then."

"Fact. "

"You could always wear light lipstick like me," she suggested.

I turned towards her. "Seriously? I'm Assyrian."

"I thought you were Kurdish-" she interrupted me.

"Same thing," I muttered, not willing to explain the difference between the Christian minority groups currently residing in the semi-autonomous region of northern Iraq.

"I mean, since the half of the people that I work with that *don't* think I'm a terrorist think that I'm Mexican, I guess that would work. Frosted pink lips and Sharpied eyebrows? Yeah, kitten ass would look pretty good. You're Mexican, but somehow so white that half the time I think I need to call Zak Bagans to come exorcise this place."

"Hey, do you ever get weirded out being here...you know? Because..." She cocked her head towards the spare bedroom across the hall. The door was closed. Like always.

I shrugged and started shimmying my way into my dress. "I mean, I'm not gonna lie and say the nights Ashley's not here that I maybe don't sleep with the lights on and barricade myself in here with a dresser. I always make sure the .9 is loaded, but I think I'm more worried about robberies. This *is* Detroit after all..."

"Grosse Pointe," she corrected, in her best British accent. She's right. An address in Grosse Pointe- even the edge of it- commanded a certain amount of respect.

"This wasn't his room," I replied, holding up my phone for the obligatory Snapchat selfie. "His was across the hall. I refuse to sleep in there. I mean, that's where..."

She nodded.

I changed the subject quickly.

"And what bullshit are you reading about words and stuff? I can tolerate the fashion and beauty crap they mass-produce, but they really need to leave the $4.99 life coaching advice out of there," I retorted.

"This was written by a PhD. It's about women who had someone say something nice *or* mean that changed their lives."

She started to read, but I turned towards her, narrowing my eyes.

"Uh oh," she said, shirking back, trying to feign fear while disguising laughter. "That's **the look**. You're about to unleash the intellectual beast on me, aren't you?"

I crossed my arms and glared at the magazine as if it had personally accused my mother of giving head for a cheap crack rock.

"I'm *sure* it was an *excellent* work of the *highest* literary standards. In fact, I'm *so sure* that woman didn't get her degree online at all from University of Phoenix and she is highly successful in her practice. She didn't want to write a silly little paper for an *academic peer-reviewed professional journal,* so she wrote three pages using small words and lots of pictures. How many years have I been writing for the Recorder?"

"Two?" she guessed.

"Correction, fourteen months, but close. In less than a year, I will have my Masters in Journalism as well. If I ever wrote as poorly as that, I'd be laughed out of the newsroom. Plus," I continued, vigorously applying lotion to my elbows, "Those magazines want to make women feel good about themselves so they'll continue to buy them. It's like vanity sizing at stores. You think a 160-pound woman is a size four? No, but if she can get into a size four at Forever 21, she's going to shop there. You think most readers of those magazines lives aren't completely pointless? They are. But as long as those magazines tell them how much they are loved, something their daddy never did, they'll continue to buy them. I'm sick of the inflated sense of self-importance they give women."

"They're just trying to give girls confidence-"

I cut her off. "People say stuff every day. The lady at the grocery store told me I was pretty. Am I going to drop everything to pursue a modeling career? No, because I don't like water going up my nose, let alone coke. That's why I don't like snorting my Adderall or jumping off diving boards. I can't deal with a chapped nose in the winter, let alone a coke nose year round. Plus, I've got to deal with reality, not someone trying to boost my confidence."

"But maybe she was just-"

I continued. "A more *realistic* statement would have been, 'You're pretty, but at only 5'8" and already an ancient relic at 27, you should probably take up a more appropriate hobby, like knitting.' Or Pinteresting."

Marissa laughed. "OK, any time I compliment you, I'll follow up with a caveat. Speaking of," she continued as she got off the bed. "That dress looks nice on you, but it would look better on me."

"No it wouldn't. You're seven inches shorter than me. It would be too long. See, there's me telling how it is."

She mumbled something from inside the closet, but I paid it no attention. I was too busy rubbing lotion into my creepy old lady elbows in a vain effort to fight off my demise towards middle age.

"Actually, I make it a point to tell it how it is. Like today." I paused for dramatic effect, "I bumped into some breeder's stupid stroller in Starbucks. She called me a bitch. Do you see me crying?"

"Wait," Marissa interrupted, poking her head out from the closet. "I know you didn't let that go. Let me guess, you called her fat?" she asked, laughing wickedly, knowing me too well.

I rolled my eyes. "Um, *no*. That would have been way too easy. Instead, I politely apologized for bumping into her granddaughter."

Marissa looked at me quizzically for a second before the realization hit her and she burst out laughing.

(It only took her five seconds. She's getting smarter by the day.)

"*Oh my God! You bitch!* That's hilarious! What did she say?"

"Meh, nothing really. But I've got twenty bucks saying she went home and burned that LL Bean coat and made a Botox appointment stat. Now hurry up, we have to leave here in an hour."

Marissa flopped back down on the bed and groaned. "Why do we have to go to this stupid art show? Are you going to buy anything?"

"Marissa, some of us are cultured and appreciate the finer things in life."

"You order mozzarella sticks at almost every meal," she pointed out, getting up to put on her dress.

"I'm thrifty. Oh, I've got an idea, why don't I write an article about that? It will be a Pulitzer winner for sure. All the money I've saved has allowed me to buy the fabulous dress you're going to see me in tonight."

"OK, how does this look?" she asked, turning around modeling her dress.

"I fucking hate you," I retorted. "*Akilu*- it means man eater. That's what we'd call you."

"That good, huh? Well, I'm going to accessorize it with your gold cross necklace since you aren't wearing it tonight."

"No!" I shouted.

"Why not?"

"Because it was my grandma's. On my dad's side. They were the Christian minority in Iraq- and that made them targets for violence and persecution. We didn't bring much stuff over from there when we came to the U.S. It was broken, but my ex-boyfriend Jeremy paid to get it fixed. I only wear it on special occasions."

"Ok, how about the silver horseshoe?"

"That's fine," I replied, adjusting my dress- a purple sparkly number from Bebe. I looked in the full-length mirror and sighed.

"I look like Amazon woman next to you," I said, turning around to analyze my back, thigh, and arm fat from a 360-degree angle. "My shoulders are so big- I heard there are going to be some pretty big names at this art show tonight. Maybe Jim Caldwell will show up and recruit me to play defensive line for the Lions."

"You wouldn't have to worry about student loans then," she pointed out, plugging in her hot rollers to heat them up.

"Come stand next to me," I said.

"I'm not playing this game," she responded.

"Yes you are, because I'm driving."

She emitted a deflated sigh and stood next to me. "You look gorgeous. If I were as tall as you and had those long legs and huge boobs, I'd probably just be a porn actress."

"Thank you for that sound career advice," I replied, unfazed. "But seriously, OK, my back fat is spilling over and look at my gross knees and bony elbows. From the back, I look like a middle age woman. You look fifteen-"

"I'm barely five feet! I'm technically supposed to be in a booster seat!" she protested, attempting to flee the scene and continue getting ready.

I yanked her back.

"Do I look like a drag queen? Or a cougar? Seriously, people are going to think I'm your mom. That guy last week thought I was really old."

"He thought you were 28!"

"Um, yeah, older than I am. He was probably repulsed by my elbows."

"You're barely 27. Plus, you told him you're almost a real writer. Excuse him for not thinking you were 19. What's your current carding rate?"

I rolled my eyes and flipped my hand, signaling for her to leave the mirror. "Seventy percent."

"Then what are you whining about? Hurry up, because I need you to show me where you keep your coats." She paused as if remembering something. "Hey, I was going to ask. What are all of those boxes doing in your spare bedroom?"

"Ugh, those are my things from my parents' and grandma's houses. My mom said it's a lot of Halloween decorations that I can put up, plus other miscellaneous crap. They had to move it to make room *for the baby*," I said, sarcastically mocking my mother's voice every time she mentioned her precious grand daughter.

Marissa realized she had hit a nerve. "How is the baby?" she asked.

"Fine I guess," I shrugged. "She's what...six months old? I mean, I guess she's healthy and good. Of course, now that my socially inept brother and whorebag sister both have children, suddenly she's Mother Theresa, he's Jesus, and I'm the sixth horseman of the Apocalypse. "

"Jesus didn't-"

I put my fingers together in a zipping motion- her cue to shut the fuck up. "Thank you for that religious history lesson. I just don't get it, right?" I asked, putting on my coat and handing one to Marissa.

"She's a stupid *bagara*, essentially a cow, goes and gets knocked up by some dude she meets at Thirsty Thursday, has an illegitimate child, and yet my parents are still on my ass about every little thing I do wrong. I'm seriously never going to be good enough for them. Or anyone for that matter. My parents feel like they wasted all of this money coming to America only to have me fail."

"Yes you are. Have you set a date for your wedding yet? I'm sure you're ready to *finally* lose your virginity," she joked, rifling through my closet.

"Probably sometime next summer," I replied, slipping on a heel, then kicking it off and replacing it with another.

"I want to wait until I've graduated so that I don't have coursework hanging over my head. Then we can let the deflowering commence," I said, winking.

She nodded her head as she pulled a coat out of a pile of clothes on the floor. "Hey, I like this coat. Why do you never wear it?"

"It was my sister's. Taline sent a bunch of her clothes to me from when she was skinny, but she's shorter than me, so a lot don't fit lengthwise. Some might be in those boxes. Tomorrow we can go through them and you can take what you want. We'll disinfect it, but I still recommend you get a prescription for Valtrex."

Suddenly, a door slammed behind me and a voice boomed, "What did I hear? There's *organizing* on the agenda for tomorrow? Because I intend to spend it watching football and drinking beer!"

I turned around to see Ashley, my fiancé simultaneously kick off his shoes, throw his coat over a chair, drop his open gym bag on the floor causing the contents to spill out with one hand, and open a bag of chips with the other.

I glared at him. "Are you just going to leave that there?"

"Mmmm-hmmm," he mumbled through a mouthful of chips. "I'll pick it up later."

I threw up my hands in frustration. "Seriously? You know I try really hard to keep this place clean! What would people think of us if they saw this mess? Do you want people thinking we just moved out of the doublewide? I'm really sorry your mom picked up after you. I guess I'm an inferior woman," I commented as I returned his sweaty socks to his gym back and put everything in the closet.

"Awww, don't be mad. We're going to see you after the art gallery thing, right?" he asked, tossing the bag of chips on the floor.

I snapped them up. "If you're lucky."

We exited and as I pulled the door shut, I heard him yell, "You look nice by the way! I get credit for saying that, right?"

My response was a slammed hard oak door.

***

"Do you have heated seats?" Marissa asked as soon as we got in the car, wrapping her arms around and rubbing her shoulders for warmth.

"Yeah, be patient," I said, backing my car out of the driveway. "You know, pioneers traveled in covered wagons and survived. You won't die. Hold on- let me tweet that."

I parked the car and began composing my tweet.

"Do we follow each other on Twitter? What's your name?" she asked.

"Oliviamizra. Same as my Instagram and Pinterest," I replied, carefully typing out my tweet.

@oliviamizra
 It's so cold in the D. Pioneers must have been tough. Thankful 4 heated seats. #winteriscoming.

"Original," she muttered, zipping her coat up to her nose in exaggeration. "I miss summer." She shivered.

I turned onto the highway as she unzipped her coat.

"Nurse Marissa, since texting and driving is illegal in the state of Michigan, will you be so kind as to put on some music?"

"What are you in the mood for?"

"Indie pop," I replied, dead serious. "Crystal Figures. No-wait! I want to get pumped. Vampire Weekend or Noah and the Whale."

She rolled her eyes. "You and that weird music. Seriously, who *listens* to that?"

"Lots of people. The people who *don't* listen to Miranda Lambert."

"I like country! I'm *from* the country," she pouted, turning the heating vents toward herself.

"You're Mexican."

"I was adopted by white people in South Carolina. I don't even speak Spanish."

"Fine, compromise. Just put on my hip hop mix, OK?"

She put it on and Pitbull started yelling about red rooms and tie-ups.

"Seriously, you know why I can't listen to this crap? Because it's overplayed. Hip-hop and top 40 just rehash the same themes. Why does middle America like this?" I joked.

"Is this what you talk about all day at grad school? Because if it is, I should seriously think about taking the GRE. I could already write a paper."

She paused and cleared her throat. "Today's music is *so* vulgar and the rappers weren't hugged enough as children."

I turned onto the highway. "Our professor for the one class is Indian. And yes, that's *exactly* what I'm writing my paper on this weekend. *'Hip-hop artists: were they hugged enough as children?'*"

"You have *another* paper to write this weekend? Didn't you just write one *last* weekend?" she whined. "I thought we were going to hang out!"

"Marissa," I said, trying to sound patient, "It's called a *thesis.* It's over 100 pages. Single-spaced."

"That sounds hella boring," she said, rolling down the window.

"If you're cold, ask me to turn down the heat!" I protested as we turned onto Woodward and into a slightly shady (even by Detroit standards) part of town.

"No, my paper is on the influence of the media with regard to bullying."

She looked confused, so I tried to explain the best I could.

"It's a really long paper in which I prove something earth-shattering."

"I love it when you talk all smart. It's so sexy. Do you put on your Sarah Palin glasses and read the encyclopedia to Ashley as foreplay?" she asked, giggling.

"Only when we do it in the university library." I squinted as I slowed down and tried to read the road sign.

"Navigate me. Your people crossed the Rio Grande to get here. You're good at this."

"Is the Rio Grande in Colorado?" she asked, dead serious.

(Jesus, is literally too stupid for words sometimes. I shudder to think that she has peoples' lives in her hands every day.)

I continued, sighing. "And on top of this damn 100 page paper, I have to do this stupid "reflection journal," which is me basically paying five grand a semester to write in a fucking diary. It's such bullshit."

"I think this is the place," Marissa said, turning her iPhone sideways, comparing the blue dot to the red pin.

"Yeah, let me parallel park over here. Not that I'm worried about anyone stealing a seven-year old BMW." (OK, it was Detroit. They steal copper from abandoned homes. Maybe I should have been a *tiny* bit worried.) I navigated into spot with the precision of a fighter pilot landing a jet.

"Not bad. Here's the deal. We're staying for an hour max. We go in, look at art, drink wine, then leave, *aight*?"

She nodded in reply, shivering as she closed the car door.

We zipped up our coats and walked across the dilapidated parking lot. This was the area of town that had just recently started undergoing the gentrification process. While the skeletons of new apartment buildings loomed in the distance, only every other light on this street was in working order. Some entrepreneurs, however, took it upon themselves to start building coffee shops/art galleries, and other semi-trendy boutiques in what had been an old barbershop at one point.

(My Middle Eastern brethren were already taking it upon themselves to set up mobile electronics stores and falafel restaurants in the area.)

Upon entrance, we were greeted by four of our friends and two people we didn't know. Pete and Christina were two of twenty or so artists displaying their work this month. Apparently the gallery was some sort of a co-op effort, but I usually quit listening when they started talking because in my head, all I heard was, '*I am an underappreciated artist who is going to work at Office Max forever.*'

Pete was there with his boyfriend Kristoff. Their combined weight was equivalent to one of my boobs, yet both were wearing skinny jeans, loafers, black-rim glasses and Affliction shirts. If irony could be bottled up, I'd sell it to Halliburton as a new resource. Kylie looked perfect as always with her jet-black straight hair framing her flawless complexion and expertly applied eye shadow (MAC's Cat Eyes collection, for the record). Christina was

the Barbie Doll of the group- a size zero with blindingly
white teeth and a perfect nose (courtesy of her father, the
plastic surgeon). While her father gifted her with a
perfect nose, he neglected to give her any of his
intelligence. Christina Jordan is quite possibly the
dumbest human I have ever met.

(Seriously, she makes Marissa look like a TED recipient.)

Delilah, at 29, was the oldest of the group, but definitely
the leader. I had known her somewhat since I was a child,
and despite a somewhat average level of beauty, she had
always been the best dressed, most put together, and in
her opinion, the most sophisticated.

"Uh-oh," whispered Marissa. "Delilah looks like she's in a
mood."

I rolled my eyes. "Delilah doesn't like art, museums, zoos,
movies, or anyplace where less than 100% of the
attention is on her. She could win a Nobel Prize and be
pissed that someone else gave an introductory speech
before her."

"Christina said she heard Delilah got in a little bit of
trouble at work, but it was just a big misunderstanding."

"Oh please," I whispered back. "Delilah probably fucked
something up, but blamed it on someone else. Come on,
you know half these people in here would stab me in the
back if it came to saving their own asses. Delilah though,
she'll stab you in the front, but the bloody knife will be in
someone else's hand."

I paused to let that sink in before continuing.

"You all underestimate her, but I've known her since we were kids. Even as a child, she terrorized people for fun. To her, life's one big game that she *has* to win. You think were her friends? No way. We're her pawns. Just remember that."

As if on cue, she came over. Although she was just slightly bigger than Marissa, she commanded a presence like no one else. Tonight, her long red hair was tightly pulled back in a bun with what appeared to be chopsticks protruding from the back.

Hugs were exchanged all around, but Delilah and I didn't hug. Delilah isn't a hugger and neither am I. I hate people in my personal space as much as she does. At least we have that in common.

I poked at her head. "Is someone hoping to have takeout later?"

I heard the others giggle as we grabbed some wine.

She swatted my hand away. Whereas the others appreciate my snark, Delilah possessed neither sense of humor or self-deprecation in any manner.

"I don't expect you to understand. You don't read *Vogue*."

"Of course I do," I retorted, continuing to poke at her chopsticks. "I look at the pictures. I can't say I read the articles. Sort of like a reverse *Playboy*," I winked as the others giggled.

"You shop at the *mall*, so I'm not going to try to explain this to you."

"In two years, I'm going to be shopping at the hay and feed store. In my motorized scooter."

She looked at me quizzically.

"Never mind, let's just get a drink and go look at some art, shall we?"

I took one last poke at her chopsticks and asked what kind of rice came with the Mu Shu pork special.

She ignored me.

I felt my purse vibrate and discreetly peeked in to read what I knew was a text from Marissa.

OMG, don't ever worry about looking like a Drag Queen. I'm pretty sure Kylie's penis is showing tonight. Delilah needs to stop scowling too. At her age, the lines stay on the face.

I put my phone back in my purse and mouthed *'you're terrible'* to Marissa.

We spent the first few minutes looking at Pete and Christina's art. To me, it looked like random splatters of paint on a canvas, but what did I know? I *oohed* and *ahhed* appropriately, wondering if they at least got a discount on this stuff through their inevitable employment at Office Max.

As we moved on, the wine kicked in and my bitchy inner art critic emerged.

"What's the title is that?" I asked, pointing to a picture of a desolate run-down house. "*Daddy got busted cooking meth and mommy is facing foreclosure?*"

The group's giggling prompted me to continue. "And look at this one. It's a bunch of blue smears with a red jagged line in the middle. This painting obviously represents a woman's heartache and the red is the jagged tear through her heart which can only be repaired with a pint of Ben and Jerry's."

I had everyone's attention now. I turned and feigned mock interest and scrutiny.

"Over here we have a painting of what appears to be a woman bearing a strong resemblance to Kirstie Alley circa 2009 in the embrace of David Beckham. I shall title this, '*Type II Diabetes Dream.*'"

By this point, I noticed the nearby hipsters in their skinny jeans actually remove their ear buds and snicker.

"Uh-oh, looks like someone vomited on this one. No, wait! This one represents the artist's inner turmoil and frustration with not yet being promoted to the day manager of Applebee's."

More laughter.

"Look at this pot," I said, examining a clay work of art. "My mom would like that, but she already has one exactly like it from Kohl's."

By this point, I had my friends (and a few others) rolling with laughter. Kylie was trying to tweet as fast as I talked. Delilah scowled, sipped her wine, and adjusted a chopstick.

We turned the corner and faced a large photograph of a naked woman taking a picture of herself in the mirror.

"*Holy hell!*" I exclaimed. "I thought they shut down MySpace. Someone has daddy issues but couldn't land a job at Secrets Gentlemen's Club by the airport!"

I was just starting to get warmed up about the benefits of a fine arts degree from Central Michigan when Kylie tapped me on the shoulder to turn around.

I was confronted with a three-dimensional full-wall display of Barbie Dolls who had been modified to resemble characters from every George Romero film created. Interspersed with the undead Mattel were burlap voodoo dolls. I cannot make this shit up.

I paused to let everyone Snapchat it first. "I'm not going to lie. This is creepy as fuck. I want to meet the artist, but

Electronic Journal of Oda Mizra

File Name: MPJ-701_Reflection Journal

I'm pretty sure she's at home writing bad poetry and love letters to Scott Peterson. I'm guessing she didn't sit at the same lunch table as us in high school, huh?"

I think Marissa actually snorted wine out of her nose.

Just then, an angry large girl approached us. I'm pretty sure she hadn't seen the sun since Bush's first term. (As governor of Texas.)

"Well, Christina," she snarled. (Girls like this never speak, they either 'state', 'yell', or 'snarl' their words.) "I'm *so* glad you and the other *plastics* can make it tonight. This exhibit is titled *Dichotomy of a Woman*. It's about reversing the paradigm of inner and outer beauty- in other words your-" she paused, looking around the group, narrowing her eyes at each of us, "worst nightmare."

We stopped, clasped our hands, and looked contrite for three seconds.

I started in with Kristoff and Kylie backing me up.

"Oh my gosh, if we are the Plastics, can I be Lindsey Lohan before she aged 40 years?"

"No, you are totally the one who can tell the weather with her boobs."

"Hello, two of us are Jewish. Who gets to be Gretchen Weiner?"

"Does that make her the angry lesbian?"

"Please tell me these are generic Dollar Tree Barbies and not the real ones. That would be such a waste of money."

"Has anyone bid on this? Because I know this would look really good in my living room next to my G.I. Joe Armageddon mural."

"On second thought, if we are plastics, can we be in your next art show? Like live art? How much are you paying?"

"Depends how much she makes posing for BBW web-cam sites."

She muttered something under her breath that suggested we burn in hell and stomped away.

I grabbed my shoulder as yelped in pain. Everyone turned and looked.

"Ouch! I think she just stabbed a pin in the voodoo doll of me. We need to take that away from her. Call Shia LeBouf and tell him we're making *Indiana Jones Five: Revenge of Jenny Craig!"*

Don't bury me in a sweater, because I'm sure I'm going to hell.

Electronic Journal of Tiffany Harris

File Name: Tiff's Life: 2014 edition

October 10, 8 p.m.

If I never have to see that bastard again, it won't be soon enough. Who does he think he is that he can just come up into *my* house, not his house anymore, and treat me like that? If I didn't need him to pay me so badly, I would have never let him in.

Hell, let me rephrase. If I never have a *day* like this again, it won't be soon enough.

The morning started out rough. The kids had just gotten on the bus and I went out to start the car, the cruel Michigan morning wind smacking me in the face. (I seriously need to move away from here.)

I turned the key.

Nothing.

Shit, I swore to myself. I tried it again.

Nothing.

I took a deep breath and popped the hood. I wasn't sure what I was looking for, but I knew that it was probably the battery.

In retrospect, was it really fair to blame the battery? I mean, the car is 15 years old. That's like a 100 year-old person dying and blaming a bad heart.

"What's the problem?" Gary asked from his porch.

Electronic Journal of Tiffany Harris

File Name: Tiff's Life: 2014 edition

Yep, good ol' Gary, always smoking outside. Sometimes I wonder if he smokes just so he can keep an eye on the neighborhood.

I jumped up, so startled that I hit my head on the hood.

"*Fuck*!" I swung around and yelled at him. "You scared me!"

He walked over, tossing his paper coffee cup into the small, pathetic hedge that was meant to separate our yards, but did little more than create an annoyance when mowing the lawn.

"It sounds like the battery."

Thank you Captain Obvious.

"Can you give me a lift to work?" I begged, panic starting to well up in my chest.

"I would, but my car is in the shop. I just got home and let Nancy take the car to work this morning."

That was right. I remember his gem of a vehicle, a truck in far worse shape than my car, being towed away last weekend. Gary had worked third shift at the factory until it closed down in 2009, but now just did odd jobs to make ends meet. His wife was a home caregiver out in the suburbs somewhere.

Apprehensively, I turned toward the house.

Electronic Journal of Tiffany Harris

File Name: Tiff's Life: 2014 edition

Gary must have read my mind. "Go ask him," he said. "He won't be mad at you."

We both looked ominously at my pathetic excuse for a house, the words between us remaining unspoken.

He paused and scratched his head. "I'll tell you what- I'll call my brother in law- that's Nancy's little brother. He owns a body shop. He might be able to get you a cheap battery. I'll see if I can't get something over here today. Maybe Nancy can pick you up on her way back from Bloomfield Hills."

I thanked him and sighed, walking up to my house, the weight of the steps creaking with every step I took. I let myself in and walked into the bedroom.

Troy lay there fast asleep, face down, spread eagle on the bed. I wanted to spend a bit more time watching him sleep. He looked almost angelic- the way his dirty brown hair flopped over his eyes. I always thought his constant 5 o'clock shadow was sexy, but the pale gray light made it look even sexier. I apprehensively approached the bed.

"Troy," I whispered softly.

He grunted something inaudible.

I poked him. "*Troy*," I repeated, this time with more urgency.

"*What?*" he yelled, now fully awake.

44

Electronic Journal of Tiffany Harris

File Name: Tiff's Life: 2014 edition

I stepped back. "My battery is dead and I need a ride into work."

"Jesus *fucking* Christ woman! Can't you *ever* do anything right?" He stood up, inches from my face, yelling at me. Any delusions of an angel sleeping were shattered.

"I'm sorry," I said, biting back tears. "I don't know...the car is old...and I just...I'm sorry, but can I get a ride?"

He stormed into the bathroom and retrieved his jeans and sweatshirt off the floor. I heard him swearing the whole time. I didn't need to hear the specific semantics, but I got the gist of it.

Fucking cunt...I can't do any of my own shit because I'm too busy taking care of yours.

I followed him wordlessly out to his truck, eyes overflowing with tears. I got in, buckled up, and pulled out my phone. Shit, I was going to be so late. Maybe Krishna wouldn't be in until later today. I pulled down the rearview mirror and tried to blot my eyes with the back of my coat sleeve. It was a fruitless endeavor. No matter how much makeup I tried, I could never cover up the dark circles below my eyes. My translucent skin only exaggerated the contrast. I kept saying that once I had some extra money that I was going to go to the tanning bed. (I was also going to buy makeup that cost more than five dollars, get some eye cream, and maybe get a facial.)

So much for that idea. Now I was trying to calculate in my head how I'd pay for a new car battery.

Electronic Journal of Tiffany Harris

File Name: Tiff's Life: 2014 edition

I took out a comb and tried to pull my hair back out of my face. I don't know why I was worried about my skin when my roots were a disaster. My highlights, which were meant to be strawberry blonde, looked almost gray. Based on the gray mixed in with my dark brown roots, I'd be fully gray by the time I was 30. I'd be an old lady with long, witchy, gray hair. Wait, that was wishful thinking. My hair refused to grow past my shoulders. It just hung there, like a deflated curtain that always looked like it needed to be washed. My hair seemed to speak to my inner psyche.

Come on Tiffany. What's the point? It ain't like you're ever gonna be a beauty queen.

"Well?"

I snapped out of my contemplative state of self-analysis (ok, self-loathing) and turned to Troy.

"I'm sorry, what?" I asked.

He sighed and shook his head. He had calmed down enough where he was just pissed off at me.

"Why is Paul Jacobi such a fucking asshole?"

I shrugged. Troy likes to constantly remind me that I grew up with Paul Jacobi, partial owner of Jacobi's Luxury Imports, 2005 Grosse Point East high school prom king, and Detroit's reigning Lord of the Douche.

46

Electronic Journal of Tiffany Harris

File Name: Tiff's Life: 2014 edition

"Why is the sky blue?" I shrugged. "He's been an asshole since he came out of the womb. He made my life a living hell. You don't have to deal with him that much in maintenance and repair, do you? Doesn't he work more on the sales end?"

"I don't know," Troy said, stopping at a red light, causing me to look impatiently at my phone. "The other day, he came in to look at some work we were doing on a Maserati that came in. He hovered over me the whole time, less than a foot away, and didn't talk at all. Made me feel like a fucking retard- that I needed his fucking supervision to do a job. I mean, Christ, can that jackass even fill his own gas tank?"

I looked down. 8:05. I was so screwed.

He continued. "I asked if he knew you. He has all of his high school sports gear up in his office like a fucking shrine to himself. He said the name sounded familiar, but he didn't think so."

"You might want to ask if he remembers the abominable snowman," I muttered under my breath as I collected my purse.

Troy pulled up and I yelled thank you as I was jumping from the car- an athletic feat for someone who hasn't jumped since middle school PE.

I ran into work and smack into Krishna. She looked at me and sighed, her long black hair looking almost blue in the fluorescent lighting.

47

"Where have you been?"

"My battery-" I started, trying not to stare. *Seriously, how was her hair so flawless?*

"Excuses!" she snapped. "I do not want to hear these things. If you are to be here at eight, then it is eight you are to be here, yes?"

I mumbled some sort of apology and scooted toward my desk.

Krishna had already moved on to berating someone else who she caught on Facebook. There is no place for fun at work.

"Do you think they implant sticks up their ass over there in India or Bangladesh or wherever she's from?" LaShawndra, asked as soon as I sat down at my station.

"It is with great regret that the sticks were so unfortunately positioned," I mocked her in my best Indian accent. "This task of stick placement was for purpose of ensuring the worker sits up straight at the Dell helpdesk to best serve customer."

I thought LaShawndra was going to have a heart attack she was laughing so hard.

"Girl, we gotta get out of here," she said, pulling out a bag of candies and extending them to me.

(Yeah, because candy was *exactly* what two plus-size women should have easy access to.)

"I heard they're going to make cuts. They're moving part of the center to Mumbai. They work for four dollars a day over there and can handle more calls."

"I heard that too," I whispered, leaning in. "Have you applied anywhere?"

"At&T," she whispered back. "Thirteen an hour. You?"

"Southeastern," I replied. "Flight attendant program."

"Ha!" cackled LaShawndra, leaning back in her chair. "You trying to land yourself a pilot? Some white Ben Affleck-looking brother?"

"No!" I hissed. "I'm with Troy."

"Which one was that?"

"You know him- shaggy brown hair. We met at Tony's watching one of the preseason games. I think it might work out."

(Yeah, like all great romances start at a cheap sports bad that reeks of cigarette smoke, motor oil, and broken dreams.)

"How long have you been together?"

"Seven weeks," I proudly announced. (OK, lie, I know, but it's only exaggerating by two....)

Electronic Journal of Tiffany Harris

File Name: Tiff's Life: 2014 edition

"And you think he's the one?" she asked, reaching her brightly colored nails into the bag in search of a Krackel bar.

"Maybe."

She raised her eyebrows. "Uh-huh. And what about all of the other 'the ones'? How many have there been this year?"

As if on cue, my phone chimed. Saved by the bell. "Two," I hissed, both of us knowing full well that I was lying.

Instagram notification. Looking around, I made sure that Krisha wasn't looking and opened the app, which for some reason prompted me to log in- again. Stupid phone.

I typed tiffanyharris1986 and my password and saw my notification. Gary liked my picture of the Marylyn Monroe quote, which read, "If you can't handle me at my worst, then you don't deserve me at my best."

Of course he did. Old people love technology. I logged into my Twitter- TiffanyHarris1 and tweeted the same quote. I don't have a ton of Twitter followers, but I follow all the celebrities.

By the time five rolled around, I was in better spirits. Krishna had only yelled at me three times today, one time for, and I quote, "speaking with the most unpleasantness."

Electronic Journal of Tiffany Harris

File Name: Tiff's Life: 2014 edition

LaShawndra gave me a ride home as my house was on the way to her brother's restaurant that she sometimes helped out with on the weekend. LaShawndra had five brothers and each owned at least one gas station, restaurant, or auto body shop in southeast Detroit. Growing up around such manliness made her the toughest bitch I ever met. Or maybe it's because she's lesbian. That too.

"Come to the restaurant tonight," she said. "You bring your man for date night."

"I wish. I have the kids tonight. The ex is picking them up from school and taking them to some Red Wings exhibition thing. Of course, the only reason he's doing anything with them is to show them off to his new girlfriend. She's barely older than him."

"Oh, don't act like you're so old. How old are you? 29?"

I grimaced. "Twenty seven." (I don't care if I had to prostitute myself, I was going to buy that hair dye. Stat.)

"Wait until you're 43, honey. Then you can talk old."

We pulled up and I got out, thanking her profusely for the ride. Dusk had already started to settle in. In a month, when daylight savings kicked in, it would be pitch black when I got home.

I went in, dropped my stuff, and started to rifle through the mail. I knew I should go for a walk, but I was so tired. I had a hard day. It was emotional. I deserved a drink.

Electronic Journal of Tiffany Harris

File Name: Tiff's Life: 2014 edition

I poured myself a glass of Jack Daniels over ice and took a sip. That felt better. I shared an Internet meme on Facebook about my workweek interrupting my weekend. That should get some likes.

I was feeling more than decent when the doorbell rang a few hours later. Emma and Tyrell ran in, eager to show off the plastic souvenirs from the hockey game.

I met Jesse at the front door, kicking aside the bills that had come through the mail slot.

He looked me up and down, sighing disgustedly.

"What's your problem?"

"I just took your kids to a hockey game. A hockey game. Do you have any idea how much fucking time and effort that was? Parking was ten-"

"*Your* kids," I corrected him.

"Emma is mine. Tyrell is Darnell's boy. When's the last time you saw that worthless nigger anyways?"

"He's in Afghanistan."

"Oh, um..." For a split second, Jesse actually looked embarrassed.

"And he sends me money *regularly*." I crossed my arms and leaned against the door, taking extra precaution against anymore paint peeling off the rotting wood frame. "Speaking of, are you going to pay me? It's almost the middle of October."

"I don't get paid until-"

"Not an excuse!" (Great, now I was channeling Krishna.)

We began shouting at each other. I was too busy fuming with anger that I failed to notice we had company. Behind him stood a girl no older than 22, her red hair strategically covering a Bump-it.

"This is Kaylah," Jesse said. "Kaylah, this is my ex-wife."

I looked down and realized I was still in my yoga pants. In the dirty reflection of the door, I caught glimpse of the rat's nest my hair had become. I guess Jack had put me to sleep for a bit.

I mumbled hello and shut the door. For the first time, I noticed how most of the flecks of paint that had peeled off the door frame revealed so much of the ugly brown wood below it. For a second, I couldn't help but think that was a sign of my life, a representation that I was slowly coming undone. In a few years, no one would want to buy this house. It was on the corner, so it would be easier to just tear it down and build a new one. Eventually, I'd end up the same way- used up and worthless.

Electronic Journal of Oda Mizra

File Name: Tiff's Life: 2014 edition

October 10, 9 p.m.

By the time we left the art gallery, the temperature had plummeted at least ten degrees. I wrapped my coat around me a little bit tighter and stopped. I pointed to the west, where the lights of the Renaissance center twinkled against the darkening sky.

"Remind me to take you up there sometime," I said. "In the fall, when the leaves start to change, you look out and see the fall colors on Belle Isle and up and down the river. My grandma used to work there and take us up there when we were little. Fall was always my favorite season."

She nodded, looking up. "When did your grandma die?"

"Two years ago."

"I'm sorry to hear that," she said, keeping her eyes fixed on the skyline.

"It's OK," I shrugged. "She had Alzheimer's, ya know?"

"So why is fall your favorite? I know this is my first winter here, but Michigan winters have to be way worse than South Carolina winters. Don't you know that the coldest months were yet to come?"

"Oh, fuck yeah. It's gonna get balls cold. It's gonna feel like Jack Frost is permanently resting his icy ball sack on the side of your face-"

"You're so graphic. Do they teach you that in journalism school?" she asked.

I ignored her and continued. "It's just that she always said fall was a time for new beginnings, the trees shedding their leaves so they could be reborn or something. I never really got it until she pointed out this tree in our front yard. I always assumed it died in the winter until she showed me pictures of it over the years. How much it had grown. The winter was the time for hibernation, like a cocooning moth I guess. And in the spring, the leaves came back and the butterfly emerged. I think that every year I thought things would be better, that I'd finally emerge into that butterfly or whatever. Like, this year was going to be my year."

I shrugged, unlocking and getting in the car. "Never happened though I guess."

"That was very poetic," Marissa said. "I bet you can ask the Barbie mutilator where you join a poetry slam."

"Fuck you. It's a long walk from here."

***

Three wrong turns and thirty minutes later, we pulled into the Greektown Casino parking garage. I pulled the car into the first handicap spot I saw and stuck the placard on the rearview mirror before tilting it down and examining my eye makeup.

55

"I think my eyebrows are too low," I stated, gently tugging the skin up, so they were higher. "Maybe I need an eyebrow lift."

"Maybe you need a brain lift," she said, rolling her eyes.

"That doesn't make sense."

"Are you ready to go? My buzz wore off three blocks ago," she huffed, pulling down the passenger side visor and applying her lip-gloss.

"Yeah I guess. Seriously though- will you tell me if I ever need to go on a diet or get Botox?"

"Yes," she responded, opening the door and stepping out. "Will you tell me?"

"Of course. You *know* I don't mince words."

"Olivia! Marissa!" came a shout from behind us. Kylie, Christina, and the girl I didn't know came running up behind us. (OK, "running" is an inaccurate term as they were all in at least four-inch heels, so I'd say it was "hobbling slightly faster than normal.")

"No way." Kylie looked between us and the parking spot. "You're gonna get towed!"

"Au contraire," I winked, reaching inside and showing her the famous blue sign. "We are handicapped until next July."

"Where did you get that? Did you sleep with someone at the DMV?"

"Um yeah," I retorted. "He was so hot too, let me tell you. He had this bald spot on the back of his head and the sexiest beer gut you could imagine. We did it right there on the germy counter. Then he bent me over the urine-soaked plastic chairs and we did it again."

"So funny," she muttered.

"No, it was my grandpa's," I said, as we started walking to the entrance.

"Isn't he dead?"

"Yep, but do you think our bankrupt city interfaces their death records with their DMV records? Seriously. One of you hobble or some shit in case anyone sees us."

Did I mention I don't have just a one-way ticket to hell, but my own private chartered G-6?

The thing about the casino in Detroit is this: you have to walk through it to get to most of the bars and restaurants downtown. In truth, Detroit is largely a sketchy place, but the downtown area where the sports stadiums and tourist attractions are is really nice. The odds of getting shot downtown are significantly lower than in most other areas of the city. As a statistician, I like to play the odds.

As we walked through the casino, I could feel the eyes on us. Occasionally I heard the catcall of, *"Damn girls,"* and *"Hold up shorty, lemme get your number."*

Who could blame them I guess? We were all well under a size four (and that's real sizes- none of this vanity crap), well dressed, and probably had enough hair products on to create a new hole in the ozone layer.

(Yeah, I'm sorry about the trees and all, but do you know how hard it is to straighten this mop of hair? If some hippie comes up with some herb sap I can use, I'd gladly give it a try. Until then, it's the Kenra straightening line.}

We approached the bouncer.

"VIP please, the last name is Buckner," Delilah said.

"You got VIP?" the Indian girl whose name I didn't know asked.

"Um, duh," replied Kylie. "You think we want to spend the night dodging some dental hygenist's bachelorette party or the fratastic white rappers?"

(Eminem, *you* brought this plague upon our city.)

Marissa looked confused. I think she was still trying to figure out how to spell VIP.

We got to VIP and exchanged pleasantries with everyone. Ashley was already there with his friends and after saying hello, returned to his immersion in the MMA fights on the big screen.

I sat down on the couch next to Marissa and the Indian girl whose name I didn't know.

"Hi, I'm Krisha. I'm Christina's friend from Lansing. I don't think we officially met," she said, extending her hand.

"Oh, nice to meet you, I'm Olivia. This is Marissa, and that over there is my fiancé, Ashley."

"He's good looking."

"Thank you," I replied, pleased that he had worn the outfit I laid out for him.

"He looks like this famous person...um... of Backstreet Boys?"

I burst into laughter. "You mean J.C. Chasez? From 'NSync?"

She lit up, her dark brown eyes widening in recognition. "Yes! Is that him?"

I couldn't stop laughing. "No, it's not, but he gets told that a lot. While he can't get you dinner with Justin Timberlake, he is however, an airline pilot and can get you discounts on Southeastern."

"That is a job of utmost importance."

Marissa got up. "I'm going to smoke. Come with me."

"No way," I replied, pouring myself and Kylie Red Bull and Grey Goose. "It's colder than a witch's tit in a brass bra out there. Plus, I don't want my hair to smell like smoke. I washed it today and don't want to wash it tomorrow. You need to quit or your teeth will get yellow."

"Thank you, Sanjay Gupta," she shot back, walking away.

"So how do you know everyone else?" Krishna inquired, sipping her drink and making a face.

"Too strong?" I handed her a can of Red Bull. "Pour some more in. I make mine strong I guess."

I continued, "Let's see, I've kind of known Delilah since we were younger. She was a few years ahead of me in school. Then we ended up at university in the same sorority."

"University? Where are you from? You have a slight accent."

"So do you," I replied. "You're not from Lansing."

"No, I am from India originally, but we moved here when I was ten. I did not speak any English," she said.

"No way!" I smiled and nodded my head. "Well, *I* was born in Irbil, Kurdistan, which is sort of a part of Iraq.

We are Assyrian though. My dad was originally from there, but my mum was Canadian. They both studied at Michigan State. They were both international students technically, but she was pretty much American. She grew up across the river outside of Windsor. We moved to the U.S. when I was almost eight- a few years after the first Gulf War was over. My dad was a scientist and came to work for a pharmaceutical company. I went to a British school over there, so I knew English already."

"Do you speak Arabic, or Assyrian?"

"Nah, I used to, but I fell out of practice. When we came back, I wanted to be so American, I refused to even speak it at home. I still know some words though- but definitely not enough to get me by."

I thought for a second. "Then, let's see, I met Kylie in our sorority as well. She was my 'little sis' even though she's our age. She didn't pledge until her sophomore year."

"Wait, where did you go to high school and university?" she asked.

"I went to Grosse Pointe East for high school. Then, I went to Southern Michigan, but after I graduated, I moved to Cleveland for a year, then back here. My grandpa died and we have the house now. We are supposed to try to sell it and split the profits with the rest of my family, but Ashley has a good gig with the airlines. What about you?"

"High school in Lansing, college at State. How do you know my friend Christina then?"

"When I came back here about eight months ago, I met her at some party with Delilah. Delilah and her didn't really know each other, but we all started hanging out. I guess I met the others through that same crowd. Marissa I met just five months ago at some charity run. She lives close to me out in Grosse Point and I offered to dog sit. Now here we are in the pretty people corner together."

"The what?" she asked, raising her eyebrows.

Kylie turned around. Apparently she had been listening the whole time, but since the conversation didn't revolve around her, neglected to chime in until now.

She sighed and looked at me, then over at Christina. "They didn't *tell* you about the pretty people corner?"

Apparently I neglected to mention that on my tour up the stairs as I tried to not fall on my face.

"It's where the pretty people - us - sit. You're pretty, so you get to sit here with us. It's above the dance floor so we can judge everyone below us. " She started rifling through her purse. "Liv, can you ask your fiancé to take a picture of us? Get on the right side."

"Ashley!" I shouted, throwing an olive at him to get his attention. "Take a pic, please?" I whined, pouting.

He groaned, reluctantly turning from the television. "OK, on the count of three…"

He took it and handed her the camera. He knew his job wasn't yet done.

"My arm looks so fat!" I yelled.

"My forehead looks too big!" Kylie exclaimed.

"I look fat because I'm in the middle. Olivia, you're the skinniest, switch me," Krishna said as she scooted over my lap.

I saw Kylie shoot Krishna the Look of Death. Uh oh, she said I was skinnier. I'd hear about this for the next two weeks. I couldn't wait to hear what Kylie had to say about Krishna.

Five pictures later, we had one we all approved, plus one of our bottle service. I posted it to Facebook and Twitter with the caption:

"Hot bitches on a cold night in the D! #yolo #hotbitches #thisishowwedo"

"Are you going to blog about the tragedy this bar has become?" Marissa asked me.

"You blog?" asked Christina, twirling the straw in her drink.

"Yeah, it's nothing big. Just a little advice site I guess. Life advice with a heavy dose of sarcasm," I replied.

"What do you blog about?"

"It's sarcasticassyrian.blogspot.com. Just relationship, dating, lifestyle stuff. Pretty much the anti-Oprah."

"So if I wrote to you asking why I was still single at 25?" Krishna joked, laughing.

I chewed on my straw in contemplation. "Well *I'd* probably tell you to ask yourself some questions. Are you fat? If the answer is yes, go to the gym. Respect yourself before you expect someone else to respect you. Are your standards too high? Are you refusing to settle for nothing less than a Ryan Reynolds lookalike who also enjoys horseback riding and plays John Mayer solos on the guitar? I'd tell you this isn't fucking Build-a-Bear and the chupacabra doesn't exist."

She laughed hard and then proceeded to Google *chupacabra*.

"Olivia is *so* funny," Kylie chimed in, with just a hint of bitterness in her voice. "Smart, funny, skinny. No wonder she's almost married."

I began to reply, but realized there was no use debating an ex-debutante drunk off Patron and Sprite. I thought about telling her that maybe the reason I'm skinny is because I drink *Diet* Sprite.

"You do look like a Kardashian- but way prettier," remarked Pete. "What's your measurements?"

I laughed. If a straight guy had asked that, it might seem creepy, but Pete was harmless.

"I'm like 34C-26-35," I said. "Probably about two inches bigger than *you*," I joked.

"Your waist is 25? It doesn't look that big!" he exclaimed.

Big? I guess I never thought of it that way....I self-consciously wrapped my arms around my waist, trying to suck in my gut, which was apparently ginormous. Leave it to the gay guy to give it to me straight. I vowed to start dieting tomorrow.

By this point, everyone had gathered back in the VIP section for shots. It was too early and we were way too sober to start dancing.

"Who is that in the VIP across from us?" Christina asked. "She looks like a *total* whore and she's giving a lap dance to an empty chair."

"Some jersey chasing club skank. Heard there might be some athletes here and she's ovulating. The needle in her purse serves many purposes- to shoot heroin in her toes and poke holes in condoms. *Eighteen years, eighteen years...*"

The random club skank looked over at us and scowled. I flipped her off.

"Speaking of, *oh my God*, is that chick pregnant and drinking?" Marissa (who singlehandedly already had consumed half a bottle of whisky) shouted, standing up, wobbling slightly as she did so. "I'm going to tell her how she should be ashamed of herself!"

She marched past the VIP bouncer, down the stairs, right up to the woman. I saw her gesturing wildly, waving her hands, then the other woman reaching out to push her.

Despite her blood alcohol level, Marissa reacted quickly enough to dodge the woman and scoot out of harm's way before her friend could intervene. Hands on her hip, she stomped back up to us.

"Let me guess," Ashley's friend Jake said, taking a swig of his beer, "She was just fat?"

We all laughed.

Marissa crossed her arms and glared at us before picking up her drink. "Well, she shouldn't be drinking anyways. Alcohol has lots of calories. Maybe she's going to go home and start dieting."

"Or maybe she's going to go home and end her life," Kristoff smarmily responded. "I hope she goes home and burns that *horrible* knockoff Burberry sweater."

"Hey, speaking of," I piped up. "I'm going to Chicago in a few weeks if you need anything. I know the malls here are *so not-fabulous*."

"Why didn't you tell me?" asked Kylie, staring in her hand mirror as she fixed her eye shadow.

"I tweeted like three days ago," I shrugged, reaching for the vodka, which much to my dismay, was empty.

"Excuse me, ma'am," I motioned to the waitress. "Can we get some more please?"

"Ma'am? Wow, who knew you to be polite," remarked Kristoff.

"Excuse me, but I did *not* know you were going to Chicago. That's *not* on my birthday, is it?" interrupted Kylie, going on her seventh minute without breaking contact from her reflection.

"No. The week after. I posted it."

"I don't read other people's statuses unless they affect me," she replied, without a hint of sarcasm.

Christina interjected. "But do you expect people to comment on yours?"

(It was a valid question.)

"Of *course*," Kylie said, rolling her eyes. "But I don't have *time* to read other people's statuses."

"That's right, she's too busy brokering Middle East peace treaty negotiations," I responded as Kristoff, Krishna, and Christina snickered.

With no comeback, she stormed off, only to be replaced by the waitress.

"Thank you ma'am," I said as she set the bottle down.

"Seriously! What is with the southern manners? Next thing you're gonna be saying, *'yes massa'* when I need a ride and *'I ain't no house nigga'* when I ask you to pick up my dry cleaning," Pete chimed, quickly looking around to make sure that we weren't in the presence of black people.

(Kylie doesn't count. She's barely human, let alone a human with feelings.)

"Please, I know full well what I am doing," I responded, pouring a drink. "I'm subliminally calling her old. And for good reason. I don't like her. I get a bad vibe. She was probably one of those bitches who thought she was so much better than me in high school, then she got knocked up, enrolled in community college, and hustles here at night. Her fucking C-section scar is showing for the love of God."

"So judgmental," mocked Kristoff, crossing his legs and picking lint off his unnaturally tight pants. "Tell me you weren't a little queen bee back in the day."

"Nope," I said. "I was just some girl."

"She's right," said Delilah, coming over and sitting on the edge of the (probably Herpes-infested) couch. "When I met her, she was a pudgy little 18-year-old rushee in a cheap sundress and bad spray tan. But I took her under my wing-"

"That dress wasn't cheap. It was from Nordstrom."

She gave me The Look. I shut up.

"But look at little Livvie now. All grown up with a fake nose and all. Your boobs, those are still real, right?" she asked.

Self-consciously, I crossed my arms over my chest and twisted my hair. "Yeah, whatever. So what's new with you?" I asked, trying to change the subject.

"Just crazy meetings with clients. It's so hard just networking all the time. I have a $15,000 check that I deposited today, but the bank is waiting for it to clear before they'd let me withdraw off of it. Can you believe the nerve of them? I've been doing business with them for so long, and they treat me like some day laborer off the street bringing in my bi-weekly paycheck?"

"I think it's a tax law, like how they do accounting-"

Just then I heard Ashley yelling my name. "Olivia! Your friend is in the bathroom vomiting. Please deal with her."

I sighed, knowing how this would end. Delilah, Christina, and I walked in the bathroom where Marissa lay on the floor gripping the toilet.

"I can't throw up, but I wanna," she slurred, lifting her head only to have it fall right back on the toilet, her black curls falling onto the toiled bowl.

"Just make yourself throw up. You look like a fool," snapped Delilah.

"I can't." She started to cry.

Jake walked up. "Oh Jesus, what a fucking cliché. You stupid hot girls can't hold your liquor. And because of that, *I* have to go find another bathroom."

Delilah leaned over her and looked at me. "Olivia, you know all about making yourself vomit, right? Show Marissa how it's done."

"Seriously-" I spun around, about ready to yank one of her stupid chopsticks out of her hair.

"You want her to feel better, don't you?"

I reached into Marissa's purse looking for any tools of the trade. The idea that using your finger makes you vomit is an urban legend. The finger isn't usually large enough to initiate the gag reflex. I found a makeup brush. Someone wouldn't be putting on anymore bronzer tonight.

"Look at me," I instructed her. She tried her best to oblige me, but her head kept lolling from side to side. I grabbed a fistful of her hair to pull her head up, instructed her to open her mouth, and shoved the brush, bristle end, down her throat. I turned her head just in time to prevent a quart of regurgitated whiskey from landing on me.

"I feel better," she mumbled, wiping her stained mascara from her face.

"Keep going until you're done," I instructed her, standing up and washing my hands. I walked out only to run right into Delilah.

"See Olivia, you haven't lost your touch, have you?" whispered Delilah in my ear. "Although I guess nowadays, it's just healthy eating an exercise," she said, almost in a taunting tone. "But I'm sure you need a little "help" from time to time now. Maybe after a big dinner? You know, your metabolism starts to slow down after 25."

I was half tempted to respond, '*Oh yeah, tell me what yours is like approaching 30?*' but I bit my tongue. Instead I smiled, and as sincerely as possible, muttered, "You're right, Delilah. Some of us just aren't as lucky as you."

We got home and I put Marissa on the couch, covered her with a blanket, and set a wastebasket next to her. Ashley mumbled something about not wanting to hear us yapping and moving around in the middle of the night, so he went to sleep in the guest room, grumbling the whole time.

I knew in my heart of hearts that Delilah wasn't completely a bad person. She used her bravado to conceal her insecurities that she felt deep down inside towards herself. She was good at a lot of things, but she was never *the* prettiest, smartest, or most athletic, so she manipulated others into believing that she was by denigrating the accomplishments of her peers. Slowly people began to assume that since Delilah was better than Kylie at this, Marissa at this, and Christina at that, that surely she must be better than everyone at everything. I knew that she always felt one step behind the curve. It took her five years to graduate instead of four, and while everyone else found jobs with relative ease, she was forced to temp at an office downtown. Now as all of her peers are getting married and having kids, she worries that she's fallen too far behind and become irrelevant. Delilah has way too much pride to let others feel sorry for her. She'd rather everyone despise her than just one person feel pity towards her.

I contemplated this as I walked into the kitchen and got a glass of water, pausing to make sure that Marissa was still breathing.

Maybe I wasn't too different from her after all. I used sarcasm, humor, and cynicism as a defensive measure on an almost daily basis, but why not? The world is a harsh place. Kristoff had no idea what he said when he accused me of being a Queen Bee.

Angry, I smacked the ice cube tray to get some ice.

What the fuck did *he* know about my life? Did *he* spend the first 18 years of his life being mercilessly taunted? Was *he* the butt of others' cruel jokes? I earned every damn right to be who I am right now. I started out as nothing and I became something. Should I have just gone and crawled into a cave because I didn't win the genetic lottery or was I right in fighting- no, *clawing*- my way to the top? Should I just let the hateful people of the world continue to shove me around or should I stand up for myself? Life fucked me over pretty damn hard in my early years, so why can't I enjoy some spoils now? I earned any right to be in the same place and treated the same as the Delilahs, Christinas, and Marissas of the world.

I knew I shouldn't let some tool like Jake under my skin, but I couldn't help it. He didn't know my struggle. If he did, he'd understand that I worked so hard for everything I had.

I looked at Marissa and sighed. Poor Marissa. She was just so damn stupid and naïve. Even asleep, she looked like an idiot. Although it was now smeared in makeup, her porcelain plump skin radiated an aura of innocence, making her seem far younger than her 24 years. I tried to warn her on so many occasions about the true nature of people, that this world is a cruel place and most people would throw you under a bus for a damn Klondike bar. I tried explaining to her that everyone is going to fuck you over- it just becomes a matter of when and how hard.

I shrugged and walked into my bedroom. I guess there are some lessons she'll just have to learn on her own.

October 11, 6:15 a.m.

What a nice, chilly, autumn morning. I love these Michigan mornings where the leaves are just starting to change colors. There's no snow yet, just a hint of frost on the grass.

Oh who am I kidding- what grass? Our lawn (if you can even call it that) has been dead since long before we moved in. I think it has something to do with Troy parking his truck out there. Haha, that will do it I guess.

I ended up finishing the rest of the bottle of Jack last night while reading the latest issue of Glamour, specifically *How* Anyone *Can Land Their Dream Guy.* The author said it's not about how you look (*all* women are beautiful), but about how you treat your man. Give him his space. But do nice things for him.

Maybe I'll clean Troy's truck today. The kids are still asleep and they are going to Jesse's house later. Troy works so hard. I feel like I *should* do something nice for him. Lately, I feel like he's been so distant from me. Is it normal for a boyfriend to come home at two in the morning on a Tuesday? It is normal for him to not come home some nights at all? He says he gets drunk and doesn't want to risk (another) DUI. I told him maybe he shouldn't drink so much. He said he had to drink to deal with me. I think he meant it as a joke, but I'm not sure anymore. Isn't there *some* underlying truth in every joke?

Electronic Journal of Tiffany Harris

File Name: Tiff's Life: 2014 edition

It's not like I'm one to talk about drinking, but it's just not fair. I've had such shit happen to me that I deserve it. I challenge anyone to find someone who's been through more shit than me. My life has been one series of heartbreaks after another.

I guess I could understand if he was fooling around behind my back. I'm a 27-year-old single mom with a high school education and minimum wage job. I know I could stand to lose a few (OK, a lot of) pounds. I'd love to be able to do something about my hair, but I can't afford it. I've been teased my whole life. I guess I should be used to it by now. When I was younger, my friend and I were called "Porky" and "Piggy." I made the mistake of telling Troy this one night after a few too many beers. Now at least once a week, it's *"Hey Porky, make me a HAM sandwich"* or *"Hey Porky, where's the beef? Or are we having PORK tonight?"*

The doctor gave me a new antidepressant this week, but so far nothing helps. I don't know if an antidepressant can help me. I wish there was a pill that could make me forget everything bad. If Pfizer makes a drug that erases 27 years worth of memories of the taunts, crushing criticism, and perpetual humiliation, sign me up as a lab rat- I'll try it out!

I believe I should get up and get going. I want to do something special tonight with Troy. Maybe I'll get online and check out cheap date ideas. Maybe there's a concert or something later. I want to show him how much I love and appreciate him- and I definitely don't want to lose him. If I lose him, I have nothing.

Well, that's not entirely true. I have the kids. But Troy's the only guy who has stuck around for more than a month. The kids are starting to grow attached to him. I don't want much- just some semblance of a happy family. Is that too much to ask?

That was profound. I logged on and tweeted and posted it. Troy never comments on my stuff. I just don't get it. He says he's too busy to be on social media, but I catch him scrolling through all the time on his phone. I know he's still friends with his ex and that pisses me off. I also don't get why he likes all these pages of hot women in bikinis. Doesn't he know how bad that makes me feel? He says that it's the Internet and I shouldn't be mad because it's not like they're real girls that he knows, but I still am.

I tell him that I'm a real woman and that this is what real women are supposed to look like. I've had two kids. I'm a single mom, which is the hardest job in the world. Nobody appreciates us though. When they make a Facebook page dedicated to *real* women, I'll happily submit a picture for that. Until then, I can only dream.

October 11

"Fuuuuccccckkkk! I feel like Satan's playing the bongos inside my head!"

I rolled over on the couch and peeked out from under the comforter, shielding my eyes from the piercing morning light, trying to discern the source of the agony.

"Rough night?" I asked Marissa, looking around for her.

"Why do I drink?" she mumbled her voice coming from the left.

I got up, wrapped the blanket around myself, looking at the clock. 10:40 a.m. Fuck. I padded into the bathroom where she lay on the floor, a death grip around the toilet.

"And why do I keep carrying you back here?" I admonished her.

"Because you looovveee meeeee." She put her head down on the bathmat. "I need to get up and get my life together."

"You do that," I replied, heading to my bedroom. "I'm going for a run. When I get back, I'll make you all breakfast. In the meantime, if you get overly ambitious, go through those boxes and look for any clothes you want."

"How the *fuck* do you go running after a night of drinking?"

"Well because I, unlike you, know my limits. Also, I don't want to get fat. And fat- it doesn't care about how hung over you are. Fat doesn't take a holiday."

"You're not fat!" she exclaimed.

"Exactly." I emerged from my room, pulling my sweatshirt over my head and putting on my sneakers. "I don't want to be fat again."

"You were never fat," she replied, opening up the cabinet and looking for a towel to wiper her makeup off with.

"Yeah, OK, whatever. I'll be back in an hour or so."

I zipped up my sweatshirt and put on my gloves. It was almost 11, but a brisk cold still permeated the air. I headed outside, turned the corner on my street and picked up my pace. If there was one thing my neighborhood was good for, it was jogging. Grosse Pointe was known for it's stunning views of Lake St. Clair, a smaller lake connected to Erie by the Detroit River. Grosse Pointe, despite bordering some of the worst parts of Detroit, was one of the nicest neighborhoods in the country. When we moved here, Ashley was pissed that we had to live in Grosse Pointe rather than the slightly trendier Royal Oak or Novi. (What could I say? *'Sorry my grandpa died in a less-than-desirable area?'*) Most residents in the area were of "old money," but lower real estate prices were bringing a new demographic to town. When we lived here, we lived further out in Farmington Hills, a bland, boring suburban wasteland. I was determined to never live like that again. In a weak economy, we were able to purchase a nice three bedroom not too far from the lakefront. Just on the edge of the uber-wealthy.

About three miles in, I was so distracted by the fall foliage that I realized I missed my turn around. I was all the way up Nautical Mile in St. Clair Shores. I thought there might be a shortcut back, but I had to consult my phone. I saw a park turned in, looking for a bench. I sat down, took off my armband and pulled out my phone. I got my bearings, put my phone back, and stood up. As I looked around, I was overcome by a sense of déjà vu.

I had been here before.

Or had I? It looked so familiar. I crossed the parking lot to the playground, which sat on a hill overlooking the small beach. No, I definitely had been here before. But when?

'*Think*,' I told myself. The playground was deserted, as the sky was quickly clouding over and the wind was picking up. I sat on the swing and closed my eyes.

I was maybe 10 or 11. We had been in the United States for less than a year. It was some sort of class trip. I remember the stupid tie-dye tankini swimsuit I wore, self consciously pulling the top down to cover my ample stomach. I sat on the edge of a group of girls- not the

*pretty ones who the boys flocked to, but the average ones.
I had a vague understanding that they didn't like me, but
I had nowhere else to go. I think one or two of them
tolerated me, so they let me sit by them on the unspoken
condition that I didn't talk. As they discussed boys, TV
shows, bands, and other trivial pre-teen matters, I
occasionally murmured in agreement or simply nodded
my head.*

*After a while, they all got up to go swim. I got up to
follow until one of them turned and said, "Won't your hair
frizz up any more if you get it wet, Orca-whale? I mean,
my poodle's does."*

I looked down, trying to hide my tears.

*"Well, at least she finally shaved her legs," continued the
second, a slightly cross-eyed girl named Kirsten with an
upturned nose (but perfect hair). "She was looking like
Sasquatch. Now if she'd only do something about her
eyebrows. There's supposed to be two, you know?"*

*"She's just trying to detract from that horrible swimsuit,"
her friend Ali chimed in. "Look at it- it's like a bulls-eye
on it. She's a pretty big target."*

*I bit back tears and looked up. "What did I ever do to
you?" I snapped.*

*"Nothing, you're just a loser. You're fat and ugly. Your
mom should have just had an abortion."*

"Looks like your mom did," I retorted, quickly spinning on my heels before they could see me burst into tears.

As I walked away, I heard one of them whisper, "Did she really just say that?"

I headed towards the bathrooms and turned the corner, only to find myself face to face with Carmine, one of the objects of desire of every girl in our school. With his curly brown hair and blue eyes, it was easy to see why everyone was charmed by him.

"Are you OK....Oda?"

I looked down, not bothering to correct him. "Yeah, I'm fine."

"You sure?" he asked.

I could see his friends looking over at us. I didn't want them to jump on the humiliation bandwagon.

"Yeah, I just tripped and I'm going inside to wash it off." I didn't wait for a response. I just darted around him and closed the door behind me.

I stood with my back to the door, taking deep breaths and trying to calm down. I felt someone pushing on the door. 'What the hell?' I thought. I had left them alone. They had no right to come bother me in here. My sadness turned to anger as I spun around just in time to avoid being hit by the door. I breathed a sigh of relief.

"Are you OK?" the girl asked.

"Yeah, fine."

"You're Oda, right? Is that how you say it?" She smiled- one of those smiles that seemed so eager to please. I had a feeling she smiled like that a lot and never seemed to be rewarded with the accolades she desperately chased after.

"Yeah." I tried to remember her name. I had seen her around, but she was one of those faceless people- the kind you tended to forget. She was plump, but not obese. Homely, but not ugly. Her hair was a dull strawberry blonde/light brown, and apart from a small scar on her cheek, she was incredibly unremarkable. "I'm sorry. I don't know your name," I blurted out.

"Tiffany. I think we were in class together, but that was only for two weeks until you got switched to the advanced class."

(In the 90s, we had different classes. There were no pretenses. We knew which kids in the grade were smart, average, slow, and seriously slow).

"Oh yeah, OK. I kinda remember you."

"Don't let them bother you. I mean, they're mean. They've been that way forever. I've been in class with Ali since kindergarten."

"Seriously?"

"She's horrible. One time she peed her pants and made another girl change with her. Then she started teasing the other girl."

"What a bitch," I replied. As young girls do, we giggled at the use of a curse word, and with that, a friendship was born.

It was easier to go out into the water, and even the world, not being alone. Maybe it's strength in numbers or maybe the biting sting of insults is diluted amongst more people, like blood in the ocean. Either way, I knew I wasn't alone.

I stood up, shaking off the memory and smiling to myself. I laughed at the thought of ever feeling self-conscious in a swimsuit. I crossed my arms and took one last look at the playground and beach, as if somehow almost two decades later, I had conquered it.

Back at my house, Marissa had woken up and was watching TV with Ashley.

"Good run?" he asked.

"Yeah, got a little lost, but that's OK. What do you guys want for breakfast?" I asked, getting out pots, pans, and eggs.

"A new liver," was all I heard from the couch.

Later that afternoon, I stood in the living room surrounded by boxes. Marissa was still on the couch staring at the TV, her arm flopping off of the couch onto the floor.

"Hey, who's that blonde girl in the picture with Ashley?" she asked, pointing towards the bookshelf.

"Ha, that's his sister. She's probably the most photogenic person I know. He has this picture of her in his wallet and everyone thought it was the stock photo that came when he bought the wallet."

I took the picture off the shelf and dusted it off before returning it. "I like her way more than I like my real sister," I replied, scooting a box into the living room with my toe.

"I have to go through this stuff," I sighed. "I want all my Halloween decorations up and I want to sort through these old clothes and crap. If I'm going to take it to Goodwill, I'm going to do it Monday." To demonstrate my resolve, I opened the box and dumped its contents on the floor.

Clothes. Some old pillows. Why did my mom keep this stuff? I separated it into piles and repeated the task with the second box.

Clothes. Books. An old keyboard. Seriously. WTF?

After a few more boxes, I was less careful as I assumed most were just old clothes until I opened the fifth box and something hard fell on my foot.

"Ow! *God dammit!* What the fuck!" I leaned down and picked up a pink photo album covered with Lisa Frank stickers.

"What is it?" asked Marissa.

"Just old pictures and stuff. I'll look at it later."

"Let me see!"

"No!"

She reached for it, but I held it above her head.

"Wait, there's another one," said Ashley, picking up another (pink) album that had fallen on the floor.

He opened it and showed it to Marissa.

"Wait, which one are you?" she asked, pointing to a picture of my 14th birthday party.

"Give me that. Now." I reached for the book.

"Seriously-"

"That's her!" Ashley announced, pointing.

"No it's not," Marissa replied, looking from the book to me.

"Yes it is. Her face shape is the same- look at her teeth. You never had braces, right?"

I put my hands on my hips. "Just give it back to me, OK?"

"*Holy shit*! That *is* you!" Marissa burst into a fit of laughter. "Is that a *unibrow*?"

"Oh, shut up. I'm sure *you* looked *perfect* when you were young."

"So what you're telling me," Ashley chimed in, "is that you really have one eyebrow. Did you get it separated? Also, was that a Tina Turner wig you were wearing?"

"I told you I was ugly when I was young. You never believed me."

"No, you didn't tell me what a man-beast you were," he said. "Do you have some Bigfoot DNA in you? Should I call Dean Cain? Wasn't he looking for Sasquatch on his reality show?"

With my secret past revealed, I sat on the couch and flipped on the TV.

Marissa picked up a yearbook and flipped to the index in the back. "You were in the Geography club?" she asked.

"Obviously. Because you can't even rely on Apple maps these days, let alone in 2001."

"What's this say in the front cover? It's all scratched out."

"I don't know," I retorted, getting annoyed. "I probably wrote my crush's name in there or something."

"No. It looks like someone wrote something to you. Ork- pork- I can't tell."

I sighed and took the book from her. I guess there were no more secrets.

"It says, '*Orky Porky, have a good summer. Hope Jenny Craig works out for you.*' From Reagan."

Marissa and Ashley burst into laughter.

"Where did that come from?" Marissa asked, groaning as her mocking laughter exaggerated her hangover.

I sighed. I knew they wouldn't let it go. "So the first day of school, my mom filled out our paperwork. Her handwriting wasn't very good, so her letter 'd' looked like the letter 'k,' and maybe there was a smudge on the paper or something that looked like an 'r,' thus causing my name to be 'Orka' on the roster. My homeroom teacher accidentally called me *Orka* and it stuck. An orca is a breed of whale. The name stuck."

"So does that mean we'll have to install an aquarium instead of a pool in the spring?" Ashley asked, causing Marissa to fall into convulsions.

"I fucking hate you both."

I spent the rest of the day sorting through the miscellaneous odds and ends and decorating the house for Halloween. By five, I was done and was vacuuming the floor, much to Ashley's chagrin.

"Do you have to do that *right* now?" he asked, turning the TV up even louder.

"The floor isn't going to vacuum itself."

"You can do it tomorrow. Just come sit over here by me." He patted the couch next to him.

I sat down and leaned next to him, patting his stomach.

"Have you been working out?" I asked, playfully grabbing flesh between my fingers.

"Just stop it," he muttered, getting up. "You know, I work a lot of hours during the week. You could cut me a little slack."

I sighed. I hated how the mood had the ability to turn 180 degrees sour in such a short time. "I'm just saying, I work really hard to look good for you. When we first met, you were really into fitness and had a six-pack.

How much weight have you gained since we've gotten together?"

"Don't start-"

"Don't start what?" I stood up, crossing my arms. "I'm just supposed to let *you* get fat while *I* work my ass off? I demand perfection of myself, so please excuse me for expecting a *little* bit of effort on your part! Our wedding is in-"

"Shut up, you old hag," he said, turning the TV even louder.

I turned and went into our bedroom, slamming the door for added emphasis. I lay on the bed and pulled out my laptop. I logged onto my website and pulled up a new blog template.

Tough Love With (not a) Doctor Olivia: Love is *not* enough

October 11

Ladies? Do you ever wonder why your husband or S.O. cheats on you? After all, aren't marriages and relationships supposed to be through better or worse? Sickness and health? Good and bad? Don't the magazines tell you that love is enough to guide the way? Or maybe that was Celine Dion.

I'm here to give you your daily dose of tough love. There are things that happen to couples that they should weather together. Then there are things that one half of the couple does that the other should not have to suffer through. Take for example the following two scenarios: In Scenario A, the man is in a tragic car accident and loses a limb. He didn't bring it on himself. His wife, knowing this, goes to physical therapy and countless doctors appointments with him because she loves him. In Scenario B, however, a man's wife lets herself go, gains a bunch of weight, stops putting any effort into her appearance, and wonders why her husband isn't attracted to her. After all, she's the same person as when he married her!

Wrong. Think about it. If you bought a Lexus, you wouldn't expect it to turn into aNeon, would you? No. So why should a man marry a seven and be OK with her turning into a two?

Ladies, if you are lucky enough to be in a relationship, you need to continue to strive to be better and better every day in all aspects of your mind, body, and spirit. Only then will your significant other see you as a prize and not a burden.

Don't like my tough love? Then go watch
Oprah. As always, use comments section
below for hate mail, comments, and
dissenting viewpoints.

#lifesabitchthenyoudie, #truelove,
#highstandards, #lastingrelationships,
#relationshipadvice

I proofread the blog, opened the story up to comments, shared it on social media, and closed my laptop. After 45 minutes, Ashley should be less mad at me. I don't know why he was pissed. Half of his friends' wives are frumpy hausefraus whose only physical activities are couponing (yep, it's a verb) and making "Kustom Hairbowz" (their name, not mine). The worst part is those bitches all think they are *so* much better than me because they have the perfect suburban life and go to Zumba in matching outfits.

I got worked up thinking about their misplaced priorities as I got dressed. I pulled a sweater over my head and yanked my arms through the sleeves. I thought about his one friend's wife, Jeannine. That bitch had the nerve to call me a whore because I wore a bikini to her pool party. *It was a fucking pool party!*

Was I supposed to wear a burquini?

My people didn't leave the suffocating, patriarchal Middle East just to replace the judgment of out-of-touch men with that of out-of-touch women.

I took a deep breath and huffed angrily as I looked for my jeans. I wanted to ask Ashley when the last time perfect fucking Jeannine put on a pair of jeans without an elastic waistband. Hell, when was the last time that bitch saw her toes? I'm willing to bet it was when wooly mammoths still roamed the earth.

I took one look in the mirror and appraised myself. I sighed. My body was decent, but my pores looked fucking huge. I seriously need to do something about that festoon line on my face. My mom swears it's a childhood scar, but I swear it's the Mark of the Middle Aged Woman. I sighed, dejectedly dropping my arms to my side. What use were the $200 Guess jeans on an old lady? I made a mental note to call a plastic surgeon first thing Monday.

October 11, 11:30 p.m.

Well, today was a waste and a disaster, caused by what else? My stupidity and pathetic longing for some semblance of happiness. Jesse came and got the kids, barely acknowledging my existence. I think he's starting to resent them too- like we're such a burden on him. He says of course, that they're fat, lazy, and stupid (and obviously got that from me). I told him I know I'm not stupid because I always did well in school and help them with their homework. I should have never opened that can of worms. Of course he took to task with his usual rhetoric.

And you flunked out of college how many times?

I didn't even bother reminding him that I didn't flunk out. I quit because I needed to get a job to raise my kids.

I remember the day Tyrell was born like it was yesterday- the cumulative, overwhelming sense of happiness, but also fear and anxiety. How would I pay for all of the things he needed? I was just 19 and a part-time waitress. Darnell worked at the auto-detailing place, but eventually got a bug to join the Army. He promised me we'd eventually get married, but as with him, most promises ended up being empty. I met Jesse when Darnell was at basic training. By the time I was 21, Emma had arrived. Jesse begrudgingly married me, but only after his parents pretty much forced him to. I had always fantasized about a wedding as one of the best days of my life. Although I've never told anyone this, I still have a scrapbook of wedding ideas I've been assembling since I was a little girl.

They didn't include a sterile waiting room at the courthouse down the hall from the license plate renewal office and an impersonal few words by a judge who was just biding his time until retirement.

Remembering this, I made the unfortunate decision of going upstairs and opening what my grandma called" the memory chest." It's not so much a memory chest, but a chest where I keep all the winter blankets.

Underneath, I have my old photo albums, scrapbooks, and journals, which would be far too embarrassing if anyone ever found them. My "dream wedding book" lies at the bottom of the pile.

I sat down and heard a noise from down the street. Gunshot or backfire? It was a game I played all too often in this neighborhood. Despite claiming that I lived in Grosse Pointe, the truth was that I lived just on the Detroit side of 8 Mile. For all the difference it made, I may have as well lived in a war-zone. I tried to take the kids on a walk up to Grosse Pointe park one day, but a Rent-a-Cop asked if I was a resident and said that the park was for residents only. Someday I promised the kids that all our dreams would come true and we'd live in the nicest house on Lakeshore Dr. Until then, all we could do was dream....

I opened up the leopard print photo book, taking care to avoid messing up the excellent rubber cement job of a preteen girl. I turned to the first page where Josh Hartnett's smiling face greeted me and remembered that day 14 years ago.

Today they had Pinterest for this. Maybe I'd create like a vintage wedding board- stuff I thought was cool 15 years ago. Tiffanylharris1 would be a Pinterest star for sure- people would think I was trendy and quirky. Perfect.

I looked down and started reading.

"OK, so what celebrity would you marry?" Oda asked, sitting cross-legged on the floor, flipping through Seventeen.

"Matt Damon," I replied.

"Seriously? Ben Affleck is SO much hotter! And he saved the world in Armageddon. Matt Damon's gonna do what- calculus problems?"

I laughed and picked up the first stack of wedding magazines we had grabbed from the dentist office where my mom worked.

"We have to get down to business. So our poster is going to be about the cost of an average wedding, right?" I asked.

"Sure," she replied, opening up Modern Bride. *"I like this dress. Do you think I could wear it?"*

"Your boobs are way too big," I replied, with just a hint of jealousy. "Do we even know how much this stuff costs?"

"Uh-huh. I already wrote it down and made a pie chart in Excel. I printed it all off. All we need to do is put it on the poster board."

I looked at her charts and graphs. Of course they were perfect. Everything Oda did had to be perfect.

"Where did you print these charts?"

"My dad's printer," she replied, nonchalantly, as she sniffed the perfume sample in the magazine and rubbed her wrist against it.

I should have known. Oda's family always had the best computer and TV stuff. Her dad had been some big doctor in Iran or something, then he moved here to work for one of the drug companies. Her parents were really old- almost as old as my grandparents, but it didn't seem to bother her. According to her, it was all part of their life plan. And like her parents, she had a life plan too.

"How old do you want to be when you get married?" I asked.

"Twenty three. Because then I'll have finished university and will be in medical school with my husband. Or maybe he'll be in law school. Lawyers are OK too. What about you?"

"Um, I don't know. My mom got married when she was 18."

"Eighteen? That's only four years away!"

"I know, right?"

"So, that would mean you'd probably know the guy you're going to marry right now. He's probably someone we go to school with." She stopped organizing her piles of flower pictures by color and looked up. *"OK, tell me who it is. Who do you want to marry?"*

I blushed. There was no lying to Oda. "I don't want to marry anyone until I go to college!"

"OK, fine, but suppose it's ten years from now and you HAVE to marry someone we go to school with now. Who would it be?"

"I don't know...."

"Yes you do. Is it Reagan?"

"No! He's too short!"

"Samir?"

"No way! He's even shorter than Reagan!"

"OK, fine, I'm going to just keep guessing. Adam, Ben D., Ben J., Vinnie, Mark with the weird last name, Mark

McDonald, Tony, Carmine, Ryan Markson, Sanjay, Ryan Sanchez, Tony-"

"He's an oaf!"

"He is not!" She doth protested too much.

"You like Tony?"

"He's OK, I guess. No, we're not getting off topic. Is it Paul?"

"I...um...no..."

"You like Paul Jacobi!" she shouted.

"Shut up! Yell any louder and he'll hear you all the way over on Lake Court."

(Lake Court was, and still is, one of the priciest streets in Michigan.)

"You and every other girl in grade eight. Take a number," she said matter-of-factly, neatly cutting out a picture of a cake that probably cost more than most cars. "Eventually, you'll get your turn."

"No way," I said, shaking my head. "He's out of our league."

"Yeah, I guess you're right," she sighed, dejected at the thought. "Like he's gonna probably marry Julie Borowitz

or Kirsten Delgado. What a stupid name anyways. Like, why not just be Kristen like a normal person?"

"Don't tell her that or she'll start in on you again. This week, she seems to be hell-bent on ruining Fat Morgan's life."

"Why?"

"I think Fat Morgan said her answer was wrong in some class and the teacher sided with Morgan. Kirsten was pissed because Reagan called her an idiot, so she told everyone that Fat Morgan got her period early and it soaked through her jeans."

"Why would she do that? It seems the crime doesn't fit the punishment."

"Because she's a bitch." I sighed, arranging our cut outs on the board as I tried to figure out if we should put Christmas lights around the board- you know, to really make it pop.

"Do you think that we'll ever get married?" I asked.

"To each other? Now, I'm not that kind of girl," she laughed, before getting serious and continuing.

"I don't know. I mean, yeah, probably. Don't most people? It's statistically proven that most people get married."

"But what if we don't?" I asked, realizing for the first time in my life that we existed in reality, not some Disney fairy

tale. *"What if no guy wants me because I'm too fat? I don't want to be an old, lonely, cat lady like my aunt. She's 35 and single."*

Oda thought about it and finally spoke up. "I guess if I'm not married by the time I'm 30, I'll just settle for some guy- any guy. But I want to at least try for the hot guy- when I'm grown up, I want to have a way hotter husband than Kirsten and whatever idiot she marries."

"Like Tony Muscarella?" I asked.

"Shut up. Tell anyone and I'll kill you."

"No, someday you're going to be a super successful doctor and Tony is going to want to marry you. I'm going to save all these pictures of dresses you cut out and put them in a book so you can remember what you liked when we did this consumer ed. project in grade eight," I responded, encouraging her.

"Why do we even have to take this class?" she asked as she peeled the glue off of her fingers. "Isn't it just home ec? I'm never going to need to know how to cook or clean. I'm going to have a chef and a maid service. And when I get married, I'm going to have it at the Detroit Yacht Club with tons of Christmas lights and you can be my Maid of Honor."

"Deal."

"But only if," she giggled and held the magazine up to reveal a putrid green frock, "You wear this dress."

"For Mr. and Mrs. Muscarella? Anything!"

I closed the book and thought about Emma. She's only six, but someday she's going to be 13, planning her imaginary wedding to the boys in her class. I worry about her ending up like me. She seems to have more friends in her class than I can recall at that age, but I forget if kids are mean that young. Kaylah, Jesse's new girlfriend, despite all her flaws, seems to enjoy buying clothes for Emma, so at least she won't get mocked for the K-Mart specials that I showed up to school in.

(I guess whores do sometimes bring small miracles.)

The doctor said that Emma's a little bit on the chubby side, so I've been trying to get her to eat healthy. I can't control what they give them at after school care and God knows I'm not a model for healthy living, but hell, I wouldn't wish my childhood on anyone else, especially my own flesh and blood.

I put the book back in the chest and covered it up with blankets. I stood up, my joints creaking in protest. I really need to lose weight- 160 (ok, fine, 182) is far too much. I started to fold the blankets when I heard footsteps behind me.

"Troy!" I announced, turning around in surprise. "You're home early! I thought you had to-"

"We got done early. What the hell have you been doing all day?" he asked, accusingly.

"I was just, um, I was…"

"Look at yourself," he said, disgusted, as he took off his sweatshirt and threw it on the floor. "Have you even showered? Did you do *anything* all day?"

"I was busy- I had to-"

He cut me off. "Oh, I'm sure you were so busy. What were you doing? Wait, let me guess, writing the next *New York Times* bestseller?"

"It's for my class. I had homework."

"Yeah, I'm sure homework from Wayne Community takes such a long time. Your school's a fucking joke. What are they gonna do? Make you CEO of the call center?"

I bit back tears, not wanting to start a fight. I picked up his clothes and took them to the hamper.

"Christ woman, do we not have any toothpaste?" I heard him shout from the bathroom.

I went in the bathroom and began rifling through the cabinets, knocking over the kids' medicine and my diet pills in the process.

Troy picked them up. "What the hell is this? Green tea weight loss? Stupid cunt."

"I'm trying!" I protested.

"How about you put down the fucking fork for once? Or just shut your mouth in general? That'd kill two birds with one stone."

"You know what? You treat me like a piece of shit!" I screamed as I slammed my fist into the wall. Somewhere down the hall, a picture crashed to the floor.

"Is that right?" he sarcastically remarked as he spit out toothpaste all over the sink. "Well, I wish you were a *silent* piece of shit, so just shut the fuck up already, OK?"

I burst into tears and turned to leave.

"Oh stop it with the dramatics. Look at you. You're a pathetic creature, you know that? You think you can treat *me* like this? You think *you* can do better than *me*? I'd like to see that. You'd be nothing without me. You'd probably still be putting out for any guy who paid you attention, which let's face it- ain't exactly a large population, now, is it?"

He turned on the shower and stepped in, his voice barely audible over the water. "Just go away and leave me the fuck alone. Why don't you go clean the house or go fucking shopping for once so I don't have to eat stale chips?"

I took a Lysol wipe and cleaned off the sink, knowing it would be a mess in an hour anyways and gathered up his laundry. Maybe I should have paid more attention in consumer ed. after all. At least my house would be in order, even if my life isn't.

October 13

I swear, if it's not one thing, it's another. When my parents decided to go into the house-flipping business, did they just assume that I'd have nothing better to do than manage their properties? Seriously. I was on my way hoe from work before heading out to my evening kickboxing class when Brenda, our renter at the Livonia property called. Apparently she got a notice on her door telling her that she was being fined $25 for having a non-regulation campaign sign in her window. I sighed and dialed Brenda's number. She picked up on the second ring.

"Brenda, does anyone else have a campaign sign?"

"Yes, everyone," she replied in her ex-smokers voice.

I'm pretty sure than Brenda had been a Vegas lounge singer or something back in the day. At 60 years old, she still had a killer body, but the largest hair ever. I swear, she is like a skinnier version of Dolly Parton. Now she's a receptionist at some dentist's office in the suburbs. She's a good tenant who pays her rent on time, so I had a hard time believing that there was an issue.

"So why can't you have yours?"

"Because the condo association doesn't like me."

"They don't *like* you?" I asked, incuriously. "You keep the place spotless. Have you been having wild parties I don't know about?"

"Well, it's all women on the board, you know."

"Yeah, like 60-year-old women," I replied, taking off my shirt and tossing it in the hamper. "No offense."

"None taken. They just don't like me. They think Judy's husband was flirting with me."

I pulled another shirt on over my head as I stifled my laughter imagining that lady's geriatric husband leaving his recliner. "Well I highly doubt that. I believe that man just probably took a too many hits off of his oxygen tank and was coughing. Aren't you still with Jim?" Jim was her ex-biker boyfriend who lived next door in the other condo that we owned. At worst, we received a complaint about him playing "Stairway to Heaven" too loudly one night.

"They don't care. I'm *telling* you, they don't like me."

I sighed. "I'll call my dad and have him call them. Just take down the sign for now."

"But the election isn't for two more years."

I paused taking out my earring. "Wait, what sign is this? What election?"

"Ron Paul, 2016," she replied without a hint of sarcasm in her voice.

"Take it down Brenda."

The day only went downhill from there. After that, my auxiliary cord didn't work on the drive to the gym, almost ruining the night. I *cannot* drive in silence. Then I was stuck next to some lady with body odor at kickboxing.

To top it all off, I get home and I forgot I had this stupid assignment for my *Journalism of Conscience I* class. Some hippie bullshit. I want to be a features reporter. I'm not gonna go to fucking Afghanistan and build schools and report on it. I want to write travel and lifestyle features about Michigan. I have no idea how this class is a Master's level course.

On top of it, I have to do my stupid journal entry. Yes, I am a grown adult writing in a journal as part of my class assignment. What am I going to write?

Dear Diary,
Today at work, I broke the copier but I walked away because no one saw me. I do not feel guilty, which is possibly a sign that I'm a narcissist.

P.S. The guy who is fixing the computers is very cute. He looks like at least one member of One Direction. I might have a crush on him. I sure hope I can give him a Hello Kitty Valentine in a few months.

Fucking shoot me now.

October 14

Ugh, I need to punch something. Anything. Or someone. Why do people suck so badly? Work today was so fucking pointless. I'm so sick of the whiny bitches that think they're so exceptional because they have their own column while I'm just the copy editor. Fuck that. When I've written the next best seller and those dumb cunts are still covering the auto show, they won't be so superior *then*, will they?

I started out the day like normal- hitting the gym before work for two hours and then had to edit three feature pieces.

I arrived at the office and took off my coat, then immediately went to the bathroom to check my hair, which had gone from super cute to tsunami chic in a matter of five minutes. Our receptionist greeted me with her usual frosty stare.

"Do you always wear high heels?" she asked, narrowing her eyes into slits and tapping her un-manicured nails against her plastic gas station cup before loudly taking a sip.

"Except when I'm running," I replied, standing at her desk with my arms crossed.

"I could never wear heels," she commented, taking another loud sip from her Big Gulp, this time making slurping noises.

(*'Maybe if you weren't a fat slob, you could,'* I thought in my mind.)

"I like to look nice." I continued to stand there, arms crossed, waiting for her to realize what I needed.

"I just spend so much time running after my toddler all day, that-"

I cut her off, bored with her worthless diatribe about her pedantic, pathetic life.

"Wow, that's admirable, but can I get some of Martin's files from last year on the new housing market data? Specifically broken down by neighborhood?" I asked, using my "nice girl" voice. "I already have the Access file, but I want the hard copy as well. He said you have it."

She sighed and turned around, like it was the biggest inconvenience ever. What the hell? She's a secretary. Didn't she go to school for this? I mean, what the fuck do they teach them at ITT tech? Their entire job is filing and answering the phone. She manages to fuck up the latter, so I guess I shouldn't expect her to excel in alphabetizing either.

I managed not to sigh too loudly or impatiently tap my foot too hard, eventually getting the files I needed.

I sat down and got to work. At least I was doing statistical analysis, which required a few more brain cells than correcting improper use of the Oxford comma. I really needed to focus, but instead was forced to endure the stupid whining, worthless drivel of eight "journalists" and 13 copy editors. They were discussing the finer points of child-raising, a battle most of them were clearly losing.

As they were yammering away and I was trying to ignore them, Mrs. Day, the 300-lb. food reporter asked me, "In your country, are the parents very strict with the children?"

"I've lived in the states for almost 20 years," I replied, not looking up.

"But you're from...over there...right?" she asked, lowering her voice as if I had immigrated from Hades.

(Last month when we were doing the September 11 anniversary special issue, this woman *honestly* asked if I knew any of the 21 hijackers. Because we all look alike I guess.)

I wanted to reply, "In communist Russia, children raise parents," but realized she'd never get the pop culture reference.

"Well, my parents are pretty much American and Canadian respectively, but yeah, they were super strict growing up. Just wanted to push us to be the best I guess."

"And they must be proud then at how disciplined you are. You're always working, always so serious," she replied, taking a sip from her Big Gulp.

(Seriously, what was *with* these people? Maybe I should open a 7-11 franchise. I made a mental note to make a joke with Krishna about that later.)

"Yeah," I replied, in a tone that was clearly indicative of an ended conversation.

"You're wound so tight though," she continued. "You know, if you spend so much time trying to prove to others how perfect you are, you're going to wind up a sad and lonely human being."

I shrugged and put on my coat, indicating that it was time to leave and therefore relieving myself of their idiocracy. "Yeah, but I guess there's worse things in life. I could be fat."

Before she could respond, I grabbed my purse and headed out into the blistery wind, sharing my hilarity with the world on social media.

After I hit "share," I texted Ashley to see what he wanted for dinner, but he didn't reply. Ever since the Malaysian airliner got shot down over the summer, Southeastern has amped up security protocols and given the pilots so much more to do during routine checks, so I totally understand when Ashley doesn't text me back right away.

By the time I got home, it was already 6:45, so I hurriedly tried to start cooking dinner.

I was pre-heating the oven and letting the water boil as I pulled out my computer and started working on my homework.

At seven, I heard Ashley's key in the door. Shit.

"I'm sorry!" I yelled, frantically stirring the pot of noodles and turning the heat up. "Dinner is almost ready. I really am sorry I didn't get home sooner."

"No," he said, not sounding sorry at all. "You're doing your thing."

"My *thing*?" I retorted, angrily turning towards him. "You mean, like, *my job*?"

"I don't see you getting paid for it."

I almost exploded with anger. "*I'm in fucking graduate school!* I'm sorry we all aren't qualified to be fucking Southeastern pilots."

"I'm just saying, it's your decision. You want to advance your little feminist agenda, go right ahead," he said, cracking a beer.

"My *feminist agenda*? You mean, earning a higher degree? Because, look at me, I'm a *real* feminist," I continued sarcastically as he took a swig of his beer. "I don't shave my leg hair, I go to war protests..."

"Just stop it with the bullshit. You know what I mean."
He sat on the couch and turned on the TV.

"No, I *don't* know what you mean. Please enlighten me,"
I snapped, standing in front of the TV.

"Oh, *mommy and daddy don't love me enough,* so I have
to prove how smart I am. I was fat and now I have to
prove how hot I am," he mocked, craning his neck to see
around me. "Come on, what am I missing here?"

"You-"

"Oh wait, you got engaged to me too, right? Marriage to
an airline pilot isn't quite as prestigious as being
married to a doctor, but hey, it's a distant third, so that's
good, right?"

By now, I was fighting back tears, but turned
nonchalantly towards the kitchen and stirred the
noodles, which were by this time starting to burn to the
bottom of the pan. I decided to try to lighten the mood.
"I'd say you were below stockbroker, but above
pharmacist."

"Jesus, you *would* have a list, wouldn't you?"

I started cleaning the counters. "In case you didn't get it,
that was sarcasm. Oh, I forgot- you just wanted a dumb
housewife who would end up barefoot and pregnant
and I just wanted a trophy husband, right?"

"Yep, well at least you got what you wanted. I got a raging feminist bitch with a chip on her shoulder."

"Then why don't you go back to your ex girlfriend? I'm sure she'd be all too happy to do your laundry and breed your children!"

I knew it was a cheap shot and I regretted the words as soon as they came out of my mouth.

"At least she'd tell me she loved me."

I put on a hot mitt and took the lasagna out, slamming the pan on the stove.

"I love you. Dinner is ready."

We ate the dinner in awkward silence, and then I retreated to my room to work on my paper. It was on childhood socialization and the effects of bullying. I rolled my eyes. Seriously? Kids are mean to kids. It happens. If I had a dollar for every time I was mocked, insulted, or generally degraded, I'd be a millionaire by now. But that was a long time ago. Even Delilah used to moo at me, an allegation she vehemently denies, although she admits that she used to make at least 20 girls on average cry per week. (She called it character building.)

I lay on my bed and thought about what I wanted to write about. It was for this stupid conscience class, which was not only a joke, but also a waste of time. Not only did I have to write that 3,000-word story, but we also had weekly assignments in which we had to read this book (written by the professor of course) and reflect on a chapter per week. The book was seriously titled *"The Human Experience."* Some tree-hugger bullshit if you ask me. I opened my book, skimmed the chapter and wrote my weekly entry. The topic was "death." We had to write just a paragraph or two.

(Seriously, I'm in a Masters of Journalism program?)

I groaned and started typing.

```
Death is sad, but a part of life. It is
hard to understand why we must die, but in
the cycle of life, we all must die in order
that a new society can grow. However, ideas
do not die with people. Ideas are what live
on. We should all try to contribute as many
ideas to our world as we can so that we
have done something productive with our
lives.
```

I rolled my eyes and hit "Submit." I turned to back my other paper and opened up the PDF files I had downloaded. I started browsing through the bullying statistics.

```
About 15% of boys and 7% of girls were
bullied and 12% of girls and 13% of boys
were victimized at age 16. Both bullying
and victimization at age 16 were associated
with a wide range of psychological problems
```

at age 8 and 16, and with referral to child
mental health services…

I yawned. This was nothing groundbreaking. I knew all
of these statistics. I couldn't seem to get an angle. Our
professor always tells us to "look for the gaps in the
research." I couldn't find anything. Surely there was
something….increased suicide rates…drug abuse…. I
rolled my eyes.

'More touchy-feely whiny liberal jibber jabber,' I thought,
as I rubbed my temples. *'Why can't these people just
toughen up?'*

I suddenly sat up.

That's it! I would write an opposing paper- sure to be
provocative and definitely controversial (the
cornerstones of successful journalism). The so-called
bullying phenomenon was nothing more than an
attempt at the liberal, whiny, media to justify their
weakening of our children. I was going to do a series of
case studies about people who had been bullied, yet
went on to become incredibly successful. It would be an
amazing feature series- guaranteed to at least get me
noticed.

I had just opened a screen when Marissa texted me. The
conversation is verbatim:

Marissa: I think I'm in love.

    Me: With whom this week?

117

Marissa: His name is Sanjaya and-

Me: Wait, I'm sorry, did you say his name is Sanjaya, like American Idol? Please tell me you met him online through his fan site.

Marissa: Hahahahaha. No. I met him at a meeting for work. He's training us how to use the new patient reporting software. He's so smart with computers. He wants to meet up Friday night.

Me: Then go.

Marissa: Will you come with? I really want you to like him. I think he might be the one.

Me: You met him yesterday.

Marissa: But he's so smart and funny and we like the same stuff.

Me: So he watches "Say Yes to The Dress" and "A Wedding Story" marathons as well?

Marissa: Go to hell.

Me: I'll meet him on Friday. Ashley might be working, but if not, I'll

```
still go. And I'll tell him how you've
already created your wedding registry.
```

I shook my head. Some people. I wrote the paper, then started in on my blog.

```
"What is a feminist? Is it a dirty word?
Are feminists bra-burning hippies or are
they Hillary Clinton-wannabes? Today we
celebrate the early women's rights
activists, yet we still say the word
"feminist" with disdain."
```

I was about to type the definition when my dad called. I could hear my niece crying in the background.

"Did you tell Brenda to remove her sign?"

"Yes," I sighed. "She said she did."

"I know, but that Judy lady from the condo association called and said that she took down the sign, but has been associating with unsavory characters," he countered before yelling at my niece to take something out of her mouth.

"Like who? Is there some septuagenarian gang I don't know about?" I snidely retorted.

"I don't know, but Christ, I can't deal with this woman. Apparently Jim had some of his long-haired ex-hippie buddies over and they were playing cards on the porch until midnight."

"So are they complaining about *Jim*?" I asked, saving my document.

"No, because they said it's Brenda's fault."

"How is it her fault? I'm confused."

"I don't know. Just call her and tell her to please keep the noise down after eleven. You're the *babu* on this one."

Did that mean doorkeeper or evening? I didn't want a lecture so I sighed, "fine."

I was about to continue when I realized that he had hung up.

"Well thanks for asking me how my day was. What's the Kurdish word for *asshole*? " I muttered to myself. I put away my computer and turned out the light.

October 14

I am completely and totally devastated. I don't know
what to do. I feel like I've had my heart ripped out. I
know that I've hit rock bottom and there's no way to get
back up. I can't bear the thought of seeing Troy or the
kids tonight. I don't know how I'm going to tell them
that I failed them all. Just last week, I thought for sure
that I was up for a promotion. I had been getting such
good supervisor reports recently. I was hoping to get a
promotion to team leader by the end of the month so
that I could buy the kids something nice for Christmas
this year and not have to put everything on layaway.
Now, I don't even know if we'll have a roof over our
heads by the end of the month.

Work started out normally enough today. I clocked in at
7:59 exactly, after getting the kids off to school. I was
going through my monotonous job with my usual level
of false enthusiasm when my supervisor came and
tapped me on the shoulder and told me to come with
her. I knew by the tone in her voice that I was in for
some form of ass-chewing. Whether it was a collective
or individual ass-chewing had yet to be determined.
When I got to her office, she asked me to close the door.
The lady from human resources was there, which I
knew was never a good sign.

I figured I was getting a formal reprimand for arriving
late, but as soon as I heard the words, "We're going to
have to let you go," the blood rushed to my head and all
I remember is crying, or perhaps more accurately,
wailing. I've never had the wind knocked out of me, but

DETROIT POLICE DEPARTMENT Case 07013091911

Electronic Journal of Tiffany Harris

File Name: Tiff's Life: 2014 edition

I knew this is what it had to feel like. I didn't hear the rest of the words- something about cutbacks, budget problems, poor performance reviews. With as much dignity as I could muster, I returned to my desk, fumbling with the keys on the computer as I deleted the few personal files on my computer- a picture of the kids here and there, a scanned permission slip. I grabbed the cheap plastic picture frames on my desk and placed them in my even cheaper bag. To add insult to injury, the clasp on my purse broke as I was trying to salvage any vestiges of what shred of my dignity remained. By now, it was obvious to my co-workers what had happened. I didn't even try to hide my tears as they ran down my face. As I stepped outside, the cold wind seemed to whisper to me, reminding me that I was a huge failure at life.

'How could you have been so stupid?' it seemed to ask. *'You've failed at everything in life. You're worthless. You should do everyone a favor and kill yourself.'*

I got to my car, the door creaking in protest as I opened it. I didn't even bother to turn on the heat (I can't even afford gas now, I guess) as I sat inside and just cried. With each one of my ragged breaths outward, the window next to me started fogging up. Out of childhood habit, I began to trace my initials in the window. I traced the "T" and the "H," then out of habit started tracing a heart, something I hadn't done in over a decade.

I remember Oda and I sitting outside after lunch break one day at school in what must have been our eighth grade year. It was the middle of winter, yet the sadists in

122

Michigan still made us go outside after lunch for "fresh air." Long before texting, note-passing was the preferred means of discussing what boys you liked. There was just the one problem of notes falling into the wrong hands. If you wanted to talk to your friends, very few places were private. Allegedly, the school administrators designed our outdoors area more like a prison yard in an attempt to thwart teenage pregnancy and sexual activity.

(In hindsight, I'm not really sure what 13-year-old boy was smooth enough to remove three layers of Tommy Hilfiger coats and get freaky in below freezing conditions.)

Because of this, and because someone seemed to hear you no matter where you were, Oda devised a method to encrypt our secret conversations. One day, after lunch, we hurried outside to chat. As we stood up, I noticed she had a new coat.

"Wow, that's so pretty," I remarked. It was one of those coats we used to call "puffer" coats that looked more suited for a space mission than the schoolyard. Hers bore a DKNY label and was pure white.

"Thanks, my mom bought it for me yesterday. I got straight A's at midterms."

"My mom took us to Frisch's," I replied, somewhat embarrassed.

"Well that's nice. She's proud of you and you got to spend time together, so isn't that what matters?"

Electronic Journal of Tiffany Harris

File Name: Tiff's Life: 2014 edition

I kind of nodded. No matter how much more money Oda's family had then mine, she never made it a big deal.

I struggled with the zipper on my coat- a hand me down from a cousin in high school. The arms were too long and the waist hung almost to my knees. Despite the added length, it hugged my mid-section, which seemed to expand daily.

"Oh crap!" she said. "The coat has black lining and I'm wearing brown shoes. Wanna swap?" she asked.

I gladly switched with her and we walked outside.

As soon as we turned the corner, we were met with our first taunt of the afternoon (if you don't count Reagan defining obesity as "Tiffany" in health class today.)

"Nice coat," said Ali, eying both of us (simultaneously somehow). "Who are you, the Michelin Man?"

"No, the Stay-Puff marshmallow man!" chimed in Julie.

"It's my coat, and it's DKNY," Oda piped up, hoping to gain their approval of the designer brand.

"Do you even know how to spell that?" Ali mocked.

"Uh, no, she's smart," Julie whispered to correct her. "She's just fat."

That was the thing about Oda. No matter how mean everyone was to her, she continued to be so nice, like somehow hoping she'd say or do the right thing to gain the approval of those whose opinions matter. I really wonder if she thought that if someday, she could just have the right clothes, the right car, the right boyfriend, those who taunted her would finally accept her. I never understood why she wanted to be liked so badly. What did she see as the metaphorical pot of gold at the end of the popularity rainbow? A date with Tony? An invitation to Kirsten's sleepovers?

Ali turned to Oda. Ali has a special hatred for Oda that would only deepen as Oda would eventually replace Ali as starting midfielder in field hockey freshman year.

"I'm sorry, I thought where you and your cave-people came from, you didn't need coats," Ali chirped, in her nails-down-a-chalkboard voice.

"I don't think it's caves. It's like mud huts," Kirsten corrected her.

While Ali turned to snap at Kirsten, we made our escape. I followed Oda over to the covered area underneath the classroom window. It gave us not only shelter from the brunt of the wind, but also a modicum of privacy.

Oda reached into her purse and pulled out two locker mirrors. The way it worked was this: you blew onto the mirror and wrote any sensitive information (i.e. initials of boys you liked) on the mirror with your finger. It faded after a few seconds.

125

Electronic Journal of Tiffany Harris

File Name: Tiff's Life: 2014 edition

I often wondered if Oda was the creator of Snapchat. She was smart enough to be.

Oda also took her security layer one step further. She didn't like us to use real initials when we wrote or spoke. We made the first letter of someone's name one letter lower in the alphabet and the second letter one letter higher. For example, if our crush's name was J.D., we wrote K.C. We usually could figure it out.

Just then, our friend Tyler came over and sat down with us.

"Whatcha doin' girls?" he asked in his singsong voice. Although he wasn't officially *out, it was apparent even at that early age that Tyler was gay. His skinny frame shivered in the winter as he wrapped his arms around his body.*

"Where's your coat?" I asked him, sounding eerily like my mother.

"Tony ripped the back of it."

"What did he do?"

"He put it on and did his fat guy in a little coat routine from Tommy Boy. Split down the back. I don't know if he meant to, so he took it to his mom to sew up." (Tony's mom was conveniently the home ec teacher at our school.)

126

"Do you want Oda's coat?" I offered.

He looked at it and shriveled his nose. "I think it's too boxy."

Oda rolled her eyes. (Yeah, no one was shocked when Tyler came out two years later.) "OK, so yeah, I'm kinda over last week and you-know-who."

I thought about it. "Wait, wasn't-?"

"Shhh!" she put a finger to her lips. Last week's crush had been Tony. As he would be for many more weeks intermitedly throughout the time we knew each other.

She wrote in the mirror, "I heart R.D."

OK, that meant Sanjay C. (I still can't spell his last name.) I could respect that. I wrote "I heart J.N."

Instantly, her and Tyler burst out laughing. "You like Kirk Moffet!" he giggled. Kirk Moffet may have been the most unfortunate looking man I'd ever laid eyes on. It wasn't his fault really- at least not the glass eye. I really hope that he discovered Accutane to help with the acne as well. His true burden to bear was his facial hair. The problem was that it wasn't limited to his face. Kirk Moffett had hair growing on his neck, his chest, and one time, I'm pretty sure I saw some poking out of his ears.

As soon as the giggling died down, they realized that I meant Kade La Bruyère (no relation to the philosopher. This guy couldn't spell philosopher.)

I guess I didn't realize how loud we had been until about ten minutes before break, Reagan, Tony, Carmine, and Paul came over and said, "Hey, you girls, come with us," pointing to Oda and I.

Oda jumped up, all smiles at Tony. Tyler stood too.

"No, not you, faggot," scowled Paul. "Just the girls, you fucking homo."

Oda opened her mouth to protest, but then thought better of it, shooting Tyler an apologetic look as we followed the guys around the side of the building, where a small crowd had congregated.

Suddenly, Oda seemed to want her coat back.

"No, you leave it on. It looks perfect on you." Paul smiled at me, revealing a row of dazzling white teeth. I always imagine he grew up to be either a male model for Crest or a professional NFL player.

Apparently he sells second-rate imported cars now.

There were about 20 people gathered around including the three guys who came and got us as well as the rest of their little dirty dozen(ish)- Ben, Mark, Ethan, Amir, Zach, Reagan, and Sanjay. Ali, Julie, Kirsten, Lynsey, Andrea, and Natalie were there as well. I began to suspect something was amiss, but by that time it was too late. "Ladies and gentlemen," announced Paul, his teeth now appearing sickenly white. "As many of you know, I am an ordained minister. I went online and got my certification during third hour. And it has come to my attention that our friend Tiffany, who, dressed in her wedding color white, looks quite like the abominable snowman," he paused for laughter.

"Wishes to marry her distant cousin the Yeti."

At this point, Kirk turned to walk away, his oafish shoulders slumped in a sort of resignation- the kind of resignation that one gets upon realizing that he would forever be the punch line of others jokes.

Tony stepped in front of Kirk, eliminating any exit options. Paul, realizing that he was about to lose his place as the center of attention, continued.

"And the wedding party is joined by their friend, the Bride of Frankenstein and bearer of the world's greatest unibrow, Michigan's very own Sasquatch."

Oda turned and ran as fast as she could. I saw Carmine shoot Paul a dirty look and head after her. Just then, Kirk slammed Paul's head into the wall and turned to punch Tony. Mid-uppercut, Mr. Haling and Mr. Pastore, our gym teachers, came over and broke up the fight. Kirk got suspended for three days and Paul was given a lunchtime detention.

(Being pretty and rich- it pays off for life, huh?)

Two things changed after that day. Kirk's family moved away to Novi soon after that and Oda became a lot quieter and more reserved. She did her best to avoid Ali, Kim, and the other girls for the rest of the year. On the other hand, she did eventually wax her unibrow, and for as long as I knew her, carried a spare pair of tweezers, just in case a wild hair ever snuck back up on her.

I've typed too long. I need to start looking for jobs. I'm really hoping that Southeastern is seriously hiring- Aimee (who already works there) says they are. Travel the world (or at least the Great Lakes Region) and meet interesting people, right? I really hope so, because our medical benefits run out at the end of the month and I can't afford COBRA.

October 15

Have you ever had one of those dreams so vivid that even when you wake up, you're still not sure if it was real or a dream? That's how my day started. I don't remember what I dreamt, but I woke up feeling more insecure than I had felt in a long time. I poked Ashley.

"Psst….wake up."

"What?" he grumbled, pulling the comforter back over him. "Go away."

"I had a nightmare," I whispered, this time with more urgency.

"Stop watching *Criminal Minds*," he muttered, grabbing a pillow and placing it over his head.

I wrapped my arms around him and hugged him in close. "Would you ever make fun of me in front of your friends?"

"Did you do something to deserve being made fun of?" came his mumbled reply from below the pillows. "Because if you got stuck in another revolving door, then yes, I would not only mock you, but video it as well."

I sighed. Clearly, this was going nowhere and I needed to get up anyways. I looked at the clock.

5:52 a.m.

Great. I was exhausted and it wasn't even Friday yet. As per my usual morning ritual, I slipped on my rabbit feet slippers, wrapped an afghan around myself, and padded to the laundry room, where my clothes lay in wait. I tossed my clothes into the dryer and set it for five minutes. I sat down on the floor and waited for the warming cycle to commence.

'Why do you work out so early?' Marissa would ask me.

'It's the only time I have,' I'd reply.

'You can take a day off, you know.'

My rebuttal argument was always the same.

'Fat doesn't take a holiday, does it?'

Admittedly, you can't argue logic.

I hit the remote start to my car and waited for it to heat up. I gathered up all of my stuff and got my lunch out of the fridge. Still half-asleep, I shuffled out to the car, pulling my hoodie over my head, cursing winter, nature, and Al Gore- you know, because I thought promised the planet was going to warm up for us or some shit and it would be nice and toasty year round.

I opened my glove compartment in search of a *Five Hour Energy*. Nada.

Shit, I swore I had one in here somewhere.

After two minutes of tearing my car apart like a crack fiend in desperate search of a fix, I resigned myself to stopping at the gas station just on the Grosse Pointe side of 8 Mile.

I pulled up, and reluctantly took the keys out of my car. It would be my luck that my car would get stolen at six in the morning while idling in a gas station parking lot.

I squinted my eyes in the bright lights of the store. Why did gas stations keep it so damn bright?

(Probably because they don't want to get robbed.)

I approached the counter and the large black woman put down the tabloid she was reading. I contemplated telling her that tabloids served no other purpose than to allow others to live vicariously through the lives of worthless celebrities, but decided it would be rude to ask her to put down her magazine when in fact I had no alternate reading material with which to provide her. Maybe next time I stopped in, I'd bring a copy of *Atlas Shrugged.*

"Two five hours please," I asked, shoving my hands in my sweatshirt pockets.

"Mmmmhhhhmmm.....I need some of those myself."

"Does it get pretty boring around this time....LaShawndra?" I asked, squinting to read her name tag.

"Honey, I like boring. Boring means ain't nobody robbing you."

Truer words had never been spoken. I laughed and handed her my money.

She looked at me suspiciously. "Anyone ever tell you that you look like one of the Kardashians? Not Kim, but maybe-"

"Kourtney?" I filled in.

"Yea! The little pretty one. Or maybe like one of the younger two. The older one of the younger two. But sort of like the Indian girl...Mindy someone...the one that comes on after New Girl. It's like New Girl but not as funny. Or maybe the chef- Pashmina something. Yeah, definitely her."

"I know who you're talking about. Yeah, thanks, I'll take that as a compliment," I said. "Have a good night! Um, I mean, morning!"

I sat in the car and placed the bottle to my mouth, using my teeth to remove the plastic wrap. I opened it up and quickly took a shot. From inside, I could see LaShawndra shaking her head and picking up her magazine.

The shit white(ish) people do.

By the time I arrived at the gym, the drink was starting to kick in, but not fully. I contemplated taking the second shot, but didn't want to have a heart attack and the program at my class reunion to read:

"In loving memory of Olivia, whose death was the result of an unfortunate complication of three ounces of manufactured vitamins, chemicals, and a Turbo3000 model treadmill."

I looked at the treadmill's start buttons with the same apprehension one would approach a death sentence.

'Would you like to start on 7.8 mph or go for the big 8.5?' I thought to myself.

Or maybe I should ask, *'Would you like to die by firing squad or by lethal injection?'*

Somewhere in the back of my head, a small voice whispered.

Olivia, you don't need to run. Go do the bike. Hell, go sit in the sauna. You're skinny now. You've earned this.

As always, her voice was replaced by Cody's and I snapped back to reality. I set the treadmill on 8.7, which in my own twisted thought process was my way of saying *"fuck you, Cody."* Every time I stepped on a treadmill, lifted a weight, or clipped my shoes into a bike pedal, Cody's voice was always in my head.

"If you just lost some weight..."

I started running and within five minutes was in the zone.

I tell people about the zone, but other than a handful of serious runners, no one really understands "the zone." It's that time when your mind wanders and thinks about anything and everything. I had just made a new playlist too- some hip-hop mixed with indie pop. I made sure to alternate the Crystal Figures with Kanye, just to keep me on my toes.

I started to think about dying. Or not *dying*, per se, but the idea that if I had indeed met my maker at Lifestyle Fitness and Sport Club, I think I'd be the first person from my high school class to die. Would I *really* be the first person to die from my graduating class? I thought about it. We had graduated almost 600 people. There was that one guy in the car crash, but he was the grade below us. There was that other one who had cancer... he was also a grade below us. I was methodically trying to go through my Facebook feed in my head when my arm started buzzing. I reached down and pulled my phone out of my armband. I knew any calls this early couldn't be good news.

It was my mom. Shit.

"Who's dead?" I asked, straddling the belt, but allowing it to run.

(In hindsight, this action was probably a notion courtesy of the Bad Idea Fairy. If she was going to

deliver bad news and I was going to pass out, I'd be
likely to end up with rubber burn all over my face.)

"Oh, you're awake."

"I am now. I was at the gym. What's the matter? And
why are you awake? What time is it there?"

"We're still in Spain. Nothing bad. I need you to go over
to the island as soon as possible and turn off the water."

Fuuuucccckkkk.

"Seriously? Why can't Pierre do it? Or why can't it wait
until you get back?"

"It's supposed to freeze this weekend. I don't want the
pipes freezing. You need to go in the attic and-"

"OK, can you just send me an email?"

"Fine. You need to do Pierre's too. You have both keys?"

"Yeah, fine, I'll do it Friday."

"Promise?"

I rolled my eyes. "Yes, I will do it Friday. How's Spain?" I
asked.

It was too late. She had hung up. Clearly this is a trend
with my parents. I got back on the treadmill, thought
about the island, and increased the speed even more.

October 15, 2 p.m.

Fucking A! I can't catch a break. My douchebag prof
emailed me and said that I needed to put more
"personal detail into my writing" or some bullshit. Like
I'm gonna tell Dr. Levenstein my life story. I don't care if
he promises the confidentiality of a priest. The last thing
I need is someone jacking his laptop (of which I doubt
he secures his password) and finding out my deepest
thoughts, fears, and desires. I flipped the book open to
what looked like an easy piece to read and reflect upon.
I had to hurry and get ready if I was going to make it out
of here by noon (luckily Fridays are half-days for me).

Battered

For this reflection, I read "Battered." I
think the authors did a great job of
comparing the woman in the story to a
battered woman. From what I understand
about battered women, they are continually
trying to appease a volatile partner, an
unending quest, which will never be
accomplished. This story teaches us a lot
about leadership and is a good lesson for
all leaders- not to become "that" leader.

I had a boss one time who was absolutely
terrible. My nickname for her was "The
Devil Wears JC Penney." Some days she'd be
tolerable and actually say things were

good. The next day, she would be screaming at me. My work was always good and consistent. She would constantly refer to herself as going through "the change." I'm sure she means menopause or something, but it was more like she was changing into a werewolf. I quit after three months. When people asked why I quit without another job (and ended up working at Macaroni Grill as a waitress), I tried to explain how awful it was.

I think as journalists, it is our responsibility to be consistent in our actions and words. By doing this, we are more likely to be perceived as competent, thus earning the respect of our peers and readers. I also think this is important as humans. I know so many people who are so volatile.

Sometimes my fiancé can be volatile. I know he is kind of mad that I don't want to stay here in Detroit forever. I just can't. It is miserable. If we stay here, then I will just die in this horrible place. I get that his job is stressful, but it's hard when he takes it out on me. He definitely doesn't beat me-or even yell at me. He just acts like I am an inconvenience at times. I don't know if he'll be annoyed or happy when I come home. He gets annoyed sometimes if I don't have his lunch made or something minor like that. I think that he wanted a different kind of wife- the one who would do whatever he wanted, submissively and without question. He had this illusion that I was just an accessory. I didn't know that when I went from a girlfriend to (almost a) wife that I was expected to change everything about me. I just wish sometimes that he'd be more stable in the way he viewed me. Hell, sometimes I just wish that he'd tolerate me.

At least I don't feel battered at my job now. I hate it because it's mind-numbing and boring, but at least I'm respected and treated fairly. For me, that makes it tolerable and at times, even enjoyable. I am actively looking for something else and I really hope that I'll find it. I have had a few interviews for some freelance stuff, so I hope those pan out. I just don't want to be a copy editor forever. I feel like I've got so much potential.

October 16, 2:56 a.m. (Saturday morning)

OMG. That's all I can really say. I guess I could say OMFG for added emphasis, but that wouldn't do it justice. I'm wide-awake and in complete and utter disbelief.

Last night was NOT real life.

I mean, it was. It was definitely not a dream, but *holy hell*- I can't believe it happened.

To back up a bit, it all started at about noon today when I convinced Marissa to come to the island with me so I wasn't bored by myself. (I also think the place is haunted, but I'll never admit that to anyone.)

"An island?" she asked skeptically as we drove down I-96 toward the bridge to Canada.

"Yes, an island. A body of land surrounded on all sides by water. I don't want to get your hopes up, but it's not going to be tropical."

"I didn't know there were islands in Lake Erie."

I rolled my eyes. She is literally sometimes too stupid to function.

"Well, you're about to see one." I opened my glove compartment. "You got your passport?"

"Yep."

"Cool, they're kind of dicks about it at the border."

"So are you Canadian?"

"Me? No, not personally, but my mom's side is. See, her ancestors were French and they came over and bought up all this beachfront property on the lake about 100 years ago. All of these French families eventually ended up splitting the land and handing it down through the generations. I'm somehow related to about 10% of the population on this island. Most everyone lives in either Toronto or Detroit and just come here for the summer. When we immigrated here, we went to Detroit and became U.S. citizens. My mom is the only one who keeps dual citizenship. My grandparents also had it before they die."

"Why are we going now? It's freezing."

"I have to go turn off the water so the pipes don't freeze and burst."

"Does the lake freeze over?"

I thought about it. "I remember it used to. At least where it was really shallow. You couldn't *ice skate* per se because the waves actually froze and made it bumpy. I heard it doesn't freeze anymore because of the global warming effects."

"So you've been coming here your whole life?"

"Yep. Lots of memories." I slowed as I merged into the traffic crossing the bridge. "It's a good thing we didn't wait until five. That's a mass exodus across the bridge with the American tourists heading to Windsor and the Canadians who work in Detroit heading home."

"How long will it take us once we go through customs?"

"Half an hour, max," I replied, pointing out the window. "Can you see the Boblo Island sign?"

"Yeah."

"That used to be an amusement park we used to go to."

"Look at you, Detroit's one-woman tourism department."

"Oh yeah, I know *all* the happening abandoned buildings and hot spots to get copper. There's a VIP section at the abandoned GM plant on the top floor."

"OK, we *have* to be back downtown at 5:30. That's when we're meeting the guys for drinks."

"That's fine. It's not even two. Where are we going?"

"Avalon. It's a new place."

"Sounds happening. I'll be sure to write a review for the Detroit Board of Tourism." I extended my palm towards her. "Passport?" I asked her as I slowed for the custom's booth.

She handed it over and I rolled down the window.

"Hello ladies, how are you all doing today, eh?" the young Canadian customs agent asked.

"Fine," I replied.

"Citizenship?"

We went through the standard questions and I noticed quite a line had formed behind us.

"Is there a problem, sir?" I asked, figuring either his computer was being slow or they knew enough to profile anyone who looked remotely Middle Eastern. I've been a citizen for two decades and never had a problem.

"No, no," he responded, smiling. "I just wanted to take my time and talk to the prettiest girls in Canada." He handed us back our passports and smiled. "Have a nice time ladies."

I rolled up the window and giggled. "He was cute!"

"Ewww, but he doesn't make a lot of money," Marissa pointed out.

"True. But he's defending Canada from terrorism." I mock saluted. "Job well done, sir."

We both laughed and headed onto the Queen's highway toward the island.

By the time we crossed the small bridge onto the island, Marissa had pointed out no less than 30 times how Canada "looked a lot like the U.S., except their speed limits are way faster."

(I didn't even want to touch that one.)

We pulled up at our house, a small three-bedroom yellow-shingled place with a wraparound deck. I parked the car and got out, stretching and inhaling the smell of beach and listening to the sound of the waves.

We made our way through the house and out to the beach. It was already 2:45

"Hey, I still have to go turn off the water at my uncle Pierre's houses. Why don't you go explore the beach?" I asked, yanking down the attic stairs and immediately jumping outside as to avoid the fallout dust.

Looking at the condition of what came out of the attic, she took off her shoes and ran down the steps towards the beach.

I went back inside and began going through the steps of turning off the water. I remembered I was supposed to go up in the attic and check for water damage. I straightened out the ladder and gingerly began feeling my way around in the dark. I turned on the overhead light and crouched down as I began to check the floor. I saw one suspicious spot below the vent. I took off my engagement ring and set it on a beam as I felt the vent for moisture. It seemed to be dry. I sat down to take a break. I forgot how hot and stifling the attic could be. I think I'm the only person in my family who has ever been up here. As kids, Taline and Zako were both claustrophobic little bitches that were scared of spiders (some things never change).

Maybe if people had been up here, they would have realized what a good spot this was for spying on everyone. The small slats on the side provided just enough of an aerial view to see what was happening on each side of the house. The ducts let me hear everything below me, both inside the house and out.

For two decades, I've heard everything. I've heard about my other uncle who didn't want to tell his wife that he had cancer. I've heard about how my mom didn't like my aunt's husband. And I've heard some things about myself.

"What do you want to do now?" Jean asked, going to the window for the fifth time in ten minutes, as if doing so would will the rain to stop.

"We could play another game," I suggested, pulling games out from under the couch.

"These games are stupid. They're all for little kids or adults. I wish we had a PlayStation up here," whined Zako.

"This one says ages '13 and Up.' I'm 13, but you guys are only 12. I guess I would be tough for you," I replied.

"It's never *going to stop raining," pouted Ana, looking out the window, where a light drizzle continued to fall for the third day in a row.*

"Maybe we can go see what Delilah is up to," suggested Jean, Delilah's cousin.

"You idiot, she doesn't want to hang out with us. She's sixteen. She's hanging out with Pierre and the other older boys at their house," countered Marie. She looked at me. "What do you do in Detroit when you're bored?"

I shrugged. "Probably the same stuff you do in Toronto. Video games. My dad says we can bring up our PlayStation next weekend."

I saw Jean's eyes light up at this notion. It still didn't solve the dilemma of what to do today.

This was long before iPads and iPhones.

"We could play hide and seek," suggested Taline.

"That's for babies," Ana countered.

"No, not if we play it my way," pouted Taline. "One person is the hider. Everyone spreads out to find them. When each seeker finds the hider, they have to stay with them. Everyone ends up in a closet or something. The last

person to find everyone becomes the hider next time. We played it at my friend's birthday party."

(Of *course* Taline got invited to everyone's parties. Everyone *loved* Taline.)

We all begrudgingly admitted it was an okay idea. We laid down the boundaries (inside or outside at all three of our families' houses). Taline volunteered me to be the first hider.

I made a big show of walking towards the front door and slamming it closed, then quietly doubling back in and entering the utility room. I pulled the attic stairs down and crawled up into the top, pulling a box in front of the stairs to make them less obvious.

A few minutes later, I heard voices on the side of the house.

"Where is she?" I heard Ana ask.

"Do you care? We got rid of her." It was Jean. "Good thinking, Taline."

Taline???

I heard my sister laugh. "Oh my God, do you know how annoying it is living with her? It's so embarrassing to tell people that Porky is my sister."

"Porky?"

"It's what everyone calls her back at school," Taline continued. "Her friend is Piggy. They're two losers in a pod."

"Why doesn't she just stop eating?" Marie chimed in.

"How hard is it to find her? She's fat. Where the hell is she going to hide?" Jean asked, impatiently.

"Probably-"

I was interrupted by a scream from downstairs. With no regard for dirt, I snapped back to the present and stood upright, nailing my head on the ceiling and fiberglass filling. I scooted toward the ladder and jumped down, knocking over a bunch of boxes in the process.

"*Marissa!*" I shouted, running towards the back of the house. "Are you all right?!"

I saw Marissa on the other side of the glass door, running toward the lake. I ran after her. "What the hell happened?"

"It....it..touched me."

I began laughing, figuring out what likely happened.

"Slow down, use your words. I know you've never seen a penis before, but you'll get used to it. Seriously, though. What happened?"

"It was *so* big," she said, rinsing her arm in the lake.

"Well, they come in all shapes and sizes. Some are circumcised-"

She started laughing.

"Was it a spider?" I asked.

"It was a really *big* spider, OK?"

I rolled my eyes and turned around.

"What's in your hair?"

Ugh, the fiberglass filling.

We went back in and managed to pick out the pieces and rinse off the back of my neck. It was getting late, so I rushed to turn off our water, then went next door to Pierre's house and turned off his. By the time we left, it was close to five. By the time we got back across the street to Avalon, it was closer to six.

Marissa was starting to stress.

"Just chill. You texted this guy and said we were running late. It's the border. They'll understand. You should make boys wait. Haven't you read *The Rules*?"

"No," she said, leaning over to pick more fiberglass out of my hair.

"Neither have I, but it sounds good," I winked as I pulled up and tossed the keys to the valet, a bored looking Sons of Anarchy-type.

"Do you think your car is OK with him?" she whispered.

"Probably. He doesn't want to go back to prison," I replied, not caring if he heard me or not, and smoothing out my hair, which under the lights, seemed to change it from jet black to purple.

I giggled and handed the bouncer my ID. I guess he had heard our conversation and looked less than amused. He extended one tattooed arm back to me and said, "Don't worry, your precious BMW isn't the nicest car we've seen today. In fact, I'd put it in the bottom third. Have a nice evening, uh, Oda."

I glared at him. *Prick*, I thought to myself.

"What did he say?" asked Marissa.

"Nothing," I snapped, shoving my card back into my purse.

We walked into the new club, dazzling white with new paint, chandeliers, rows and rows of mirrors, and even fountains.

"No, I heard him. He called you something."

(Oh great, *now's* the time she chooses to pay attention?)

"I haven't changed my first name on my ID. Olivia is a shorter version of my name" I put my ID away and abruptly changed the conversation. "So what's this guy's name? Sanjaya?"

"He's right here," Marissa said from behind me, tapping me on the arm as I spun around.

"Oh my God," I whispered

Part II: This is what you made me

Hi my name is-
You won't remember
Wait till December
Cuz you thought that I was pure as snow
Guess you didn't know
Hold tight, surprise
Open your eyes, its springtime
Flowers blossoming, I am one of them
Bet you like how I've grown

Cuz now I'm that bitch
You'll never get to
Can't get what you want
So you're acting like a punk
You were too fly then
So fly away now
Now I'm that bitch
And you're just a clown

-Livvi Franc, "Now I'm that Bitch"

October 16, 3:43 a.m.

> ***Sidebar: Had to take a quick break to cook some
> mozzarella sticks...totally had munchies***

Now, where was I in my story?

Ah, yes...

I just stood there like an idiot, my mouth hanging open
and my feet unwilling to move. I had to take in the
scene. In front of me was hands-down the most
gorgeous guy I had ever seen. He was tan with dark
brown hair, light blue eyes, a chiseled jawline and six-
pack abs. I could tell this based on his extra-smedium
(you know, a small-ish, medium-ish size meant to show
off biceps) Affliction shirt.

My first thought was that this was the only man besides
Kid Rock who could pull off an Affliciton shirt.

(Side note: I met Kid Rock. Once. For five seconds. And
by meet, I mean I awkwardly asked him how his day
was going as his bodyguard opened his car door. He
didn't reply.)

Beside him were Sanjay Choudhary, Paul Jacobi, Tony
Muscarella, and another black guy I didn't recognize.

It had been damn near a decade since I had seen them,
but there was no mistaking.

(Birds of a douche still flock together long after graduation day, apparently.)

I didn't have time to explain anything to Marissa, so I wordlessly followed her to them, my knees turning to jelly.

"Marissa!" Sanjay exclaimed, hugging her. "Good to see you again. Who's your friend?"

They looked at me. I stood frozen in place, no words coming out of my mouth. They looked at me quizzically. Marissa appeared the most perplexed of anyone. I guess it must have looked confusing to the outside observer. Here I stood, amongst the sparkling white walls and decorative chandeliers, looking nonsensical, scared to talk to a group of average-looking guys. For some reason, the water from the fountains seemed louder than ever, creating a rushing sound in my head.

I opened my mouth, but couldn't think of anything to say. Why hadn't Paul made a Porky joke yet? I was wearing a white, long-sleeved sparkly shirt. Surely one of them would have made a joke about the Michelin Man coming out of the closet. I waited and it didn't happen.

Marissa stared at me and mouthed, "*What the fuck?*"

"This is Olivia," she said.

I nodded as if hearing the name for the first time.

'Yes, I am Olivia,' I told myself. In my head, I repeated it as a mantra. *'You're Olivia. Not Oda. Olivia.'*

Sanjay made the first move to break me from my trance.

"Hi, I'm Sanjay."

I wanted to scream, *'I fucking know who you are! You were a huge asshole and probably still are!'*

I shook his hand and mumbled something about how nice it was to meet him. I shook hands with Paul and Tony, waiting for them to make some joke about catching the ugly virus, but it never happened. The black guy's name was Brandon and I knew I didn't know him. The hot guy came up last and shook my hand.

"Hi, I'm Carmine."

No. Fucking. Way.

"No fuck-" I started to say before catching myself. He looked at me quizzically.

"I mean, um, sorry, that, I, um, I had a friend by that name..." I trailed off.

He kept smiling, showing a row of perfectly white teeth.

"I hope he's a cool guy."

"He's dead," I blurted out.

What the-? Where did that even come from? Get your shit together Olivia...

Marissa must have been thinking the same thing because she quickly made an excuse about needing to use the restroom and dragged me with her.

I let her lead me to the bathroom where I collapsed on the chair in the corner.

"What the *hell* is your problem? Since when did *you* become socially awkward?"

I just stared up at her, unable to formulate my thoughts.

"Look, I get it. That guy is fucking hot. I'd be nervous too. But he's not the first hot guy you've ever seen. You met *Kid-fucking-Rock* in Greektown after a Tigers game and actually managed to throw a line at him. This guy looks like he missed the bus to the Ultimate Fighter tryouts."

I nodded and took a deep breath. She was right. I needed to pull it together.

"And furthermore, you have a dead friend named Carmine that I don't know about? When did he die?"

"Um, a long time ago. In Iraq."

"So now your fictional dead friend is a *war hero*?"

158

"Sorry," I said, trying to snap out of it. I got up and headed over to the mirror where I managed to find more fiberglass in my hair. "I'll do better," I promised her. "I just need a drink."

Before walking out of the bathroom, I turned to her and said, "Look, just whatever I say, please go with it. I don't have time to explain now. As far as they know, you barely know me. You only met me a few weeks ago. Share *nothing* about me. Got it?"

"Okay, but-"

"*Nothing*!" I snapped, running a brush though my hair one last time. "Not where I live, where I grew up, not my last name, not where I live, not even that I work at the paper."

She looked confused, but nodded in agreement.

By the time we got back to the table, there were drinks waiting for us.

"First round's on me!" announced Paul, patting for me to sit next to him in the booth. I hesitantly sat down, waiting for him to make some crack about the bench breaking. I braced myself for it, but it never came.

"A toast!" He turned to me and said, "to new friends." He then paused, looking at my chest. "Both of them."

The table, including myself, erupted in laughter. I raised my glass and cheered with the rest. Hesitantly

Over the next two hours, I found out that Paul ran one of his dad's car dealerships, Tony worked at his dad's law firm, Sanjay customized software for hospitals, and Carmine- well Carmine was living every Detroit boy's childhood dream. He was a Detroit firefighter. I had to look away so I didn't picture him shirtless....like in the scene from Magic Mike.

Really, Olivia? He's a professional public servant, not a male stripper.

The other guy was Brandon and he and Tony played football together in college. I thought a lot about him. He seemed so nice. I wonder if he would have been a dick to me like the other guys or if he would have been different.

Truth be told, all the guys seemed really nice. Sure, they were borderline inappropriate and possessed a falsely inflated sense of confidence, but no more so than most guys my age.

"So you're not married?" asked Carmine.

"I'm actually engaged." I held up my hand to show my ring. '*Oh shit!*' It was in the attic. Dang. I'd have to go get it tomorrow.

"Crap, I left my ring in Canada. Dammit. You?" I asked, finishing my martini.

"No," he said, looking straight at me.

Damn, he was so hot. Why did he have to look at me like that?

"Why not?" As soon as the words came out of my mouth, I regretted it.

"I mean, I'm sorry, it's none of my business. I mean, I guess you guys just always had- or seem like you're the kind of guys who could have had- or I mean- you know....any girl you want...not that I know you or anything. I mean, I just met you. Um, sorry."

He looked perplexed. "Uh, just haven't found the right one I guess."

Tony ordered the next round. I ordered a long island and got a text from Marissa.

```
Marissa: Slow down there, killer.
```

I rolled my eyes and told the waiter to make it extra strong. I caught Tony's eye and for a split second, I expected him to crack a joke about the amount of calories in a long island. Instead, he looked at the waitress and told her to make sure they used good vodka.

The drinks arrived along with a round of shots Tony had ordered. He handed them out and we raised our glasses. I was *not* prepared for what happened next.

"G-G-G- to the R-R-R- to the O- oh......"

NO. FUCKING. WAY.

He was singing our high school fight song. I didn't think
I could imagine a bigger cliché until Paul pulled out his
phone.

"Hey, check out this commercial for the dealership. We
got the hottest chick ever to come do it," he said,
extending the phone to the table. Everyone gathered
around with rapt attention. "I might have tapped that,"
he smugly added.

By this point, my liquid courage was starting to kick in.

I piped up. "Wow, I half expected after that little display
of glory days nostalgia for you to pull up tape of your
senior year football season on YouTube."

Everyone turned and looked at me. I didn't know if I
outed myself or hit a nerve, but I didn't care. I
continued.

"Or is the file too big? You probably have it on a thumb
drive."

At this, everyone burst into laughter. Carmine and
Sanjay high-fived me while Paul scowled, unable to
deny that such a thumb drive existed.

"Yes! Score one for the girl who's witty and has
nice....eyes!" Brandon joked. "Another round!"

Marissa looked relieved that I had reverted to my former self and seemed pleased with the direction in which the evening was headed.

"So Olivia, where are you from?" Carmine asked.

"Cleveland!" I announced quickly, shooting Marissa a look.

She looked confused, but I continued. "Um, yeah, I live here now and I used to have some family here and over in Canada."

"Is it still tough to get back across the border?" Tony asked.

"Only if you look like Sanjay," I replied.

Again, the table started cracking up and I was rewarded with adulation and high-fives.

"No, seriously, though. U.S. Border Patrol agents are like the ultimate club bouncers. If you're a girl, it's all 'Welcome to America.' If you're a guy, it's all, 'Sorry bro, party's full.'"

I thought Tony was going to start crying, he was laughing so hard. By this time, the appetizers we had ordered arrived and I knew I had charmed the table appropriately. Sanjay was very much into Marissa, which in a way pleased me, but also worried me. I knew it was just a matter of time before they figured me out. I had seen Sanjay add Marissa on Instagram. I knew my clock was ticking and before long, he would start creeping and find me. Even though I went by Olivia, my last name was still unique enough that eventually someone would put two and two together and that would be the end of this little charade.

They dimmed the lights and started playing music, which at least gave me a sort of break from my worrying.

"Oh my gosh! This is Air Dubai! I love this band!" I shouted, excitedly.

(Way to go, Olivia. Now they're going to think you're retarded for sure.)

"Well let's dance then," suggested Tony, taking my hand as we pushed our way into the throng on the dance floor.

Let it burn hot without letting it smoke
Pieces hope she gets blowed
Leaking those secrets, but put the past away
I never let it drown what we have today

We pressed close together, his hand resting on the small of my back, the weight of the crowd forcing us together. With my heels on, my chin was almost at his shoulder. Tentatively, I put my right arm around his shoulder. Someone bumped into me, throwing me off balance, causing me to tighten my grip around his neck and put my other hand around his waist.

I could feel Paul behind me. Standing behind me, he wrapped his arm around me and sang into my ear.

She's the belle of the ball, cream of the crop
No wonder you never forgot her
And all the drinks are flowing
Not a good time to phone the bell of the ball, cream of the crop
Mirrors all over the wall
And now all the lights are flashing
And all of the people dancing

We moved with the music, and as we did so I tried to reckon the giddiness that my twelve-year-old self felt with the anger that I should have felt.

I can't let go
It's never been easy for me
I can't let go, it's never been easy for me
Baby that's just a warning

"Let's go to another bar," I suggested, pushing Tony away before he could protest. "It's too hot in here."

"You sure? I mean, you could take off your clothes. No one would mind," suggested Paul, who was instantly rewarded by a fist bump from Brandon.

We eventually adjourned to the next bar, but not before Tony made a big show of picking up everyone's tab.

This is not real life, I told myself.

"Am I okay dressed like this?" I asked the guys. I was just wearing jeans.

"Oh, you're *more* than OK," Paul responded, not breaking eye contact with my chest. "You just bring Montezuma and Fiji and don't worry about the rest."

Creeper, I mouthed at Marissa.

"We're not going to a dive bar, are we? I hate dive bars," Marissa whined, leaning on Sanjay for support.

"Of course not. Dive bars are for ugly people," Tony added as we paused at the crosswalk.

I wanted to make some smartass comment, but my face was frozen. I was shivering and cold, despite the copious amounts of alcohol coursing through my blood stream.

"You look cold," Carmine said, putting his arm around me. "Here, I'm not trying to be creepy. I'm just making sure you stay warm."

I didn't mind at all. I wrapped my arm around his waist. (I was right about the six-pack abs.)

"You smell good," he said. "What is that?"

"Burberry," I replied, trying not to blush at how physically attracted I was to him. We were both fairly intoxicated and had fallen a bit behind the group.

"Burberry fragrance my shirt when she hugged me," he sang. *"Hard as a rock when she touched me, thinking oh, she wanna love me."*

I tensed up.

"What it is, what it ain't, tell me what to do. I know it's late but destiny brought me back to you. Time went by, turned you into a butterfly..."

"You OK?" he asked.

"Yeah," I said, letting go of his waist. "Who sang that? Fabulous?"

"Um, I think so. Are you sure you're all right? If you want, we can just go get like coffee or something. Or do you prefer hot chocolate?" he inquired as we caught back up with everyone and turned towards the door to the next bar. As we stood there and basked in the glow of the neon lights, I knew I had to tell him.

"ID?" the bored-looking bouncer demanded.

"Just a second!" I said, frantically scrambling through my purse. "Carmine, just go in there. I'll meet you inside."

"No, I'm not leaving you on the streets of Detroit alone. Am I *that* big of an asshole?"

"Carmine Vincent, just give me a second!"

"Wait, how do you know my last name?"

I stood, stagnant, my feet glued to the ground, unwilling to look at him.

"Oh my God," he whispered. "I *knew* there was something about you-" he started to raise his voice.

"Shut up!" I hissed.

I leaned in closer and he pulled me in for a hug. I clamped my hand over his mouth.

"Shhhh...." I whispered. "Don't say anything. Not yet."

"I won't, but I can't believe it's you. My God," he cupped my chin in his hand and ran his other hand through my hair. "You're beautiful."

As I stood there on the street corner, shivering, I didn't know what to say. We had lost most of the group, but I noticed Brandon had turned around and saw us.

"Thank you," I whispered back, my face inches from his as I tried to blink back tears. "Just promise you'll let me do this on my own accord? Let me tell everyone, okay?"

He nodded and wiped the corner of my eye where a tear had started to form.

Eventually we caught up to the group and sat down. I already had a drink waiting for me. Carmine pulled out his phone.

"I should get your number. You know...because you said you needed work done on your house and all..."

"Yeah," I responded. That statement wasn't completely false. I really needed work done on...stuff...

Jesus Olivia, get your mind out of the gutter!

He unlocked his screen to three text messages from Paul and Sanjay.

`Paul: Get iiiiittttt booooooyyyyy!!!!`

`Paul: I'd tap that.`

`Sanjay: Dude, if you want to bail and tap that, I would.`

Realizing that I had read the messages, he tried to mumble and apology, but I simply held up the phone to Paul and Sanjay with an expression of '*Really?*'

Meanwhile, Brandon was giving me a dirty look.

By then, we were feeling pretty good, but I noticed Sanjay was on Instagram looking at Marissa's pictures. I was running out of time.

I deserved to be the one in control. I earned it, dammit. And I was hell-bent to go out with a bang.

"Order a round of shots," I whispered to Carmine.

He nodded and went to the bar.

"Hey Sanjay," I said, trying to distract him from his phone, literally swatting my hand in front of the screen. "You work in IT, right?"

"Yeah."

"So tell me, what do you think is going to be the new Facebook? I mean, it's getting too commercialized, right? And like, *everyone* is on it. Really, who wants to be friends with their great aunt?" I said desperately, trying to buy myself some time.

"Fuck, tell me about it," Tony chimed in. "I don't give a fuck about anyone from high school or their stupid problems. Like, your kid is sick. Who gives a fuck?"

"You know who tried to add me the other day?" Paul asked, scrolling through his phone. "Tiffany Harris. What a fat slob. The abominable snow woman."

I winced upon hearing the name.

Carmine had arrived with the drinks. I sent a quick text to Marissa.

I'm sorry.

I piped up. "But surely not *all* the girls you went to school with are fat? Are there not some attractive ones?"

"Fuck no," Tony retorted, reaching for a shot. I slapped his hand away. "Dumb, lazy bitches. I wouldn't sleep with them if they paid me."

"None at *all?*"

"Not a chance," he replied, hungrily reaching for the shot.

Simultaneously, I saw Carmine wince and Marissa begin texting in frustrated confusion.

"It's my turn to do the toast," I quietly said. I sat on the edge of my seat, my purse in my arm as if I was just about to get up to use the restroom. My left hand gripped my driver's license, the plastic digging into my skin.

With my right hand, I lifted a glass and took a deep breath.

"As my boy Kanye would say, 'Here's to the douchebags, here's to the assholes.'"

They looked confused, so I continued.

"Tony, you're wrong. You couldn't pay *me* enough to sleep with *you*." I threw my license on the table. "You should be more careful who you call a lazy bitch."

With that, I took my shot, slammed it on the table, and walked away.

I didn't look back, but I can guess what probably happened next. They looked at the license, realized who I was, and Marissa filled in the gaps. I anticipated Carmine running after me, so I quickly ducked around a corner as he ran out. I saw him head around the corner as I slipped into a cab.

■■■

3:57 a.m.

It's almost four and I have thirteen messages from Marissa and five from Carmine. I still have no idea where my license is, nor do I particularly care. I'm not ready to deal with the fallout yet, but consequences be damned, the look on Tony's face was worth it.

October 17

I'm a mess. I really don't know what to do. Troy left me. He said he couldn't be with someone as unstable and emotional as me. I don't know what he's talking about. I know the last few days have been rough, but Jesus, doesn't he understand that I'm a single mother who lost everything?

This morning was the straw that broke the camel's back. I had posted on Facebook the day I lost my job. The support was overwhelming. The comments were so sweet:

```
Girl, forget that job.

Your boss is a royal bitch.

You'll get through this. When God
closes one door, he opens another.

It's always the darkest before the sun
rises.

God never gives you more than you can
handle.
```

Over the next few days, I had tried to post inspirational pictures and quotes. I needed to believe that someone or something was going to come and make my life better.

I guess the kids had gotten up and gone to school on their own. I vaguely remember Emma coming in and giving me a hug before she left. I rolled over in bed and picked up my phone to check my Twitter news feed. I only had two notifications. How the hell was that? I posted last night how badly I was in need of an angel to come save me. You think that people would be a little more sensitive. I was about to throw the phone on the floor and go back to bed when it started buzzing. It was a text from LaShawndra.

LaShawndra: How are you doing?

I texted her back.

Me: Depressed. Why can't anything good ever happen to me?

LaShawndra: Do you want me to come over?

Me: No.

LaShawndra: Are you in bed?

I sighed. I texted that I was indeed not in bed.

LaShawndra: Liar. You haven't posted any words of self-pity yet this morning on the Book of Faces. It's almost noon. I took a power nap. I'm coming over.

I knew she wouldn't take no for an answer.

"Bring me some cigarettes," I texted her.

Electronic Journal of Tiffany Harris

File Name: Tiff's Life: 2014 edition

I had barely gotten up and brushed my teeth than I heard the front door open. For a split second, I thought about grabbing the .9 my stepdad gave me out of the nightstand until I heard LaShawndra's voice booming from the kitchen.

"Were you robbed or does it always look like this?"

I shambled out into the living room, not even making the effort to put on a bra. In the light of day, the kitchen really did look worse for the wear. Piles of dishes and pans sat haphazardly in the sink, the pans crusted with an unidentifiable substance. The mail lie strew all over the foyer, now covered with wet, muddy footprints. I hope Detroit Power and Light didn't mind getting a soppy bill. Hell, who was I kidding? They're not getting any payment from me this month.

I sat down on the couch and lit a cigarette.

"Cigarettes?" I asked LaShawndra.

She sighed and took them out of her purse, today revealing lime green nails with black jack-o-lanterns superimposed on them.

"Don't you want to smoke outside?" she asked.

"Nope. I don't want to go outside looking like this." She started to say something, but I interrupted her. "By the way, what were you thinking, just walking in here? You're lucky I didn't shoot your ass."

"With what?" she scoffed, waving her hand to blow the smoke away from me.

"I have a .9. My dad gave it to me a few years back. It's legal, don't worry. I sleep better knowing it's there." I paused and sighed. "But I sleep way better knowing a man is next to me."

I laid my head back, letting my hand fall to the couch. LaShawndra quickly grabbed the still-smoldering cigarette from my hand and put it out in the overflowing ashtray.

"You need to get a job."

"I'm trying to collect unemployment. They pay fifty percent."

"You think you can survive on half of what you were making at Telcon? We made, what, $360 a week, *before* taxes? How much is rent for this place?"

I shrugged, shoving the reality of the math out of my head. "I'm going to try to go on disability."

"For what?"

"Depression," I said, getting up and making my way to the kitchen, where a nauseous smell seemed to permeate the air. "I've been diagnosed, you know." I poured myself the rest of the Jack, not even bothering with ice. (OK, to be fair, the ice cube trays were on the counter, now filled with water.)

I returned to the couch and started drinking. "You know, why did this happen to me?"

"We all lost our jobs. You, me, Frank, Whitney, Mohammed-"

"Yeah, but why *me*? I'm a single mother. *Nothing* has gone right for me. Ever. In my life," I pointed out as I took another swig.

"You're still here, aren't you? You woke up this morning. My daddy always said that every day you wake up is a gift from God to do something new."

I pulled out another cigarette and took a drag. "If I want a lecture about God, I'll listen to my fucking stepdad. I'm surprised he hasn't been over here yet."

Holding the cigarette in my left hand, I turned on the television and flipped through until I found one of the Real Housewives.

"Why can't I land a man like that and just be a trophy wife all day?" I moaned, tears filling my eyes. "Why are *they* so lucky? I need a man who's going to take care of me."

LaShawndra got off the couch and marched over to the television, unplugging it from the wall. I thought about plugging it back in, but realized Comcast was probably going to shut it off next week anyways.

"No, what you *need* is a job."

I started to protest, but she interrupted.

"My brother Joe says he needs some help at the gas station. Day shift. When your kids are at school. The pay isn't great, but it's better than nothing. He says he can get you ten an hour."

"I'm going to try to get on disability."

"That pays worse than unemployment. The gas station is almost as much as you were making at Telcom. You might even get some overtime. Joe really needs help and he only wants to hire people he knows and trusts. I already told him about you."

I sighed and took another drink, flopping onto the couch, spilling Jack on my already stained sweatshirt.

"I don't *want* to work at a fucking gas station."

"Is it because you're too good for a gas station?" she asked, cocking an eyebrow and crossing her arms over her ample chest.

"I want to be a *real housewife*!" I protested, starting to cry.

She stood up, grabbed her purse, and walked towards the door, muttering something to herself.

"Where are you going?"

"I can't help you if you're not willing to help yourself. I'm giving you a gift. You live in a city with the highest unemployment rate in the country and someone is offering you a job! You should be thankful."

She opened the door and turned toward me. "You're welcome for the cigarettes by the way."

With that, she slammed the door behind her. Somewhere in the hallway, a picture crashed to the floor.

I had no sooner gotten up and plugged back in the TV than my phone started ringing again. It was my mom. *Shit.*

"Hello?"

"*What* is your problem?" she yelled.

"What do you mean?" I asked, walking into the kitchen and returning with one of Troy's Bud Lights.

"I came over this morning and took the kids to school because Emma called me. She said you were sick. I was worried so I came over. Jesus, Tiffany, that house should be condemned by the board of health."

"I've been busy."

"Looking for jobs I hope."

"Look, just shut up. I can't deal with you right now, OK?"
I flipped the television back on. One of the housewives
was busy accusing another one of ruining her dinner
party.

"I'm picking the kids up from school. They can stay with
me for a few days. I'm bringing them back Friday. Roger
and I are going to Mackinac this weekend."

I rolled my eyes at the thought of her and my stepdad,
Roger, going on vacation. Roger is a retired Detroit
Police officer turned mall cop at Partridge Creek mall
out where the rich people shopped in Sterling Heights.
All Roger seemed to do was guard the Cinnabon. I
imagined they were going to Mackinac more for the
fudge than hiking through the fall foliage.

"Fine."

I hung up, finished the rest of the beer and rolled over.

I checked my phone. No new notifications. Of course
not. No one loves me. The big news was Kim Cho's
announcement that she had passed the bar. Fuck Kim
Cho. And fuck everyone else who got what they wanted
in life. I wished it was ten years ago and I didn't have a
daily electronic reminder of my failure. Kim Cho was
going to be a lawyer. Nina Mancinni owned a hair salon
in Warren. I just wanted someone to love me. It was all I
ever wanted.

*"This is too hard," Kim complained, throwing down the
scissors.*

180

"Um, no it's not," Tony replied, picking up the scissors and enthusiastically cutting Randy Moss out of a Sports Illustrated magazine. "It's the easiest thing she's had us do. Come on, a 500 word essay about where we see ourselves when we're 30 and a photo collage. You'd think we were in remedial, not advanced, English."

"I want to do so much though! I can't decide!" Kim pouted, a piece of her jet-black straight hair falling out of her barrette.

Our teacher, Ms. Smyth, had arranged our desks in circles, so we could "interact with each other," or as Olivia put it, awkwardly stare at Sanjay, who sat directly across from her.

"He thinks I'm staring at him," she whispered to me after class. "I'm only looking at the board!"

"Don't you people all have to be doctors or something? Or if not, they send you back to the motherland to work at Microsoft?" Tony joked, directing the joke towards Kim, who just rolled her eyes.

"Nah, that's Sanjay's people. His graduation present is going to be his own 7-11 if he doesn't get into Michigan," joked Carmine.

When everyone (including Ms. Smyth) laughed, Carmine stood up and bowed. "Thank you, come again."

Sanjay took it in stride. "What about you Carmine? You're never going to get into college. Did your dad give you a choice between his restaurant, his other restaurant, or maybe his other restaurant?"

We all snickered. Carmine's dad owned a chain of Italian restaurants and sub stores.

"Maybe he'll let you open your own," Olivia piped up. This was one of the first times she had spoken since the Abominable Snowman incident. We both felt more comfortable in this class. It was the only hour that we could be 100% certain that neither Paul nor his sidekicks would bother us. Paul couldn't spell English, let alone survive in an advanced class. The rest of the guys (even Tony) were tolerable when they weren't around Paul.

She continued, "And then, whenever Tony is-"

She paused and looked at him. "What is your career? You have 10 pictures of Randy Moss. Are you going to be Randy Moss?"

The whole table snickered.

"I'm going to be a professional athlete."

(I'm friends with Tony on Facebook. He's definitely not a professional athlete. Unless you count beer pong as a sport.)

*"I want to be a sports reporter. I want to be on ESPN,"
interjected Maria, a quiet girl with braces who never said
much.*

*"Ha!" snorted Sanjay, flipping through GQ (Ms. Smyth
later docked him 5% because apparently "rich" wasn't a
valid career option). "You have a mustache and a lisp." He
paused as if to think. "But I guess that could work out for
you. Everyone would be too focused on your mustache to
think about your lisp."*

*The other guys high-fived him. Maybe Sanjay should have
tried to be the next king of comedy.*

*"Mr. Choudhary! You better be working!" Ms. Smyth
yelled from her desk.*

*I looked at Olivia's poster. She had drawn a timeline with
dates, notes and pictures on hers. Graduate high school at
18, Notre Dame at 21, married at 22, complete med
school at 26, first child at 27, second child at 28, and
published author at 30.*

*"How are you going to have kids a year apart?" Tony
asked, leaning over with a picture of Tiger Woods.*

*"It only takes nine months. This first one will be at the
beginning of the twenty seventh year and the other at the
end of the twenty eighth." She frowned as if something
was missing. Glancing at the picture in Tony's hand, her
eyes lit up. "Can I use that one?"*

He handed her Tiger and she stuck it above the number 22.

"You're going to marry Tiger Woods?" Sanjay asked.

"Or Ben Affleck. Someone successful and clean-cut," she replied in all seriousness.

"Does Ben Affleck know this?" Allen asked. "Because I think Kim's already glued him to her *board."*

Olivia frowned, then burst into laughter. "OK, but no one steal Tiger, all right?"

I guess she said that a little too loudly because Ali turned around from her table and chimed in. "Really? Do you think Tiger Woods is going to want to be with some sea pig with bad skin?"

(Side note: as we all now know, Tiger Woods would probably have sought out a sea pig if he thought he could sleep with it.)

Her friends giggled, a signal for her to persist in her needless mockery. "Seriously, we can all see your acne under whatever orange paste you use on your face. You should probably become lesbian with your bull-dyke friend there," she nodded her head towards me, "and go live in the U.P. somewhere as loggers, or whatever lesbians do."

Olivia ignored her and turned away. I could tell she was trying not to cry. I think she could tell I was trying not to cry.

She looked at mine. "What is yours?"

"I want to be a writer," I said. "See, here's a few books. I want to write children's books as well as all kinds of adult books. I want people to always wonder what kind of book I'm going to write next."

"Isn't it hard to be a writer?" she asked. "Like don't most of them end up working at Starbucks?"

"I guess," I replied, realizing that I hadn't given it much thought.

"It is," she said matter-of-factly. "When my parents made my ten year plan, they told me that if you go to university to become a writer, you'll end up working at Starbucks until you die."

"Your parents have a ten-year plan for you?" I asked incredulously.

She nodded, indicating the board. "This is it. They'll be so proud of me. I bet they'll probably make me hang it up in my room as a reminder."

"Do you want to be a doctor?" I asked.

"Of course." She leaned in and whispered. "If nothing else, than to perform the world's first brain transplant on Ali

185

over there. A chimp's brain will be a significant improvement."

I rolled over and pulled up my computer. I highly doubted writing status updates counted as a career in writing, but now, it's all I've got. Through all this, I realize that Troy has never posted anything on my Facebook. No words of encouragement, no sweet messages. Nada. He said he was sorry the first night, but after that, he keeps telling me to look for a job. If he made more money, he could support us both. I just want someone who cares about me.

I was lying there feeling sorry for myself when my chat window popped up.

```
Mitch Francelli: Sup?
```

I smiled. Mitch was a guy I hooked up with a few months ago. We met at some dive bar off Six Mile and three hours later, we were back at his place. He was just my type- tattooed, muscular, and pierced in all the right places. Best of all, he drove a Chopper. He was like my own personal Jesse James. The Chinese symbol on my shoulder was his idea. Oh sure, it fizzled after a week or so, but I always knew he'd come back around.

I typed back. "Just hanging out. Bored."

```
Mitch: That sux. U working 2day?

Me: No. Lost my job.
```

Electronic Journal of Tiffany Harris

File Name: Tiff's Life: 2014 edition

Mitch: Bummer. Wanna hang out?

I thought about it. Mitch might be just what I needed. He's sweet, kind, caring, sensitive. Maybe he's what I need to get out of this funk, I thought to myself.

Me: Car's broke. Can u pick me up?

Mitch: Only got the Chop. Can I come over?

I looked around my place and down at my sweat and alcohol-stained sweatshirt.

"Give me an hour," I replied, hopping up and taking off towards the shower, laptop under my arm.

An hour and a half later, I heard a knock at my door. By this time, I had put on a pair of jeans and a low-cut shirt that showed off just a hint of the tattoo on my chest.

I opened the door. Damn, he looked even better than I remembered him.

"Come in. Want something to drink?" I asked.

"Sure, beer if you have it," he said, eyeing the place.

I brought it over and invited him to sit on the couch.

"So, uh, what's been going on?" he asked, leaning over to put out his cigarette in the ashtray. Oh my God, he smelled so good- some sort of musky combination of cologne, aftershave, and cigar smoke. I wondered if it was on his coat. After all, he *was* a bouncer at the club we met at.

I started in on my story. I was at the part where I was talking about unemployment benefits when he interrupted me.

"So just get a new job," he said, draining the beer can and tossing it to the side atop one of the kid's homework.

"I'm trying."

"You apply a lot of places?" he asked, awkwardly avoiding eye contact by looking up at the ceiling.

"Yeah," I lied. "It's just so hard. I just feel so alone."

"You're not alone," he said, opening up his phone and checking it. I noticed he still hadn't taken his coat off. I scooted closer to him on the couch. Damn, there was that smell again!

He continued. "I mean, you got friends. And your kids."

OK, not *quite* what I wanted to hear.

"And I'm here, ya know." He leaned forward and put out his cigarette.

There, that was better!

"That means a lot to me." I smiled as seductively as I could and leaned forward so he could get a good peak at the full hibiscus tattoo under the shirt.

"Well, well, what have we here?" he asked, pulling down my shirt.

I giggled and playfully swatted away his hand. "You've seen this before!"

"I don't know," he laughed, reaching down and pulling my shirt up over my head. "It was dark. When did you get this little gem?"

"When I was eighteen. It was my first one." I self-consciously covered my flabby stomach with my arms.

"Look at you. Such a *bad* girl." He reached and unbuttoned my pants. "Got any other surprises for me?"

"Come on back and we'll see," I said, getting up and leading him to by bedroom.

***

By the time it was over, I was exhausted and out of breath. Mitch was every bit as passionate as I remember.

I turned and rolled over, putting my arm on his chest. "That was amazing."

"Yup, it was pretty good," he agreed, sitting up and looking around the bed, gathering his clothes.

"Do you have to go so soon?"

"I have to be at work in a few hours," he said. "Gotta be there for happy hour."

"Sharkeez has happy hour?" I asked. Sharkeez was the kind of bar known for pool hustling and Lions games, not après work martinis.

"I don't work at Sharkeez anymore. I work at a new place in Greek town. Avalon." He pointed to his black t-shirt with Avalon emblazoned across the chest. "Real uppity and shit, but it's got a pretty nice rooftop setup."

"Oh." It was all I could think to say. I was waiting for him to tell me I should stop by sometime, but it never happened.

He laced up his boots and put his jacket on. I put my shirt on and got up to walk him to the door, but he was one step ahead of me.

"It's cool. I'll show myself out. I guess I'll talk to you later."

"Yeah, later," I replied, trying to keep it casual.

As soon as I heard the door swing close, I flopped back down on the bed. I smelled the blankets. They still smelled like his cologne. What kind was that?

Something about it smelled so familiar. I leaned in and tried to smell it more, but it seemed to have evaporated.

I must have fallen asleep because by the time I woke up, it was almost dark. I sat up, my head still spinning. I must have drunk more than I thought. I looked at my phone. One missed call and a voicemail from an area code I didn't recognize and one text from my mom reminding me to take care of my battery. Nothing from Mitch. I sighed. Well, he *was* working after all.

I heard the door open and the familiar cursing of Troy. Probably bitching about the mess, the lack of food, the lack of beer, or some combination thereof. I walked out into the living room. None of the lights were on, making it difficult to see. I tripped over some toy and fumbled for the light.

"What the fuck were you doing all day?" Troy yelled.

"I was busy," I mumbled, attempting to clear up the mess on the table.

"Doing what?" He indicated the disaster around the room. "Day drinking? Who was over here?"

"LaShawndra. She came over to see how I was doing."

"Jesus, you bring your ghetto ass nigger friends over here. Around my shit! Bitch, this TV is worth more than your fucking pathetic life!"

"LaShawndra isn't-"

191

"You know what? I don't fucking care! I'm done with this shit." He walked over to the entertainment center and began pulling out cords. "Why don't you just go on welfare with your crack whore friends? Maybe have yourself another nigger baby-"

I don't know what came over me, but I hit him. Hard.

He put down the Xbox, stunned. For a second I thought he was going to hit me, but he just looked down and kept unplugging his electronics.

"What do you think you're doing, Tiffany? Here you've got a decent guy and you piss all over it."

"*Decent*?" I spat out. "You don't even care about me! You're an insensitive asshole!"

"Oh please. What do you think you're going to get, Tiffany? Prince fucking Charming? You're 27 with two kids and no job. It's about time you grew up and started taking responsibility for yourself. Did you think this was fucking *Mad Men* or something- that you'd go become a secretary, bang your boss, and end up married and living out in Novi, shopping at Whole Foods and going to Pilates?"

I started crying as he headed toward the bedroom.

I followed him. "I deserve better than you!"

"Fine." He pulled his gym bag out of the closet and started putting his clothing in it.

"You don't-"

"Just shut up and stop talking. I know what you're going to say." He started clearing out his shoes, throwing my stuff on the floor. He stopped and looked up. "Let's talk about what you *don't* do. You don't look for a job, you don't-"

"I *have* looked for a job!"

"Really?" he asked, looking skeptical. "I pulled up your Internet browser. Yeah, I know, you think I'm just some dumb illiterate mechanic, but I know how to check history. You've been on no less than seven gossip sites, everyone and their mom's Facebook page, two dating sites, and exactly zero job sites."

I started to protest, but he just held up his hand as he zipped up his bag.

"I'm done. I'll come back tomorrow for anything I've left. I'm going to my mom's tonight."

Before I could plead with him, he slammed the door behind him. I burst into tears as I locked the door behind him. I heard the car door slam as he drove away.

Instinctively, I went to the kitchen and poured myself another drink. I picked up my computer and carried it into the living room to charge it. I reached down and picked up my phone.

Where was area code 214 from?

I pressed play on the message.

"Hello, Ms. Harris, this is Tawanna Huggins from Southeastern Airlines..."

October 18

I am still in disbelief. I know I shouldn't get my hopes up, but I think I'm one step closer to becoming a flight attendant. I posted to my Facebook:

```
Got the call from Southeastern! Things
are looking brighter for me and my
kids!
```

I actually put forth some effort and cleaned the house this morning. I want Troy to come back and see what he's missing out on. I read *Glamour's* career section. They are completely right. I shouldn't have to settle for less of a career than I'm worth.

I went ahead and updated my online dating profile. I don't have money for the fancy, paid sites, like eHarmony or anything, but the free one has plenty of men to pick from.

Most of the guys on there write that they're just looking for "kickback friends"- whatever that means, but I'm cool to just browse for now.

I added a little bit to my profile and decided to take a better picture. I backed up from my webcam and attempted to look as sexy as possible. I didn't want to catch my midsection so I moved the camera up a little bit on some of my books. There, that was better, but you couldn't see my tattoo.

I went and changed into a tank top. I put on some lip-gloss and made a pouty face for the camera. I backed up

and waited for the countdown. There, that was better. I
looked like a plus-sized model. I uploaded the picture
and left the window open. Not but a few minutes later, I
heard the familiar ping of a message. I moved my cursor
to wake up the screen.

```
Message from CaliBred83
```

```
Sup?
```

```
So what's up. Saw u on here and thought you
looked like a cool chick. Wut u like 2 do?
```

Ignoring the improper grammar, I emailed back.

```
Re: Sup?
```

```
Hey there, I got your message. Thanks!
Well, my name is Tiffany and I like to
spend time with my kids- I have two. They
are seven and nine. I'm in between jobs,
but I'm hoping to start working as a flight
attendant soon. What about you?
```

```
Re:Re:Sup?
```

```
That's coo, whatchu doin right now?
```

'OK, that was brief,' I thought to myself.

```
Re:Re:Re: Sup?
```

I'm cleaning my house, waiting for my kids
to come home.

I waited a few minutes and he never responded. I
shrugged it off and continued my chores. I checked my
phone a few times. I just had one message from my
mom telling me that she was bringing the kids back
around four.

By the time the kids came home, the house was looking
clean and she actually stayed off my case for once.

The kids started to watch TV and I checked my inbox
again. Damn, four new messages. I took my time to
respond to each. All of the guys were my type- loved
tattoos, piercings, and bikes. I gave Mike878787 my
number so he could text me.

No later had I given it to him then my cell phone started
buzzing. I was so excited. Mike seems like a really great
guy- way better than Troy. I was on my third text when
Emma threw down the remote.

"How come the Xbox is gone?" she whined.

"Well, it was Troy's, and he is an asshole, so he doesn't
live here anymore," I replied.

"Are we going to get a new one?" she pouted, sitting on
the couch.

"When we can afford one," I replied. "Which I think will
be soon."

"Did you meet a new, rich boyfriend?" she asked, picking at the cigarette burn on the couch.

"I might have a good job," I responded, to which she seemed less than thrilled.

"Doing what?" she asked, picking her paper out from underneath the discarded beer can.

"Well, hopefully I'll work as a flight attendant."

"So you'll get to go on a plane every day?" she asked.

"Almost every day. Some days I won't work." I explained.

"Where will we go when you're gone?" Tyrell asked.

"Grandma's probably," I replied.

"The plane won't crash like the ones from Malaysia, right?" he asked, very seriously.

"No, of course not. American planes are very safe."

I felt a twinge of guilt. I *would* be getting on a flying deathtrap every day. I didn't want to leave my kids mother-less, but I had to think about all of the other people who flew for business. I have to do it for them.

"Can we have dinner now?" he asked.

I fixed them macaroni and cheese and sat back down with my phone. It was Mike again.

Mike: What u up to tonight?

Hadn't I told him already?

Me: I have my kids.

Mike: Can u drop them off sumwhere?

Me: No. But maybe we could hang out this week.

Mike: Yea, maybe

I got the kitchen cleaned up and did the dishes. It was almost ten by the time I was done and I hadn't heard anything from Mike (or anyone else for that matter). I sighed. During this week, I had been neglecting my assignment. I am so glad that I am taking all online classes. That's going to help a lot if I get this job. I clicked on this week's assignment. It was titled, "Narrative and Anti-narrative." The description read:

In a narrative, a story is told from one person's perspective. In an anti-narrative, a story is told from the opposing perspective. In this assignment, you are to write a story from both perspectives. The story should focus on a certain event. For example, in the case of a story about a robbery, you should write from the victim's perspective as well as the robber's. What made

him (or her) do it? Try to get inside both characters'
heads. Length: 4-5 pages, double spaced.

Rough Draft Due: October 20

I thought about it and started typing.

"Can we have a snack before bedtime?" Tyrell asked.

I nodded. "Just clean up after yourself."

"What are you doing?" asked Emma, sitting next to me
and pulling the comforter over her feet.

"I'm writing a story."

"What's it about?"

"It's about a man and a women who meet each other
and fall in love. I have to tell the story from the man's
side and the woman's side."

"Are you going to let us read it?" she asked.

"Of course," I said. "But I need to get going on it, so why
don't you take your snack and go watch TV in my
bedroom?"

She was more than happy to oblige.

What should I name my first character? Should I name
her Tiffany? No, that would be too obvious. I settled on
naming her Annabelle. I named the man Cody. I decided

to make the character a little bit older than me. Maybe a little fatter too.

Great, I thought to myself. Now I'm making myself feel better by creating imaginary characters.

I started typing.

Annabelle

Fat. Broke. Thirty-five years old. Single mother. Ugly. Wrinkled. Saggy. Invisible.

Have you ever met someone and thought, "Wow, their life must really suck?" I'm not talking about the starving kids in Africa wearing ill-fitting Crocs and Broncos 2014 Superbowl winner t-shirts. I'm talking here. In America. Someone you actually know or met, not just the homeless people shuffling through the soup kitchen. The people who a suicide hotline member couldn't even give valid reasons worth living. Upon meeting them, have you ever wondered how they got there? Where did their lives derail so badly that they ended up in a position?

That was me a month ago. I was sitting at home when I realized that I had to go to the gas station. I didn't want to wait until morning when it was too cold outside.

I wrapped up my daughter in her little coat and hat and put her in her car seat. It had just started to snow and the roads were icy and I was being extra careful. I knew I needed to get new tires, but I couldn't afford them. I was just about to turn the corner, when BAM!

Someone had rear-ended me. We were both OK, but I knew there was some damage to the car. I got out as the frigid winter wind blew around me. Through the thick snow, I saw an SUV with its blinkers on. Standing next to it was the most gorgeous man I had ever seen in my entire life.

Cody

I was just coming home from work when the weather started getting too bad. I had evening patients. Believe it or not, people have dental problems late at night. I was trying to build my client base at my new practice. I knew I was going a little too fast when I saw the brake lights in front of me. I tried to stop, but being an Alabama boy, I'm not used to these winter driving conditions. I was going about 20 mph when I hit the van in front of me. I got out to inspect the damage and saw the woman with the kindest eyes I had ever seen.

Eventually, the rest of the story will have them falling in love and getting married, but I still have yet to figure out where I want that to take place at. Do I want a quickie Vegas wedding or a summer Mackinac Island wedding? Decisions, decisions. The only decision I'm making now is to go to bed.

Electronic Journal of Oda Mizra

File Name: MPJ-701_Reflection Journal

October 17

Eventually I woke up when Ashley came home about 11 in the morning.

"Productive day?" he asked, turning on the light and taking off his shirt.

I mumbled something in reply.

"Where's your car?"

I pulled the covers over my head. "Downtown-ish. Don't judge me!" I mumbled through the covers.

I could almost see him rolling his eyes. "So do you need me to take you to it?"

I peeked my eyes out from under the blanket. "No, Marissa can take me. How was your day?"

"You mean, how was my *twenty hour shift*? It was fucking fabulous. I thought after they fixed this sequester thing, the air traffic controllers were supposed to pull their heads out of their collective ass, but I guess that's asking too much."

"I'm sorry," I said, giving him my best pouty face. "Wanna get in bed and cuddle? I've kept it warm."

He looked at me and sighed. "What I'd *like* is to come home to more than cereal in the cupboard. What the hell have you been *doing* all morning?"

"Don't be mad," I said, trying to keep it playful. "I have the funniest story to tell you."

"I'm sure you do." He got up and went into the shower. "I can't *wait* to hear about what your idiot friends did this time. Let me guess, someone mixed plaids and stripes?"

I sighed and got up. "You don't need to be mean. I'll go to the grocery store right now."

I went to the bathroom, brushed my teeth, and pulled up my hair. "Can you make me a list of things you want?" I called out to him.

"Jesus, why can't you just be a wife for once?"

I came out of the bathroom and crossed my arms.

"Excuse me? I'm supposed to be a mind-reader now?"

"If you'd take any time to care about me, you'd know that I fucking hate Rice Krispies and that's all you buy," he complained as he lay on the couch.

"I'm sorry, sir," I said sarcastically, "but I'm not one of your flight attendants. Now, rather than making you undergo the difficult task of writing out a list, could you please at least *tell* me what you'd like?"

Ten minutes later, I was out the door and driving his car to the grocery store. I was well aware of the fact that I hadn't looked at my phone. Pushing my cart through the store, I unlocked my screen for the first time all morning.

WTF?

Where are you?

WTGDFF?

Srsly, where the hell did you go?

Are u OK?

WHAT. THE. FUCK. WAS. THAT.

Call me. Text me. Srsly. We're worried.

You single yet?

(The last one was from Paul.)

I clicked on my Facebook icon. Five new friend requests. Tony. Carmine. Sanjay. Paul. Brandon. Well, they didn't waste any time, did they? I approved them all, knowing that full well I'd have to face them eventually.

I finished up the shopping when Ashley texted me.

Don't forget we have that dinner tonight. I need you to pick up some beer to bring.

A 'please' wouldn't hurt, I thought to myself. *I'm not one of your stupid flight attendants.*

Crap, I had forgotten all about that. Ugh, I hated going to his co-workers' houses. They were a bunch of self-righteous assholes with perfect Stepford-type wives, wives who I'm sure were not hung over at noon debating whether or not to get Americone Dream or Chunky Monkey ice cream.

I eventually got home, went for a jog, and showered. By five, I was feeling alive again. I had replied briefly to Marissa and Carmine letting them know that I was indeed breathing and that I'd talk to them tomorrow.

"Is this okay?" I asked Ashley, emerging from the bathroom and turning around to reveal a low-cut purple shirt with black leggings.

"Aren't you going to be overdressed?" he asked.

"Um, *no,* it's an *evening* social activity," I said, putting my hands on my hips and turning sideways to appraise myself.

He sighed.

"I look ugly? Fat?"

"No, no, you look hot...just overdressed."

I rolled my eyes. "Then I don't see the issue. What are *you* wearing?"

"Is this OK?" he stood up, revealing a button down and khakis.

"Fine. Can we get this over with?"

The drive there was mostly silent.

"What did you do last night?" he asked. I could tell he didn't really care, but was just asking out of politeness.

Stirred up some shit, I thought to myself. "Well I met up with Marissa and her friends, who coincidentally I went to high school with."

"That sounds fun."

"It was aight I guess, just ya know, did some Detroit shiz...made meth in an abandoned house and then burnt it down. Typical Devil's Night prep work. How were your flights?"

The rest of the drive he spent talking about the particulars of budget cuts and their effects on air travel. By the time we arrived, I had tuned him out.

He turned off the car. "Promise you'll be nice?"

"I'm always nice," I replied, checking my makeup in the visor mirror.

"When have *you* ever been nice?"

I thought about it. "I told that one lady that one time that I thought it was great that she was a preschool teacher."

"Yes, but then you followed up by telling her that you were glad other women chose simple-minded professions like teaching and nursing," he pointed out.

I thought about it. "I don't think I used the term 'simple-minded.' Maybe 'pedagogic?'"

"Be nice," he snapped.

"*Be nice*," I mimicked sarcastically, following him up the driveway.

We walked in and I politely shook hands with everyone. Ashley walked out back as if to smoke and I followed him.

"No, you stay here," he instructed me.

I stood in the kitchen and looked around. "You want me to *stay in the kitchen*? What are you doing out there?"

"Having men talk. Just stay here with the other wives."

Great.

I stood there and leaned up against the counter, checking my phone for messages. I crossed my arm under the other, hopefully accentuating not just my ample bosom, but the fact that I didn't have a drink in my hand while the other wives (the minority who were not pregnant) did.

"Can I get you something? A water?" the hostess, Amy, asked.

"Wine would be great. Or maybe a beer, please."

She glanced sideways at her friend. "Um, should you be drinking?"

I looked up from my phone. "I didn't drive," I responded.

She looked back at her friend. "Well, aren't you trying to have a baby?"

I almost snorted with laughter. "Ha! No, you must have me confused with someone else."

"No, we *know* who you are," Amy responded. "You're what, 28 now? Clock is ticking."

I raised my eyebrow, both indicating annoyance and implying that she should work harder to get me an adult beverage.

"I'm 27 and you should get me a drink."

"I thought your people didn't drink," another one piped up.

"My people? Oh yeah, you mean all of us towel-heads. Yeah, well after three of my cousins, hijackers three, seven, and 18, were killed on September 11 upholding Allah's wishes, we were all kind of sad, so we took to the bottle."

They all looked shocked.

"Kidding," I muttered. "I'm not even Muslim."

(I wanted to follow up with a caveat: *'But if I were, odds are that I'd probably still wouldn't be a terrorist,'* but decided not to press the issue.)

She handed me a beer and looked at me. "The dip is very good. Where did you get the recipe?"

"Thanks. I got it off the Internet. Speaking of the Internet-" I brightened at the thought of attempting to engage these idiots in an intellectual conversation, "What do you think about the new copyright and patent laws with regard to third world Internet usage?"

Blank stares.

"Well, I mean, what were your takes on SOPA?"

Silence.

"I'm sorry," I said. "What's new with Jessica Simpson?"

With this prompt, they broke out into animated conversation, mostly comparing their little bundles of joy to those of the former pop princess turned Sea World exhibit.

I smirked with superiority, yet found myself rather disappointed that my clear mockery of their intellectual perception went unnoticed and therefore unappreciated.

I tried my best to make small talk with her and the others. Just when I thought I'd die of boredom from hearing about their kids and potty training, my phone buzzed. It was Carmine.

"Excuse me, I need to take this call," I said, politely making my exit.

"Hello?" I whispered.

"Hey! What are you doing?" he shouted. I could hear loud background noises, leading me to believe he was in a bar.

"I'm at a thing, " I whispered.

"What?" he shouted as I heard Paul yell something in the background about making someone his bitch.

"I can't talk," I hissed. "I'll text you." I hung up and turned around.

"What are you doing out here?" Ashley asked as he stood there with his boss.

"Oh, sorry, I didn't want to take the call inside. It was just some friends." I extended my hand to his boss. "Hello, my name is Olivia. Nice to meet you, sir."

He gave me a weird look and tentatively returned my handshake. "Likewise."

"Thank you for having us, sir. The food is delicious," I continued.

"Oh yeah...about that...my wife sets that all up....and...uh..."

It was clear that he was uncomfortable and didn't know what to say. "So, what did you bring?"

"The dip," I replied. "I must confess that I'm not a very good cook."

"Well, you'll get better," he said confidently, swigging his beer.

"Um, yeah," I replied. "Maybe when I'm done with school, I'll take classes for fun. I want to learn a foreign language. Maybe I'll take cooking classes as well."

"You're still in school?"

I cocked my head. Ashley had been working with this guy for almost three years. "Um, yeah, I'm working on my Masters in Journalism. I work at the paper. Mostly copy editing, but I've had a few pieces published. Ashley didn't tell you?"

"No. He just said that you worked part-time at the paper. I thought you were a secretary."

I felt the anger rush over me in waves. I gritted my teeth and tried to smile.

"I work 32 hours I'm trying to get a diverse writing experience before I figure out what I want specialize in."

I felt my phone buzzing again.

"Well, uh, that's really nice." He looked around as if I had just told him the most uncomfortable and deeply personal information ever.

"Why yes sir, and after my twelfth abortion, I did decide to get my tubes tied. Wanna see the scar?"

I guess he was scared of a female with a brain. I decided to make him squirm a bit more.

"You know my friend Veronica is actually an engineer and she works on your engine components. What kind of engines are in the planes you fly? I've been meaning to ask Ashley, but totally forgot."

"Your friend Veronica is an engineer?" he asked skeptically.

"Yes, a mechanical-"

He cut me off. "What kind of engineer? A sandwich engineer?"

He started laughing as if he were the new king of comedy. I politely excused myself by asking where the restroom was. He pointed down the hall and high-fived Ashley.

Jackass, I thought to myself.

I guess since I was by the back door, he sent me to the restroom by the kids' bedrooms. I didn't really need to go, I just wanted an opportunity to escape. I put down the toilet lid and sat down. I looked in the corner and saw a little kid's potty.

Eww, gross.

I checked my phone and started composing a text to Carmine. I heard voices, so I got up. I wouldn't want them thinking that I was taking too long and had clogged up the toilet. Looking in the mirror, I noticed that I had a smudge of black under my eye.

Gingerly, I opened the medicine cabinet, taking care to ensure that it didn't squeak.

Holy meth lab! This bitch apparently kept all her shit in this cabinet. Vicodin, Percocet, Xanax, Adderall…

I opened up the Adderall and slipped two into my purse. I debated crushing up the third, but just popped it instead. I went to replace the bottle and looked at the label.

Damn, this bitch was only 30. I guess that would make sense. Ashley's boss was maybe in his late 30's. In fact, while I thought all those women were older than me, the truth of the matter is that they are probably my age or just slightly older. Hell, some may be younger. I sighed. Nothing like missing my benchmarks, huh?

I pocketed two more Vicodin and Xanax and closed the medicine cabinet. I was washing my hands when I heard voices.

"Could she not find a shirt that fit or does she just *want* everyone to look at her?"

"I wonder how much she pays for those hair extensions."

"They're not extensions. Those bitches over there have real hair that long. She should have stayed back in Saudi Arabia or wherever she came from."

"She's just a gold-digging slut who got lucky and landed a pilot."

"Maybe she needs her green card."

I whipped my head around and thought to myself: *slut?* Really?

I had been called many things, but it had been a while since I had heard that one. How could I be a slut? I had never had a one-night stand. I only had like four boyfriends in my entire life. Ever. One of whom I was currently engaged to. I thought about the last time I had been called a slut and how much it hurt.

"What are you doing after school?" Tiffany asked me, standing by my locker, eating a candy bar.

"Practice," I replied, removing my field hockey stick and gym bag from my locker and blowing a kiss at my poster of Justin Timberlake. "Until about six or so. What about you?"

"Choir. We get out at five. My mom is going to pick me up. Do you want me to have her wait for you so she can give you a ride home?"

"Oh no, I don't want to do that to your mom. If I'm done, I'll run right over to the choir room, but don't wait for me, okay? My dad can get me later."

I closed my locker and sighed. "It's going to be so nice having a car next year!"

"How many months until you get your license?" she asked.

"Eleven! I'll be older than you!"

She laughed. "For like a week. You'll be one of the first sophomores to get a license."

"I like to do everything first," I reminded her as we walked toward the locker room. "Speaking of, our coach is going to decide who gets the varsity spot today: me or Ali. Wish me luck?"

She hugged me. "Hit her with a hockey stick."

I walked in the locker room, almost running into Delilah.

"Are you ready to play on varsity?" she asked.

I nodded. This was the first time that Delilah had directly addressed me in her life.

"Yes, I hope to really show you all what I can do," I mumbled in reply as I looked down and dug my toe into the chipped blue linoleum.

"Ok, well good luck."

Wow. Delilah just wished me luck? I was feeling more confident already.

We took to the field and started doing drills. From there, we transitioned to a scrimmage. I was running down the line, Ali close at my side, when she muttered, "Fucking porky, just go back to Afghanistan or wherever you're from."

I glanced sideways and saw our coach's attention focused on activity at the other end of the field. My anger welled up inside me.

Who the hell is this *bitch to make my life miserable?*

I tried moving to the left and (completely accidentally- at least I think so) whacked her in the shin with my stick, throwing her off balance. Seeing my opportunity, I dug my elbow into her collarbone (I had about three inches on her), causing her to collapse.

She cried out. I was stunned, but quickly snapped back to reality when I saw my opportunity. I deftly cut around her and before I could call to Delilah that I was open, she was already shooting the puck my way. I got it and made a perfect goal.

Fifteen minutes later, the game was over and the coach announced varsity.

I had made it!

I was so elated! Some of the older girls and even a few in my grade congratulated me. I was on cloud nine as we lined up to get uniforms issued for our first game. I could not believe that I was going to play varsity! I couldn't wait to tell my parents!

By the tine we were done, it was close to six. I knew Tiffany was gone. I was headed to my locker to call my dad when I heard a voice behind me.

"Nice move out there. I didn't think you had it in you," Delilah said, letting down her auburn ponytail, her red hair flowing down her back.

"I don't know what you mean," I retorted, avoiding eye contact as I meticulously folded up my school clothes in my bag before setting my books on top of them.

She looked at me. "Yes you do. You were smart about it. You were angry, but you weren't irrational." She took off her shirt, revealing perfect, porcelain-white skin.

Self-consciously, I wrapped a towel around myself, covering up my ample midsection as I wiggled my way out of my shirt. "It was an accident. I never meant to hurt anyone."

"You don't need to apologize. It's okay."

OK? I didn't press the issue anymore. I pulled out my cell phone.

"Damn," I muttered.

"What?" she asked.

"No bars. I have to call my dad for a ride."

"I can give you one. You live off of Jewett, right?"

I nodded. How did she know where I lived? Until today, I was unaware that she knew I existed.

"How do you know where I live?" I asked.

"You have the brown one with the balconies on it, right?"

I nodded.

"Our moms went to high school together. Didn't you know that? I always liked that one. When you moved back, my mom said she knew the lady who lived there- she said she was the lady who always wore the pink hat in Canada. They graduated together."

I was confused. My mom had never mentioned that. Weird.

I followed her out of the locker room and called my dad, leaving him a message letting him know that I had a ride home.

"Where do you live?" I asked, feeling rude that I didn't know such information.

"Off Lakeshore," she said, pushing open the locker room door.

I hustled to keep up with her, dodging the boys who had just emerged from football practice. "That's so far away! Are you sure it won't be a big deal taking me so far out of your way? I can give you gas money."

(My parents had always told me that anytime you felt as if you were inconveniencing someone to offer them money. Even if they didn't accept it, it made you look classier.)

"I don't mind," she replied.

"That's nice of you. There are no young people who live around me. It's all really old people. One day I'm going to see the grim reaper driving his hearse down Jewell."

"You live on Jewett?" I heard a male voice ask.

I turned around. Shane Carson, aka Senor Senior, was perhaps one of the most well-liked boys in his class. Not only was he a football star, but on Fridays, he dressed up in a sombrero, fake mustache, and cape for the morning announcements.

I blushed and looked down. "Um, uh, yeah, I um..."

(Seriously, what the hell was wrong with me? This guy was going to think I didn't know my own address.)

"I live right around the corner on Lincoln."

"Oh, OK, I know where that is."

(Did I really just say that? Of course I knew where it was. It intersected with my street.)

He looked at Delilah. "I can give her a ride home."

Delilah shrugged, oblivious of how meaningful this event was to me. "Sure, fine with me." She looked at me. "Is that okay with you if Shane gives you a ride home?"

She may as well have just asked me if I'd rather have Kobe steak for lunch rather than our stale burgers. I just nodded, realizing that forming any more words would brand me an even larger moron.

I followed Shane out to his car, a late-model Jeep Cherokee. He opened the door for me. "Excuse the mess," he said, closing the door.

I gingerly sat down, carefully kicking a plastic dip cup out of the way.

We started driving home with him making small talk and me replying in one-word answers, lest I limit my stuttering and decrease my odds of sounding like a complete simpleton.

"So Oda, do you smoke?" he asked, flashing his pearly white teeth at me.

"Sometimes," I stammered.

(Lie. I had never smoked a thing in my life.)

"You want to go smoke?" he asked.

"Sure," I replied, pinching myself to make sure I wasn't dreaming. I desperately ran my fingers through my hair and tried to tame my frizzies. I sat up straight and sucked in my stomach.

By this time, the sun was starting to set. We pulled into a little park by the electric field.

The electric field actually ran parallel to a small creek. On both banks of the river was a small forest. I had heard that kids had all kinds of forts and secret hideouts back here. I had also heard that they found dead bodies, but put that thought out of my mind.

"Come on, I know the perfect spot."

I followed him into the woods and a few minutes later, we were at the base of a tree house.

"This yours?" I asked.

"Yep. Pretty sweet, huh? It's actually my cousin's, but I hang here a lot." He pulled out a baggie and put some weed in a pipe. He lit it up and inhaled, then passed it to me.

Oh shit, I had no idea what to do.

Luckily, he was nice about it. A few minutes later, we were laughing and I had no trouble talking at all.

Suddenly, he leaned in and kissed me. I was so caught up in the moment that I didn't realize it was happening. Truth be told, it was the first time I kissed a boy. It would be the first of many.

(Hey, I said I only had four serious boyfriends.)

He didn't press for anything further and we eventually knew we had to go home. He dropped me off and I went inside the dark house, trying to sniff my sweatshirt to catch a trace of his Abercrombie Woods cologne.

"How was practice?" came a voice from the darkness.

I jumped and screamed, then upon realizing it was my mom, turned on the light.

"You scared me!"

"Where have you been?" she calmly asked.

"Practice! I made varsity! Sorry, Shane Carson gave me a ride home."

"That's good. Did you beat out Ali?"

"Yes." I sat down at the table, my heart still racing. "Why are you sitting in the dark?"

She didn't answer me. "That's good. What did you get on your Geometry test?"

"Ninety seven," I replied. "I'll have all A's on my progress report," I assured her.

"Is Shane going to ask you to homecoming?"

"I don't know, mom!" I got up and poured myself water. "I'm already going with Tyler. Just as friends."

"But Shane is more popular than Tyler."

"I could never do that to Tyler even if Shane asked me." I took a box of rice from the cabinet and poured it into the rice cooker. "Brad just gave me a ride home. We're not picking out our bridal registry at Bed, Bath, and Beyond."

I knew this kind of disappointment. It was her passive-aggressive way of trying to make sure that I lived up to her (downright unrealistic) standards. I get it, her life sucked growing up, and now she wanted to live vicariously through me.

I paused as I buttered my rice. "You didn't tell me you went to high school with Delilah's mom."

"I did. Her mom and her real dad."

"Her dad's not her dad?" I asked.

This wasn't unusual, lots of people had divorced parents, but their last names were the same.

"No, Delilah was born out of wedlock."

I opened my mouth, shocked. Delilah was a bastard baby? No way! I made a mental note to save this in my arsenal of information should I ever need it later. Of course, my mom changed the subject back to one that suited her.

"What did Shane say when he dropped you off?"

I sighed and threw up my arms. "He told me to have a good night and he'd see me tomorrow! What the hell? Did you think he was going to ask when we'd go to Jared to pick out rings? I got a good grade on my test and made varsity. Isn't that good enough?"

I didn't wait for her reply. I took my rice upstairs and turned on my TV. I wanted to call Tiffany, but I'd wait until tomorrow. I sniffed my sweatshirt one last time and then drifted off to sleep.

The next day, I could sense something was amiss. I caught Paul giving me weird looks. At one point, I swore he was winking at me.

In third hour, I was walking to the stapler when I heard Kirsten cough, and under her breath, mutter, "whore."

I turned towards her.

"What did you say?" I whispered.

"Dirty whore," whispered her friend Kaylee, a bit louder.

"Shut up. I don't know what you're talking about."

"I heard you gave Senor Senior the dirty Sanchez," Kirsten said, not even bothering to whisper.

"I have no idea what you're talking about. Nothing *happened between Shane and I."*

(I didn't even know what a Dirty Sanchez was until I was 24.)

They looked at each other and laughed.

"I hope he closed his eyes when he was on top of you so he didn't have to see your unibrow."

Self-consciously, I touched my face. I did not *have a unibrow.*

(OK, maybe I did.)

I went back to my seat and finished out class. At lunch, Tiffany practically ran to the table.

"Oh my God, is it true?" she breathlessly asked.

"Is what true?"

"You and Shane!"

"No! Nothing happened!" I protested. "Ok, I mean, we kissed, but that was it. I swear."

"I heard you gave him head in his Jeep."

"Eww! Oh my God. No way. That's disgusting!"

"Did you touch his, you know-"

"No! Absolutely not!*"*

The rest of the day continued like that. I tried to dodge as many people as possible, but I couldn't block out the whispers and stares.

Finally, when school let out, I caught Shane.

"Why did you tell people that we hooked up?" I asked accusingly, this time not stuttering at all.

"I didn't tell anyone anything, relax."

"Why do people think we hooked up?"

He shrugged. "Maybe someone saw you getting into my car with me. Just chill."

"People are calling me a whore!"

"Don't worry about it. They'll get over it. I gotta go to practice," he said, changing directions and heading to the locker room. "I'll talk to you later."

Red-faced, I headed into the locker room.

"Are you sure you can play today?" asked Ali, as she smugly stood by her locker. "Should you maybe get tested for STDs first?"

"Nah, I'm cool...I haven't been touching your stuff," I replied right before turning my back to her so she wouldn't see my tears and got changed. Slut or not, I had to keep playing.

I turned off the water, feeling the first effects of the Adderall kicking in. I listened to my teenage self. Slut or not, I had to keep playing the game. And I was not about to lose.

I walked back out into the kitchen, smiling as big as could be. I guess they hadn't realized that I was in the bathroom.

"Can I have a wine please?" I asked, tossing my beer in the trash.

"Um, sure," said Amy.

I pulled out a stool and sat down, smiling and propping my hand up on my chin. "So, girls, what did I miss?"

They looked dumbfounded.

"Um, well, we were just talking about how hard it is to be married to a pilot."

"I don't think it's hard at all," I confidently replied, taking a sip (scratch that- a gulp) of wine.
"I mean, let's face it. My fiancé's going to Sacramento at the furthest. He's not exactly on a Mars exploration mission."

They stared. I took this as my cue to continue.

"I mean, I guess if I were a sad and pathetic co-dependent excuse for a human being, I might be depressed. But think about it- what's the worst that's going to happen while he's gone? The garbage disposal breaks? They have YouTube videos that show you how to fix it." I drank more wine. "In fact, when stuff breaks around our house, I make it a point to fix it. I don't want my man to come home to a laundry list of chores."

Cricket-cricket. Silence.

Finally, one spoke. "You fixed a garbage disposal by yourself?"

I finished the glass and indicated to Amy that she should pour me more. "Oh yeah, it's not hard at all. I mean, you have to know how to read and all, which might be a stretch for *some* here, but it wasn't too hard at all."

Amy glared at me, untying her apron. (Yes, this dumb bitch was wearing an apron. I guess in breeder-speak, removing the apron means that shit's about to get real.)

I went on. "I mean, sure, people have asked me if I worry that Ashley's cheating on me while he's on the road. Really? With who? Have you seen the flight attendants today?" I snorted and slammed the rest of the glass. "None are below a size eight. He's not a chubby chaser."

Several women's jaws dropped open. Hey, size eight's a goal for some I guess.

I sighed and continued, subtly scanning the room. "I mean, I guess I could see why *some* men cheat."

Just then, I caught Ashley out of the corner of my eye. I knew he had caught the tail end of our conversation. I stood up.

"Well, it's been so nice to meet you all or see you all again, but we really have to go. We have another event to attend to. Thank you for the party. It was lovely," I said as I put on my coat.

They glared me down. I saw Ashley shaking hands with his co-workers.

As soon as we got out to the car, he laid into me. "What the *hell* were you thinking?"

"They called me a slut!" I protested. "I was in the bathroom and they said-"

"Oh Jesus, Olivia, get over it. They did not."

"They did *too*! They made fun of this shirt!"

"Can you not just keep your mouth shut for *one* night?" he shouted as he turned out of the subdivision.

"So I'm just supposed to let them walk all over me?" I cried. "I've worked *way* too hard to make something of myself! I'm done being pushed around by dumb bitches!"

He rolled his eyes. "That's right, Olivia. The whole world is out to get you. Get over yourself."

I turned away so that he wouldn't see me cry.

"You know, I'm thirty two years old and I'm trying to move up in the fucking company. I don't need my crazy future wife ruining that."

I turned as if slapped in the face. "So is that why you didn't tell your boss that I was working on my Masters? You thought being married to a hausfrau would look better on your resume?"

"No, but unlike you, I don't feel the need to flaunt how much better I am than everyone."

"So what? Would you rather be married to one of those fat cows in there?" I screamed, slamming my fist into the window. "Because last time I checked, you were *more* than satisfied with my physical appearance! Three times satisfied in one night, if I recall correctly!"

"Jesus Christ, I'm done with this."

"Fine," I said, throwing my hands up in the air. "You think you can do *so* much better than me? Be my fucking guest. But let's face it- you've got a receding hairline and haven't seen your abs since Obama's took oath. The first time. I'm *sure* you'll land yourself a fucking Victoria's Secret model!"

We drove in silence the rest of the way. We got home and he went to bed. I stayed up and was watching TV when I realized that I never answered any of Carmine's ten texts.

Me: I'm so sorry. I was so busy. Long story.

> Carmine: No, just wanted to see if you wanted to hang. Your friend came out with us.

Me: Oh, bummer, yeah, I had to go to this thing.

> Carmine: Hey, what are you doing next Saturday?

Me: Nothing that I can think of off the top of my head. I think my fiancé is gone. I have no plans as of yet.

> Carmine: Do you want to be my plus one to Alex Giancarlo's wedding? I told him I'd find someone and it's either you or Craigslist personals. Marissa is going with Sanjay.

Me: Haha, yeah sure.

> Carmine: Your man won't be mad?

Me: You and I are going to a friend from high school's wedding. Unless we have sex on the dance floor to the Harlem Shake, I think he won't be too worried. He knows I

can't even twerk. Damn, he's getting
married?

> Carmine: Hellz yeah, another one
> bites the dust. We're taking him
> to Diamondz later this week if
> you'd like to join us.

Me: Uh, no, I'll pass. Body glitter takes
forever to come out of my clothes. But make
it rain for me, K?

> Carmine: Word.

Me: Two words: midget stripper. Good night.

October 20

I had my first interview with Southeastern today. I had hoped for it to go better than it did, but this was just an initial interview. They said they'd call me later this week or early next. I'm so upset. I don't think they understand how badly I need this job. *Right now.* I'm *so* desperate.

I haven't heard from Mitch, Mike, or anyone all weekend. I saw on Troy's Facebook that he was back with an ex-girlfriend from Saginaw. Go figure. I needed to find something short-term. I started looking on Craigslist. Cleaning houses? Ha, yeah, right, I could barely clean my own house. Baby-sitting? Again, I had my own kids to worry about. All of the sudden, one ad caught my eye.

`Wanted: Waitresses!!!! All shapes and sizes welcome. Diamondz Gentlemen's Club. Apply in person between 1 pm-5 pm.`

'Are you out of your mind?' I asked myself. *'There's no way.'*

Then another voice popped into my head. *'You're sexy. You've been sexy. You've stolen boyfriends away from other girls. Maybe you don't have the body of a supermodel, but some guys like thicker girls.'*

I decided to go for it. I *could* use the money after all. It wouldn't be the first time that I took my clothes off for money. Maybe I'd meet a guy there- who knows? Maybe some guy at a bachelor party. I heard a lot of Detroit Firemen and Police went there. Those are good jobs.

And I wasn't *really* taking my clothes off, was I? I was waitressing. It was different.

To get a little bit of courage, I took a few shots before heading out. By the time I pulled up in the parking lot, I was feeling good. Anyone who's ever been to a strip club in the middle of the day knows that it's probably one of the most despondent sights in the world. I looked up at a dilapidated sign and pushed open the door, my nostrils greeted with the smell of stale cigarette smoke.

"Be right with you!" a voice shouted from the back.

I took the opportunity to check my reflection in the mirror. I had put on more makeup and tried to tease my hair to give it some body.

"Can I help you?" a man asked, emerging from the shadows. He was young- about my age. He didn't look like the typical strip club owner. I don't know if I was expecting an unbuttoned shirt, gold chain-wearing skeeveball, but this guy was definitely not it. I handed him my resume. He chuckled. I guess he wasn't used to getting resumes at a strip club.

He glanced it over. "No shit! We went to the same high school!"

He had introduced himself as John, which didn't set off any bells.

"Yeah," I replied, desperately trying to place him.

"You graduated the same year as me! No way!" He looked up at me as if trying to place me. "My last name's Grambling."

"No way!" I said. "I think you sat in front of me at graduation. You had a little portable TV so you could watch the Pistons game?"

"Yes! And they lost. Those bastards. Do you remember Ranjit's valedictorian speech? Where he quoted the late, great, Tupac?"

I thought back. I remembered a lot about that night. It was early June. We had to graduate late because we had too many snow days. Graduation was at six in the evening, but they wanted us there by five. Kim, Oda (who had since taken to waxing her eyebrows), Maria (who had since taken to waxing her mustache), Tyler, and I sat in her bedroom fiddling with our caps and gowns. I turned sideways.

I looked like a bloated whale.

Oda was painstakingly applying layers of makeup to cover up her eczema. After every layer, she applied a layer of powder to set it.

"So, does this mean that you're salutorian?" I asked her.

She threw up her hands in frustration. "No! And my parents are so pissed! There were so many of us that tied for the same GPA that they took into account other factors such as sports and extracurricular to determine who got to do the speech. Jenny Wright beat me out. It's stupid. She does more sports. Who the hell wants to do sports in the winter?"

"Well, I bet she didn't get thrown out of a hockey game for beating another girl with a stick- twice," Tyler piped up, looking applying some of the powder to his nose. (By this time, Tyler was completely out of the closet.)

Oda paused. "Ok, I didn't beat either of them. Neither was hospitalized. Plus, I was a sophomore. One was some senior named Regina who apparently started rumors that I was a slut the prior fall. Remember, she was the one who told everyone that I hooked up with Shane? She had it coming."

"Probably the first time in history that someone has tried to whack a player on their own team," Maria pointed out.

"Like I said, she had it coming." She turned and looked at me. "Ok, I think I'm done. How do I look?"

"Good. How about me?" I asked.

"Excellent," she replied as she started putting things back into her purse. She looked around the room, about to ask one of her famous questions. "So what are you guys looking forward to most about graduation?"

"College?" Kim asked, confused. Even though we were all going to separate colleges, we had promised to stay close.

"No, no," she paused. "Like what will be best about being done?"

"Oh that!" I smiled, just thinking about it. "I won't miss being called a cow, pig, or any other variation of farm animal. I won't miss stupid Paul Jacobi putting a Weight Watchers pamphlet on my desk during chemistry."

"What an asshole. I hope someday he gets fat himself." She plugged in her hair straightener and started straightening for the hundredth time.

"I won't miss Paul calling me fag every day," added Tyler.

"I won't miss Tony copying my homework and then saying, 'Me love you long time China girl' and doing his stupid squinty eye thing," Kim chimed in.

"He does accents very well," Oda said thoughtfully as she straightened the other side of her hair.

"Your hair is straight! We have to get going!" I reminded her, looking at the clock.

"It's going to frizz. All of the rest of us who tied for salutorian have to get up on stage. I guess they're giving up some award for being in a 20-way tie for third place."

"That's cool," I said, just happy to be graduating.

"Are you kidding me? My parents are just devastated that it's not an acceptance letter to Notre Dame," she moaned.

"Notre Dame is a hard school to get into," I reminded her.

"Yes, but if I were prettier, maybe I'd have a chance."

"That makes no sense," I replied, already sweating through the blue satin material of our graduation gown.

"I'm looking forward to just being able to go and be myself for once, you know?" she asked, un-pinning and re-pinning her hat to her hair. "No one to tell me what to do. Not worrying about getting hit with some new insult every time I turn a corner. I don't want to be 'Porky' anymore. I just want to be me. I'm tired of being beat down."

In that moment, she looked far older than her eighteen years, as if she had been battling demons for so long. Her eyes belayed exhaustion and pleaded for relief. I knew how bad everything had hurt her. I tried to blow it off, but she internalized everything. Whereas I knew what I wanted (a man), I think she wanted so much more. She just didn't know what it was yet.

"Are your parents coming tonight?" she asked.

"Yep, mom and stepdad, dad and girlfriend, both sets of grandparents," I replied.

"That's sweet."

"You?" I asked.

241

She sighed. "My parents are going to probably bail because they're too ashamed. I'm sure Zako and Taline will be there," she rolled her eyes.

"That is so weird that you're just a year older than them, but you all don't get along."

"Oh please, they're way too good for me. Did you know they told Mrs. Horowitz that I was just a distant cousin?"

"They're not that special," I remarked.

She shrugged. "They're B-team popular and they both know it. Problem is that I'm D-team. I can't wait until college when there's no more teams."

"I want to meet my husband," I said, changing the subject. (Trust me, Oda could go on and on about how much she couldn't stand her brother and sister.)

"Yeah, I bet college guys are more mature. Hey, speaking of mature, I got something for us," she winked, puling out two Pepsi bottles. She handed me one. I tentatively removed the cap and took a sip.

I spit it back up. "What the hell is this?"

"Rum. Drink up."

"Something to drink?"

I snapped out of it. I realized John had asked if I wanted anything to drink.

"Rum, please."

An hour later, I had secured a few shifts. I don't know if John was so impressed with my drink serving skills or he just felt bad for me. Either way, I was glad to have the opportunity.

Electronic Journal of Oda Mizra

File Name: MPJ-701_Reflection Journal

October 22

I had to meet with Dr. Levenstein today for my
quarterly meeting. So far, he said my case studies for my
paper are going well. He suggested I use less "harsh and
judgmental" language. Whatever. He's probably a whiny
liberal who doesn't believe in winning and losing teams
in Little League.

Right after that, I headed over to Canada. I needed to get
my engagement ring. I made it in 35 minutes. Record
time.

I went up to the attic, got the rings, and got the hell out
of there. I don't care how big and bad you are, being
alone in an attic is scary as fuck. My dad had asked me
to go around the side of the house to check to make sure
that the crawl spaces were all closed up; not because he
was worried about thieves stealing all of our valuable
rafts, but because several years ago, raccoons used our
crawl space as their own personal swingers club.

(Despite my pleas, we were not allowed to keep the
twenty or so baby raccoons that were born below us.)

I started around the right side and worked my way
around to the beach side. It was in the 60's-
unseasonably warm for this time of the year. I couldn't
tell if the last panel was locked up, so I knelt down to get
a closer look at the rusty lock. As I leaned down, I
caught the sickingly sweet smell of something. Hibiscus.
Either my grandma or mom had planted them there

every year. Most of the flowers are dead this fall, but I guess fifty years of history hangs around.

I sat with my back against the side of the house, not caring if my jeans got dirty, my head resting on the wind-battered siding. How was it that a smell could make you remember so much? How can a scent so seamlessly bridge the gap of all space and time and take you back to places you thought you were gone from?

It was right before the fourth of July after I had graduated high school. By this point, my friends and I came over to Canada every weekend pretty much. I was a hostess at my uncle's restaurant in Greek town, so I could even drive back and forth to work. I had invited Tiffany and Kim over several times, as well as Tyler, who by this time had not only come out of the closet, but had made it a personal point to start a GLBT club at our school. Because of him, at least ten other kids came out our senior year.

We were sitting on the deck drinking long island iced teas I had made from the liquor in my parent's cabinet. I had taken to watering it down, figuring that in less than a month, I'd be legal to buy alcohol, so I'd replenish their supply later.

Taline and Zako were begrudgingly forced to hang out with us. Both were in trouble because of their grades their junior year, so my parents were keeping them on a tight leash. They were semi-grounded to Canada except to go in for summer school sessions. The only reason they even tolerated me was because I provided ample amounts of alcohol and did their summer homework for them.

"What should we do today?" asked Tiffany.

It was before ten in the morning. Back then, I never thought about working out, jogging, or anything of that nature.

"We could go to Pelee Island and rent bikes. Ride around. Check out the vineyards," I suggested.

"It's going to be too hot today," Kim complained.

"Hot? Bitch, you're going to university in Florida!" I reminded her. (Kim's uncle was the head of the physics department at some school in Florida. He got her a sweet discount on tuition, plus, in obligation to fulfill her Asian destiny, she was going to get her PhD in physics. Her words, not mine.)

"I can't believe I leave in two days for summer session," she mused. "I haven't even packed."

"Fine, we can take the boat out and go from there," I suggested. "But let's wait until-"

I sat up, staring down the beach.

"What?" asked Tiffany as her and the others followed my gaze.

"Hold up, just don't stare. Who is that?" I asked.

"I don't know, but he looks yummy," Tyler noted.

Even from here, we could all tell that whoever he was, he was beautiful. He was standing around with Jean, trying to figure out what was wrong with a jet ski.

"Get me the binoculars," I whispered to Tyler, waving my hand. "They're in the front drawer under the green glass fish."

He returned with them and I took off the cap, trying to look inconspicuous.

"Why do you have binoculars, you creeper?" Tiffany asked.

"Bird watching and looking at the boats on the horizon," I replied, trying to focus.

"Yeah," snorted Taline, looking up from her People magazine. "When we were kids, my parents used to tell Oda to sit out here and look for pirate ships and report any possible sightings in a notebook. Talk about how to entertain an idiot for hours. She had so few friends that she had to look for imaginary pirates."

"I'm the idiot?" I yelled, getting up and stomping over to her chair. "I didn't fail consumer math." I snapped the magazine out of her hand. "Think about that the next time you expect me to do your work."

She put her hands up in mock defense. "Chill Godzilla. If you fall, you're going to crush me."

She was right. At the time, she was the size of an Olsen twin. Maybe 95 pounds at most and barely 5'2." I, on the other hand, may have just tipped the scales at 160.

"I'm going to fucking beat your ass!" I shouted.

"Girls! Girls! Stop it!" Tyler hissed.

We both turned around. Jean and the unidentified hottie were walking our way. Even my sister was smart enough to recognize that this guy was hot. I made a mental note to punch her later.

"Hey Oda! Does your dad have jumper cables in the boat shed?" Jean called out.

"Yeah," I replied, thankful I was wearing sunglasses as not to appear as if I were staring at the guy with him. "You need a jump?"

(Wow, way to dazzle him with your intellect and reasoning skills, Oda.)

"Yeah, can we borrow them?"

I nodded, indicating that they should follow me around to the shed.

"How have you been?" I asked Jean.

"Good, graduated. About to go to university in Toronto this fall. You?"

"Same. Heading to Southern Michigan, but hoping to transfer to Notre Dame after two years. I didn't get in, but the admissions counselor said that if I get good enough grades at another school, I'd have a better chance even against high school seniors. But that means by the time I graduate, I'll probably be 24," I sighed.

We stood at the shed and I opened the door for Jean. There was only room for one person, so I figured I'd let him get what he needed.

"Hi, I'm Cody," the uber-hottie said, extending his hand.

"I'm Oda," I replied, getting a good look at him for the first time. He was perhaps the first guy I had ever seen that was so ridiculously good looking that I blushed when I saw him. He looked exactly like a young Kevin Bacon circa the Footloose era. I figured him to be maybe a few years older than me. He had the kind of body that had inspired generations of sculptors and artists. If I had any artistic skills, he would be the model for my David statue. I was subtly trying to count his ab muscles when Jean yelled out from the back.

"Yeah, sorry! That's just Oda. Oda, meet Cody."

"Ok, I guess my full name is 'Just Oda.' 'Just' is the first."

He laughed. I made a mental note to high-five myself.

"So what are you and your friends doing later?" Cody asked.

"I don't know. Might go out on the boat."

"Are one of those guys your boyfriend?" he asked, smiling to reveal a row of dazzling white teeth.

Dammit, why did he have to be so hot?

I made a face. "Eww, gross, no! That one is my brother and the other guy is my gay friend. How do you know Jean?"

"I'm actually friends with his older brother. We're on the diving team together at State."

I tried to remember how much older Jean's brother was. Twenty-three?

As if reading my mind, he said, "I'm twenty two."

"Oh cool, I'll be nineteen soon," I replied, looking down at the ground, suddenly aware that my feet were very hot standing on the cement.

"Ah, well I'll have to take you out for your first celebratory drink," he winked at me. Fuck, was this happening or was I still dreaming?

"Sounds good. I made some Long Islands if you guys want one."

*"How could I say no to a pretty girl offering me a drink?"
He leaned into the shed where Jean was also rummaging
for some tools. "I'll meet you back at your house buddy. I'll
bring you one."*

*He mumbled something in reply and we walked indoors. I
could feel his eyes on my backside and tried to suck in my
stomach.*

*In the kitchen, we made small talk as I mixed another
batch.*

*So, what kind of music do you like?" Cody asked, scrolling
through my playlist on my computer.*

*"Oh everything," I replied, desperately trying to think of a
hip new underground band that sounded impressive.*

*"You like Dave?" he asked, which should have been
obvious given that I had a whole playlist dedicated to
musical genius and variety of Mr. Matthews.*

*"Yeah, 'Spoon' with Alanis Morisette is my favorite song,"
I said.*

*"I play the guitar. I should play for you sometime," he
said.*

This was just getting better and better.

"Awesome," I replied.

"So you wanna hear me sing to you?" he asked, smiling

that dazzling smile again. "I mean, tonight. We'll sneak out onto one of the beaches down the way. Or a boat."

"Yeah, that sounds awesome," I said, leaning into the fridge and rummaging for lemons as to avoid him seeing me smile like a retard.

"Have you ever put cranberry juice in instead of Coke?" he asked, coming up behind me. He was so close. I could feel his breath on my neck and feel the warmth of his body almost pressing into my back.

"Um, yeah, isn't that called a Grateful-"

We were interrupted by the slamming door and Zako's little bitch voice whining about my mom's inability to buy the right kind of sunscreen.

"Whoa, uh, sorry, didn't mean to break up anything in here," he said, not even bothering to conceal his surprise about seeing Cody and I together.

"It's fine, we're just getting drinks."

"Are you gay, bro?" he bluntly asked as he tried to figure out the child-proof lock on the sunscreen.

"Zako!" I shouted.

"What. I'm just asking? I'm down with the homos. I mean, Tyler is gonna hook me up with a hot chick he knows from Express."

"Why do you think he's gay?" I yelled.

Cody turned towards Zako, obviously wondering the same thing.

"Uh, cuz you're a fag hag and no straight dude would hang out with you."

"Well I happen to think she's beautiful," Cody said, defensively, putting his arm around me.

"Whatever, it's okay to be gay" Zako mumbled, giving up on opening the bottle and throwing it on the couch.

We eventually returned to our respective beaches and made plans to hang out later in the day.

"So how hot is he?" asked Tyler.

"Soooooo hot!"

The rest of the day I had trouble focusing. I wondered if this was what love felt like. Sure, I had gone on dates with a few guys. I went to prom. I had kissed boys. But none made me feel the way Cody did. Why was he paying attention to me? No one ever paid attention to me. I was so distracted thinking about him that I barely ate anything all day.

That evening, Cody came down to us and invited us to a bonfire. After showering and taking full advantage of my makeup (I had invested in the entire MAC collection I swear), I admired myself in the mirror. "Not bad," I

253

murmured out loud. I was still a little heavy, but I was tan and my white shorts looked awesome against my skin. I headed downs to where the music was and my friends were waiting for me.

"Wow! That was you playing?" I asked as I saw Cody strumming his guitar.

"Yeah, I sing too. What do you want to hear?"

"Um....how about something you've written yourself?"

"You got it babe."

Now, to say Cody was a talented guitar player would have been a blatant lie. He was marginally tolerable at best. I'm pretty sure his "original" lyrics went something along the line of:

"Your eyes are your soul/i love you under the sun/for a long time"

(I should have just had him play some Dave.)

Jean's brother, Chad, and some of his other friends came down and sat there with us. I recognized one of the guys from my stint as a hostess at Coney Island in Sterling Heights. I lasted all of two months, mostly because I hated the entire staff- primarily college dropouts and single moms. There was this one guy in particular, Jesse, who used to be so mean to me. Since my eyebrows were a little dark and had the tendency to form a unibrow, he called me "The Fat Bride of Frankenstein." His minions thought he was hilarious and it caught on. So I quit. I didn't worry too much if he showed up. I was sitting next to a hot guy now. Nothing could phase me.

After he was done playing, we sipped our drinks and began talking. He seemed genuinely interested in me, asking me about my plans for college, my family, my friends, and other normal first date topics.

All the sudden I heard him mutter, "Oh shit."

"What?" I asked, looking around, the dancing flames obstructing most of my vision.

"That's my ex-girlfriend," he said, slinking down in his seat.

I tried not to be conspicuous as I looked around.

"Which one? There are about twenty girls out here."

"The one in the blue striped shirt," he said.

I looked. "Her? She's like twenty three!"

"She's twenty five actually," he said. "We only dated a few weeks."

I wondered how I could hold a candle to a twenty five year old with perfect hair and fake breasts. All I could notice was how hot she was! She was rail thin. Suddenly, I felt very fat in comparison.

"I don't think she sees you," I said reassuringly, knowing she full well saw him and was sending daggers our way.

Sometime around midnight, the party started to wind down. My parents had just gotten up here and wanted us to come back. (Probably to bitch about the mess we made.) Plus, I had to say goodbye to Kim and Tyler.

"Well, I had an awesome time tonight," he said, leaning over towards me.

"Yeah, me too," I said, trying to decide if I should turn towards him or away. Suddenly, he leaned over and kissed me. It was the best kiss ever. I must have stayed out there for fifteen minutes before I told him I had to go. (I didn't want my dad to rethink his decision to send me to the nunnery rather than Southern.)

That night, I couldn't sleep. All I could think about was Cody, in all his awesomeness, and the fact that he wanted me when he could have had any girl. What was he doing with me, a four at best? He was clearly a ten. Or what if I wasn't?

The next few weeks, Cody and I were inseparable. He was sensitive, caring, kind, and always knew what to say. I knew there was a bit of jealousy amongst some of the friends around there as well as with my sister. There always was. But now, for the first time, the tables seemed to have turned.

It wasn't without a few warnings from Ana though.

"Oda, I don't want you to get hurt," she said, looking me dead in the eye as I raked the seaweed off the beach. "Cody is a liar, a cheater, and he will hurt you eventually. I'm not telling you what to do. Just don't get attached."

"Whatever Ana. Are you jealous or something? That you never got with him? Or that Cody and I have something special you'll never have? I like him and he likes me. The end. I'm a big girl, I can handle myself."

With that, I threw the rake on the ground and stormed up the deck to the house, slamming the door before she could come up.

Later that night, before Taline and Zako's combined birthday party, I told Cody what happened.

"Ana's just jealous baby," he said, stroking my hair. "You know you're the only one for me. I want us to work out. I'm going to come see you every weekend until we can be together in a few years." He put his hand under my chin and lifted it up. "Now cheer up and let's go to the twins' party."

That was one good thing about Cody. He got along with everyone. He charmed the ladies and found ways to joke around with the guys. All of Taline and Zako's friends became his friends.

There were about 35 people at Taline and Zako's party on the beach. Most had come over from Michigan and were just staying for one night, but some were going to stay over. I was planning on going back that night since I had to work in the morning.

"You guys, I have to go," I said, as the little hand on the clock passed two. "I'm exhausted. I taught swim lessons this morning, then worked a seven hour shift. It was ninety three degrees, and I am so, so tired! I'll catch you in the morning."

"Bye!"

"See ya later!"

Cody walked me to my car. It was just Tiffany, Taline, Zako, and five friends left there. Tiffany had her own car so she could find her way home.

"Night," I said, kissing him goodbye.

"Night, sweet dreams."

I was about halfway to the bridge when I reached into my purse for a pack of gum and realized I had left my cell phone there.

"Damnit!" I cursed. "Fuck, fuck, fuck!" I slammed my hand on the steering wheel.

I knew I shouldn't be driving without it, so I made a U-turn to go back to get it. I pulled up to the house and all the lights were off, but Taline and Tiffany's cars were still there. I didn't think much of it. We had had two extra rooms and plenty of couches and it wasn't uncommon to fall asleep there. If everyone was sleeping, I'd just creep *in, get the phone, and get out. No problem.*

I went around back, quietly stepping to the side to avoid the creaking steps. I opened the back door, taking care not to let it squeak. I tiptoed over to the couch to look. Wasn't there. Crap. Checked the floor. Not there either. Where could it be?

Oh yeah, I borrowed Cody's charger, so it was at Jean's house. I walked down to his house, quietly letting myself in. I didn't want to wake anyone, so I tried to be quiet. I opened the door and-

What the hell???

Cody and Tiffany were in bed together! And they weren't just cuddling.

"What. The. Fuck. Are you doing?" I screamed.

"Oda, we-"

"You fucking asshole! You're cheating on me with her?" I pointed towards Tiffany, who was scrambling to put on her clothed. "Are you serious? You told me you cared about me, that I was the only one-"

Cody had quickly regained his composure after being barged in on and was trying to find his own pants.

"Look Oda," he said, calmly holding up his hands. "I can't help it. This isn't my fault."

"What? She tied you down and forced you?"

"No, but let's face it, she's hotter than you. I had to upgrade eventually."

And there it was- a slap in the face to the reality I had created in my own mind. No, I wasn't a ten. No, I wasn't witty, charming, fun, or cute. I really was just a big fat, unattractive slob who no one would ever want.

I guess since he had been caught, he figured it was no-holds-barred time. Adding insult to injury, he unleashed the floodgates. "By the way," he continued, "I also slept with Ana. And your sister. Taline. Last Thursday."

My stomach dropped out from under me. There was no way. No way. This couldn't be happening.

"Are you serious? Where's that whore now?" (I meant my sister. Ana I could handle later.)

"I'm right here," she said, coming up behind me with Chad, whom had apparently decided that her seventeenth birthday meant a special treat for him. "Cody, shut up, nothing happened between us. He tried, but nothing happened." She glared at him, clearly displeased she had been woken up to such unpleasantries.

"Shut up Taline. It's better that she knows. You called her porky every day and asked how I was porking the porkster."

I turned toward her and smacked her across the face.

"The only thing that shocks me there is that your simple mind could come up with something that clever!" I screamed as Jean pulled me off of her.

"Whatever," she said, clearly unapologetic, as she returned to Chad's room.

"And you," I turned toward Tiffany. "Get the fuck out of here, you lazy, stupid, worthless cunt. You're nothing more than a sad, portly, pathetic wannabe whore. You can't even do anything for yourself! You just pick up everyone else's scraps. You should do the world a favor and go fucking kill yourself."

After a few more minutes of cursing, screaming, and crying, I grabbed my phone and left. I ran down the small path in the dark, stumbling and tripping. Someone had planted hibiscus plants along the path. The sickenly sweet smell made me want to vomit. The whole ride home, I bawled like I had never before. I cried and cried and cried. I got home and didn't sleep- just cried more. I didn't even go in to work. I went back over to Canada where I cried some more. I knew that everyone had left. I didn't want to go back to my parents, lest they see me like this and ask what happened.

I was sitting alone in the dark crying and wondering how I was going to go to college in less than a week. I was a wreck.

'Why was I even going to college?' I wondered. I was nothing. I wasn't smart, pretty, funny and would never

really amount to anything. Cody had told me all this, sure; but more importantly, my whole life I had been told the same thing.

I was just destined to be alone forever. But maybe that was better than trusting anyone.

A few more hours of crying ensued. I cried so hard that my head throbbed every time I opened my eyes. I felt like the pressure and intensity of a million weights were crushing down on my temples. I could barely open my eyes- the skin around them was so puffy. I cried so hard that I couldn't speak, then I cried so hard that I had no more tears and all I could do was rub at the skin around my eyes which had become worn, rough, red, and patchy- not dissimilar from the way I felt.

My self-wallowing was interrupted by a knock at the door. I had to answer it- whoever it was knew that I was here. Not giving a damn about personal appearance, I opened the door to find Delilah standing there.

"What do you want?" I asked her. "Come to rub more salt in the wound?"

She looked confused. "Uh, no. I came to ask if I could borrow a few chairs. It's my grandma's birthday and we're having a party."

"Fine. Go out back and get them yourself." I started to close the door, but she pushed it open.

"What's the matter?"

"None of your Goddamn business," I said, surprising myself with the boldness with which I spoke to her.

"Really? You look like a disaster."

"Who cares? I'm fucking fat and alone. I'm ugly and my life is pointless. No one's ever going to want me. Not here, not at Southern-"

"Wait, Southern?" she interjected.

"Yeah," I replied.

"That's where I go."

I had forgotten that. "Great, so you can just continue your mockery there. I can't wait. I'll save you some trouble. I'm living in Brigham Hall dorms." I went to close the door again.

"Someone called you fat?"

I nodded.

She shrugged as if someone had just told me that I had spilled my drink on my shirt. To her it seemed like a non-issue.

"Then fuck them and prove them wrong. Turn the tables on them. Go get skinny. Fix your hair- your skin. Success is the best form of revenge."

She turned around. "You can come down to the party if you want to hang out with 82 year old women. If not, see you soon." With that, she was gone.

I went back and lay on the couch until finally, almost 24 hours after the world came crashing down, I went to the bathroom to shower. I looked at myself standing there in the full-length mirror- my hair a disheveled mess, my eyes bloodshot with dark circles underneath them, and my disgusting fat hanging off me in rolls. No wonder no one wanted me. I was almost 19, but I looked 40.

Then it occurred to me. I was only 18. I wasn't yet one of those desperately single 40-year-old fat ladies you see at the grocery store buying Lean Cuisines and cat food. No, I still had a fighting chance, goddamnit.

I stood up, turned on the shower and stepped in letting the water spray on my face. I had a plan. It might take some time, but I could make it. I'd prove to everyone I wasn't a huge pile of fail. By this time next year, I vowed to be hotter. In ten years, I'd be the hottest 28-year old around. If not, I'd simply kill myself. I was going to be beautiful, sexy, and hot. Freshman year, here I come.

I must have been sitting against the wall a long time in contemplation because I didn't even hear the man yelling out to me.

"Irene!"

I turned and looked. There was an old man- well over 90- hobbling down the street towards me. I stood up and rushed to help him, afraid that he might lose his footing on the uneven paths.

He stared at me. "Irene, I haven't seen you all summer," he smiled, tears welling up in his eyes as he took one of my hands in his frail, wrinkled hand. "You came back!"

I guessed he was suffering from Alzheimer's, so I tried to break it to him as gently as possible. "I'm not Irene. That was my great aunt. What's your name, sir?" I asked, slowly and deliberately.

Apparently he didn't understand. "I came back, you know?"

Patiently, I tried to play along. "Where were you?"

He looked shocked, as if he couldn't believe I didn't remember. "Well, over there, fighting the Japs."

Just then a middle age woman came rushing out of the house, clearly embarrassed after hearing the Japs reference.

"Dad!" she gasped, clearly breathing a sigh of relief. "I was so worried."

"I'm talking to Irene," he snapped at her, willing her to go away.

I looked at her and shook my head.

She sighed. "Dad, this isn't Irene. This is..." she looked to me.

"Um, great niece I think," I replied. "Irene was my mom's aunt."

He appeared very confused, but crestfallen at the same time. He mumbled something about knowing that I was Irene and wondering why I didn't want to talk to him.

I felt terrible, so I tried to help out. I whispered to the lady, asking what his name was.

"Frank," she mouthed back.

"Hey Frank, how about I walk with you guys? We can walk home together?" I looked to the lady for approval and she nodded, probably just happy that she had found the old man.

I walked with them to their house and sat inside as he regaled me with stories from yesteryear. Finally, I had to get going. I promised him I'd visit soon, but knew that by tomorrow, he'd forget my visit.

His daughter walked me to the door. "Thank you," she said. "He never forgot Irene. You look just like her with the long black hair." She paused. "Is she...?"

"Yeah, she died a few years ago. They knew each other?" I asked.

"Oh yes, Irene was the love of his life, but see, back then, they couldn't get married. She was five years older than him and Catholic. We're Jewish."

"That's crazy," I replied, trying to wrap my head around something that today wouldn't seem too controversial.

"Well, I've got to get going, but I'll see you around," I said, heading back towards my house. She said goodbye and I got in my car and left.

When I got home, I told Ashley the story as I put the finishing touches on our dinner- chicken marsala- yum!

"And can you believe it? They couldn't be together because of five little years and a religious difference? You're five years older than me."

"It's not so different today," he said, thoughtfully as he cut into his chicken.

"What do you mean? Women marry men who are five years younger all the time. It's not like once you're over 21, it's a big deal anymore."

"No, but if you want to get ahead, you have to date someone who is societally acceptable. Maybe it's not about age or religion anymore, but there's other factors."

"Oh yeah? Why do you want to marry me? Because I'm such an awesome cook?" I joked, noting that a hacksaw would have been more appropriate for cutting the chicken.

"Well obviously not. But I thought you'd make a good wife."

"Wait, what do you mean, *make a good wife*?" I replied, forgoing my rubbery chicken and focusing on the rice.

"You're pretty, intelligent, well-spoken. You seemed to be on track with your timeline..."

"I have a timeline?" I wondered out loud.

He realized he had misspoke and tried to backpedal. "Well, not a timeline, but blueprint-"

I glared at him as he realized he was digging himself into a deeper hole.

"So you thought you could take me and *turn me into a housewife*?" I asked.

"No," he assured me. "Why do you want to marry me? You don't believe in love."

I nodded. This was true. Love is an abstract construct made up by philosophers who attempted to qualify hormonal feelings of attachment and sexual attraction.

"Well, you're smart, successful, and came from an acceptable family. You're good looking and we get along," I stated matter-of-factly.

268

"There you go. But you couldn't marry someone who just worked in fast food because then you'd be mocked by your peers, right?"

I shrugged. He had a point.

"I guess you're right. So my great aunt did the right thing by marrying someone more socially acceptable so that she didn't spend the rest of her life getting mocked by others?" I questioned.

"I wouldn't say mocked, but I'd say judged. Judgment never ends. You know this better than anyone, Liv- you're still living in the same high school world as all those people you despise," he said, getting up and clearing the table.

"You're right, I hate being judged *still*," I replied, starting to rinse off the dishes.

He snorted. "That's not what I meant. You judge people all the time."

I stopped and turned off the water, staring at him. "I do not!"

"Yes you do. Anyone who isn't as good as you- you judge them. Your sister, your classmates, my friends' wives-"

"My sister is a stupid whore who deserves judgment! Do you know what she did to me? She made my life hell growing up!"

"OK, well what about everyone else?"

"They're the *kind* of people who made my life
miserable," I said, finishing up the dishes and wiping
down the counter. "I spent two decades letting them
push me around. It's *my* turn to be on top." I knew that I
had adopted a defensive tone, but I wasn't willing to
back down.

"You just keep telling yourself that," he replied, turning
on the television.

I rolled my eyes and stomped into the bedroom, pulling
up my laptop. I opened up the revision file along with
my file and started typing. I made the first part sound a
little bit nicer and the lead a bit more enticing, then
started in on the second part- my case studies.

Bullying is deeply engrained in American
culture. Despite efforts of psychologists,
experts, and lawmakers try to limit its
scope, it continues years after Columbine
brought it to our national attention.
According to Donegon (2012), "Our society
illustrates the pinnacle of capitalistic
competition. This win-or-die-trying
atmosphere, the competitive college
acceptance process, and much of the
corporate world, contribute to many of the
bullying problems that we battle today. The
issues of bullying and cyber bullying can
only be contained in the short term and not

eliminated completely due to how deep-seeded they have become in our competitive society." This begs the question as to whether or not the focus should be on eliminating the competitive framework that currently exists in schools today, or harnessing that competitive nature so that children can find ways to succeed without doing it at the expense of others.

I was about done when I got a text from Marissa.

Marissa: Wut r u doing?

Jesus, couldn't she fucking spell? I rolled my eyes and replied.

Me: HW. U?

Marissa: Watching TV. U wanna get mani/pedi tomorrow?

Me: I can when I get off work. I'll text u then.

I tossed my phone back on the bed. She's such an idiot. But she's not the kind of girl you can be mean to. She's just so nice, yet stupid at the same time. I sighed. Oh well, I needed a mani/pedi before the wedding on Friday.

I typed a bit more and logged into my writing class. I checked my grade. An F???? I immediately thought there must be some sort of mistake. I clicked on my last assignment and read Dr. Levenstein's comments along with an email he had sent.

From: Dr. Levenstein

Topic: Journalism of Conscience (MPJ-701) grade

While you have committed your ideas to paper, your lack of insight and depth of reflection is inadequate. The undergrad students in my community college class put in more effort than you have on your answers. I want you to take some time, think about these answers, and not just use the text to respond. I want you to include your own personal experiences and feelings. Everything you say is 100% confidential. This class is not just about writing, but about detailing the human experience. I will give you one week to make up your past assignments for full credit. I'd suggest that you start a reflection journal. Nothing formal- just an outlet for your thoughts and feelings.

I rolled my eyes and checked back to see how many assignments I had to make up. Three. *Fuck!* I decided to go ahead and knock one out tonight. I leaned over and broke an Adderall in half, crushed it, took out a business card, made my line, and snorted it. I flopped back down on my bed and began typing.

Selfish Behavior

Today I read the piece titled "Selfish Behavior." The writing about selfish behavior is timely, especially as more and more young people enter the workforce. Many leaders feel that younger people are selfish because they are only thinking of their career interests and financial gain, not necessarily the good of the company as a whole.

Rather than fighting this, leaders should harness this energy in a positive manner. They need to acknowledge that these "selfish" urges exist and find ways to align the goals of the individual with that of an organization. Perhaps leaders could offer incentives, financial or otherwise, for going above and beyond for the organization. They could also make it apparent that there are many opportunities for advancement within the organization. These tactics will not only appeal to the "selfish" desires of many, but also serve to benefit the organization by having more motivated employees.

I admit to being selfish at times. I probably am. I am a huge fan of Ayn Rand who said in Atlas Shrugged that, "I swear

by my life and my love of it that I shall
not live for the sake of another man nor
ask another man to live for mine." I think
this is true in that I should be able to do
what I want, buy what I want, and go
wherever I want so long as I do not harm
others in the process and have obtained the
financial means to do so myself. If it is
my money and I have earned it, I should be
able to spend it how I wish. The same
applies to my job. I have bills to pay and
things I want to buy, so why shouldn't I
want to make as much money as I am capable
of making? Is it selfish to not want to be
stuck in a dead-end job? I don't think so.
However, that being said, I realize that
money is not everything. I understand that
I can't just arbitrarily ask for a raise
whenever I see fit, but if I am expected to
do the same thing, day after day, month
after month, year after year, I can see why
I'd get terribly bored and frustrated. I
have left jobs because I wasn't pleased
with how things were progressing. I am
trying to leave my current job right now,
but it is very hard as there are not a lot
of opportunities and I am moving in a few
months, thus severely limiting my options.

To combat this, I have decided to become a
journalist where there will be no shortage
of challenges for me to tackle. I believe
that my intellect, knowledge, skills, and

training, have prepared me to handle these
challenges and enhance the lives of others.

I get really annoyed when people say I'm
selfish. I work so hard to earn money. What
kills me more is the people who do not work
and expect things to be handed to them. I
have several girlfriends who have blatantly
said, "I can't wait to get married so I
don't have to work anymore." None of my
fiancé's friends' wives work. They see it
as a status symbol to not have to work and
just be able to hang out and do whatever
all day. I couldn't live like that. I'd
feel like I was mooching off of someone
else. Some women, such as these, feel that
they are entitled to someone else's money
because they are attractive, or managed to
get married, or whatever. (I can't get in
their heads.) It's this sense of
entitlement that really makes me mad. I
definitely do not feel entitled to anything
more than I have earned or worked for.

As a journalist, I know that I will have to
work with many of these entitled people-
largely women who feel that work is beneath
them and that they are entitled to
something better due to some birthright or
something. I have a seriously hard time
dealing with people like this, but I am
trying to at least understand their mindset
so that I might someday be a better writer.

I really hope that I can at least learn
something about human nature from them.

In essence, I think "selfish" and
"entitled" are two often confused concepts
that ought to be more thoroughly clarified
before being used arbitrarily.

October 24, 3 a.m.

Dear self, kill Carmine when you see him tomorrow. He called from Diamondz gentleman club ranting and raving about seeing a stripper named Jezebel and swearing that I knew her. He said 12 dudes ran a train on her once. I told him that he must have her confused with one of his pornos and he was projecting some weird fetish on me. Sigh. Now time to go back to sleep (and try to avoid dreaming about Carmine as a male stripper).

October 23, 4 p.m.

I got lucky! Southeastern called me today! I had my second interview. I go in Monday to their Detroit office for my third interview. I can't wait.

Tonight I have my first shift at Diamondz. I'm a little bit nervous. I haven't told anyone I'm working there. I know LaShawndra wouldn't approve and I can only imagine what Troy would say if he found out. My "dancer" name is Jezebel.

However, in other exciting news, I had a date with Ethan, who I met on Tinder. I'm trying to decide what I think of him. He has a girlfriend (technically), but says they're about to break up. I feel kind of bad, but men want what they want, right?

We met up at this restaurant in Dearborn (kinda far away). He seemed a little shorter than online. We exchanged greetings and had a nice dinner. He has two little boys and is separated from his wife.

"So do you live in Dearborn?" I asked.

His eyes darted around nervously as he took a sip of his drink. "Uh, no."

I was confused. "So where do you live?"

"Up north," he replied vaguely. Seeing the skepticism on my face, he continued. "My ex wife and I are in a custody battle and I just don't want to have to risk running into any of her friends or co-workers."

I understood. We started making small talk. "Do you have any tattoos?" I asked.

"Yeah, I got a back piece," he said, showing me a cell phone pic of the intertwined pieces making up a larger masterpiece on his back. "You?"

"Seven," I replied.

"Wow," he said. "Which one was your first?"

"The hibiscus on my back."

"How long ago?"

"A lifetime."

I had just turned eighteen when I met Cody. He was beautiful in a way that men can indeed be beautiful. The first time he smiled at me, I melted.

"Where's Oda?" he asked, coming around the side of the house.

I put down my US Weekly *and adjusted my tankini. "I don't know. She might have gone back into the city to work."*

"That's cool. What are you doing?"

Electronic Journal of Tiffany Harris

File Name: MPJ-701_Reflection Journal

I looked around. Wasn't it apparent? I clearly wasn't experimenting with nuclear fusion.

"Wanna go for a boat ride?"

"You have a boat?" I asked, incuriously,

"It's my parents, but they let me bring it over here from Lake St. Clair."

"Sure," I said, shyly. Oda was right. He looked just like Kevin Bacon circa 1987. I got up and followed him down the stairs.

Suddenly he stopped and turned towards me. I expected him to say something cruel, like, 'Are you kidding? You'd sink the boat!'

Instead he paused and looked at me, thoughtfully, with his hand on his chin.

"You know what?" he scratched his chin. "That suit is pretty, but you need to accessorize."

I looked down at the dowdy green suit. A tankini is just a fat girl's way of covering up without going full on granny suit. This one was dark green with light green trim. Only the finest of the Old Navy collection for this gal!

"Here," he said, leaning down, and picking a hibiscus. "A sweet flower for a sweet girl."

Hesitantly, I let him place it behind my ear as he tucked away the flyaway strands.

We walked to the dock, got on the boat, and once we were outside of the No Wake zone, took off.

"Where do you want to go?" he asked.

I didn't care. I remembered the sun shining against the pristine blue sky. I remember the emerald hue the water took on, as smooth as glass the further we got from shore.

On the coldest, darkest, gray Michigan days, when things seem at their worst, I think back to that day and my troubles seem a little less substantial.

"Pelee?" he asked. "I know a spot. If we're feeling really crazy, we can even go to Putin Bay."

I nodded. We headed out to the middle of the lake where the water changed from a cerulean shade of blue to a deeper almost turquoise. We arrived at Pelee and dropped an anchor on the far side of one of the beaches. Since it was a weekday, not many people were on the island and we had the whole beach to ourselves. There was an old fort there that looked like a medieval castle. Cody grabbed two beers and we hopped out into waist-deep water and made our way to the shore.

We must have sat on the shore and talked about everything and anything for an hour. I had my legs stretched out in front of me and was propped up on my back elbows when all of the sudden Cody's hand landed

281

on my knee. I paused what I was saying, but only temporarily as I figured I should just let it happen. If he wanted me, that was his thing. Him and Oda weren't married, right?

I don't remember what I was even saying. By this point, it didn't matter as his hand found its way up my leg and he started pulling my swimsuit aside.

"Let's go back to the boat," he said, looking around. "More privacy."

I nodded and followed him back. On the boat, he wasted no time taking off my shirt and pressing his mouth to my breast.

I gasped. "What about Oda?" I asked.

"Forget her. She's going away in a few weeks. She's going to find some new guy at university. You're not going far. Plus, I think you're prettier than she is and have a way better body She's too tall."

This was true. Over the summer, I had lost weight while Oda seemed to have gained. I couldn't argue his logic.

I didn't want to tell him it was my first time, but I think he could tell. It was amazing and magical. I remember lying on the floor of the boat afterwards, the smell of hibiscus still lingering from the flower in my hair. For the first time in my life, I felt loved. Like someone could actually care about me. He was the first person to ever tell me that I was beautiful. I felt like I had just entered a dream world, a place in which a man as hot as Cody actually loved me. I was beside myself. I turned over, lightly stroking his chest.

"What are you thinking about?" I asked.

He sat up. "Well, I'm thinking that we should probably get heading back."

OK, not exactly the answer I had hoped for, but whatever. We drove back pretty much in silence and docked in front of Oda's house. Luckily she wasn't there, but her sister was.

As we walked up the stairs, I heard that Taline was playing music. More specifically, she was playing Usher's song, Confessions, where he cheats on his girlfriend and gets another girl pregnant. Ouch. I couldn't help feeling a little guilty. I had just lost my virginity to my best friend's boyfriend. I was the "other woman" in this case.

"Where did you go?" she yelled at us, hands on her hips as she held my US Weekly magazine.

"We went on the boat," Cody said, unapologetically.

If Taline knew something was up, she didn't let on. She wasn't the brightest bulb in the lamp. Plus, based on the stack of magazines, she appeared to be more engrossed with Angelina and Brad's impending affair than any affairs of her own world.

"But you said you were gonna take me!" she whined.

"Fine, let's go," he said, rolling his eyes at me, as if to say, 'Look what I have to deal with now.'

She set down her drink and they went off. I took her chair and picked up one of the magazines. So Brad Pitt, sexiest man in the world, was going to leave Jennifer Aniston for Angelina Jolie? Well, what was the big deal? I mean, if Angelina was hotter, it's Jennifer's fault, not Angelina's, right? The heart wants what the heart wants. I began flipping through the pages. It all made sense. If a man fell in love with someone else, he should be able to have her then, right? Of course, right.

"Ten years ago," I answered, thinking that it seemed like a lifetime since that summer afternoon. "It was a thing with a guy, you know? Embarrassing."

"Naw," he replied. "Tattoos reflect your experiences, ya know? You had a meaningful occurrence and you memorialized it in ink."

I laughed. I had never thought of it that way. "So what do you do again?"

"Baggage handler at the airport. Exciting stuff," he replied.

"Oh wow! I'm trying to become a flight attendant!"

"Ha, well maybe you'll actually talk to me. The flight attendants are too busy trying to hook up with pilots and first class passengers that they barely acknowledge my existence," he scoffed.

I assured him that I would definitely still talk to him, but what he said got me a little bit excited. I was completely on board with any opportunity to find true love on a plane. It would be like a Lifetime movie of the week. I'd meet my soul mate on a flight to Denver or something.

We finished dinner and he paid the bill. I promised to call him this weekend and we parted ways. Now I'm just praying that I get the job and everything works out. Unconsciously, I reached back and touched my hibiscus tattoo. Almost a decade since I had been searching for love. It was time to find it.

October 24, 11:30 p.m.

So I am officially nervous. I didn't realize who all was going to be at this wedding. I texted Carmine this afternoon to make sure that he was alive. He replied that he was indeed alive, but his car was still at Diamondz. I asked if he needed a ride. He promised to take me out for happy hour appetizers. Sold.

I picked him up at his house and he looked worse for the wear, laying on the couch next to an empty bag of Doritos and bottle of mustard.

"I don't even want to know," I said, brushing crumbs off of the couch cushion and gingerly sitting down next to him.

"But I have an awesome voicemail from you telling me something about a stripper and a train of guys."

"It was some chick we went to high school with! I don't remember!"

He sat up and immediately groaned from the sudden movement.

"What is her real name?"

"I don't know. I'd have to check the yearbook."

"Oh my God, *please* tell me that you have your yearbook and homecoming crown prominently displayed in your room along with your framed football photos."

"What? No way. I live with four guys." He paused and grinned.

"But that shit's at my mom's house! Sandy built a shrine to me in my old bedroom. High five!" he held up his hand.

I burst into laughter and high-fived him.

"I like to think that when I bring girls over that they're turned on by my memorabilia. When I bang chicks in my childhood room, I want them to shout out my football number."

"You are retarded!" I laughed, as we headed out to the car and began to drive. "Where is Diamondz even at?"

"Turn left up here," he instructed.

I did as he said. Trust me, there is no sadder sight than seeing a strip club in the light of day. His black SUV sat alone under the marquee sign that now just proclaimed "GIRLS! G RLS! IR S"

I dropped him off and followed him to Fishbones, a popular restaurant in St. Clair Shores, where we were by far the earliest patrons.

We sat in the back corner with our beers and began to catch up. I wanted to hear all about his cool firefighting stories but I figured I should hear his backstory first at least.

"So after you graduated? You went to school at Southern?" he asked, grimacing as he looked at his beer.

I nodded. "And you went to...Iowa?"

He nodded proudly. That's where my family's from originally. My grandpa was a donor, so I got to go cheap.

"That sounds cool. I've never been to Iowa."

"It was fun. My frat used to-"

I cut him off. "You were in a fraternity?" I feigned mock surprise.

"Well color me shocked! I figured you more for the Renaissance reenactment club."

"Oh what, you weren't in a sorority?"

"I was, but-"

"But what?" he countered playfully. "You were too cool for fraternity guys?"

"I will have you know that I also played field hockey *and* I wrote for the newspaper. My article on marijuana legalization was very popular."

"What sorority were you?"

A sorority or a fraternity pretty much dictates your place in the social structure of college life. At a smaller school, unless you're an athlete, you pretty much have to enter into the Greek system. At our school, rush was held the first week of classes. This was so the older girls met the younger girls without any preconceived notions (allegedly). All of us freshmen girls knew which sororities and fraternities were better than others. There were eight sororities. The best was Omega Mu, the next best was Delta Mu, and the third best was Rho Lambda. Only 70% of girls who went through rush even got a bid. Of those who did get a bid from a lesser house, many rejected it in hopes of trying the following year.

I had already been to the freshmen athlete orientation. There were so many hot boys. So, so, many hot boys. I was still reeling from the Cody incident, so I calmly told myself to wait until I was skinny to make a move. In the meantime, I'd lay the groundwork.

I was walking out with two of the other girls on the field hockey team when I heard a voice behind me.

"Daaaaayyyyummm girl.....I didn't know yo' fine ass was gracing my school with yo' sexy presence."

We turned and spun to see what jackass possibly said such things out loud. At an institute of higher learning no less.

"Jeremy!" I shouted, running over and giving him a hug. "My mom gave me your email, but I didn't want to seem like a creeper by hitting you up."

"Nah girl," he said, rubbing his hands on his chest. "Creep away all you want. And bring your friends." He winked at the other two girls. I slapped him.

"Hey guys, this is Jeremy Montoya. Our parents are friends. He's been hitting on me since he realized that he stopped liking men."

The other two girls giggled, taken aback by an attractive senior paying them attention.

"What sport do you play?" Aubrey asked.

"Baseball," he said. "Speaking of," he looked at me. "We're having a party tonight. You all should come."

We giggled. Aubrey spoke up. "Of course we'll be there. After rush. *"*

We parted ways and I went home to get ready for the night. The first night was casual- shorts and t-shirts. The second night was sundress attire and the third night was formal- party dress.

We got to spend ten minutes at each of the houses. At the Delta Mu house, I ran into Delilah. She seemed to pretend not to know me that well. I was kind of upset. It was clear that she was paying more attention to the more attractive girls. At the fifth-ranked houses and below, I got a bit more attention, but it felt like a horrible consolation prize.

That night, we went to the party at the baseball house. There were so many boys. I felt like a kid in a candy store, but reminded myself that I wasn't going to pursue a boyfriend until I had lost at least 40 pounds.

Jeremy and I sat out on the porch, drinking our jungle juice.

"Hold up, you got an eyelash. Let me get it." He leaned in, plucked it off with the tip of his finger and held it up to me.

"Blow on it and make a wish."

I did.

"Yes, you can have sex with me tonight."

I burst into laughter. "I'm not like that!"

"I didn't say you were." He paused.

"But you could be."

I knew he was joking, so I laughed it off. "No sex or boyfriends until I've lost 40 pounds."

"You don't need to lose weight, but if you want to, that's your thing."

291

Electronic Journal of Oda Mizra

File Name: MPJ-701_Reflection Journal

I looked down, tears welling up in my eyes. "I'm not going to get into a good sorority," I mumbled, my voice shaking.

"Why not?" he asked. "You're every bit as pretty as girls in any of those houses."

I shrugged. "I'm just not. The ugly ones get in because they're legacies. My mom wasn't in a sorority. The unsightly ones that do get in have that leverage."

"Get leverage of your own," he said, putting a dip in his mouth and spitting it back into the cup. "Hell, Jen Shake got caught cheating on a geology exam last year." He spit onto the ground again. "How the fuck do you get caught cheating in a class about rocks?" he mused. "Minnie VanSloten had an abortion."

I shook my head. "That's all hearsay. I don't know any of these people..." my voice trailed off as I looked off to the side. Suddenly, a realization hit me and I snapped back up, turning towards him, grabbing his arm.

"I've got it!" I shouted, standing up, spilling red sticky liquid all over us both.

"What?" he asked.

"I can't tell you, but I think I know how to get into the number two sorority." With that, I got up and took off running to find my friends and head home. The next day would be a new day.

*The next night I walked into the Delta Mu house in a
bright yellow Old Navy sundress with my head held high. I
could tell that they were grouping us by those they were
definitely interested in, those they were maybe interested
in, and those who didn't stand a snowflake's chance in
hell. I was solidly placed between the latter two groups.*

*Ignoring the girl who was politely talking to me, I made
my way over to Delilah and stood next to the pretty girl
whom she was speaking with. Delilah clearly looked
confused, as I had committed some horrible social faux
paux. She wrapped it up with the girl and turned to me.*

*"Oh, I just wanted to come say hi," I said, smiling as nicely
as could be.*

*"You know, I saw your parents before I left. Or, I guess I
should say your mom and your...step-dad? Now, I didn't
know that. You guys have the same last name...wow, it's
really cool that this sorority is so accepting of all kinds of
families..."*

*She yanked me aside into the corner. "How did you find
out about that?" she hissed, looking around like the NSA
had tapped the sorority house for the latest intel on fall
fashions.*

I smiled and calmly replied, "You know...around."

*She looked around. "You haven't told anyone else, have
you?"*

"Of course not!" I said. "I mean, it seems like your sorority sisters really respect you. You are the president, after all."

I paused.

"This seems like a great sorority. So far, it's my favorite. Your mom was a legacy....but wouldn't a legacy be considered invalid if the birth was illegitimate? I don't know all the rules....maybe I could ask someone." I said, looking around.

She glanced around. "Shut up about the rules. You know that legacies are guaranteed spots," she whispered through gritted teeth. "Wasn't your grandma a Delta Mu?"

"Oh my gosh! Yes she was," I said, understanding what she was getting at. (My grandma never even went to college.) "Didn't I mention that on my form? Silly me, I was just thinking of my mom."

She smiled a pained smile and returned with me to the group. The difference was- I was now on the opposite end of the room knowing that I'd be invited back for many nights to come.

"Wait, you *blackmailed* someone to get into a sorority?" Carmine laughed, choking on his beer.

I shrugged. "Blackmail is such a harsh word. I dazzled them with conversation."

He leaned back. "Holy shit, Oda- I mean Olivia, you are something else." He shook his head, smiling. "So is that when you changed your name?"

I nodded. "I wanted to shed some old skin I guess." I took a drink and quickly changed subjects. "So tell me about this wedding. What should I wear?"

"Uh, it's an evening wedding, so...a dress?"

I smiled. "You know how I know you're not gay? That was a straight man's response, through and through."

"I don't know. Do you want me to ask the other girls who are going what they are wearing? I can ask Ali, Kirsten, Kim-"

I cut him off. "Wait, Ali's going to be there?"

"Yeah, she married Wes Martin. Kirsten married Reagan, and Julie used to be married to Paul."

My heart started racing. Was I really going to *voluntarily* subject myself to the humiliation and torment of these girls? I didn't have a choice now.

We finished up and parted ways. I spent the rest of my night going through my closet looking for the perfect dress. I finally settled on a dark green one-shouldered Bebe number. I laid out my shoes and accessories. I am so nervous. I'm going back into the lion's den.

October 26, 3 a.m.

Wow, just wow. I can't even believe that tonight....was just tonight. I suppose that I should type quietly. Sanjay, Carmine, Marissa, Tony, and two other girls who were in my siblings' grade are all passed out in the living room. I don't know if I ever want to take off this dress. I'm lying here stretched out on the bed, feeling like Cinderella (you know, sans the whole fairy godmother thing).

I was so nervous that when Carmine picked me up, I was pacing. At his suggestion, I downed two shots of Bacardi (and did a line of Adderal) before heading out the door. I felt a bit more at ease as we drove downtown, looking for the church.

"I should know where this is," I said, rapidly, the combination of stimulants and alcohol not doing anything to calm my nerves. "My parents got married here." I consulted my phone again. There were so many one-way streets.

"Are you Catholic too?" he asked.

"Yeah, sure, I guess, I mean, I don't know...I don't know if I buy into the whole thing...like no room for questioning. Is that bad? Am I going to hell?" I giggled.

He started singing, "*Girl, you and I will die unbelievers, bound to the tracks of the train*...Quick! What song?"

"Um, um....I closed my eyes. "Vampire Weekend! *Unbelievers!*"

"Relax," he said, navigating through a narrow alley and pulling into a parking lot that charged $20. "Weddings never start on time. Besides, we have fifteen minutes."

I got out of the car and wrapped my coat around me tighter. I had chosen my long black pea coat because it was the warmest thing I had. I had accessorized it with a camel scarf and a black hat (seriously, it was below freezing).

We quietly slipped in the back of the church five minutes before the ceremony was supposed to start. They say it's impossible to walk in St. Mary's and not look up. The ornate ceilings and wall art rival mimic the Italian renaissance churches. When I was younger, I used to look up and daydream whenever church got boring (90% of the time).

We were seated next to Sanjay and Marissa. I removed my coat, scarf, hat, and gloves, subconsciously checking my hair in my compact.

"How long is this gonna be?" whispered Marissa.

I looked at the program. "It's a full wedding mass, so I dunno...an hour and change?" I guessed.

Marissa made a face.

"Jesus saw that," I whispered.

The wedding began and as per usual in church, my eyes started wandering. I tried to look around the room to see if I recognized anyone, but I mostly saw older and middle age people. I fiddled with my nails. I looked up at the ceiling and tried to guess how long it took to paint it. I wondered how many people it took. What kind of paint did they use?

(I am a horrible Catholic.)

Finally, it was time for the "peace be with you" part. I leaned into Marissa and Sanjay. "Just shake hands or do an awkward ass-out hug," I instructed them.

Next, it was time for communion. Carmine and I scooted closer to the edge, leaving Marissa and Sanjay seated.

"Heathens," I whispered. "Stay here and be judged by *that* guy," I whispered, pointing to a very judge-y looking Jesus.

"Do you have to go up there?" she asked.

"Yeah, because I'm saved in Jesus's warm, loving embrace while you are all cast out into the sixth circle of hell."

"Ha. But you have to walk by all those people you're scared to see," she whispered as we all stood up and they backed out to let people by.

"Nah," I whispered back. "They won't recognize me. I'm just Carmine's last minute date- some random. We probably met on Tinder." I stepped in front of him as I followed the people filing out from the row in front of me.

I felt him lean in. "Actually," he whispered. "I told them you were coming so they could put your name on the place card." He paused. "Uh, everyone knows you're you."

I spun around and gave him a dirty look, but there was no way I could turn back. (I swear the priest was eyeballing me, knowing that I was thinking unholy thoughts.)

I kept my eyes forward and my hands clasped in front of me. As I walked, I tried not to look from side to side. I heard the whispers and felt the daggers of a thousand glares in my back. I turned briefly to see where they were coming from. It was a group of the middle age women.

Wait- holy hell! Was that Ali? Oh my God! And Kirsten? What. The. Fuck. It looked like a failed Jenny Craig support group. I half-ass tried to suppress a smile as I bit my lip, lifted my chin, and walked with a bit more confidence. I was so scared of laughing so hard and spitting up the communal wine, that I barely let it touch my lips.

On the way back to our seats, I smiled and cast a sideways glance directly at them. They tried to look away, but knew they were busted. I couldn't believe it.

When the ceremony ended, we went outside for a break before blowing our bubbles. (I guess throwing rice isn't environmentally friendly- damn you, Al Gore.)

"There is no way that was Ali," I commented, absentmindedly playing with my bubbles and shivering in the cold.

"Yep," Carmine replied. "She's right over there. Why don't you go say hi?"

I rolled my eyes.

"I will," Marissa piped up, rubbing her hands together and blowing into them. "I should say that *I'm* Olivia."

"You would," I muttered.

"I bet you would," Sanjay interjected. "You're the wild card."

"Does that mean I'm the brains?" I asked.

Both guys broke out into laughter and started high-fiving us. "You like *It's Always Sunny*?" Carmine asked, to which I nodded in the affirmative. "No way! You're like the coolest girl *ever*!"

I laughed and replied, "So who is the muscle then?"

We were discussing our favorite quotes when the bride and groom finally emerged. After we blew our bubbles and they took pictures, we headed out to the wedding reception at a place out in Warren.

We pulled up and the valet took our keys.

"Last name?" he asked in a bored tone of voice.

"Vincent," Carmine replied.

The valet stopped writing and looked up at him. "Oh yeah, I should have known you'd be here. Birds of a feather..." he began, mumbling something inaudible under his breath.

"Do I know you?" Carmine asked.

"I guess not, must have thought you were someone else," the guy said, handing Carmine a ticket, and getting in the car, adjusting the seat to accommodate his bulky frame. He drove off and we looked at each other, shrugged, and walked in.

We got in and started cocktail hour. I was incredibly nervous and downed my first class of cheap wine in under a minute. Carmine laughed and motioned for the waiter to bring me another one.

Marissa, Tony, and Sanjay had joined us and I was almost through my third glass when the three women who had been identified as Ali, Kirsten, and Julie walked up to us.

"Hi Carmine," Ali said loudly pointedly, giving him a hug, shooting a sideways glance in my direction.

I rolled my eyes as the others followed suit, fawning all over the guys like nothing had changed.

"Hey guys, you remember Olivia?" he asked.

I smiled. "Hi, good to see you again. Hey Ali...how's that leg doing?"

I couldn't resist. They glared.

"Sanjay, why aren't you guys sitting with us?"

"I didn't make the seating charts," he replied, ordering another round of drinks.

"But we *always* sit together," whined Ali. "Just like at prom."

I couldn't take anymore. I half-laughed, half-coughed, half-snorted wine out my nose.

They looked at me.

"I'm sorry," I said, my confidence emboldened by my liquid courage. "But did you reference *prom*? Because I could have sworn you did..."

Apparently realizing the ridiculousness of her statement, she recanted.

"I mean, we just should catch up. It's been so long. What are you *up to*? Save any lives recently?" she whined, clearly not directing the question at me.

Carmine began telling a story that I had already heard several times. As they talked, I couldn't help but gawk at how much they had changed- all for the worse. They had put on an average of 40 pounds each and Kirsten's once-beautiful mane of hair had been transformed into some sort of dirty blonde mom haircut.

I smiled and nodded as they chatted, trying my best to be nice. They hadn't said anything to me, so I figured it was best to let sleeping dogs lie. I mean, maybe they had matured. I was willing to put the past behind me.

The DJ came on and announced that it was time to take our seats. We did so and soon after, began to eat.

"So do you like to bike ride?" Carmine asked.

"Ha, a little, but I'm not very fast," I replied.

"We should go up to Mackinac Island. They've got great biking in the fall. I want to get a group together."

"That would be fun. Do you like to bike?"

"I did RAGBRAI with my brother," he responded. Just then, he reached in his pocket. "Damn it! Speaking of, I was supposed to call him and remind him to pick up something in the morning."

"So why can't you call him or text him?" I asked.

"Battery is dead," he replied, looking forlornly at his cell phone. "I have to take it out to the car to charge it."

"Do you know his number?" I asked.

"No, crap. I haven't memorized anyone's number since like 2001." He looked around. "Julie probably has it though. Her and Andrew are friends."

He turned around to Julie, who was also suffering the same fate as sitting at a different table than Ali and Kirsten.

She handed him her phone and he texted his brother. He turned back to hand her phone back to her, but she had gotten up to use the restroom.

"So what is that bike thing?"

"It's the RAGBRAI- or Regents Annual Great Bike Across Iowa. My whole extended family rode across the entire state."

"Wow! That must have been fun."

"Yeah, there's pictures on my Facebook." He used Julie's phone to look up his own profile and showed me the pictures. "Go ahead, take a look," he said. "I'm going to get another drink. You want anything?"

I nodded and began skimming the pictures.

Just then a text popped up.

Kirsten: I cant believe he brought that whore- he can't just bring some random girl to OUR friends wedding.

My jaw dropped, but I clicked back on the pictures. Maybe they weren't talking about me. There were lots of females here. I kept scrolling.

Ali: Could that dress be any tighter? Hello???? Boob job? Nose job much? Cheek implants?

Kirsten: How much liposuction did it take to get rid of that jelly belly???

OK, maybe they *were* talking about me. I put the phone face down and turned to get up, tears stinging my eyes.

"Where are you going?" Carmine asked as he returned with the drinks.

"I'm going outside to smoke. Let me have your phone I'll take it out to charge it."

He must have sensed that something was amiss
(probably because I had never smoked in my life), but
he handed me the phone and I walked out to the valet.

"Can I get the keys for Vincent please? I just need to
charge a phone."

"Yeah, sure, you want me to bring it around?"

"No. You just park them right there, right?" I asked,
indicating a lot about 100 feet from me.

"Uh, yeah."

I smiled. "I couldn't justify wasting the gas."

I went out to the car, got in the driver's seat and turned
on the car. I didn't know if it needed to be on to charge,
but it was cold and I didn't feel like going back inside
just yet.

Just then I heard a rap on the passenger's side.

"Jesus!" I shouted, my heart pounding. Luckily it was
only Carmine.

"What are you doing out here?"

"Charging your phone," I said, opening the door for him
and scooting over. "And trying not to get raped in a dark
parking lot. You're lucky I'm not carrying. I have a .9 at
home."

"You have a .9? Damn girl," he said, turning up the heat.

"It's my husband's but I know how to use it."

"Look, I saw what was on that phone. I'm sorry."

I shrugged. "Not your fault. Sorry you brought 'the slut.' The fat slut, I guess."

"Awww, come on. Cheer up. You're not fat at all. Plus," he reached into his coat and produced two bottles of beer, "We can have our own party out here."

"I hope it's light beer," I smiled.

"Cheers," he said, clinking bottles.

"So I have a question," he asked. "Don't get offended or anything, but how *did* you lose all that weight?"

After I had gotten in the sorority, things started to go very well for me.. I realized that once I had an in with Jeremy, the boys on the baseball team, basketball team, football team, and pretty much every other team seemed to accept me, as Jeremy's approval was like gospel to them.

That's the thing with cliques. You just have to get in right with one key person and you're golden. Never go for the top dog- always his right hand man. Carmine had been Paul's right hand man his whole life. Some things never change. So long as I had Carmine in my corner, I knew that I was golden.

We were at a sorority meeting one night when Delilah started passing out our t-shirts that we had ordered for winter Greek Fun week. She tossed me mine. It was a large.

"I didn't order a large," I said. "I think I asked for a medium."

"You're a large. Trust me," she said, continuing on.

We all put them on for our group pictures and admittedly, the large was a bit snug on me. On the way home, I got a text from Jeremy asking me to come over and help him with his paper. It was snowing really hard already by the time I got to his house. I parked and trudged through a snow bank and rapped on his front door.

Joey, his hot roommate answered.

"Jeremy! Your friend is here."

"Who?" I heard Jeremy call from the back.

"I don't know," he shouted back. "The tall pudgy Middle Eastern-looking one."

"Let her in jackass!" he yelled, emerging from the bedroom where he was apparently blasting R&B music.

I looked down so that Joey wouldn't see me cry and I walked back to Jeremy's room.

"What's wrong?"

I sat on the corner of his bed and cried. "I'm fat!" I wailed.

"No you're not."

"Yes I am! Did you just hear what Joey said?"

"Joey's an asshole-"

*"No he's not! He's right! I'm fat!" I took off my coat and
threw it on the bed. "I'm a large! Look at this t-shirt," I
said, yanking the tag around to show him.*

*"Why don't you take off your shirt and show me?" he
smirked.*

I half-smiled and playfully slapped him. "It's not funny!"

*"Come on, you're not fat. Now look, I had this whole
romantic night planned out. I have fine wine coolers,
good music, and I even made the bed."*

*I looked skeptical. "This is good music?" I pondered as
Usher sang in the background.*

*"Even before,
All the fame and people screaming my name,
I was there, and you were my baby...
Started when we were younger, you were mine..." he sang
(poorly).*

I giggled.

"It's ambiance," he said.

"You're so romantic. I think I love you," I playfully retorted.

"There's no such thing as love, Olivia. You'll realize that someday. It's just a feeling of sexual attraction to someone that eventually fades. Everything ends. Everyone's gonna screw you over sooner or later. It's just a matter of when."

"You don't think anyone can ever really love someone unconditionally?" I asked.

"You don't get something for nothing. All love comes with conditions- with ulterior motives. Remember that you're the only one looking out for you."

I rolled my eyes. "You're so jaded. I'm going to prove you wring someday. Now let me see your paper."

I went through and made some basic edits as I bitched out loud about how I hated being fat.

"So you really want to cut weight?" he asked.

I turned and looked at him, shutting the laptop. "Have you not been listening to me for the last hour?"

"Look, I have some stuff. But you can't tell anybody where you got it from."

I perked up. "I won't! Please! Just give it to me whatever it is!"

He reached in his desk drawer and pulled out a bottle written in Chinese.

"It's ephedra. Pure."

"Isn't this illegal?"

"That's why you can't tell anyone where you got it."

I nodded. "I won't."

"Be careful with it," he said. "It's strong."

I thanked him, hugged him, and ran out the door to my car. The next morning, I woke up and took just one pill. Halfway through my eight o'clock class, my heart was racing faster than Seabiscuit. I could feel my armpits dampening up with sweat. I felt jittery and kept nervously looking towards the door. I needed to get to the gym ASAP.

"-is it, Olivia?"

I snapped my head back to the front of the room. My professor (and the rest of my class) was staring at me.

"Um, it's....I'm..." I fumbled for the page in my book before piping up.

*"The magic bullet theory states that there is no magic
way to interact with consumers."*

*However, my speech was so rapid, it sounded more like,
"Themagicbullettheorystatesthatthereisnomagicwaytoint
eractwithconsumers."*

The class broke into laughter.

*"Someone stopped at Starbucks on the way in I see," Dr.
Tyndall said with a smile.*

*I smiled back. Of course that was the logical explanation.
I was a straight-A student, not some illicit drug user. No
one would ever suspect me of taking more than Aspirin. I
was good. I just needed to be a little less paranoid.*

*As soon as class was over, I bolted out the door and ran to
the gym. I didn't even bother to stretch out before
jumping on the treadmill. I kicked it up to 8 mph, faster
than I had ever run before. I felt like I could run forever.
After an hour, the machine automatically went into cool
down mode.*

*I started hitting buttons. "Stop it," I muttered to no one in
particular. "I want to keep going."*

"Your time is up. You get an hour max."

*I looked up to see some girl in rival sorority letters, arms
crossed, staring at me, impatiently tapping her foot. All of
the other treadmills were taken.*

"All yours," I said, hopping off and walking away.

"Aren't you even going to wipe it down?"

"Nah, I don't have any diseases," I retorted. "You might wanna get checked though."

(Where did that come from? These pills were not only making me jittery, they were kind of making me pissy.)

In the full-length mirror, I saw her jaw drop and saw her mouth 'Bitch.'

With my back turned to her, I flipped her off before going over to the only available cardio machine- the elliptical. Then, when my time was up, I went to the bike. After that, I hit the weights. Before I knew it, it was almost one. I could have kept going but I had a class at two. I showered, went to class, then came back and went for another round. When I felt my energy waning, I took another pill and perked right back up. At six, I finally called it quits after exercising for a grand total of seven hours.

"Holy shit, you worked out for *seven* hours?" Carmine asked.

"My record for one day was nine."

"So how much weight did you lose?"

"By the time I went home for that summer, I had lost like 20 pounds," I said, sipping my beer.

"My brother thinks he remembers seeing you that summer. You looked good, he said."

I shrugged. "It was better, coming home I mean. I worked at a fitness center and for the first time, guys actually looked at me. Like *really* looked at me."

"Well there you go! Good for you! I mean, it's not good that you took ephedra, but you know what I mean."

I looked at my empty beer bottle. "Yeah, it's whatever," I said. "No regrets."

"So how did you lose the rest?"

"My beer's empty," I responded, dodging, the question. "Time to go back inside."

We went back inside, handing the keys to the valet who shot Carmine a dirty look.

"Where have you been?" asked Marissa.

"Giving Carmine a hand job in the parking lot," I replied with a straight face as I grabbed her drink and downed it.

"We can go if you want," Carmine suggested, clearly alarmed as I grabbed Sanjay's and did the same.

"No," I said, flipping my hair as the cheap alcohol coursed through my veins and emboldened me. "Let's go say hi. I'll play nice, I promise."

"Jesus," he muttered. "Do you think-"

"I think we should say hi," piped up Sanjay, smiling and taking his phone out of his pocket. "Just let me get prepared in case we have to send this into Tosh for web redemption."

I rolled my eyes.

Luckily they were standing around Paul, so we had a means by which to segue into the conversation.

"Hey girls, you all remember Olivia?" Carmine said.

"Yah," snapped Kirsten, folding her arms in front of her chest, revealing *very* chipped nails.

"How are *you* all?" I asked, smiling, trying not to grit my teeth, hoping that my hair hadn't caught any static electricity from my coat.

"Fine."

Paul looked at her quizzically, clearly unaware of the girl drama that was unfolding in front of him. As he did so, I couldn't help but notice the middle age paunch that was already developing around his mid-section.

She sighed and continued. "What are you up to these days?" she asked reluctantly.

"I'm a reporter and copy editor for the Detroit Recorder and I'm working on my Masters in Journalism. I'm engaged to a pilot. What about you?

"I'm a consultant for Thirty-one."

"Thirty-one what? Thirty-one companies?" I raised my eyebrow, feigning interest.

"It's a home-based business that sells embroidered goods and-"

"Oh like those lunch sacks with your initials on them?" I asked, barely unable to contain my laughter.

"Yes, and-"

"Got it, you sell lunch sacks with peoples' names on them. What about you?" I turned to Ali.

"I have my own business."

"Really? What do *you* do?"

"It's Scentsy-"

"The candles! Oh, those smell great. I have one in my bathroom. So you sell candles. That's nice," I replied in the most patronizing tone that I could conjure up.

"What do you do, Julie?" I continued, sipping on my wine and feigning mock interest. (I really hope Sanjay caught this all on video.)

"I work in the health industry."

"Nurse?"

"No, health and fitness."

"Personal trainer?" I asked, attempting to choke back laughter.

Ali, clearly pissed off that I had just mocked her and Kirsten, wasn't about to let Julie off that easily. "She sells weight loss shakes."

I couldn't take it. I burst into laughter.

"Are you *serious*? Isn't that kind of like a Mormon selling beer?" I paused, letting her absorb it as I drained the contents of my glass.

"Speaking of, I need another drink. Nice catching up. Glad to see you all have *such* fascinating careers."

I walked away before they could add anything else, or ask me for more detail about my job. I wasn't about to tell them that I spend most of my day editing for the proper use of the Oxford comma. Let them think that I spent my time doing undercover investigative work into Hoffa's disappearance. They sold fucking candles. I still win.

By midnight, the party had would down and we went out to get the car. Carmine had gone to use the bathroom and Marissa and Sanjay were outside smoking.

"Vincent," I said to the valet, barely able to stand, my feet painfully squeezed into my too-small heels.

"Already on the way over." He appraised me. "You his girlfriend?"

"Oh no, we just went to high school together."

"Really? What's your name?"

"Olivia Mizra."

"Holy shit!" he shouted just loud enough for people to look over. He lowered his voice. "I knew you looked familiar. Kirk Moffett," he said.

I put my hand over my mouth. "Oh my gosh! Why didn't you say something sooner? How the hell are you?" I asked, giving him a hug.

"Oh great, just living the dream," he said, a touch of bitterness in his voice. "What about you? How the hell did you link back up with these assholes? I thought you hated them as much as I did."

I looked down sheepishly. "I, um, I mean….well….it's a long story…"

"Ready to go?" Carmine asked, helping me with my coat.

"Yeah, I was just....yeah, I'm ready." I looked at Kirk, unsure of what to say.

"Have a good night," I muttered, averting my eyes and stepping out into the windswept parking lot.

"What was that all about?"

"Nothing," I mumbled. "I think Marissa's drunk. Can we go to Denny's?"

By the time we got to Denny's, my stomach was growling. We walked in, clearly not the only ones under the influence of alcohol (or bath salts from the look of it).

The beleaguered hostess appraised us. "Four?"

"Yes, please," slurred Marissa, trying to stand up.

We sat down and ordered our food after the waitress brought us our water.

"I wonder if these glasses are clean," Marissa wondered aloud, holding hers up for inspection. "We could totally get salmonella."

I rolled my eyes. "You can't get salmonella from a glass. That's what you get from handling uncooked poultry."

She laughed. "My bad."

Idiot, I thought to myself.

"I would have totally gone to bat for you," Marissa piped up, checking her reflection in her phone.

"Not necessary," I said. "I can handle myself."

"What's your deal? Why don't you let anyone stand up for you?"

"Because I don't need it. I'm fine on my own."

"You've got trust issues," she said, her head lolling to the side and falling on Sanjay's shoulder.

"Where did you go to college again?"

"Central Carolina Community-"

"So you never actually *attended* medical school, yet you think you're a psychologist?" I snapped.

I guess I said it pretty loudly because the group of African-American women next to us turned around.

"I'm not saying that, I just-"

"Food's here," I interjected, placing my napkin on my lap as I prepared to devour some mozzarella sticks.

I don't know if it was bad oil that they used to deep-fry
the cheese or the combination of several cheap open bar
grain liquor drinks, but I wasn't feeling good. I got up
and went to the bathroom.

I knew I was going to vomit. I wasn't worried. I had a
toothbrush and toothpaste with me (old habits die
hard). I closed the door, noting that they were playing
Lana Del Rey over the speakers. I knew from experience
that I had one song length before anyone got suspicious.

'This Denny's has good taste in music at least,' I thought
to myself.

*Don't break me down, I've been traveling too long, I've
been trying too hard.*

I went into the furthest stall and hung my purse on the
hook. I turned my necklace around and pulled my hair
back with my left hand- sorta like they make you do at
TSA. With my right, I reached down and tickled the back
of my tongue. I gagged, but nothing happened. I tried
again.

I hear the birds on the summer breeze, I try to drive fast.

I gagged a bit more, but nothing. I reached and tried to
tickle my ulua. Nada.

I've got a war in my mind...

I reached into my purse and grabbed my bronzer brush.
The handle was about a quarter of an inch in diameter.

I shoved it in, choking, tears welling up in my eyes.

I'm tired of feeling like I'm fucking crazy, I'm tired of driving till I see stars in my eyes...

The third time was the charm. I managed to regurgitate not just the mozzarella sticks, but also the crackers from the hors de oeuvres tray.

I'm trying hard not to get into trouble, but I've got a war in my mind...

I flushed the toiled and walked out. Under three minutes. Not bad.

People think that bulimics wake up one day and just think, 'Hey, I'm going to make myself vomit my lunch.' That's a fallacy. It's a gradual descent into utter madness, obsession, and an all-consuming fear of losing control.

I had been back at school for two months into my sophomore year. Everything was going well, but my weight had hit a plateau. I couldn't break 130. I had tried everything. Anthony was providing me with an endless supply of ephedra. I had refilled an old prescription of Adderal, so I was about one shot of caffeine away from a full-fledged cardiac event.

Over the summer, I had gone to Weight Watchers with my mom, mostly as moral support, but I had learned to count calories. It worked for the first month. I lost a little over two pounds, but then I hit the 130 wall.

I went to my weekly weigh-in with my mom. She had lost three pounds and I had lost an ounce.

The lady weighing us in looked at me and laughed. "You know you don't need to lose anymore weight. You've got a good bone structure. If you lose anymore, you'll be a skeleton. We aren't even charging your mom for your membership since you are right on target for your health."

I scowled. Oh great, I was good by fat lady standards. Fuck that. Did she have to go back to sorority rush? Did she know what they did with fat girls at sorority rush?

They hid them in the closet and put them in charge of playing the music.

I had to up my game. I didn't like dark, confined spaces. Plus, no one wants to be the fat girl in the closet.

By that August, I started restricting myself to 1700 calories a day. By Halloween, I was down to 1100 calories a day and working out two extra hours after lacrosse. My performance on the field had slipped, a fact that I attributed to a stress fracture in my foot.

It was Halloween night and I had dressed up as a sexy ladybug. We were at a soccer party.

"Ryan Young looks so absolutely hot tonight," I whispered to my friend Aubrey.

"He always does. Stop drooling."

"He looks especially like Josh Hartnett tonight," I commented, sipping my beer (140 calories).

(My love for Josh Harnett will span decades.)

"He looks nothing *like Josh Hartnett."*

"You didn't have a poster of Josh Hartnett in your locker all through junior high. You don't know what he looks like."

"Well maybe you could stop staring all creepy and go talk to him. Seriously, you look unsettling."

"He's out of my league."

"No he's not."

"How the do you girls make looking like a bug so damn sexy? Baby, I'll be your Orkin man any day," boomed a voice behind us.

I turned to see Jeremy in the costume I helped him make, a torn up shirt with lipstick marks all over it.

"What are you supposed to be?" Aubrey asked.

"The Axe man. Ladies can't resist me."

"Jesus," Aubrey rolled her eyes.

"No, just call me Jeremy. What's the situation over here?"

"Tell Olivia to go talk to Ryan Young."

"Aubrey!" I exclaimed, slapping her.

"Hey Stretch Nuts!" Jeremy shouted.

I looked perplexed as Ryan waved at Jeremy.

"What-"

"Come here and bring my girls another drink," Jeremy instructed him.

"Don't say a word," I hissed.

Ryan came over and handed us each a cup of jungle juice (which I estimated to be 270 calories).

"Do you know my best friend Olivia?" he asked.

"Oh yeah, we were in media design together last year," he said.

I nodded, unable to speak, fixated on his hotness.

"What's up?" he asked, downing his drink.

I guess I somehow managed to stammer through an entire conversation with him. I even let my guard down, forgetting about calories as he handed us each two slices of pizza that they had ordered.

I thought things were going pretty well. I even managed to crack a few jokes (whether or not he got them, I may never know).

About two in the morning, as the party was winding down, I got up to use the restroom. When I came back, him and Aubrey were gone.

'Maybe they went to go smoke,' I thought, knowing full well that neither of them smoked. I went out on the patio. They weren't there. I looked around the first floor.

"Are you lost?" some lineman asked me.

"Um, I'm looking for Aubrey. She was in a bumblebee costume?"

"Oh yeah, she took off with Stretch Nuts. I think they went back to his place. She's gonna-"

My heart stopped and tears welled up in my eyes. How could she do that to me? Wait, what was I saying? It wasn't her fault. She was skinnier than me. Of course he'd want to hook up with her.

I found Jeremy and he walked me home, arms wrapped around me as I shivered and sobbed in the early morning cold.

As soon as I got back to the sorority house, I ran upstairs and locked myself in the bathroom. I started crying harder, the sobs racking my body. Of course he wanted her. Who would want me? I was a disgrace. Not only was I fat, but I had no self-control. How much had I eaten anyways?

I leaned over the toilet and tentatively stuck a finger down my throat. I gagged a little. I knew it wouldn't do much. I remembered a Cosmo article that I had read about oral sex. I giggled a little, thinking about my immaturity. If something was too big-

'Great Olivia, you can't even think about sex without giggling. This is why you're almost 20 and still a virgin,' *I thought to myself.*

I had my bathroom caddy with me. I looked through all of my stuff. My toothbrush holder was big...and long. Again, I laughed to myself. God, I was so immature. How was I ever going to lose my virginity without laughing?

I stuck it down my throat and gagged. Twenty minutes later, I finally made myself vomit. Until then, I had only thrown up when I had the flu. This felt different. I felt good! I felt like I had regained control. I had conquered the calories. I was taking back my body.

Somewhere in my head, a small voice told me that what I was doing wasn't good.

'It's just this once,' *I told myself.* 'I made a mistake. I'm fixing it. I'm not going to do it again.'

I knew all along that it was a promise I'd never keep.

As I brushed my teeth in the Denny's bathroom, two of the large African American women walked in.

"Ha! Well, what do we have here? A walking stereotype. Skinny bitch ain't gotta do none of that Crossfit when she can throw up dinner, huh?" the first one chortled, pulling out a tube of clear lip gloss and applying it.

"Watch out, honey," the other one said. "Don't wanna rot those pretty teeth you spend so much money getting bleached."

I glared at them, ready to say something, but then thought better of it. By the time I left the bathroom, the opening cords of the next song were starting. Under five minutes. Go me.

October 28

I'm trying to debate what to wear for me Halloween costume. For the last two years, Delilah has had us all do a group theme. Last year, we were sexy barmaids. This year, we're going to be the "Queens of the Insect Kingdom."

I am going to be a butterfly. I have wings from a costume that my mom wore a few years ago to a party. I'm going to rock it with the blue bodysuit that I wore a few years ago when I was a character in Avatar.

(The blue paint was a bitch to wash off.)

Delilah is going to be a Bumblebee (the Queen Bee if you will), Christina is going to be a ladybug, Marissa is going to be a caterpillar, and Krishna is going as a spider. (I know, spiders aren't insects, but do you think anyone is really going to call us out on it?) Kylie is mad because she thought that she wanted to go as the spider and instead is going as a sexy caterpillar.

I wish Ashley could come, but he's working overtime. He keeps picking up extra shifts. He says it's because they're short-staffed, but part of it wonders if he wants to just get away from me. I hate to think it, but even when he comes home, he blatantly ignores me and acts like I'm an inconvenience.

In the meantime, I have some serious work to do. I'm trying to get caught up on the back assignments for Dr. Levenstein's class. I swear, I have no idea what he thought when he wrote this book. Was he high? I sighed and picked my reflection piece.

The Lunchroom

I read "The Lunchroom" for this week's discussion board post. My first thought was about high school lunchrooms, where you're stratified by social grouping. To go and sit at another clique's table would be social suicide. It was strange how badly I wanted to sit at the table with the popular people. Now it seems that I'm not just sitting there, but I'm the one making the reservations. My friend Marissa and I were at the mall the other day and saw some overweight "emo" looking girls, decked out in their black outfits and dog-collars. I wondered out loud what possessed people to dress like that (again with the first impressions) and Marissa replied, "I don't know, but I doubt we sat at the same lunch table in high school." Of course I laughed, but I wondered if Marissa and I would have even sat at the same table. Christina has always been beautiful and had things come to her very easily. At the same time, she has somewhat of a case of entitlement. I met this girl Marissa a few months ago and we've all been hanging out. Marissa isn't the brightest bulb in the chandelier, but she's nice. Delilah says she doesn't want to hang out with Marissa because Marissa is a moron. In reality, we all know it is really because Delilah feels threatened by Marissa and the attention that people showing Marissa is starting to anger her.

In regards to work lunchrooms, I thought it was really good and made a lot of sense. Maybe 20 years ago, the lunchroom was where everyone went to vent and talk about their problems. (Today everyone can privately text each other, either individually or in a group text).

In an organization where the culture is positive, people eat their lunch and talk about normal everyday stuff. In an organization where the culture is negative, the employees view the lunchroom as a "safe zone" where people are not under the control of the boss. In our company, our boss eats in her office and the sales staff eats in the lunchroom and the staff (my people) eat in our back office room. This says a lot about the animosity between the two offices. We barely speak to each other (most of us don't know the sales staff's names) and our boss removes herself from everything. I know personally that I sometimes wonder about the people in the sales office. Some of them are closer to my age (most of the people I work with are well over 40) and look like the kinds of people I'd be friends with. However, it's just customary that we don't talk to them and they don't talk to us, nor do we eat together. If I were our manager, I'd try to facilitate some sort of way for us to get to know each other. Maybe we would realize that they are not all greedy, self-important idiots and they would realize that we are not as unimportant as they think we are.

One could still return to the high school lunchroom with this equation. If we all had just openly and honestly talked to each

other more, maybe we wouldn't all still
have lingering issues a decade later.

I decided that was self-exploratory enough and closed
my computer. I got up and started putting together my
outfit.

October 31

4:30 p.m.
I wish that I could just say how excited I am! I got the job!!!! I start next week. It's an 18-day training program, but it's all paid! Apparently, they need flight attendants really badly. Who knew? I can't wait! I'm off to celebrate with LaShawndra. Cocktails at the Avalon tomorrow night!

I'd like to say no more nights serving at Diamondz, but unfortunately I still need some money to get me by because I won't see my first paycheck until next month. Until then, I have some government benefits and my SNAP card, but that's not a whole lot since they took my unemployment payments into consideration when determining my eligibility. I am so excited!

I heard that if I complete my college degree that I have the chance to move up to a supervisor position. Now I'm double motivated to finish my degree. I logged into my class. Dr. Levenstein had called my story "idealistic," "unrealistic," and "pedantic." He said that I needed to develop a stronger set of central characters or something- that most of the time people do not meet due to random car accidents, but through their own actions and conviction. He wants to see a story about characters who are trying to better themselves so that they are ready to meet a person who lives up to their ideals and expectations.

I got a B- on the paper, but the next one I should do better on. The assignment is to read a CNN article by one of his former students, a girl named Zoe Zorka, who apparently came out of nowhere to write a front page opinion piece on her belief that it was OK to not have kids. We are supposed to choose between two options. We can either writer an opinion piece about something that we are passionate about or we can write a counterargument to her piece. I'm choosing the second. I don't know who she is, but I already dislike her. She looks smug, self-righteous, and condescending- the kind of dumb bitch who used to make my life a living hell growing up. She has probably never worked a day in her life.

Getting more and more angry at this chick who I didn't even know, I got up and put on my costume. This whole week, we are allowed to dress up. I am going to be a sexy Dr. Seuss.

Can Dr. Seuss be sexy? I hope so!

Only a few more shifts and then I'll be a sexy flight attendant- for real!

November 1
2:17 a.m.

I have never been so humiliated in my life. I'm finally home, smelling of cheap beer, cigarettes, and well vodka.

The night started out just fine. I was feeling self-assured as I started the shift. Since I lacked seniority, I had to cocktail, which doesn't pull in as much money as bartending. It was fine. I was used to dealing with drunken idiots.

At about ten, it started getting crowded. A group of guys fresh out of Wayne State were having a bachelor party by the stage.

"Can I get you anything?" I asked.

They looked at me and grinned. "Yeah, pussycat," the one said, cracking up.

"So what do we need to do to get in your hat?" his friend chimed in.

I rolled my eyes. "Will you be starting a tab?"

One of the guys handed me his credit card and ID. The card still had the paper strip on it for activation.

"Is this card active?" I asked, getting testy. "I need to make sure it is because I have to preauthorize it for

$200- it's our policy. If it's not, I need to come back and then your order will be delayed."

"Oh yeah it is," he assured me. "Just got it in the mail Wednesday. First credit card baby!" he hollered, fist-bumping his friend.

I looked at them. They were probably only five or six years younger than me, but it seemed so much more. It wasn't just their baby faces, unmarked by lines or age spots, but also their exuberance- a certain kind of youthful hope that everyone is born with, but gradually dies as we age and life's realities set in upon us.

"I hope so," I muttered, as I walked over to the computer, sweating through my costume.

Why had I painted my *entire* face and body white? I was really starting to regret not only that decision, but also the decision to apply fake whiskers to my nose.

I preauthorized the credit card and sure as shit, it went through.

The rest of the night went on like usual until about midnight when it started to get crowded, as it typically does on nights such as these.

On Halloween, people tend to go out early, get to the bars, ogle over costumes, and then realize that the combination of various plastic appendages, props, and makeup gets a bit hot, especially in already sweltering clubs. It's usually about that things start to take a turn downhill as parts and pieces of costumes disappear somewhere on the floor, makeup gets smeared, and shots are consumed faster knowing that last call is approaching.

The guys ogled over the strippers, and one of them proceeded to crawl on stage to put a dollar in her bikini bottom in a slightly inappropriate manner (pushing the limits) as the bouncer scowled and began to walk toward them to sternly instruct them to sit down.

One of the guys waved me over again while immaturely screaming..."Bartender!" I was sweaty, so I ripped the whiskers off my face because the itching was irritating as hell. My only saving grace was daydreaming about getting out of that hellhole.

The guys wanted another round of shots....GREAT. Just what they needed.

"Hey pussycat! What happened to your facial hair?"

Meanwhile, another one of the random guys walked up behind me attempting to "smack dat", as I spun around one-footed and screamed at him.

"What the hell?"

I couldn't believe this. Standing at the bar were familiar faces, but they looked a little blurred from losing my shit with those rich spoiled brats who were in the process of getting the boot.

'OMG...please tell me this is just a nightmare,' I thought to myself.

I looked like a total loser. I was so irritated, and I could have done the rest of my life without *ever* seeing *them* again. I remembered them clearly...Sanjay, Carmine, and Paul.

"Shit!" I mumbled under my breath. Now I get to make my debut with white smeared makeup and a big hat, starring as the crazy impoverished waitress at a strip club.

I turned my back to them and high tailed it to the next group of idiots to take any last drink orders, then took a peek behind me and saw them sizing me up. I wondered what nicknames they had for me tonight, or if they remembered me.

Clearly they didn't because they barely glanced at me as they took over the table from the Wayne State guys. They ordered a round of drinks and I took Paul Jacobi's credit card to hold the tab.

No sooner had I opened it then a loud, obnoxious, gaggle of girls entered and joined the guys. They were all dressed as various insect breeds, complete with wings, antennas, and...large breasts. The dancers onstage glared at them as they walked in, clearly not cool with the diversion. I knew these kinds of girls. Even under their makeup, you could tell they were beautiful. They were the girls who pretended to "be cool" with their boyfriends going to a strip club, but secretly harbored just a bit of jealousy.

I noticed two of the girls, the Avatar-looking one and the one in all black stayed huddled in a corner, whispering almost the whole night.

Probably boy drama, I figured to myself.

At least they ignored me. The worst had to be the constant harassment from Paul Jacobi and whatever bimbo was sitting next to him in her stupid bumblebee outfit with some chopsticks doubling as antennae. I couldn't help but overhearing their inane conversations as I cleared their glasses.

"Allright," he said, throwing a $20 down. "Double or nothing, the one on stage has been to rehab."

"I'm gonna say 'negative Ghostrider' on that one," Sanjay replied, putting down his own wad of cash.

They called Charlise over and I saw Paul stick a $10 in her g-string. As she grinded on him, much to the annoyance of his lady companion, he asked her something. Although I couldn't make out all of the words, I heard 'rehab' in there.

With a look of disgust, she stood up and strutted away towards a group of military guys at the next table over. I saw Paul toss his money at Sanjay.

I used this as my opening to go collect the glasses that had accumulated on the table in order to make room for their next round.

"OK, let me win my money back," Paul said, waving his hand and indicating that the other men should throw some cash into the pile. He made hand signals to the other guys that I couldn't quite understand.

I looked at it longingly. That was almost a month's electricity bill right there.

"OK, so let me ask you a question. How many kids do you have?" he said, sliding me a $5, just enough to keep me there.

"Two," I stammered.

"And how many fathers?" he continued.

"None of your business!" I snapped.

He waved a $10 in front of me.

I took it and sighed. "Two."

"And are any of them black?" he asked, handing me another $10.

I started to protest, but stammered, my hesitation clearly confirming his suspicions.

"Look, I'm just doing this between jobs, to get through school-" I protested, trying to make my case.

(Seriously, what kind of case was I making with my makeup running down my face? I looked like Gene Simmons after a two-day coke binge.)

"Jackpot!" Paul yelled, cutting me off. "Suck my left nut!"

He looked at me. "Oh, I'm sorry. Not you, him."

I nodded and tried to reach over and grab a glass.

"I know what you meant," I muttered.

"I mean if you want to...."

"That's all right, I think I'll pass," I replied, praying that he didn't look at me too closely.

He began scooping all the money off the table. "The perfect stripper cliché! I win!"

His friends groaned and handed him *more* money from their wallets. Jesus, what did these guys *do* for a living?

"So how do you end up a stripper?" the bumblebee asked, rubbing Paul's shoulders.

"I'll be back with your drinks," I replied, tears welling up in my eyes as I marched away from the table.

The truth was that I never set out to be a stripper, a dancer, a single mother...or a cliché, as Paul so aptly put it...

I was 19. I had failed out of college and was back home at community college, living with my mom. I wasn't bad at the school part, I was just so sad. Cody broke my heart and I missed him so much. I kept trying to replace him, but no one else could make me feel the way he did. I just ended up feeling empty inside.

I was walking through the Kmart on 13 mile and Schoenner one day picking up some stuff from my mom when an attractive black guy appeared around the corner.

"Hey girl," he said, smiling at me.

I mumbled 'hi' and smiled back.

About 20 seconds later, he passed the aisle I was walking down.

"You know, if I see you again, I'm going to have to come back and say hi," he said, winking.

I looked at him, quizzically, as he entered the next aisle over. Just then, I heard his voice behind me.

"Oops, I see you again. I guess you have to give me your phone number now."

And so it began. He was good-looking, sexy, just a bit dangerous. Granted, things weren't perfect. He had a tendency not to call when he said he would. Sometimes a few days would go by before I'd hear from him. He wouldn't let me post pictures on MySpace of us because he said he was "private." (Translation: he had another girlfriend.) I should have known something was up when he didn't spend Valentine's Day with me and instead brought me discount chocolates the day after.

(From Kmart. Obviously.)

When I found out I was pregnant, he promised to be a better man. Hell, he promised me we'd get married someday. All of that turned out to be smoke and mirrors. When I was a month away from giving birth to our son, I caught him with another girl two apartments down from the small, rat-infested hellhole we were sharing.

He stuck around for the first few months of Tyrell's life, but after that, his involvement was sporadic at best. By the time Tyrell's birthday rolled around, I was back living with my mom and flat broke. I told her that I got a job as a waitress at IHOP and was working the overnight shift. I'm sure she knew all along, but never said anything. Money is money, right? I came home, kicked in some money for utilities and groceries, and we all just tried to live our own little American Dream.

November 1

Well, if it isn't Day of the Dead, it sure as shit feels like it. I am so exhausted from last night. Seriously, why do we keep feeling the urge to turn up until sunrise *every* damn weekend?

The whole day started off on the wrong foot. Ashley overslept and yelled at me like it was my fault or something. (To the passengers who were delayed on their way to Minneapolis, I'm sorry.) Then, I got to work and everyone was in a bad mood because two of our feature writers screwed up in a big way by reporting information about zoning plans that turned out to be speculative at best, completely false at worst. Of course this wasn't discovered until after yesterday's paper was printed and the story was shared over two thousand times on social media. While this might be good news for me in the long run should one or both of these jackasses get the boot, it made for a long morning at work.

I got off at noon as per usual and headed home in hopes of wrapping up a little homework before I got ready, but of course, best-laid plans often fail. Krishna called me all upset because during last night's storm, a tree fell on her car, totaling it.

I made a joke about karma, but apparently Indians take that kind of stuff really seriously. Who knew? Kidding.

(I'm so going to hell.)

Electronic Journal of Oda Mizra

File Name: MPJ-701_Reflection Journal

She needed to go out to Sterling Heights to a costume shop and pick up her costume that she had ordered, but she didn't have a ride. She offered to buy me dinner, which I told her was nonsense, and I offered to take her. I shouldn't be mad. She's never asked me for a thing since I've known her, unlike some people (ahem, Delilah, Kylie).

As we navigated our way through Warren, she got a call from her insurance company. From the sounds of it, you could tell that things were not going well.

"No, the tree was *not* already on the ground when I parked last night!" Pause. "*No*, I didn't think to park anywhere else...I've parked under trees since I've been 16 and this is the first one that's fallen....no, I do *not* think that anyone cut down the tree because they wanted to sabotage my car....how do I know this? Because I heard the crack of lightning and the fire department showed up, you moron!"

She listened.

"No, I will not hold! Let me speak to your supervisor."

She paused again.

"Supervisor!" she shouted more angrily this time, her veins visibly bulging in her beautiful forehead.

I tried not to snicker as she argued with them for a good 20 minutes until finally they agreed to send a representative to her house tomorrow.

"Morons," she muttered, grabbing her water bottle and gulping it down. "These GED rejects can't do anything right. No wonder this country is going to hell."

"Oh my God, totally!" I agreed, slowing down as we approached the turnoff for 13 Mile, and my old house.

"Is it better in India?"

"Oh hell no," she said. "Women are treated like, how do you say…second class citizens?"

I resisted the urge to turn down 13 Mile and continued north.

"It's better here, yes, but many Americans I meet are lazy. And fat. In India, we have so many people who cannot eat and starve to death, yet here, the workers at my job get fat and eat McDonalds. Then they wonder why are they fat."

I was starting to like this feisty foreign chica.

"OK, we're here," I said, pulling up to the costume store, which was already packed.

We got out and navigated our way through the throngs of people getting last minute costumes and accessories. While Krishna went to customer service and signed for her order, I picked a headband with sparkly balls on the end for my antennae.

"I want to try on," she said. "Where do we go?"

We navigated our way towards the back of the store and got in line for the changing rooms. We immediately looked at each other and started laughing. Every morbidly obese girl in the state of Michigan must have been there trying to squeeze into "slutty nurse" or "slutty maid" outfits.

"Why do they dress like this?" she asked, just loud enough for a few people to hear. "It looks ridiculous and they are making a spectacle of themselves."

I shook my head. "Hey, they tell each other they look good. It's complacency in mass and the majority rules I guess."

"You will tell me if I look bad, yes?" she asked.

"I can already tell that you're going to look just *awful*," I said as the line slowly moved its way forward. "I hope you ordered a plus size costume."

"Yes, I get biggest size they have. That is why they special order. I am so very fat," she joked.

Apparently some oversized train wreck heard us and ambled over to us. She looked like the offspring of Honey Boo Boo and Larry the Cable Guy. She was wearing leggings as pants, which would be fine maybe if her shirt was long enough. Instead, it crept up her midsection revealing a lower back tattoo covering her pasty, flabby skin. Her copious stomach hung over the front of her pants, just sticking out enough to reveal a C-section scar.

Placing her hand on her ample hip, she stuck her finger in my face.

"Why don't you two get the hell out of here and go back to Persia or wherever the hell you came from?"

I tried not to snicker as I replied, calmly, "Persia ceased to be an autonomous kingdom around 1100 A.D., so going back there would be a *little* tough." I paused to let it sink in and lowered my voice.

"Why don't *you* get your cheap acrylic nail out of my face and go back to sucking dick at the truck stop off I-94?" I asked.

Her face reddened. Krishna looked scared, but I knew it this lady was just posturing.

"You're not going to hit us," I calmly continued, looking her dead in the eye.

"There are cameras everywhere and I'm clearly not touching you. Hell, I'm nowhere near your personal space. You know that if you throw a punch, I'll own you for the rest of your life. You also know that child protective services will probably take your kids away, if they haven't already, and you'll be the subject of investigation by every state agency from whom you're currently receiving assistance."

I paused as if thinking.

"Oh yeah, and one more thing. Since my tax dollars are paying for your costume, I'm kind of like a stakeholder for the corporation of welfare queens. I'd advise you go with the Queen of Hearts costume. It's more your color."

She opened her mouth and balled up her fist, but her friend was already dragging her away.

Krishna looked at me, mouth agape. "How did you know that about her?"

I rolled my eyes. "Please, what a fucking cliché. Look at her. Plus, if I was wrong, wouldn't she have called me out?"

By the time we were done, it was close to five.

"I'm so hungry!" she said. "Have you eaten yet?"

"Not yet," I replied, secretly starving as well. (I skipped lunch because *someone* needed a ride to Sterling Heights.)

"Do you want to eat at happy hour over there at Coney Island?"

I winced, looking across the parking lot. Of course, it was the one I used to work at.

'Grow up Olivia,' I told myself. *'It's a fucking chain restaurant. No one remembers you. You're not going to*

349

walk in and have someone get on the PA and say, "Here comes the Bride of Frankenstein" or announce that Sasquatch is in the house. You worked there a decade ago. No one you know could possibly still work there.'

"Yeah, sure," I agreed, popping my trunk so she could toss her costume in the back. "I could go for some potato skins about now."

I wrapped my coat around me tighter as we crossed the parking lot. How ironic was it that just seven years ago I wouldn't have dreamed about eating potato skins, or anything for that matter, if I hadn't exercised for at least five hours?

I hugged my arms to my chest as I walked back to my sorority house. It was almost nine thirty at night. Why did I think that taking a night class would be a good idea? Oh, that's right, because it didn't interfere with my workout schedule. Since I was a sophomore, I was the last year group to get to register for classes, so I ended up just picking whatever elective sounded tolerable. In this case, it was Women in Art History. My professor, a militant feminist, strongly believed that every piece of art from prehistoric cave paintings to Sports Illustrated's *latest swimsuit issue either depicted women being objectified or repressed. It was the longest two hours of my life.*

The light to cross the street was red, so I sat down on a bench to catch my breath. I couldn't believe that I was so tired. I had only worked out for five hours today- three before my nine a.m. class and two after my ten. I put my elbows on my knees and placed my hands in my head. The

350

light changed to walk, but I figured I'd just wait for the next one. What would another few minutes hurt?

I coughed into my gloved palm. It was a deep, hacking cough, like I had mucus that I couldn't get rid of. I pulled a Kleenex out of my backpack and coughed into it. It was red. Great, I was coughing up blood- again.

I stood up, slowly, feeling slightly dizzy.

"Are you OK?" I heard a woman behind me ask.

I turned around to face Dr. Pritchard, my militant feminist professor.

"I'm fine," I replied. "Just trying to kick this cold."

"Are you sure you're okay? You've been looking really sick the last few weeks," she said.

"I'm fine," I replied. "I just can't get used to the cold weather I guess."

"Are you eating enough?" she asked. "I noticed you didn't touch any of the doughnuts that I brought."

"Oh, I'm fine," I said, nonchalantly. "I just had a huge dinner."

The light changed and I commenced the arduous task of crossing the street, the wind whipping at my hair and stinging my face.

"But thank you. Have a wonderful evening," I politely spoke to her as I walked away.

The truth was that I hadn't had more than 800 calories so far that day. I knew that because 800 was the magic number. After field hockey season, I started to really ramp up the cardio sessions (and the ephedra intake) while simultaneously cutting calories. At first it worked and I got down to about 120, but then I plateaued. Jeremy said I needed to eat more, but what the hell did he know. He threatened to stop giving me ephedra pills, but I also threatened to show his professors his emails and texts to me begging me to do his homework for him. It was a Mexican standoff and I was winning.

I had also managed to convince my family doctor that I was having trouble and needed Adderall. He had no problem prescribing it to me. To ward off any concerns he might have had about weight gain, I wrapped my mom's ankle weight belts from the 1990s around me under my coat, so it would look like I only lost four pounds, not 23, since my last visit.

I finally crossed the street and let myself in the house. As I crossed the foyer, a few of my sisters mumbled greetings, but remained aloof. I had no idea what had gotten into them, but there was something definitely off about the way that they had been treating me lately.

I let myself into my room, throwing my backpack on the chair and collapsing on my bed.

"Rough day?" my roommate Sammie asked.

"Yeah, just long, but whatever. I'm just gonna read a little then go to bed," I said, changing out of my jeans into my American Eagle sweatpants.

"It was Katie's birthday tonight," she said, opening up our small fridge. "I saved you some cake and ice cream."

"No thanks," I said. "We had doughnuts in class."

She looked exasperated. "Will you just eat already?"

"I'm not hungry," I replied, getting under the covers and opening my book.

Why was it so damn cold in here all the time? How was Sammie wearing just shorts and a tank top?

"Can you turn on the space heater?" I asked.

"No, because it's boiling in here already! I'm opening a window!" she announced, making good on her promise and letting the Michigan night air in.

"Sammie! No!" I protested, wrapping myself up in the blanket.

"Then eat the cake."

I thought about it. There was no way in hell she was going to let this go. The bitch drove a hard bargain. I sighed, taking the paper plate from her. She was considerate enough to provide me with a plastic spoon.

How benevolent. I figured I better get used to eating with plastic silverware for when I became a single, poor, lonely, plump, old cat lady.

As I took the first bite, panic welled up inside me. I could literally feel the lard sliding down my throat and sticking to my stomach. I estimated the cake to be about 175 calories. It was too late to go for a run. I was so fucked.

"Stop watching me!" I yelled at her. "You're being creepy as fuck."

"I'll close the window when you eat it all."

"Bitch," I mumbled under my breath.

I managed to choke it all down, and sure enough, she kept true to her promise and closed the window. I wanted to go vomit so badly, but there were at least five girls in the bathroom right now. My heart was racing and I was in full-on panic mode. In my mind, I could literally feel myself getting fatter.

I tried not to think about it and opened my laptop, pulling up my Facebook profile.

"Are you on this Facebook thing yet?" I asked her.

"No, what is it?" she replied, still staring at me.

"It's like MySpace but with less hoochie mamas. You have to have a university email address. So far, there's like a

354

thousand people from our school on here. I have seventy friends."

"Sounds just like MySpace," she replied. "I'll pass."

I clicked on Ryan's profile. He had posted that he was "at practice." I scrolled through his pictures and my chest tightened. In every picture, he was with some beautiful blonde girl. She had flawless skin, perfect teeth, and was incredibly thin.

I sighed and set my computer down, overcome with shame at the fat slob I had become. Why did I take that cake? I had no fucking self-control. I deserved to be fat. I was 20 years old. I was supposed to be engaged by now.

"What are you moping about?" Sammie asked.

"Ryan's new girlfriend. She's so attractive- striking, actually. I bet she's a horrible bitch and a mean person.

"That's not very nice. You don't even know her. Do you even talk to Ryan?" she asked.

"I know girls like her and that's all I need to know. And yes I talk to him...sometimes....I mean...I don't know....I will when I'm skinny, OK? I'm laying the groundwork here."

"Seriously? At this rate, by the time you actually talk to him, he won't recognize you because you'll be sixty years old."

"Two months, tops. Then I'll make my move."

She rolled her eyes and turned off the lights.

"You are skinny," she muttered. "You just need to get your head on straight."

I lay there in the dark until I knew that she was asleep and I crept out of my room and padded down the hallway, casting furtive glances over my shoulder as if I was on a top-secret mission.

The bathroom was clear, which was a good sign. I went into the end stall and pulled my makeup brush out of the sleeve of my sweatshirt. (I had gotten used to buying them in bulk from Wal-Mart.) I leaned over the toilet and stuck it down my throat, gagging. Nothing. Ten minutes later, I had only managed to cough up blood and a few pieces of cake. The rest of it was already being absorbed into-

"Two?"

I shook my head, breaking my daze. The bored hostess looked at me, trying to conceal her cell phone under the ledge of the hostess desk as she pretended not to look at it.

"What?"

"It is just you two or are you waiting on someone else?"

"Oh, yeah, just us two," I replied, cringing and waiting for her to make a mocking comment about my eyebrows, my nose, or my weight.

Seriously Olivia, she doesn't even know you. She's like seventeen. She was a kid when you worked here.

"OK, follow me then. I like your coat."

"Thank you," I replied.

We sat down and ordered and started talking about tonight's activities. Our food came and we began eating. As I was showing her a picture of how I was going to do my hair, we were interrupted by a male voice.

"How's everything going ladies? I just thought I'd stop by and check on everything," the man, apparently the manager, asked.

"Good," she said, absentmindedly, zooming in on the picture.

"Yeah, everything is great," I responded, looking up and-

HOLY HELL!

My jaw dropped open. His hairline had started to recede quite a bit, but there was no mistaking him. The nametag confirmed it- Jesse, my former tormenter, was now an assistant manager.

In a split second, I regained my composure. "It's delicious."

"That's good. So what are you ladies up to tonight?" he asked. "I know you're too pretty not to be going out."

Oh. My. God. This was *not* real life.

We mumbled something in reply and he kept up with his pathetic lines until he finally got the hint that we weren't interested and decided to try his luck elsewhere- probably with the high school girls' cross country team that had just been seated.

When we were done eating, we paid the waitress.

"Hey….Kaylah," I said, looking at her nametag, "so what's the deal with the manager? You know him?"

"He's my boyfriend," she replied defensively.

"No kidding?" I asked, trying to hold back laughter. "He just looked like someone I used to know, but his name was…Chad. That's fun that you all work together. I wish I could work with my fiancé sometimes."

"Yeah, I mean some of the other girls are jealous because, you know, he's the *manager* and all," she said, lowering her voice as if she just disclosed that she was dating Prince Harry.

I muttered something about how nice that was and she went away. I waited until I saw him emerge from the kitchen empty-handed and put on my coat to leave.

"Hey!" I called to him. His eyes lit up and he came over. "Everything was awesome. I mean, our waitress was amazing," I gushed. "What are *you* up to tonight?"

"Nothing, girl. I get off at eleven. You wanna give me your number?" he asked, pulling out his cell phone, which I could swear was the same Motorola Razr that he had in 2004.

I smiled and wrapped my scarf around my neck. "You know, I just thought of something...I knew someone who used to be a hostess here...back in 2004...her name was Oda..."

He thought about it.

"She had kinda frizzy black hair, about my height, same skin color..."

"Oh yeah, *unibrow*! How the hell do you know her? You cousins or something? I mean, not that all you people are related, but you know...and I don't mean you people like *you people*...."

I smiled and pulled my keys out of my purse and leaned in to whisper into his ear.

"Because I *am* her."

A look of confusion passed over his face before he registered what I said.

"Holy shit! Wow, I-"

"Save it," I retorted, touching my fingers to my thumb in the universal sign for shut up.

"You know what? You are *so* pathetic. In ten years, when that waitress is long gone, you're still going to be the same miserable, pathetic asshole you were back then and are now. But maybe with less hair."

Before he could reply, I turned and walked away.

And *that*, my friends, is how you make a statement.

***

By nine, we were already in full costume mode at Christina's house. Delilah and Kylie had already gotten into a fight as to whether or not their antennae were too matchy-matchy. I wanted to shoot myself.

"I made Halloween drinks!" Christina announced, bringing out a tray of drinks that looked as if they had seriously just been featured in *Martha Stewart Home Living.* (Damn Christina, she was just so artistic.)

As if reading my mind, she piped up. "I found the recipe on Pinterest."

Of *course* she did.

I picked up one of her scrapbooks. Yes, this chick scrapbooked. If it was anyone else, I would have mercilessly mocked her, but she was just so freaking good at it. Plus, she was hot. Her hobbies could have included insect cataloging and no one would have said a word.

I flipped through the book, admiring her use of accouterments and trying to ignore her glaring grammatical errors. I stopped at one picture.

"Hey, who's this guy?" I asked, holding the book up.

"Oh, that was Ryan. We dated when I was like...eighteen?"

"I know him!" I exclaimed. "I thought he was cute. I mean, just for a little bit. Like a week."

(Lies, all lies.)

I felt a pang of guilt for the things I said about her seven years prior and the assumptions that I made. Even if I had met her back then, Christina would have probably bent over backwards and then some for me. Hell, I could have been a 200-pound midget with leprosy, and she still would have offered me the coat off her back. I cringed a little inside and made a mental note to try to be *slightly* less judgmental.

"So why did you break up?" I asked.

"Oh you know, just went our separate ways I guess. We're still great friends! He's a lawyer in Indianapolis now."

"That's great," I muttered.

"Oh, he said he remembers you," she said, looking at her phone and taking a sip of her drink.

"You texted him?"

"Yeah, just did. Like I said, we're still great friends."

Her phone chimed and she read the text. "He says that he didn't think you liked him. Said you never talked to him."

"Well, that's not true," I protested, but before I could continue, she interrupted.

Her phone chimed again. "He said he just sent you a Facebook request."

Great. A little late on the draw there, Olivia.

"I just texted Kristoff and asked if they wanted to come out with us," Christine piped up.

"Fine," I replied. "Just don't let them bring their fag hag-the one with the bleached blonde hair. Last time we were out, she called us vapid."

"I hope you didn't let that slide," interjected Delilah, applying another coat of eye shadow.

"No, of course not," I snapped at her. "This isn't amateur hour. Do you think that I'm going to let someone talk to *us* like that? I told him to put his fag hag on a leash and keep her chained up at home whenever we went out."

"Good girl," smiled Delilah.

I don't know why I should have been pleased that I was so mean to another human, but Delilah's praise still meant something to me. Old habits die hard I guess.

We eventually adjourned to Avalon, where we met up with Paul, Sanjay, Carmine, Brandon, and Tony. It was too crowded though. Even in VIP, I was sweating through my makeup and couldn't seem to get any air. We kept doing shots and by eleven, just as Marissa tweeted #whitegirlwasted, the Bad Idea Fairy made an appearance.

(Hash-tagging #whitegirlwasted is like saying 'Bloody Mary' three times in a dark bathroom. A demon appears. Usually in the form of Fireball.)

"Strip club!" bellowed Tony, to no one in particular.

I had to admit that it was an enticing prospect. It was hot and humid in the club and drink service took forever. At least us girls would get to drink free at Diamondz (our destination of choice apparently.)

363

Marissa, Sanjay, Krishna, and I piled into the back of Paul's Mercedes SUV as Delilah got in the passenger seat. Jesus, what was going on between the two of them? The collision of their combined egos could potentially cause a cosmic event unseen since the big bang.

(Or a black hole. More likely a black hole.)

By the time we got there, the place was packed. Lucky for us, a bunch of jackasses from Wayne State were in the process of being "escorted out" so we took their table. We ordered drinks and critiqued the dancers.

"She's not bad," I said, pointing to a redhead. "I mean, if you get past the dead eyes and meth teeth."

We kept going, because there's nothing like a night at a cheap strip club to reinforce all the positive decisions one has made in their life. As soon as the waitress approached our table, Krishna pulled me to the side and turned her back towards the group.

"Don't look!" she hissed. "I think the waitress used to work for me."

"Liar," I said, "You can't even tell what she looks like with all that makeup on."

"I recognize her stupid voice!"

I agreed to stay huddled in the corner until she left.

"What are you two doing over here?" Carmine asked, wheeling his chair towards us.

(Yes, this strip club had wheeled chairs- like office chairs. I wondered how they cleaned them. No wait, I don't want to know...)

"Nothing," I replied innocently before turning back to Krishna.

"I'm not getting involved in your stupid games because *I* don't want to be shanked by a stripper in a parking lot though. Can you imagine if I was the first person to die in our class? What would they say in the program at our reunion? She was suffocated with body glitter and drowned in body oil?"

"You wouldn't be the first to die. Not even the third," Carmine piped up.

"Oh no, who died?" I asked.

"Remember a girl named Morgan?" he asked.

"Yeah, you used to call her 'Fat Morgan.' That's awful. How did she die?"

"*I* didn't call her that. Paul did. Suicide."

I almost choked on my drink. "You're kidding! When?"

"Uh, in May I think. Then a girl named Maria and another one named Chelsea or Chloe."

"How did they die?"

"Suicide as well."

I almost choked on my drink. "No way! Were they all friends?" I didn't remember them hanging out together back then, but hey, times change apparently.

"Morgan and Maria were kind of friends, but Chelsea wasn't. I guess they all wanted to be in the 'Forever 27' club."

I shook my head. That was insane.

"What's the 'Forever 27' club?" Krishna asked.

"The famous people who have died at 27- Kurt Cobain, Janis Joplin, Tupac, Amy Winehouse, Jimi Hendrix...." Carmine explained.

I still couldn't believe it. How could someone so young decide to just tap out on life? It blew my mind.

While I was busy contemplating this, I saw Paul say something that must have offended the waitress (shocker) and gave us the cue to leave, which we probably needed to do as it was almost three in the morning.

We left and all went back to Christina's house, save for Delilah and Paul and Marissa and Sanjay. I was pretty sober, so I drove Brandon's car back. I needed to wash

all the blue off my body, so I went to take a shower.
Thirty minutes later, I emerged, my skin red from
where I had to rub really hard to get the blue out.

Despite the late hour and the fact that some paint was
still crusted into my hair, I emerged from the bathroom
smiling.

"What are you so happy about?" Carmine asked me as
he flipped through one of Christina's art portfolios.
Apparently he and I were the only ones still awake.

"I don't know...I mean, I just had fun tonight, you
know....like isn't this awesome?"

He laughed. "It was an all right night, I guess. But
nothing special."

I sat down next to him on the couch and started fiddling
with the sleeves of my sweatshirt, looking down.

"I don't know...I mean, I don't think you can appreciate
something like this until you've gone without it for so
long."

"Like sex, right?"

I laughed.

"Well, kinda, but not like anything physical, ya know..."

I crossed my legs and brought them to my chest, wrapping my arms around them, resting my chin on my knees.

"How can I explain it? Okay, so I'm reading this book- it's called the *Atlantis Gene*- it's just some fiction book or whatever, but there was this quote, and I found it rather profound, ya know. I memorized it. It said, '*We so often seek what we're deprived of in childhood. Sheltered children become reckless. Starving children become more ambitious...and some people want to have genuine human contact, to see their life mean something.'"*

All of the sudden, I could feel myself getting incredibly tired. I lay down on the couch, positioning my head on the pillow and pulling a throw blanket over myself so that my feet were almost resting on Carmine's lap.

As I started to fade into sleep, the last thing I remember saying was something to the effect of, "I never wanted much- just the friends that I never had growing up. I wanted to be accepted, to know what it was like to truly belong. Maybe that sounds stupid, but it's my own little version of the American dream..."

November 7

One week down, three to go! I am officially excited to be in paid training.

So far, it's been mostly basic and boring stuff- there's so much more studying involved than I would have thought! Oh well, it's not *that* bad. I've always been really good at taking tests. I got a 97% on the one this week- highest grade in my cohort!

Lucky for me, I got my home study packet in the mail a week before I started training, so I was able to study. Dr. Lowenstein agreed to let me complete all of my work prior to starting training. He said that he was very proud of me for taking initiative and responsibility with regard to my career- or something like that. He said that he hopes to see me in his master's level classes in a few years.

So far, the other girls are nice enough. They're all different ages- some younger than me, some older. It's mostly women, but a few men. I've met one girl, Rose, who seems pretty cool. She's a single mom about my age and has two young sons. We haven't met any pilots yet.

(Which is just the tiniest bit discouraging.)

In other, brighter, news, Jesse finally brought me some money after I threatened to take his ass to court (again). Sometimes I wonder what I ever saw in him. Oh yeah, that's right- he had a stable job and didn't expect me to sleep with him on the very first date. Sad as it is, that's probably the nicest that a guy's ever been to me :/.

It's going to get better...it has to.

November 13

I 'm just finishing up in class tonight, trying to write my thoughts as they remain fresh in my mind. We had to do our individual meetings with Dr. Lowenstein, who happens to also be my program mentor, tonight.

I walked into his office, wrapping my arms around myself to keep warm and taking a seat amongst the piles of papers, journals, and newspapers from 1974-2013. I gingerly moved a *TIME* magazine featuring Bill Clinton onto a stack of papers whose corners had started to yellow with age.

This guy was the epitome of the eccentric professor. A dying potted fern was perched precariously atop an old typewriter and I could literally see the dust bunnies on the windowsill.

"Olivia, what do you want to do with your life?" he asked, moving the *TIME* magazine into a different pile.

Oh great, he was going to be one of those people. Were we going to start talking about my relationship with my mom now?

I shrugged and looked down, trying not to roll my eyes.

"Write, I guess. Probably features pieces," I replied, already bored.

"Well that's good. I think that would be a nice fit for you, he said, making a note in his spiral notebook.

'The man probably doesn't even own a computer,' I thought to myself.

"So what pieces have you submitted and where have you submitted to?"

"I don't really have any pieces yet," I mumbled.

"Sure you do! You've been in this program for what- almost two years? Surely you haven't been twiddling your thumbs the whole time, have you?"

I looked down, picked at my nails and focused on my dark blue nail polish. There were still traces of blue paint in my nail beds from my Halloween costume.

"I'm not- I mean, the article's- not good enough yet."

"Well how do you know that?"

I sighed. "I submitted the piece about the cleanup efforts on Lake St. Clair to a few places, but no one responded."

"You submitted *one* article? To how many publications?" He paused, put down his pen, and looked at me.

"Like two...or three..." I replied, avoiding eye contact.

"And that was enough to call it quits? I submitted to fifty plus papers before I got published. I had to type it out on a typewriter and then make photocopies. I addressed each envelope by hand."

"Well, when we did the peer reviews of each other's work, Brianna pretty much said my stuff sucked, and Raj referred to it as 'trivial' and 'monotonous,'" I argued.

"So what am I going to do? Waste my time on sending something out that sucked? Plus, I'm nobody- just some girl from Detroit. I don't have anything good to write about. There's enough articles about how bad this place sucks. Unless the actual portal to hell opens up, I can't exactly break new ground."

"Just some girl from Detroit, huh?"

"Well Grosse Pointe if you want to be technical about it. Which is even less exciting."

"Ah, *now* we get to the core of your problem! I've heard this excuse before," he said, reaching under a TV Guide from 1992 and pulling out a brand-spanking-new shiny MacBook Air.

Seriously? WTF. That's one way to avoid getting robbed I guess.

Perplexed, I leaned in to see what he was pulling up. He clicked on Chrome and went to a CNN story in his bookmarks.

"I want you to take a look at this," he said, turning it towards me as he printed me a hard copy.

I shrugged. "Look at what? The news story? Zoe Zorka? I don't know her. What's this story about? Opinion? I don't want kids? Why do I care?"

"The author," he paused, looking for a stapler under a pile of yellowed *Weekender* magazines, "was one of my former students. She thought that she was just a 'random girl from North Carolina.' In fact, it was the name of her blog. She wanted to be a writer, but was too scared to submit because the humor book she submitted to publishers in 2012 got rejected."

He handed me the papers and I flipped through them. He continued talking.

"I'll be honest. She wasn't the best student in the program. She probably wasn't even the best writer in her class. But one day, upon realizing that her family had neglected to invite her to her grandfather's birthday party because she hadn't produced them grandchildren, she got incredibly angry. She channeled all of her anger and passion into writing. Do you think that she made it big because she wrote about cleaning a dock on Lake St. Clair?"

I shook my head. She looked somewhat cross-eyed and possibly hunchbacked.

"She wrote about something she cared about."

"And let me guess," I interrupted. "Everyone loved her and she was great and now she's on the New York Times bestseller list?"

"Quite the contrary. She faced unrelenting criticism. You should look up the article online. There are over 8,000 comments, quite a few of them very negative. Even after that, she didn't quit. In fact, she's hosting a small segment on an Internet news show and working on a novel now."

I shrugged and flipped through the pages.

"Whatever it is you're angry about, start writing about that. You may find out that you have more to say than you think."

"OK, I'll work on that," I said, smiling, and getting up to leave.

"Keep journaling," he said. "Your posts are getting better. Go back and read them. You might just find that you already have something to write about. You just don't know it yet."

■■

I pulled into the driveway, and upon seeing Ashley's car wasn't there, breathed a sigh of relief. I hadn't made him anything for dinner yet and knew how upset he got when I was late with that.

It wasn't always that way. When we first started dating, he used to be happy just to see me. Now, it was like nothing I did was good enough. The harder I tried, the more I seemed to push him away.

I took off my coat and hung it up in the closet. I opened up a Stouffer's *Dinner for Two* and transferred it to the pan before burying the box under a few layers of trash.

(Ashley says that pre-made meals are a lazy woman's way out.)

I sat down and started reading the article.

In the wake of the Supreme Court decision that struck down key portions the Defense of Marriage Act, I celebrated this historic milestone like many Americans as a step toward acceptance of all people. Even though I'm straight, I relate to my LGBT brothers and sisters as I also struggle for others' acceptance.

By all accounts, I appear to be a completely average 27-year-old female. I was never the kind of person who thought I'd champion for individual rights or equality. Sure, I believe in it, but I'm not the stereotypical "Occupy" protestor or gay rights advocate.

On the outside, I look like many of my peers; I wear skinny jeans and Abercrombie. I play on my iPhone, Facebook and Twitter. I tend to blend seamlessly into the background of average female faces.

However, I realize that my life as a typical twentysomething will not last long. As time goes on, I will start to become more and more isolated from my peer group as my secret comes out...

I read the whole thing. It was good, but I don't know why he said people were angry. She was pretty respectful and didn't resort to name-calling or breeder-bashing. I scrolled down to the comments section.

"Who does this liberal feminist think the is?"

"What an old hag. Her husband probably is just repulsed by her."

"She probably can't have kids because she's defective."

"This dumb cunt is going to hell. She was put on this earth to reproduce."

"If all other women have to have kids, then she shouldn't get a hall pass."

"She should probably do the world a favor and kill herself."

I raised my eyebrows at some of them. Holy hell, these people were *tearing* her apart. There were a lot of positive comments interspersed in with the negative. I was trying to decipher what SteelersFan42 meant by, *"She's trying to advance the Jewish agenda"* when the door opened.

I dropped the laptop on the couch and stood up, the same level of shame washing over my face that I could assume would have occurred had he walked in on me watching foot fetish grandma porn.

"Hey," I said, rushing to the kitchen "I, uh, didn't know when...but dinner is...I thought you might be late...and already had eaten..."

"Nope," he said, opening the fridge. "Delay. Ice on the wings at O'Hare."

"Well sit down, dinner will be ready soon," I said, waving him towards the couch.

"Yeah, good," he said, flipping on the TV. "Can you make me some cornbread too?"

"Sure," I replied, getting out a box of cornbread, breathing a sigh of relief that he hadn't caught me in the act of cooking a ready-to-eat meal.

"What are you reading?" he asked, looking at the printout of the article.

"Some chick, she wrote this article and got a lot of backlash. It's for class."

He started reading it, then after the second page, tossed it on the couch and sighed.

"This is why we should only let women write about recipes and fashion."

"Funny," I retorted, pouring the can of soup in the pot.

"I'm serious. Women can't handle this kind of bullying. She probably cried and gave in. I bet she's going to have twenty kids. Or she's already drank herself to death. Do you see Wolf Blitzer doing that? No, you don't. *Women* can't handle criticism."

"Yes they can!" I protested, spinning around. "I've had to deal with a lot of criticism and look how well I've done."

"Yeah," he snorted, "think again. You've turned into a shrewd, manipulative, cynical person with a chip on her shoulder and an inferiority complex."

"Yeah, well at least I'm not an asshole with a passive-aggressive inferiority complex," I retorted, pouring his dinner onto his plate, walking into the bedroom. "Dinner's served," I muttered, slamming the door behind me.

November 14, 6:13 a.m.

Today is my last day of official training before I am on my own on my first flight tomorrow! One of the things I've been worrying most about it making sure I get there on time, because I've seen so many people let go for little things like being five minutes late to training, not completing a health screening on time, or failing an examination. My trainer, Pam, is direct, and there are no second chances. There is no time for me to not have my shit together, or this will cost me big time. One clueless girl came in four minutes late from a break, knocking on the window for someone to let her in the door, and was dismissed during the next round of instruction.

'Damn,' I thought.

I looked at my watch once again and made sure that it kept the right time.

Training has been grueling, but the pressure has made me feel like I'm accomplishing something. I haven't felt this way since I was in school. For once, my house is clean, I haven't needed a drink as badly, and I haven't had any sobbing episodes. The longer I stay away from Troy, the more I realize how much he really screwed with my emotions and made me feel totally useless. I'm amazed I kept *any* job while I was with him.

I've had plenty of time to think about all his stupid insults and the way he treated me. And what did he give *me*?! No extra money, big ass headaches, and never-ending streams of tears. Honestly, the sex wasn't even that great! Mitch was a lot better than Troy ever was.

So, here's my new start. And I know I can do a lot better in the man department. When I get my first paycheck from Southeastern, I'm going to make sure I get my hair highlighted and cut with sexy long layers. I already managed to purchase some eye cream and new makeup with the godforsaken money I've earned doing those long nights at Diamondz.

***

November 14, 11:07 p.m.

Okay! I am tired, but I feel all excited and nervous. I hope I don't embarrass myself tomorrow, especially being the "new girl" on this flight. We will be flying into Atlanta, GA, the hub of hubs, and back. If I do these shorter flights successfully, I will be going the week after on a flight to San Diego, California, which means I will get to pack and spend a night somewhere cool!

"Mom, when do we get to fly? We want to fly to see palm trees!" Emma exclaimed.

They both traipsed around my bedroom listing off all the places they want to see, starting with tropical islands and Disney World.

Tyrell piped up. "My friend Savannah just went on an airplane to Orlando. She told us about the cool parade with lights and the roller coaster that takes off in the dark. She said it's been there since her mom was young, but that it was still cool, even for an antique roller coaster... " he trailed off as I interjected.

"How about you guys tell your dad all about it too? Maybe if he paid me on time and helped out a little more, we could afford a family vacation. He's more concerned with entertaining his red headed post-teenage girlfriend. I will eventually score us a flight or two in the future, but I'm just getting started with this job, so there will be no vacations for a while."

Dismayed, the kids lumbered off into their bedrooms and shut the door, while arguing about whether they wanted go to Disney World or Lego Land first.

I shut the door and stretched out across the bed, while turning one pillow long ways like a blockade. Not quite the same as a man, but it's all I've got for tonight. I should ask Santa Clause for a "personal massager". It's probably not as good as the real deal, but whatever. It might get me through until my sexy uniform scores me a *real* clean cut man with a nice ass and a lead foot.

November 14

```
Soooo...exciting news! You're looking at
the Detroit Recorder's newest feature
reporter! First piece is set to be
published by the end of the month!
#hired #imarealwriternow
```

Almost as soon as I hit enter, my phone started buzzing as the little Twitter blue jay relayed messages of congratulations to my phone.

OK, before I start writing my Pulitzer acceptance speech, I better back the train up just a little bit. I didn't *technically* get a new job, but I'm going to be at least assigned one feature piece a week. I guess they decided it was more economical to let me write every now and then rather than hiring two full-time staff members.

(They already hired one full-time guy. He starts Monday.)

For each piece, I will receive a whopping $35 per 500 words. Before taxes. Oh well, everyone has to start somewhere, right?

I had slipped my resume and a few sample pieces into my boss's, Mr. Broussard, mailbox last week. I had no idea if he even got them. I didn't want to bother him.

Well, I guess he did, because he called me into his office this morning. At first, I wasn't sure if I was going to be in trouble for just putting them out there like that.

"Olivia, hey, come in, have a seat," he said, looking clearly disheveled and harried.

I walked in and hesitantly began to sit down. "Close the door," he instructed.

Oh, great.

'I'm probably getting fired,' I thought to myself.

I closed it and resumed my position, sitting gingerly on the edge of my chair.

"So you want to be a writer?" he asked, opening up a folder and rifling though it. I saw my sample articles sitting on the corner of his desk under a Tim Horton's box.

(He lived in Windsor and brought TH at least once a week. Based on his ample girth, he probably ate half of them on the drive over.) The papers were marked with several coffee cup rings.

"Um, I mean, yeah, but I'm sorry, I shouldn't have bothered you…"

"No, it's fine. We hired one guy, but our budget never really called for two in the East Metro section anyways."

He handed me a job description and W-2 form. "Pay's thirty five for 500 words. I'll assign the first few, then it will be up to you to send me a list of ten potential story ideas at the beginning of the week."

Electronic Journal Oda Mizra

File Name: MPJ-701_Reflection Journal

I wanted to scream, but managed to hold it in and bit down on my lip, trying not to grin like a huge goofy idiot.

He shuffled through his papers, looking confused. "I don't know if you have to fill out a new W-2, or maybe it's a 1099, but you have to fill out this...it's a job description." he handed me both papers.

"Just take those to Rhonda in HR and she'll tell you what else you need."

"Thank you, sir," I squealed, resisting the urge to get up and hug my own personal middle-age, grumpy savior.

He waved his hand. "You can thank me in a year if you haven't jumped ship yet."

He paused.

"You know what I like about you Olivia?"

I shook my head, waiting for a compliment about my writing.

"You're agreeable. You don't make waves, you don't whine. You're a good writer and you stick to neutral, safe topics. We need neutral now after that little debacle last month."

He kept going.

"This isn't Watergate. It's the East Metro features section. Do you think you can stick to writing about sunshine, happiness, and puppies for awhile?" he grumbled, looking for something and then finally opening a drawer.

"Absolutely."

"You're going to work with the new guy. He's...I don't know what I'm supposed to call it....flamboyant? Uh, possibly enjoys an alternate-"

"He's gay?" I offered.

"Yes, but if I say that and HR finds out, I can probably get fired. You're going to like him." He reached down and pulled something out.

"You can share an office with him, but don't get too excited. It smells like old soup in there- and the wheels are broken on both office chairs."

(I know where he can probably get some new ones.)

"So I can expect ten story ideas by Monday morning?" he asked.

"It would be my pleasure," I reached across the desk to shake his hand.

He held the signature red cardboard box out to me.

"Donut?"

I knew it.

November 15

I am so exhausted. I thought this job would be pretty easy, but it's definitely harder than it looks. On the flight to Columbus this morning, I stood up to give the passengers their safety directions, and in the midst of it totally blanked out while holding a seat cushion and showing how to hold it as a flotation device. I was so embarrassed! Any idiot that flew on a plane enough probably could have filled in the blanks for me. I managed to muddle through the rest of the presentation and take my seat while gritting my teeth and cussing myself.

I sat down and wiped my sweaty palms on my polyester flight uniform. On TV, the uniforms always made the flight attendants look sexy. Mine made me look boxy and awkward.

It was right about that time that I took a good look around the plane for the first time. The other flight attendants were a little smug towards me, but no different than anywhere else I've been. At the back of the plane, I noticed Cassandra and Thomas sit next to each other for take off, and it's fairly apparent that they are more than "just friends". She cocks her head, grins and blushes as he whispers something in her ear. I turn to look away, but too late, they saw me looking their way, and then they started to whisper again.

I slide to the side a bit so I'm facing the side and front of the plane, and then start looking toward the front. I

389

heard the pilot and copilot having a conversation up front, but just vaguely.

"Ashley, dude, quit making a big deal about Rice Krispies. Who cares?"

The pilot (I'm assuming his name is Ashley) muttered, "Jake, it's not about the damn cereal, man. I'm engaged to a freaking college kid and she embarrasses me in front of my friends with her 'I'm smarter and hotter than you' antics."

Jake didn't have much to add except, "Well, let me know when she's available. I dig a tall smartass with big tits. Plus Mamie isn't putting out much anymore since she had the baby. I don't know when the last time was that she actually showered. At least your girl's still showering."

Silence.

After the takeoff it was up to do my rounds with drinks and snacks. I was slightly nervous about my weight and running into someone as I passed through the aisles. I passed my physical, despite the doctor warning me that my BMI classified me as 'overweight.' So far I hadn't run into anyone. Drinks handed out, people were acting decent, and I hadn't spilled someone's drink on them yet. There were two college guys sitting together in the middle of the plane...I dubbed them "Bozo #1" and "20-year-old virgin".

"Yes sir, what can I get for you?" I asked nicely, for the third time.

"Something strong," Bozo #1 said.

"I'll take two shots of whiskey on the rocks," squeaked the 20-year-old virgin.

Great. I hope these guys keep it under control....this isn't Diamondz or "da club". I didn't want to have to be a bitch on my first real day here. The other flight attendants noticed them and rolled their eyes. Guess they were leaving the pain in the ass customers to the newby.

Another woman in her early forties, Martha, walked up and patted me on the back. "You're doing fine, Tiff. It will all come naturally in time. You looked a little nervous after you sat down from speaking to the passengers."

"Thanks Martha, I'm feeling fine, a little overwhelmed at times, but great actually. Thanks for checking on me."

Martha walked off to finish detailing the snack cart.

Meanwhile, in the front of the plane, I tried to get a better view of the pilots. I had seen the copilot walk through earlier. He was incredibly young- maybe 25 at the oldest. He was skinny and awkward, with the brightest red hair I had ever seen in person. I hadn't seen the pilot from the front, but did notice his sexy

391

dark hair and nice body from the back. And apparently there's no ring.

I think I'll just forget he said anything about being "engaged." He sounded pretty available to me. Obviously they won't be getting married.

It seemed as soon as we ascended, it was time for the landing. All went pretty smoothly. The pilot and copilot said 'good afternoon' to all of the passengers as they stepped off the plane. Good grief, the pilot was hot! I swear he used to be a member of N'SYNC when he was younger. His hair was clean cut, but just messy enough to be sexy. (Maybe his hairline was receding a *little*, but it wasn't that bad.) I could tell he spent at least some time in the gym, because his pecks looked perfectly toned though his shirt. His face was chiseled, his face just starting to show a five o'clock shadow, and his eyes were blue green, the color of the ocean.

I bet he smells good too.

After all the passengers got off the plane, I wanted to make sure I completed my duties on the plane completely. While tidying up a few blankets and picking up a stray pair of headphones, I couldn't get the latest vision of the sexy pilot out of my mind.

'Just stand tall and make sure to keep my butt poked out just a little...' I thought.

When a guy is unhappy in his current relationship, I know they're keeping their eyes peeled, despite what they say. And, if his girlfriend had stopped trying to make him happy, then perhaps it's time to show him that someone else *will*.

As I stepped off the plane, I made sure to keep the stroll confident and not too slow, not too fast. There he was, and I could see his nametag clearly now.

ASHLEY.

A pretty boy name to go with a pretty boy face. I prepared myself as approached him.

"Hello, I don't think we've met, but my name is Tiffany," I said with a little bit of flirtation and a slight smile.

Ashley looked a bit surprised, but maybe he hadn't had a chance to notice me yet on the plane.

"Well hello," he stammered. "Welcome to the crew...Tiffany," he said as he looked at my nametag.

I blushed as his eyes looked at my chest.

"Did you do the announcements during takeoff?" he asked with a grin and slight chuckle.

I blushed like crazy, but maybe he was just trying to be cute. He was the kind of guy that you blush when you look at. He was just *that* hot.

"Yes, it was my best imitation of Jessica Simpson meets airline stewardess."

He looked a little confused, but politely laughed at my pathetic attempt at humor.

"Well, it was nice to meet you. I'm sure we'll be seeing each other again soon," he said.

As I strode away, I hoped he was watching my backside. Even though the top made me look like a Redwings goalie, the bottom isn't bad. I actually think I look pretty hot in this pencil skirt. At least the jacket hides my extra fluff. I think my new makeup really made a big difference.

(I was also wearing Spanx under my uniform, so that might have had something to do with it.)

November 17

"Oh my gosh, it *does* smell like soup in here!"

At the sound of the voice, I snapped to attention and jumped up, almost tripping on the wheel-less office chair.

The guy walked- I'm sorry, *sashayed-* into the tiny excuse for an office, looking at the industrial metal desk with disdain. If the argyle sweater vest and bow tie didn't give his sexual orientation away, the large potted plant and J Crew bag stuffed to the brim with decorative trinkets did.

Mr. Broussard just stood in the doorway, shaking his head as he introduced me to what I assumed was my co-worker.

"This is your office. You and Olivia will share a desk. She sits on that side and you sit on that side."

"Can I sit on that side?" he asked. "I don't like my back to the door."

I shrugged. "Suit yourself."

Mr. Broussard wasted no time adjourning and promising that he'd be back in an hour and advised us to 'get to know each other.'

"I'm Olivia," I said, extending my hand.

"Nice to meet you. I love your boots! Guess?"

I nodded.

(Yep, he was gay. No straight guy would have known that.)

"I'm Tyler." He looked around, wrinkling his nose. "So this is just horrible, I can't believe-"

"Wait," I interrupted. "Tyler what? I mean, what's your last name?"

"Uh, Winters."

"Oh my gosh!" I shouted, attracting stares from the people out in the office.

"Sorry, got a little carried away." I announced to the general cubicle region. "I just really love his sweater. Carry on."

I lowered my voice and closed the door. "It's me, Oda- I mean, I go by Olivia now."

He dropped his bag to the floor and a South Park bobblehead doll rolled across the floor.

"Oh my God!" He embraced me in a hug. He was still so skinny. "How are you? What are you *doing* here?"

"Oh you know, just living the dream...."

"You look great!" he said, stepping me back and appraising me. "What did you-"

"Well thanks, so do you. So how did you end up here?" I asked, cutting him off.

"Well I worked at the paper in East Lansing for a while after school and then my husband got a job working for Google in Ann Arbor. We live in Dearborn."

"Wow, that's pretty cool," I said, not even acknowledging that gay marriage was still illegal in Michigan.

We got caught up and before we knew it, Mr. Broussard had returned.

"So, Olivia, I want to run with that story about the Lake St. Clair cleanup. Just check to see if anything more has been done on it and then update it as necessary."

"Yes, sir," I replied, standing at attention like the good little agreeable employee I was.

"Don't 'sir' me." He looked at Tyler. "You can 'sir' him. *He* has the snazzy sweater."

His face turned red and you could tell that he was wondering if that was OK to say.

"Uh, there's donuts in my office," he mumbled, closing the door behind him.

Tyler and I both giggled as he left.

"Doesn't he remind you of Milton from Office Space?" Tyler asked.

"Oh my gosh! Yes! Or Ron Swanson from Parks and Rec!" I replied, bursting into laughter.

We spent the rest of the day goofing around and catching up. I mean, the last time I saw him was at my beach house. I had avoided his calls for close to two years before he gave up. We didn't talk about that summer. I figured it would come in time, but for now, we were good to just make small talk.

"Do you talk to anyone from high school?" he asked.

"Yeah, I talk to-" I stopped, abruptly.

"Who?" he asked inquisitively as he arranged his bobbleheads and pictures on his desk."

"Oh no one, just Ranjit Mohapta. He's my dentist."

(That was the truth.)

"You let him drill- your teeth? Didn't he almost lose a finger in shop class when he tried to make a jewelry box?" he asked, raising his perfectly groomed eyebrows.

"Haha, yeah, but he gives me free whitening treatments too."

I picked up a framed photo of him and another man in front of a palm tree.

"So what are all these pictures of?" I asked, changing the subject.

He went through and preceded to tell me in detail about all the vacations he and his partner went on together. By lunchtime, I was only midway through hearing about their 2010 cruise.

"So where do we eat?" he asked, pulling out his monogrammed Thirty-One lunch bag.

(So someone really does buy that crap, huh?)

"Uh, we can go down to the lunchroom," I replied. "I usually just have a PopTart or something at my desk and do homework, but let's go meet some people."

We went to the lunchroom...a drab, gray room that reeked of asbestos and shattered dreams.

"Hey, you," said Nicole, sliding in the seat next to me. "How's your new 'office?' I heard it smells like a dead body."

"Meh, not too bad. This is Tyler, Tyler this is Nicole."

She extended her long, bony ebony hand and shook his.

"How was your weekend?" she asked.

"Not too bad," I replied. "You need to come out with us when you move down here. Doesn't that drive suck everyday coming all the way from Ann Arbor?"

"Yes, but I can't seem to-"

We were interrupted by a cackling noise behind us.

"Uh-oh, looks like the Wicked Witch of the Weightwatchers is back," I muttered.

Our receptionist and her gaggle of morbidly obese cat ladies walked by our table, glaring at us.

"She probably slept with Brousssard," one of them said, quietly enough that she wasn't yelling, but loud enough that I overheard.

"Yeah, why else would she get that job?"

Nicole stood up to say something, but I motioned for her to sit down.

"Are you going to let them say that?" she asked.

I shrugged and broke off a corner of my Pop Tart. "I know it's not true. You know it's not true. Broussard certainly knows it's not true." I paused and took a bite.

"Seriously, having an affair with *anyone* here would mean he'd have to do extra work. I can't see that happening." I swallowed and broke off another piece. "I mean, Sofia Vergara could probably offer herself to him, but he'd bitch about not getting paid for it. Plus, I didn't even get a new job. I got a slightly more private desk and about $50 extra a week."

"Well damn, sign yourself up on sugarmama.com," she joked, digging into a bag of Reese's Pieces. "It's just a matter of time before you'll be making those Oprah dollars."

"They're not worth your time anyways," she continued, glaring at them. "You know you're good and when you're great, there's no need to hate."

That was really profound. I decided that I liked it and was going to use it for this week's reflection journal.

Blame

It's easy to be super nice and easygoing when things are going my way. It's whenever I'm confronted with a challenge that I go on the offensive. I don't know why I do that. I've faced down some pretty tough stuff in my life. I guess I just feel that I've had more than my fair share of setbacks and obstacles. The deck was stacked against me the day I was born, but I overcame so much to make something of myself. I don't know if I believe in an all-powerful deity who controls our fates or destinies. I can't buy into a benevolent God that blesses Dwayne Wade

with the ability to put up 40 points in
a single game, yet lets hundreds of
innocent children and animals die
horrific deaths every day. So no, I
don't blame God. I can't really blame
my parents- they didn't think of how
hard their child would have it growing
up. I'm pretty good about blaming
myself for things I've done wrong.
Heaven knows that I'm a sadist for
self-punishment. I know I take out my
frustrations on other people- but they
are usually the source of my problem.
Even if they're not directly the source
of my problem, I have no qualms
snapping at the first person I see,
perhaps in a manifestation of my anger
at society as a collective. I guess
despite all my accomplishments, I feel
like I'm still trying to assimilate
into society and that I haven't quite
yet been accepted, despite my
accomplishments. And for that, I can
only blame myself.

I had just hit submit and was about to start editing the
massive amount of files that had accumulated in my
inbox when Nicole walked in.

"Hey, I have an idea for a story."

"Oh yeah?" I asked, mesmerized by her hair. She usually
wore it in an afro, like today. She was one of the only
black girls that could pull it off, probably because she
was so skinny. Today, she had a pink flower tucked
behind her ear.

As if reading my mind, she continued.

"Next month's the hair show. It's going to be huge this year. We should do a behind-the-scenes thing, you know...featuring the local hair artists."

I thought about it. "I'll add it to my list. Broussard will go for it. It's non-controversial and upbeat."

She cocked her head to the side, looking confused.

"Never mind," I mumbled, wanting to add, *'I'm supposed to stick to sunshine, rainbows, puppies, babies, and happiness.'*

Plus, I needed the idea. I had three ideas jotted down so far and they all sucked. My phone buzzed and I flipped it over. Krishna.

Krishna: Are we still going to your friend's dealership to look for a new car tonight?

Crap, I forgot I was supposed to accompany her to Jacobi's Imports tonight. She finally got her insurance check.

Me: Hold on, let me check something real quick.

I thumbed through my phone until I stopped at Ashley. I winced when I read our last text. He was bitching at me because I forgot to get energy drinks. I guess I can only blame myself for that one.

Me: When do you get home?

Five minutes later her texted back.

Ashley: I'll be home when I get there.
I'm working. Unlike some people.

I wanted to text him and ask what he meant by that, as I
was clearly sitting at my desk, but I didn't want to start
a fight via text.

Me: OK, well I just wanted to know if
you'd be home by dinner because if not,
I'm taking Krishna to get a new car.

Ashley: Fine. Go hang out with your
stupid friends.

I ignored it and looked up his flight schedule online. He
was scheduled for the evening flight to LaGuardia, so
weather permitting, he wouldn't be home until late.
Great, I was going to get to drive my friend to a car
dealer and spend time with Paul Jacobi tonight.

And they say no good deed goes unpunished...

November 17

I got a good review on my first few days alone in the field, so I have to admit, I'm pretty damn proud of myself. And what's more, I'm about to get paid! I know it's not a big enough salary to go around bragging about, but at least it will put food on my table and keep us from getting kicked out. Better yet, I feel like a real professional.

I did some sit-ups in the living room after eating some cereal for breakfast after I sent the kids off to school. Then I went and used my new Artistry facial scrub in the bathroom and noticed it made my skin brighter.

(One of the girls from high school sells Artistry makeup. It's expensive, but I like it.)

Next, I opened the box of Revlon hair dye. I couldn't take my gray roots any longer, so the box of reddish brown hair dye would have to do. My flight to LaGuardia wasn't until three p.m. today, so I knew I had extra time. Maybe he'll notice me with my sexy new hair color. I decided to post something ubiquitous to social media- let my ex-boyfriends get jealous.

New guy....new hair color....gotta keep it sexy...

Okay, so I finally got the whole "speech at takeoff" thing down. The flight was a little bumpy though, so we had to wait a few extra minutes before the fasten seatbelt signs were off due to turbulence from the windy day.

They said there was a possible threat of a thunderstorm. Eeek. Anyway, so when we were given the go, we started with snack cart. I was so damn nervous. A few times I propped myself up just a bit by pushing one hand on the cart and the other on the headrest as firmly as I could with my arms locked. I was trying as hard as I could to not end up lying in someone's lap.

After that it was just another landing, another round of cleanup, and another opportunity to bypass the pilot at some point before our trip back to Detroit. When I got off the plane, I noticed first of all how huge the airport is. Martha had told me that we have an overlay in this airport for an hour and a half, so just long enough for us to go and grab a bite to eat. She had asked if I'd like to join her at Andrew Carmellini for a bite. I politely accepted, even though I really don't have the money to be eating out right now. Martha and I walked to the restaurant and found two seats at the bar because every table was taken. I ordered an appetizer and she wolfed down a meal for two. Meanwhile, I noticed "Captain McDreamy" at the other end of the bar with his copilot.

He was sitting there with a look of frustration on his face. He kept looking at the beer and was wishing he could down one himself. Then his head was lowered as he sent a text, which I noticed ended with him abruptly shoving his phone back away in his pocket. Following that he grunted and started talking to Jake some more, obviously complaining about something.

Martha and I paid our tabs after some small talk and continued to sip on coffee.

(This coffee was definitely better than the 7-11 coffee back home.)

Correction...Martha talked and I nodded and managed to respond with, "uh huh". My eyes were drawn to those super sexy lips and ocean eyes. We got up and I excused myself and told Martha I would see her back at the terminal. I pulled out my cell phone to check Twitter. One notification- two people liked my new hair color. Okay, well nothing interesting there. Text messages? One from my mother pulling a sudden guilt trip about raising my own children for me free of charge or return favors.

Whatever. I put my phone back in my purse and went to freshen up my makeup. On the way out, I purposefully walked within a few feet from the end of the bar where Ashley and Jake were sitting.

Ashley looked over and said "Hey Tiffany! How's your induction treating you?"

At this point Ashley introduced me to Jake, who gave me a quick handshake and nodded with a cordial, 'nice to meet you' reply. I piped up and said that it was all going pretty smoothly, and I looked forward to checking out new cities at some point with the free flights. Then I pranced off, even though I wanted so badly to stand there and just stare at him. It was at this point that I caught a glance of three other female flight attendants who saw me talk to him. They rolled their eyes at me. Guess they were jealous.

On the plane ride back to Detroit, one of the girls named Julie noticeably kept going to the front to "wait on Ashley". Ashley didn't seem to mind this at *all*. First I saw a soda and pretzels, then another soda, then I saw her put her hand on his shoulder as she laughed and spoke to him. Ugh...what a stupid bitch. That is so obvious.   At least while I'm on duty, I keep it professional.

I noticed when we got off the flight that there was another girl who ran up and handed him his hat and winked at him. I didn't want to appear desperate, so I just tried to do my best to put on a sexy strut and act like I didn't see that. I made it out to the parking lot while keeping my composure.

As soon as I started in my purse for my keys, I felt a hand on my shoulder. It was Ashley.

"So, where are you headed off to?" he asked, the white glow of the parking lot lights framing a halo behind him.

(Is this a trick question?)

"Well, I think I forgot. Can you help me remember?" I joked with a giggle, making a mental note to high-five myself later for being so clever on the draw.

"Well, have you heard of a place called Lucky's? That's where I go sometimes to unwind and it's not too far from here. You look like you could use a little of that treatment yourself. No offense." He smiled and swirled his keys around his finger, his breath fogging up the cold night air.

"Well, I guess I could come out for a *bit*. My mother has my kids tonight... I wasn't sure what time I'd get home."

"You have kids?" he asked, looking slightly surprised.

(Dang, maybe the hair dye *was* working.)

"Yes, two."

"You married?" he asked.

"No, been divorced for a few years now. You?" I asked, pulling my coat closer around me, despite the fact that my armpits were sweating profusely due to my nerves.

"No," he simply stated. I decided not to push any farther.

"Let's get out of this cold. Do you have GPS?" he asked.

"Yes, I know how to get there. Plus it's on my way home, sort of. I live in Grosse Pointe," I replied.

(OK, *that* was a lie, but a block away is pretty much GP.)

I could tell that he was about to offer a ride, but he realized that I had a car. We agreed to meet at Lucky's.

I'm not sure if he's just lonely and wants someone to fill the void, or if he really *is* attracted to me. It's kinda funny he never mentioned his supposed girlfriend, fiancé, whatever. If he did, I would think he would be in a bigger hurry to go home and see her instead of inviting me out to the bar for a drink. And geez, it's been wwaaayyy too long since I've had a drink.

All the way there, my palms were sweating just thinking about what he looks like under those clothes. He had changed into some Buckle jeans and a plaid button up top. He looked super sexy, and he did smell good. I recognized the cologne he was wearing, Polo Blue, my favorite. Mitch wears the same thing. For a second I got turned on thinking about the last night Mitch and I had together, but that son of a bitch never called me after the last time he came over. Way for him to be "there for me."

Whatever, I'm about to have drinks with someone way hotter and more successful. Who's Mitch? Haha. Forget him.

I pulled up and checked my makeup in the mirror. It looked awesome- and so did my hair. I walked in the bar and looked around. There he was at the bar, with an open seat waiting for me. There were small groups of people standing around the bar, some college kids, and some adults in their mid-thirties having their night off from the kids. I walked over and nonchalantly slid into the chair beside him, hung my purse on the hook below, and made sure to keep my phone on silent. I didn't want any interruptions during this date.

410

He started to talk about his coworkers and how they can sometimes take a while to warm up to new people, but not to worry, they will all come around. He mentioned "good ole' Martha", the "one woman welcome wagon".

We made small talk. He asked where I was from, why I was single, and he grinned as I blushed at the mention of being single.

I asked where his girlfriend was, and he looked at me and smirked, "Well, you tell me? Have you seen her? Because I sure haven't."

He took another drink and caustically continued. "Look for the nearest group of popped-collared douchebags and superficial plastics and odds are, she won't be far away."

He took another swig of his beer and put his glass down while checking football stats on the television screens. The Lions and Cardinals had played yesterday and he was mentioning to me how his fantasy team did. He didn't seem to really care that much though. I wonder what he really cared about.

I ordered another vodka and cranberry, but being careful to not get too drunk and say something stupid in front of him. He picked on my "girly drink" and complimented my hair color. "I've always had a thing for red heads, you know."

I remarked, "I thought you said blondes were more fun."
I giggled and he put his hand above my knee.

He turned and looked at me and said, "Yeah, but red
heads are known for being firecrackers. You're a
redhead now, so can you clarify *exactly* what that
means?"

I just looked at him and as seductively as possible
replied, "Well, we know how to fire things up, if that
helps clear up any confusion."

He seemed to like that answer, because his eyebrows
rose up. He took another swig of his beer and loosely
said, "Well, I'd be interested in learning more about that
sometime."

He checked his text as he finished up his beer and
slammed the glass down.

"You good to go?"

His tone changed as he asked it. I assumed it has
something to do with the text.

I went to pay my tab, but he grabbed the check.

"I got it. When you start getting your overtime pay, you
can treat me. Deal?"

I nodded in reply.

As he pulled out his wallet, I got a glimpse of his fiancé. She was beautiful- blonde hair, perfect teeth, smooth skin. She looked just like a model. If I hadn't known better, I'd have thought that it was the picture that came with the wallet.

He walked me to the car and I was so nervous at this point that I didn't know what to do. I wanted to grab him and make out with him. Instead, he grabbed me around the waist, feeling around just a little, and kissed me on the cheek. I couldn't stand it, so I turned my head towards his, and his lips touched mine. They were so soft and supple. I was throbbing. When his tongue touched mine I felt like I might erupt right there! Then he leaned back and whispered into my ear.

"Well, I'll see you later."

In an instant, he was gone, nothing but the scent of Polo Blue lingering on my coat.

November 18

It's fucking snowing out. It's not even Thanksgiving yet. How is this OK? I took my sweet ass time coming into work this morning, knowing full well everyone would be late due to the weather, except for the jackass reporters who get a hard-on every time it snows. Those fuckers wake up at three in the morning just so they can go get shots of the streets before they're plowed.

(They're like the lazy distant cousins of storm chasers.)

I hope Krishna likes driving her new Audi in this crap. I shook my head, laughing to myself as I pulled up on Jefferson behind a car with Florida plates that had slowed to twenty miles an hour. I could see the driver gripping the steering wheel, a look of sheer terror plastered on his face.

We went to the dealer last night as planned. It was a Monday night, so it was pretty slow. When we arrived, the first thing I noticed was the added presence of an evil force...oh wait, that was just Delilah. I guess her and Paul are a thing now?

Great, just what the world needs- a cheap, local version of Kim and Kanye, but with less talent (if that's at all possible).

Carmine and Sanjay were also lurking around, presumably waiting for Paul's dad, Paul Jacobi Senior, to leave.

"I want to spend no more than $23,000. After taxes, title, and fee. I have eight thousand as down payment and I already have financing through my own bank. I want the 2012 Audi A4. You have one in silver, yes?" Krishna asked, business-like.

"Hey, hey, girl, slow your roll, now let me show you what I can get you into," Paul said as he sidled up to her, now in full-on snake oil salesman mode.

She glared at him. She didn't like him and felt little need to hold back.

"You know, my dad owns this place, so I can probably get you a real good deal on something newer...a pretty girl like you needs a car of equal beauty," he spoke in his smoothest voice possible.

Listening to his sales pitch was enough to induce a wave of vomit, but her comeback was epic.

"My dad owns the largest pharmaceutical distribution center in Calcutta. I will gladly get you a real good deal on generic Viagra. We will make a trade, yes?"

Sanjay and Carmine snickered. Delilah opened her mouth, but thought better of it, and closed it.

"OK, let's go look at the Audi," he muttered, glaring at Carmine and Sanjay.

"Let's go wait in Paul's office," Carmine whispered to me. "You *need* to see this."

We turned the corner and walked into his office, which was…I can't even describe it. 'Epic' would imply amazing or awesome. It was definitely awe-inspiring to say the least.

The walls were covered, literally covered, in his football photos- action shots, team shots, articles, and no less than fifteen black and white candids. Behind his desk, a massive trophy case was built into the wall. The case displayed not just an assortment of trophies, but his letter jacket as well.

A giant East Grand Rapids High flag was meticulously fastened to the wall next to the case.

I pursed my lips together, trying not to laugh. I lasted approximately 30 seconds before bursting into a fit of laughter.

I took out my phone. This was going on Snapchat and Vine. Stat.

"No way," I whispered to Carmine. "This is not real life. It's a shrine to…shattered dreams? Missed opportunity?" I looked at him.

"Seriously, help me out here."

Sanjay stood reverently in the middle of the room as if in prayer or meditation before speaking.

416

"I believe this room is a time portal back to 2005, or what is commonly referred to as the 'Era of the Paul.' While President Bush laid the smack down on Iraqi insurgents, Paul did the same with fat kids, 'queers,' and 'homos.' He was convinced that he too would eventually rise to the highest office in the nation. Or end up selling crappy previously-owned cars."

"You're terrible," I said, playfully smacking him and walking around. "Where did he get all these pictures of himself?"

"You're not going to believe this, but he asked the girl who took photos for the yearbook to take a bunch of him and then give him the copies."

"Oh no, I believe that," I replied, looking at his trophies.

Just then, we were interrupted by a rap on the door frame. Paul's dad poked his head in.

"Careful that you don't touch the glass. He doesn't like fingerprints blocking the view of his jersey," Mr. Jacobi joked.

"Oh, I'm sorry, I was just-"

"Kidding!" he laughed, tossing a set of keys at Carmine.

"Brand new 911 just came in. Take a plate and take her for a spin." He looked around. "But if you wreck it, I'm telling the police you stole it."

He winked and put on his coat. "You kids have a good night."

With that, he turned and walked away.

Carmine and I looked at each other, no words exchanged as we raced to the front desk and grabbed a plate. Before Sanjay realized what had happened, we were gone.

Carmine hopped in the driver's seat and I slid in the passenger seat. It was so low to the ground.

"Gentleman, start your engines," he said, as he pressed the start button and the engine purred to life.

"I hope you're ready to drag race this thing with the next middle age man you see," I joked, "because that's all that drives these kinds of cars."

He pulled the brim down on his hat. "Well you're in luck, because for the next hour, I'm forty years old, and *you* are the new hot, young receptionist I met at the hair replacement clinic."

I nodded. "Let's see what this baby can do."

We took off, going just slightly above the speed limit until we got on the highway.

"Oh this thing has an iPod jack," I said, plugging my phone in and scrolling through to my latest playlist. "Let's see if you know this one."

The music started playing and I sang along.

If your trials end, are really getting you down
We had a close call, I didn't even see it, then another one,
I hardly believed it at all.

"Band of Horses, *General Specific*. Too easy. Give me a harder one.

I started to change it, but he stopped me. "No, I like this song."

Knowing up here, there comes a fork in the road,
Pants have gotta go, we're on an island on
The fourth of July, looks like the tide is going home.
In time I'd find a little way to your heart, down to the general store for nothing specific,
Gonna wash my bones in the Atlantic shore - only for you and me

We followed the river north as the lights from Windsor twinkled and sparkled on the water.

"Look, I like your playlist, but we need something more upbeat," I suggested, scrolling through my list. "Check out this remix of Ellie Goulding's Lights. This underground rapper I know from Utah named TreMC did a remix. It's hella tight."

"They have rappers in Utah?" he asked quizzically. "Are there black people there?"

"I think there's a quota, but yeah, they do."

As the song ended, he said, "Nice remix. Now maybe some old school?"

"You got it. How old do you want to go?"

"Way back in the day."

"I don't think you can handle the awesomeness of *my* old school playlist," I slyly replied.

"Try me."

I put on some FloRida. "*Low*, get it...because we're low to the ground, right?"

He rolled his eyes. This isn't old school. That's from 2008. I have the same pair of dress shoes from 2008. Do better.

"Challenge accepted."

This shit is gonna be bigger than the OJ case.
What?
This dick.
Another blast from the Long Beach session...

"Snoop Dogg! *Yes!*"

We high-fived each other and started singing along.

"East side, GPE, is where I claim, fu-"

I turned down the music.

"What did you say?" I asked.

"Uh, nothing."

"Yes you did. You said 'East Side GPE.'"

Realizing that he had been caught, he continued. "We had this thing in high school. We modified the lyrics to rap songs."

I snickered. "Because you were so hardcore?"

"Stop laughing!" he said, realizing that he was laughing himself.

"Did you guys have a *gang*?" I asked, trying to maintain a straight face.

"Yes, we were incredibly hard core. Our colors were khaki and hunter green."

By the time we got back to the dealer, it was almost seven and most of the staff had gone home. Paul and Krishna were standing in front of a Mercedes G-Class wagon. I heard him repeat the word 'financing' several times.

Bored, Carmine and I joined Sanjay and Delilah in Paul's office. Delilah was on the computer, checking her Facebook.

"Ashley Merkel died," she announced with all of the emotion of someone who was reading stock quotes. "Suicide."

Sanjay and I shouted out at the same time.

"Wow! That's horrible!" I said, shaking my head.

"Suck my nuts Jacobi!" Sanjay shouted, making an obscene gesture towards Paul.

I looked at Sanjay. "What are you *talking* about?"

"She was on my list."

"Your list?" I asked incredulously. "Like a list of girls you want to have sex with?"

"Bets on who offs themselves next."

"Are you fucking serious?" I asked, looking from him to Carmine, who looked down in embarrassment. "You guys have a *bet*? On who *commits suicide next?*"

"Uh...."

"It's more like a wager," Paul piped up as he walked in, a visibly annoyed Krishna in tow.

"And I heard you, Choudhary. The people at the Volvo dealership next door heard you," he snapped at Sanjay, tossing a twenty at him. Carmine reluctantly followed suit, avoiding eye contact with me.

I rolled my eyes, refusing to participate in the morbidity that was unfolding before my eyes.

"So guess who I work with? You guys remember Tyler Winters? I work with him now!" I cheerfully interjected.

"Fucking faggot," Paul muttered, handing Krishna a stack of paperwork to fill out. "Initial where it's highlighted on those first three, then sign at the bottom. Is he still a homo?" he asked without missing a beat.

"Uh yeah, he's still gay. That's usually how it works," I replied, still glaring sideways at Carmine. "He's doing great though. He has a life partner and they seem really happy."

"Well, fuck, guess I have to cross him off my list," Paul said. "That leaves Melissa Sorrolis, Tiffany Harris, and Walt Fisher. I already got Maria and Fat Morgan right."

Even Delilah looked disgusted. Carmine and Sanjay looked embarrassed (and rightfully so).

Krishna finished signing her paperwork and we all went out to look at her brand-new car, which she managed to convince Paul to sell to her for $21,000.

(Including tax, title, and fees.)

By the time I got home, Ashley was already home. Dammit. I looked at my phone. What time *was* it? Ten already? Shit.

I opened the door and cheerfully called out.

"Helloooooo! I'm hooooommmmeeee!"

"Shut up, would you?" he piped up from the couch.

"Sorry!" I whispered, backing off.

"God damnit, why can't you just shut up for *once*?"

"Sorry," I whispered again, backing into our room. "You said you weren't going to be home until later."

I laid down on my bed and put my phone in the speaker cradle. I hit shuffle and of course, the first song that came up was Trent Dabbs *"The Odds of Being Alone."* Ironic, huh? I was terrified that Ashley was going to leave me for someone else- someone skinnier, prettier. And I'd end up alone. I shuddered to myself to think that I'd end up back on the "suicide list."

I decided to do something about it. I took off my shirt and walked out into the living room, revealing a purple and black lace bra.

"What are you doing?" he asked, looking clearly annoyed.

"I thought maybe we could...you know..." I tossed my hair over my shoulder as seductively as possible, figuring that he wasn't an idiot.

"Just go away," he mumbled.

"Do I look fat?" I asked, suddenly ashamed to be standing in front of him, crossing my arms over my chest, just now aware of how cold it was.

He didn't answer me, just rolled onto his side so that he was facing the back of the couch.

"Good night. I'm sleeping out here. Turn out the light."

Crying, I went back into the bedroom and laid down, crying even harder. I knew he must have heard me. I knew he didn't care. I could only remember feeling this low once before in my entire life, but then when I was at my lowest, a miracle seemed to happen. I didn't think any miracles would be happening tonight.

November 18

I've been on cloud nine, and all I seem to think about is kissing Ashley in the parking lot after drinks. I'm not sure if he was drunk or tipsy, or if he really remembers. At work, he still holds a cordial face and smiles as usual, but I did see him wink at me a time or two.

I joined the gym down the street from my house and started doing some elliptical and weight exercises. I don't see any improvement yet. I know that I only worked out for fifteen minutes, but those were the longest fifteen minutes of my life. I figure *something* is better than nothing at all. Besides, I think Ashley and these other guys like my curves.

"Mom, why are you all sweaty?" Emma asked.

"Well, I went to the gym," I replied.

"That's just weird. You've never been to a gym before. Why did you go there?" she asked.

"Because I'm tired of being fat. Now go put away your clean clothes and stop making me feel like a slob."

She rolled her eyes, but finally complied.

My house is turning into a wreck again. I haven't really thought much about the dishes. Crap, I don't need my mom on my case again about that. I started putting away dishes and mopping the kitchen floor. I sent the kids to clean up their rooms and vacuum. I think they each put away a sock or two and then went on to complain again about the PlayStation being gone. I ignored them until it got annoying, and then told them to get a job if they want extra stuff.

Jesse was coming to pick the kids up today for the weekend. I wanted to be cleaned up before that happened, especially since the last time he brought his underage girlfriend with him I looked like a total piece of trailer trash. I don't want to give her any ammunition to make any more judgments against me.

I'm so excited because tomorrow we're flying all the way to California! Another crew is on suspension after the pilots landed at the wrong airport, plus half of the flight attendants have the flu, so they're letting me go to California! I can't wait!

As I showered, I made sure to shave everything extra smooth, and after I dried off I made sure to pluck my eyebrows, tidy up my face, and put spray in conditioner on my hair. I wanted to look my best for Ashley. I don't really give two shits about Jesse or his red headed sexpot teenybopper girlfriend. Hopefully he won't see me and claim that he's paying me too much child support money if he sees I'm starting to attempt to take care of myself.

November 19, 9 a.m.
I had my small bag packed and was glad to be at work
with my kids squared away, and finally, for the first
time in a long time, feeling put together and fresh.

'I've got to keep it cool,' I kept telling myself.

I keep hoping that some of the other flight attendants
will talk to me, and some of them have. Others still give
me the stank eye, especially when they see me speak to
Ashley at all. I've overheard some of them ask him
sarcastically about his fiancé, and he tells them to shut
it. None of them seem to like her, and I heard one of
them refer to her as "the whore". Well, that explains a
lot then. No wonder he doesn't feel guilty about being
out with someone else. Eye for an eye, as they say.

Tonight we'll be staying over in San Diego, California.
We're staying in a Sheraton close to the airport, but our
flight tomorrow doesn't leave till noon, so that leaves
enough time to see a sunrise and eat a nice breakfast.
I've only been to a Sheraton once. It was my stepdad's
family reunion in Chicago and it was really nice. I hope
this one is every bit as nice.

7 p.m., California time
The day went as usual, with the routine becoming more
natural. All I could think about were the possibilities
later after the flight landed. I would be so disappointed
if I ended up eating and drinking alone, but I was bound
and determined not to let that happen.

When we all got off the plane, the group decided to go check in and meet at a little restaurant in the Gas lamp district. We would cab it there and cab it back to the hotel. Ashley, Jake, Cassandra, Pam, Thomas, Lindsay, and Katie were amongst the group. Cassandra and Thomas caught a cab with Jake and Katie.

(Yeah, apparently they are a thing now. Katie can see her toes, unlike Jake's wife.)

Ashley, Lindsay, Pam, and I all piled into a second ride. There was normal small talk on the ride, and our happy hour and dinner was casual and relaxed. Everyone seemed kind of tired, and Cassandra and Thomas did their little secret conversation deal as they sat at the end of the bar.

The sunset was beautiful. Ashley winked at me a few times, then turned and continued whatever conversation was going on with Jake, Lindsay, and Katie. Pam had been telling me how proud she was of my quick learning in flight attendant training and asking questions about my kids. She seemed to care more than I did at that moment, because I had something else on my mind. I hoped Ashley wasn't sleeping with those girls too. I don't think so, but they would definitely do so if they had the chance. The little giggles and the head turns- I can tell he likes the attention.

I saw him walk away and pull his cell phone out of his pocket.

"Yes," he said. "I'll be there tomorrow around noon.
You and your stupid friends try to stay out of jail, okay?"

He hung up and put it away quickly. He sounded
frustrated. Must be one of his frat buddies.

Pam and I joined the rest of the small group and stood
for a bit. Lindsay looked strained to speak to me, but
she complimented my hair, and I complimented her too
tall pencil heels that seemed ridiculously like she was
trying too hard. She was divorced too, in her mid-
thirties, and has no kids. You can see the lines forming
on her face, and she acted as though she were so put
together that she may not ever be able to deal with life
being just a little, messy.

It would suck to be so old and alone. I'd probably kill
myself before I let myself turn 30 while still single.

We cabbed it back to the hotel. The group parted ways.
There was a tapas and wine bar down by the lobby, so I
meandered over there and sat at the bar. I had eaten a
little bit, but the Latin inspired tapas looked really good.
I was worried that I may be sitting there alone and
missed my chance, until I turned and saw Ashley
standing twenty feet away. I smiled, looked at him, and
motioned him over with one finger and *that* look- the
seductive one that I had been practicing in front of the
mirror for days.

He wandered over after he saw that the others were
making their way to their rooms or other locations in
the hotel for the evening.

He sat down and said, "Have we met before?"

I laughed and said, "I guess not. I was saving this seat for someone I met out the other night."

He feigned mock disappointment.

"But he's not here," I replied with a wink.

He seems to like this flirtatious banter. He seems starved for a little romance in his life. Every man deserves to feel loved and appreciated.

"Ah, so do you...come here often?" he joked as he played along.

We sat there and I had several martinis. Someone was playing the piano. It was so beautiful. I could hear the waves crashing on the beach. The last time that I heard waves was the day I went to Pelee Island with Cody almost a decade ago. I took the kids to Lake St. Clair quite a bit during the summer, but there were no waves there.

Ashley sat there and drank a few Jack and Cokes. As he seemed to loosen up, so did I. My shirt started to show my tattoo a little on my chest.

"What *is* that?" he asked, moving the collar of my shirt a little bit to the right, my skin almost catching on fire from his touch.

I told him that I had a few secrets that were only to be shown in private.

His eyebrows peaked again.

"Well, then...." He trailed off.

I could tell that he was trying to not act too interested, because isn't that what all guys do? Why did he choose to sit down here with *me*? I think my efforts are paying off. My heart was beating fast, so the more I drank, the better. I didn't want to act nervous in front of him. I didn't want him to think that I'm self-conscious.

After a few drinks, I was giggly and feeling very fun. He put his hand on my knee several times and I noticed once that his hand meandered up just a bit.

I leaned into him and whispered, "You look like you could use a nice backrub, Mr. Pilot. I'm sure *all* that steering must make you *very* tense."

He looked like he was pretty tipsy, closed his tab, and mine, and bluntly said, "Let's go."

OMG....Omg....I was *so* horny. We got into the room and as soon as the door slammed shut it was like my wildest dreams. He kissed me and started yanking off my skirt. I started pulling off his pants and taking off my shirt and bra. He kissed me all over and commented on my sexy tattoos. His hair was so soft and thick...his face looked even sexier in the dark, and his lips!! We made love against the wall, in the chair, on the bed, and finished off

432

with me on top. He screamed, I screamed, and then, total silence. He jumped up to the bathroom and I laid there motionless, feeling like I was high on the best drug ever.

He came out and passed out on the bed. He rolled over, and I rolled over to put my arms around him.

I whispered in his ear, "Ashley, that was so amazing..."

He didn't respond, so I guess he really was asleep. This truly was a dream come true!!! It really is happening! The pilot himself is falling for me! Screw all those other guys, this one is way better looking, has a way better career, and is *way* better in bed!

The morning after came, and I didn't want it to end. He woke up and trudged straight to the bathroom. Geez, is he even going to shut the door? I guess he feels really comfortable around me, so that's cool. He came out and saw me naked in bed.

He said, "Are you going to get dressed, or are you wearing that birthday suit for the flight today?"

"Well, I figured I'd catch more attention this way."

I got up and awkwardly put on my clothes from last night. I gave him a kiss and left the room to go to my own to get ready for the day.

November 19

I'm at work, so bored, and so cold. I'm trying to get motivated to edit this huge piece that I wrote on the budget cuts affecting the Detroit Fire Department (Carmine's idea), but I'm too cold and tired. I hate winter. Ugh, I only have three of these stupid discussion posts left. Today I'm going to write on action, which is super hypocritical of me, as I haven't even gotten up to get coffee yet this morning.

Action

I read action. I know people like sloths. They just kind of plug their way through life, never really doing anything. They say, "I'll do that someday." These are the kind of people who wake up one day and realize that they are 50 or so and haven't really done anything. Then they say "I'm too old. I wish I would have done that."

I've made it my life goal to refuse to be like that. I've always wanted to be a high-profile journalist, so I'm going for it, full speed ahead. I like to think that I attack opportunities in life with the ferociousness of a dog and a new chew toy. Maybe I find out that some of them aren't for me, but at least I can say that I tried. Maybe I've failed a few times, but I don't think that means I should quit

434

trying. I have been rejected for a lot more jobs than I applied for, but that doesn't mean that I stopped applying.

I know it sounds cliché, but I really do live by the idea that you only live once (I'll refrain from #YOLO-ing). The sloth lives a long time, but doesn't really go anywhere or see anything besides his tree (yes, I just Googled "Where do sloths live?"). That doesn't sound like much of a life to me, and the only way to prevent that from happening is to take action every day.

In the grand scheme of things, I wonder if I am taking enough action. This isn't where I thought I'd be at 27.

I still have so much to prove; yet I feel like I'm getting sucked back into the very same world that I tried to rise up and get away from.

Every time that I sit down to actually write or to try to submit my pieces to a magazine, it seems that someone texts me for one of two reasons. Either they want to hang out or they want to gossip. The logical part of me knows that I need to focus on my future, but it's hard when this was the future that I once dreamt of.

Be careful what you wish for. You might just get it, huh?

If that wasn't bad enough, I had one of the news reporters, a young guy fresh out of college who specializes in politics and foreign affairs, pop his head into my office and ask for my opinion on the situation in the Middle East.

I looked up from my computer, annoyed. "I don't know. I'm pretty sure that ISIS is fucking up any chance at democracy and Israel and Palestine are still shooting at each other."

"Do you have any people over there...you know....who you could put me in touch with?" he asked, earnestly chewing on a pencil.

"Oh yeah," I replied thoughtfully. My cousin Ahmed is a goat herder, my cousin Mohammed is a poppy farmer, and my other cousins have all gone to be with Allah after their suicide missions. I might have one or two that designs roadside bombs."

I stared at him with a deadpan expression.

"Is that sarcasm?" he asked, wiping his hands on his skinny jeans.

Ugh, skinny jeans on guys. Ick.

"Yes it was. Christ, I don't know anyone over there and I haven't known anyone for awhile. I'm an American citizen and have been so for quite some time. Everyone in my extended family lives either here or in Pennsylvania. Sorry."

Crestfallen, he walked out of the office, adjusting his stupid hipster glasses and chewing on the end of his pencil. Was I too hard on him?

"Wait!" I called out to him. "Look, I do know some people in the area. They just run an electronics store, so I don't know how much they can help you, but maybe you can take another angle. I don't know- about how there are a lot of good people in that part of the world- Muslim, Christian, and Jew alike- and how they're just trying to live a peaceful existence, yet remain straddled between the archaic misogynistic dictatorships of years past and the hope for an opportunity at capitalism. Maybe?"

I paused as he furiously jotted notes in the notebook he definitely got from Urban Outfitters.

"Not everyone over there wishes death to America. In fact, many wish they could come here, but it's a lot harder to sneak across the ocean than the Rio Grande."

I paused and let that sink in before promising him that I'd send him over the email address of a distant second cousin that still lived in Irbil.

See, I'm not so mean after all.

November 22

I heard bouncing around in the living room, as the kids were banging kitchen cabinets and fighting over who got the last cup of Cheerios from the almost empty cereal box.

"Mom!! All I got was cereal dust!"

Normally, this type of commotion irritates the living shit out of me, but lately, the sky could fall in and I would just stand there in awe and watch. I rolled over and ignored them.

Why are kids always complaining about something? Why can't they be grateful for *anything*? All I wanted to do was have a peaceful morning before going to work. All I could think about was what I was going to wear, and hope that the pimple I had on my cheek last night went away enough to not be noticeable. One week till my next period; I'm glad I'm still "safe" for a little while.

The idea of going to work made me feel like I was ten years old and going to ride the roller coasters at Cedar Point again. I love the way he jokes with me, the way he touches me, his smile…ugh…I am *totally* overwhelmed by my feelings for him.

Ugh, here we go *again*!

But really, I think Ashley is worth the tightness in my chest. I wonder when he's going to break it off with his fiancé? He doesn't seem like the type of guy that doesn't know how to be alone. His confidence is so sexy. How could he not already be married? There are plenty of women around who love to wait on him hand and foot (and service him with a smile).

I spun wheels into the parking lot and whipped into the closest parking space at work.

'Damn, how did I get here?' I thought to myself.

I realized that I had been so preoccupied, that I didn't even remember the drive there at all. I reached for my phone and checked my messages, but there was only one from Jesse complaining about getting the kids earlier than was convenient for him.

Next, I checked Facebook. Should I friend Ashley? No, no, I'll hold off. Guys never like being stalked on Facebook. Besides, I have him face to face, which is much better. I briefly imagine him jumping out the bathroom again, grinning at me and asking me if my birthday suit would be my uniform for the day. Today, I felt my stomach, which felt a little slimmer, by boobs a little perkier in my black lace bra, and made sure to include a matching g-string underneath my skirt.

(We should definitely make sure to add each other on Snapchat though.)

I flipped my hair as I strutted into the front doors of the airport through the blustery wind. I admired my new mini print chevron scarf that draped over my black knee length belted coat. I dug into my purse to grab my

439

lip plumper and slap a coat of that on before heading to my flight. I was so distracted that I bumped into a small child and a fat old man who shouted a few obscenities at me. I wanted to laugh, but I politely apologized and kept hurrying through the terminal toward the plane to prepare.

As usual, Ashley was trying to prepare for his day, while three perfectly groomed females grinned with gleaming teeth and fresh lipstick and perfume, one standing with her hand on her hip and the other holding a cup of coffee, sipping as though she were a model for "Starbucks Meets Fredericks" catalog.

Um, didn't they know that he was *mine*?

I was feeling a bit jealous, but then again, I know that seems to be a part of his job...humoring the ladies.

Preparations and the flight speech came much more naturally than it did the first time that I gave it. There were two cats in crates on this flight in first class that were screeching, and a few annoying babies who were screaming. Their little heads and faces were as red as Fireball candy.

The plane was shaking as I rumbled the snack cart down the aisle. Ashley announced that snacks would have to be delayed again because of the turbulence. This was the first time that I have experienced flying into a thunderstorm. But at least the nervous crowd seemed to be quiet except for the screaming babies. I still hadn't had direct eye contact with Ashley. The other crewmembers went on as usual, but all I could think about was casually catching up with him after the landing.

Was I a one-night stand?

So many thoughts and questions kept rushing through my head. I'm glad I didn't run right up to him earlier as it may have seemed too forward.

Well, the longest flight ever finally came to an end. It seemed to be stressful for everyone. We all had to keep our seatbelts buckled the rest of the way to Chicago.

After landing, the hungry and tired passengers stumbled off of the plane. One guy was barfing in the trashcan as soon as he exited. Thank *God* he didn't puke on me. As I stared at the guy in disgust, I felt eyes watching me. Of course, Ashley was amused by the fact that this dude made me feel like I was gonna puke as well. No matter the situation, his eyes and smile were all I needed...

Dinner came and went for our little group of weary, beat down airline attendants. Southeastern announced that the return flight would be delayed until morning since it was already too late. It was raining like crazy outside, and no one wanted to go out and weather the storm.

This time Ashley casually walked toward the bar, nodding and urging me to follow and have a seat. I'm pretty sure it was obvious to his copilot, who seemed delighted to see Ashley eyeballing me up and down. He muttered something under his breath to him before he walked away. I slowly slid onto the bar stood beside Ashley, with my elbow on the table propping my chin as I stared at him with a playful look. He put his right hand above my knee, turned to look at me, and looked at me while raising his eyebrows repeatedly.

"Is that secret code for something?" I asked, hoping that my hair didn't look too stringy and my makeup still looked fresh.

"Maybe," he answered slyly, grinning and winking at me, my heart melting as he did so.

I noticed the way he looked me up and down. My mother says that kind of look is the true sign of a womanizer, but I find it to be a compliment. It's a silent stamp of approval. I wanted so bad to stay with him, but I didn't want to be the one to bring it up. We sat there, with a beer and a martini between us, and things got quiet. I heard his phone buzz a few times in his pocket. He pulled it out and sent a quick text, rolled his eyes, and put it back in his pocket.

After our drinks were empty, he looked at me, told me to grab my bag and follow him.

"Where are we going?" I asked.

"We're going to get you a nice, warm shower, if that sounds good to you..."

It did. I didn't need to be asked twice.

The shower was steaming as he slid my g-string down with his teeth. I had already unbuttoned his shirt, removed his undershirt and boxers, and nibbled at his ear. He reached his hand up and grabbed me while he finished sliding off my panties, afterward using them as a slingshot across the hotel room. In the shower he washed my hair, running his hands through my hair, touching my face, my lips, and then grabbing my ass to bring me closer to him. His chest felt so good, so manly, just right. I wanted him so bad right then, but I made him wait until we got out the shower. He dried me off, limb by limb, while kissing me deeply. I tried to do the same for him, but he abruptly pushed me into the bedroom, on the bed. It was even better this time- better than it had ever been. I crawled on top of him, trying some different positions. He seemed to like watching me from behind. We made love over, and over, and over all night long in between spats of passing out on each other.

November 27

I'm still not sure whether or not I'm happy, sad, or relieved. I'm sitting on the guest bedroom at my parents' house in Chicago. It feels really weird and formal, like a hotel room, but with cat hair on the bed. They sold or boxed up all of my stuff. Taline and Zako's kids each had one of their own bedrooms down the hall. I could hear them snoring through the high-tech baby monitor/intercoms my dad had installed in each room. I tried to turn it down, but could still hear them. I put on some music and lay down on the bed.

I couldn't even say "my bed" because it wasn't. This wasn't my bed, my room, or in any way identifiable as mine. There was no pink wall, no posters or trophies, no stuffed animals, just sterile white walls and generic Bed, Bath, and Beyond sheets and comforter. What an end to a day.

Kylie and I left Detroit at about four, hoping to make it here by eight. Wishful thinking. About 200,000 other people were also trying to make it to Chicago by eight.

"Where do your grandparents live?" I asked as we passed Ann Arbor on I-94.

"Chicago. I have the address. I'll put it in my phone."

"Well please put it in now," I asked. "Chicago is huge. Is it one of the suburbs?"

"Maybe," she said, fumbling through her purse looking for the address.

"Great," I sighed, exasperated. "They probably live in freaking Springfield or something."

I passed a minivan on the right.

"Passing lane only!" I shouted.

"Calm down, we'll get there."

"I don't want to hit any traffic," I said as I flipped off a Prius going 55 in the middle lane.

"Where's Ashley? Wasn't he supposed to come with you?"

"Uh, yeah, he was. Until two of his coworkers landed at the wrong airport."

"That was people he knew?" she asked. "Didn't they land 100 miles away?"

"Uh, yeah, so the whole flight crew is on suspension pending investigation."

I couldn't really be mad at him for that. Things had actually gotten better in the last week or so with us and I was really sad that he couldn't come back with me. But it was no one's fault.

(Other than the pilots who were too busy tweeting to
notice that they overshot the airport.)

I was just inside Indiana on the twenty-odd mile stretch
of highway around Michigan City that skirts Lake
Michigan when it happened. The flashing red and blue
blinded me as the cop pulled up behind me. I looked at
the speedometer- 80 mph. Holiday weekend. I was
fucked. I had no idea how badly until I rolled down my
window.

Without looking at the cop, I handed my ID and
registration over.

"I know, I know. I was speeding. Let's just get this over
with," I sighed, his flashlight blinding me.

I heard him whistle. "Well Miss Olivia went and got
herself a BMW, didn't she? Let me guess. Rich
husband?"

I looked up at him. "What the hell? That's none of your-"

He lowered his flashlight, revealing the shiny badge
emblazoned "Officer Montoya."

No freaking way. When was the last time I had seen
him? I scrambled to think of it, but could only focus on
one thing.

*It was the spring after I had just turned 21. I was at some
Cinco de Mayo party at a frat house next to the football
house, where Jeremy was still living. By now, Jeremy was*

finally in his senior year and in the middle of training for his Detroit Police entrance exam that he was set to take in the spring.

I sat on the edge of a railing on the porch as I listened to Aubrey yammer about something useless. Taline was down visiting from community college. She was honing in on Ryan Young. She could have him. And his herpes.

I looked into my red plastic cup, trying to assess what kind of beer it was so I could add it into my calorie counter. I was at 785 calories for the day. I had made margaritas with low-calorie mixer, but I left them at Jeremy's house. I saw Jeremy come out and motion for Taline to follow him into his room, which she willingly did. I don't know why, but it stung.

Why did I care who Jeremy dated or hooked up with? I didn't have any mark on him. I felt tears well up in my eyes and I was about to leave when this frat guy named Steve came down.

Steve was one of the only frat guys I could tolerate. He, Jeremy, and I had a class together. He had promised burn us some song files and compressed them onto zip drives for us.

"Where's Jeremy?"

"I don't know and I don't care," I mumbled, straightening out my dress and adjusting the pink sash that went around the middle. "I'm leaving."

"But don't you want-"

"Yes we do! Steve man, what's up!" I heard Jeremy shout behind me.

"Hey, I'll be up in just a sec. Gonna drain the snake. See if Olivia wants another beer."

Annoyed, I rolled my eyes and followed Steve to his room.

He closed the door and wiggled his mouse, waking up his computer.

"So I have a treat for you. You're gonna love this band. Girl Talk. They do these awesome mash-ups."

He started the playlist as Jeremy walked in. He was right, they were good. I tried not to look at Jeremy.

Why was I mad? I had no right to be mad.

About 20 minutes later, Jeremy and I walked out, zip drives in hand.

"Fucking whore, she was in there with both of them?" I heard a girl ask.

"Stupid slut," her friend chimed in.

I recognized them from another sorority, but didn't know their names. I just kept my head down, face burning with misplaced shame, and kept walking until Jeremy grabbed me by the wrist and pulled me back.

"What the fuck did you say?" he asked them.

"Oh, Jeremy, hi, how's it going?" the first one stammered, batting her eyelashes.

"Shut up, Michelle. You too, Britney. Do you even know this girl?" he asked, still holding my wrist.

I looked down, averting my eyes. "Just stop, it's not worth it. They-"

Ignoring me, he continued.

"She's the sweetest, nicest, smartest girl you've ever met. You'd know that if you ever talked to her. In fact, you should. Olivia could teach you a few things about being a decent human being. She's a way better person than you're ever going to be- the two of you combined. She's prettier- both inside and out. Now you two can shut the fuck up."

All three of us girls stood there with our mouths open. I had never had someone say something that nice about me in my entire life.

Jeremy could tell I was about to cry, so we headed back to his house where I sat down on the bed and burst into tears.

"Why did you do that? You didn't have to."

449

"Because I'm your best friend. I love you and I'll always defend you from your worst enemies. Even when that enemy is yourself."

Shocked, I sat on his bed in complete silence before finally speaking up.

"I'm fine. Thank you for defending me. But now they're going to think that we hooked up."

"And that would be the worst thing in the world? To think that you and I could possibly be in a relationships?" he retorted, tossing the thumb drive on his desk.

"You probably better go see what Taline is up to. I'll leave you two alone," I mumbled, standing up while avoiding eye contact with him.

"What do I want with your sister?"

"I don't know. You tell me. You were the one who was with her earlier, not me."

"Yeah, because she made me a playlist. I texted her earlier in the week. I can't figure out that shit on the magic Google machine you call a computer. I wanted to surprise you, so she helped me."

"Wait, so you didn't sleep with her?" I asked, still fighting back tears.

"We were gone for ten minutes. It took two minutes to cross the lawn. Do you really think I'm that bad? Come on, give me some credit."

Through tears, I responded, "I don't know, I guess not..."

"I love you Olivia. I've loved you since the day I met you when you were 14. I just didn't know it yet I don't care if you're 100 pounds or 500 pounds. I want to try this. For real. Let's give it a year," he said, moving closer to me and putting his arm around me.

"And what happens after a year?"

"Then I'll marry you. And we'll live happily ever after.

I tapped my fingers on the steering wheel, unsure of what to say. I drew in a sharp breath.

I couldn't think of what to say, so I said the first thing that came to mind.

"It's a 2007 model, so it's not that expensive. I'm not married yet- I'm engaged though. Yourself?" I asked, the wind biting at my ears and nose.

This was definitely going down in the record books as the most awkward traffic stop ever.

"Yep, married- wife and two kids." He pulled out his wallet and showed me a picture of a homely looking blonde woman and two toddlers. "Indiana Highway Patrol now for five years."

"That's nice," I said, unsure of what else to say.

"Well, uh, just slow down, OK?"

"Yeah, I will. Don't worry."

"Take care, Olivia."

"You too, Jeremy," I mumbled.

■■

I adjusted the pillows below my head and propped myself up on my elbows. I reached under the pillow and tore off the tag.

$8.99 at Target.

I threw it on the floor and turned on my side.

I found myself wondering about Jeremy. What was he doing tonight? What was his life like? Was he happy? Did he make his wife playlists? Did he still joke around with his cheesy pickup lines? As I drifted off to sleep, I found myself too tired to even care about his snide "rich husband" comment.

November 28 (Thanksgiving)

Well at least I'm thankful that today's over. I spent all of today listening to my mom bitch at me about my failure to live up to her impossibly high standards. Fuck that.

I woke up and drove downtown for a Turkey Trot that I had registered Ashley and I for. I wistfully looked at the t-shirt that they gave me for him, missing him as I ran through the early morning sleet.

I had even bought us matching sweatshirts from Downwithdetroit.com. Mine said "Hand Made" and had a picture of the mitten where the 'a' in 'hand' was and a picture of the Ambassador Bridge where the 'a' in 'made' was. Ashley's was a mock vintage Tigers sweatshirt made to look like the ones from the 1970s.

It was freezing and by the time I got home, I was ready for a nice hot shower. Of course, my sister and brother were already there with their respective significant others.

Great, just great.

I walked in, the smell of Chamusta and Kubeh simmering on the stove already. We always made it a point to blend traditional American Thanksgiving treats with Middle Eastern dishes. No matter what, I could always count on my family to have dates and chickpeas and any holiday celebration.

I mumbled hello, and went up to take a shower. I had turned on the water and was letting it steam up the room because I was still shivering and not in any hurry to remove my cold, damp clothes. I heard Taline's voice from downstairs.

"Where's Ashley?"

My mom must have responded that he was working.

"She should have just married Jeremy."

I pressed my ear to the door to hear more.

I couldn't hear my mom's reply, but Taline's came through loud and clear.

"Well now look at her, she's a total cliché- almost a spinster and her fiancé isn't even spending the holidays with her."

I recoiled in horror and stepped into the shower, not wanting to hear more. What right did *she* have to judge me? I began scrubbing at my skin until it became red.

Jeremy broke up with me that following fall. I didn't even remember his reasons, but they were something to the tune of the idea that he could do better and we ought to not waste each other's time anymore.

'We should quit while we're ahead' were his exact words. I didn't speak to him again.

After him, I dated some guy named Wes, but broke up with him because I wanted something more. I wanted to leave Michigan, if only for a while. I knew what kind of life I'd have with Wes- that would be a cliché in of itself. I would end up back in Warren with two kids while he worked as a logistics manager in a factory, moonlighting as a security guard in an effort to save up for a four-wheeler or something. That was no kind of life. He was obviously devastated when I told him, but clearly he got over it. It probably all worked out for the best, but I'll never forget the sadness when he showed up at my apartment to get his stuff.

I noticed a bandage on his arm.

"You got blood drawn today?" I asked.

"Yeah, I had my physical for work."

"How'd that go?"

"Well, my TB test came back that I had possibly been exposed to TB, so I had to go for a chest X-ray. When the nurse ran the machine over me, I told her to look for a broken heart too."

I sat on the edge of the tub, kicking my niece's plastic duck to the side. My whole family sucked. I made one decision for myself and judging by the way they reacted, one would have thought that I ended up in rehab or jail.

I finished my shower, dried off, and headed downstairs. I tried to avoid my family for the rest of the day until we all had to sit down for dinner, where I was met with the usual barrage of questions.

"Why don't you have a better job?"

"When are you getting married?"

"Why don't you have any kids?"

This continued until my niece thankfully vomited everywhere, thus ending my misery. I'm so glad I'm going home tomorrow.

(I'm taking it incredibly slowly through Indiana.)

November 28-

I was so excited. Buffalo is the perfect place to spend an overnight for Thanksgiving. Ashley had already hinted before the weekend about wanting to make sure my turkeys are stuffed right, which is the absolute worst pick up line I've *ever* heard, but he keeps it going and said he would make sure to bring the gravy. He seemed more relaxed than he usually does, like this is vacation for him.

He had texted me this morning as I rolled out of bed and asked if I wanted to grab a coffee at a Starbucks down the street from the airport before going to work. He had been texting me more lately asking me things like "what am I wearing" or for a naked pic. My reply to his invitation for coffee...

"Why are you there when you could be here laying with me and helping me wash my hair?"

He replied, "I will be helping you shampoo your hair tonight, after you polish my hard on.

Guys- they really don't beat around the bush I guess.

After work, I could hardly contain my excitement. He approached me after we left our duties and I could tell he really wanted to kiss me, but he kept it to himself. His phone kept buzzing in his pocket, but this time he ignored it.

I asked him, "Do you need to get that?"

"Nope," he replied, turning it off.

We ended up at a little diner near the airport where we ate a big breakfast and had coffee. I think the built up sexual tension kept the conversation short and dinner fast. He grabbed for the bill, threw down a $20 in cash, jumped up, and we flew through the door.

When we walked into the hotel room, there was a romantic surprise waiting for me, roses, wine- the whole nine yards. Were we falling in love? Each night we're together is more exciting than the time before it. Hot showers, our hands rubbing every inch of each other's bodies, and intimate and hot sex.

It was too silent so I decided to put on some music. I plugged my phone into the iPod dock on the hotel nightstand. Of course the first song that came on was Dierks Bentley's "Drunk on a Plane." Oh, the irony.

He was rubbing my back when I decided to broach the topic.

"So are you sad that you can't be with your fiancé for Thanksgiving?"

I was a little disappointed in his reply. I expected him to say that he wanted to have nothing to do with her, but his response was very different.

"Kind of," he spoke, absentmindedly running his hands through his hair and over the tattoo of a sun on his shoulder.

"I mean, we do have fun sometimes. We always do a Turkey Trot, then we come home and she tries to impress everyone with her drink-making skills, which solely consist of pouring lots of liquor into coffee. Then she tries to dress her nieces, nephews, and parents' dog up as elves and take pictures. It's completely ridiculous, but everyone gets a good laugh."

I didn't know what to say, so I remained silent.

As if reading my mind, he piped up.

"But now I'm here with you, and that's all that matters."

However, this time after we were done, he abruptly rolled over and fell asleep.

December 3

Tonight was a disaster of epic proportions. I invited Ashley out to Marissa's birthday party at the Avalon. It was the same people as were with us just a little under two months ago- Kristoff, Delilah, Chelsea, plus Carmine and Sanjay and a few of Marissa's other friends. The night was fairly normal, and Carmine and Sanjay actually made an effort to be nice to Ashley despite his apparent distaste towards them. By eleven, he was so angry that I begged off, saying we had to get up early because my parents were coming into town.

"What was wrong with tonight?" I asked as I teetered on my heels trying to walk as fast as him, occasionally slipping on the ice. "Were my friends not tolerable?"

"Your friends are morons," he replied, turning the radio up. "I don't care what some idiot 25 year old girl thinks of me. You've set the bar real low for you friends," he scoffed.

I reached to turn down the radio, but I paused.

"Is this country? Since when did you start listening to country?" I asked.

"I don't have to answer to you," he snapped back, yanking the wheel to the left to avoid a pothole and sliding on the ice momentarily.

"Can you please be careful?" I asked, gripping the "oh shit" handle. "I'd like to make it home in one piece."

"Just shut the fuck up."

"So is that it? If I ditch Marissa, Carmine, Delilah, and Sanjay, will I be good enough for you then? I'm so sorry I don't hang out with your friends' wives in their *perfect* houses with their *perfect* children and their perfect lives," I spat out, starting to cry. "Is that what you want?"

"It would be a start," he muttered, turning on our street.

We got home and he immediately sat on the couch and turned off the TV, effectively shutting me out.

Resigned and too tired to fight, I made myself a bowl of ice cream, pouring a generous amount of Sanders hot fudge on it.

(Calories be damned.)

As quietly as possible, I went in the bedroom, turned on my iPhone, and synced it with my wireless speakers, searching for my depressing playlist, which I had been listening to all too frequently. By the time I had changed into my pajamas, I had already hit repeat twice on *The Head and the Heart*.

While you're sitting alone, in your room on your bed, and your windows are open but you won't go out- no, heaven go easy on me.

I lay on my side, clutching the pillow to my chest, the remnants of the hot fudge sauce licked clean from the bowl. I saw two texts from Marissa.

```
11:14 p.m.: R U OK?
11:23 p.m.: Thx 4 coming. TXT tomorrow.
11:38 p.m.: Srsly. Let me know u made it
home
```

I ignored the phone, turned it on silent, and curled up in a ball. I knew I couldn't tell her why I had to cut her out. Carmine, maybe. I could make up some B.S. about having feelings for him, yada yada, which might not be a *total* lie.

I picked the phone back up and looked at it like it was a Magic 8 Ball and it was going to provide me with some direction, someone to call at least.

I realized how alone I was. My fiancé had completely shut me out of his life. My parents barely knew I existed anymore. To talk to one of my friends would violate the trust between Ashley and I, and it would expose a weakness that I wasn't ready to expose yet. I scrolled through my list....Abbie, Adam C., Adam K., Adriana, Ansley, Anthony, Antoine...

344 contacts, yet I had no one I could call or text when I was sad. What kind of life was that? I choked back tears and put my phone back. I set my alarm for five and turned on the nightlight out of habit, knowing that Ashley would probably opt to sleep on the couch again

462

rather than be forced to spend the night sharing a bed with me.

December 3

I'm kind of bummed out. Jesse had the kids tonight, so I invited Ashley to come over, but he declined, stating that he had a function to go to with his stupid fiancé. He didn't even want to go. I just don't get it. Why is he still *with* her? Is it because he needs a place to live? He could totally live here. The kids would love him.

I sat down and poured myself a glass of vodka. I wondered if I hadn't started drinking so heavily if I would have gotten into the mess that I did after Darnell. I mean, he *did* cause me to end up the way I did. He left me- and *our* baby. Ashley doesn't seem like the kind of guy that would do that. He seems super responsible- and I bet he'd make a great dad.

Darnell should have never been anyone's dad, at least not at that age.

After Darnell and I broke up, I found myself spiraling down a rabbit hole. I was dancing a few nights at the club, but I rarely got Friday and Saturday night shifts. I was barely pulling $80 a night. I was getting some help from the state, but they just gave me food stamps and a small monthly cash stipend.

It was a slow Thursday night and I had only made about $20 so far- and that was before I even paid the house fee.

A group of guys came in and sat down at a table. They were all pretty tall, but definitely not NBA. Three were white and two were black.

The tallest one- a goofy looking white guy- flashed some cash and I came over.

"You want a dance?" I asked as seductively as possible.

"Yeah, sweetheart, what's your name?" he asked with just the slightest hint of a southern drawl.

"Corrine," I answered as I straddled him and placed my arms around his shoulders. (It was the best name I could come up with.)

"Well Corrine, let me tell you this. You are beautiful. What's a girl like you doing working in a place like this?"

I blushed. No one had called me beautiful since I had my son. "I....um..."

"You know, we host some...uh...private parties," he stated as I turned my back to him and showed him my thong. "We pay pretty well. Two hundred a night, minimum."

Abruptly, I turned around. "Really?" I asked.

"Yes, really. Now, my name is Jacob and this here is Jason, Marcus, Josh, and Dwayne. We all played basketball together at college, and now that we're retired, we're in the party and event planning business."

His friends all nodded in unison.

"So what do you say? Can I get your number and maybe we meet up for dinner tomorrow? My treat?"

I put down the glass. It sounded so familiar. It all started the same- even with Ashley. Dinner. Drinks. My treat. And look how it ended up?

'Stop that, Tiffany,' I keep telling myself. *'Ashley is different.'*

I hope that little voice in my head is right. In the meantime, I am feeling pretty damn beautiful right now- or maybe it's the vodka talking. Either way, it's time for a new Facebook profile pic. I turned my phone's camera to face myself and smiled, taking a few pictures until I got the right one.

There, that was it. I posted to Facebook, Instagram, and Twitter. #selfie #brandnew me

Within 30 minutes, I had over 50 likes. The people have spoken.

December 10

I can't believe that Ashley says he doesn't have a Facebook. That's just sketchy if you ask me. Seriously. Everyone has one. He claims that he doesn't like people up in his business.

I logged on to mine. Time to post a new picture. I scrolled through my phone and found a great one with the kids. It was a bit blurry, but it would do. I posted it and got several likes within minutes.

Great, Facebook changed their damn layout again. I can never keep track of where stuff is. I began scrolling through the "People You Might Know" section.

'Whore, whore, slut, jerk,' I mentally thought to myself as I ignored them. 'Skank, asshole- Olivia Mizra?'

Wow, she was on here. I clicked on her profile pic. It was a group of people- I couldn't tell which one she was. They almost all had dark hair and were standing outside in thick coats during the winter. I hit the 'add; button and Facebook asked if I'd like to send a message. I thought about it and began typing.

```
Oda (or I guess it's Olivia now),
Hey, how are you? I hope you're doing
well. I know it's been a long time. I'm
sure you're really successful and
living in California or New York or
something. Probably New York because it
looks cold in your picture. Anyways,
```

I'm doing good. I'm a flight attendant. I still live in Detroit- right across 8 mile from Grosse Point on West Beverly. It's right across from that house on that we used to think was haunted.. (They actually tore it down and built a 7-11 there.) Mine's the little yellow one.

Anyways, I hope you're doing good. Hope to hear from you soon. Take care.

Tiffany

I read it again. Heartfelt, but sincere. It was the best I could do. I hoped we could put the past behind us and be friends again. I bet she was the kind of person who travelled for business. Maybe we could go on trips- she'd use her frequent flier miles and corporate account and I'd use my free flights. I pictured us vacationing in Hawaii together- her and her husband and Ashley and I.

I dozed off with the image in my head of the four of us laughing and drinking martinis on the beach as she told us about whatever computer program she had just invented or whatever she did. Someday we'd mention the silly bullshit, but that was all in the past now.

December 13

I can't believe that Brandon is such an asshole. He needs to stay the fuck out of my business and start minding his own. We had all gone out for Paul's birthday last night when Brandon accosted me as I came out of the restroom.

"What are you doing with Carmine?"

I looked around, realizing that we were alone. "What are you talking about? I'm about to bring him a shot."

"You're playing these games with him...and you have a fiancé. Are you such an attention whore that you can't stand not to have guys ogling you?"

"What the hell are you talking about?" I whispered at him. "We're just friends."

"Bullshit. You're the kind of girl who can't stand to have a guy on standby at all times. You need to know that if things don't work out between you and your man that you've got Carmine as a backup plan."

"You have no idea-" I interjected, but he cut me off.

"You...you stupid...cliché...center of attention. If you think that he's interested in being 'just your friend,' then you're an idiot. You're one of those girls who's gotta have a whole *starting lineup* on standby just in case she ends up single. Hey, at least Carmine's the first draft pick, right?"

"Get out of my way," I said, pushing him to the side. "You don't even know me."

"Oh yes I do. Come on, I know a million girls like you. You've got something to prove, don't you? Well guess what? You're not alone? You know I had to prove-"

I turned around and rolled my eyes. "Oh geez, let me guess, that you grew up in the hood and now you're doing *so* much better than everyone you grew up with. Is that it? Because that's pretty played out. And your teeth are too straight to have grown up in the hood."

He stood perfectly still and just shook his head.

"My dad and both of my brothers were military officers. One has the bronze star. The other died a few months ago- killed in action. I have that to live up to. Yeah, life's a bitch. Kinda like you."

He said a few other things that really stung and pretty soon, I really wanted to leave. Luckily, Paul ended up passing out and Carmine, Brandon, and Delilah took him home. We went to another bar where I had to deal with another gaggle o' douches. At least it fit in well with this week's assignment for class.

Judging

I know my post is late and that has a bit
to do with why I picked this story. I do
not have a valid excuse as to why I didn't
post last night. I'd rather lose some
points and tell the truth.

I was sitting on my couch, crying, and
listening to the Twilight soundtrack until
four this morning, texting with my best
friend who was doing likewise at her house.
You see, yesterday I was the judger and the
judgee. My participation in the former
resulted in instant karma in the latter.

I was at some bar and a group of guys we
know were talking to my girlfriends and I.
The long story short was that this
incredibly good-looking guy was talking to
me. I figured he was the kind of guy who
girls threw themselves at (just based on
his physical appearance) and trying to make
his way through all of the female
population of the city. I was kind of
snotty with him. I guess I figured he
expected me to worship him like everyone
else.

We were getting ready to leave and his
friend came up and just lit into me. He
said, and I quote, because this probably
will not leave my memory for a long time,

"Look at you- you're the most pretentious person I've ever met. You think that everyone should worship you. You're not even all that pretty. You're artificially pretty. Binging and purging has it's perks, huh?"

I tried to interrupt him, but he continued. "If daddy hadn't bought you a nose job, no one would even know you exist. I'd hate to see what you look like without makeup on. You're an artificially pretty seven at best, so get over yourself."

I was shocked and obviously laid into him. I left, but as more and more texting went on between people, several things came to light. First of all, I do not have any eating disorders, nor have I ever had a nose job. I have zero idea where this guy came up with that. Second, I didn't really know the guy that I was judging. He had just been through a terrible loss and I didn't even think of that. Third, my friend had just told that guy that she was not at all interested in him. He believed that this was my fault because I somehow tell everyone what to think. (I wish I had that power.)

Then an all-out Twitter fight ensued between approximately six people.

I was just devastated and really hurt by those comments, but more importantly, I realize I've said much worse to people in flippant retaliatory statements. I learned an important lesson last night. No one in the group was innocent and everyone got hurt. We all judged and got judged in return. None of us are bad people, I don't think.

I've never really been judged this unfairly and this was a wake-up call for me. I really hope that I can keep my judgments in check in the future and be more considerate of others' feelings.

As soon as I turned off the computer, I looked down at my phone. I had a Facebook notification and missed call from a 219 area code. Where was that?

I looked at the Facebook notification first. Friend request and message from Tiffany Harris. Great, let me guess- she is trying to befriend me so she can sell me diet shakes or whatever she does for a living? I clicked on her message, rolled my eyes, and promptly ignored her request.

I Googled the 219 area code. Northern Indiana. They didn't leave a message, so it could have been a telemarketer, but they wouldn't be calling so late. I hit redial and a man's voice answered.

"Hello?"

"Who is this?" I asked, not bothering with pleasantries.

"Jeremy."

"Oh hey," I said, relaxing. "What are you doing? Wait, how did you get this number?"

"You haven't changed your number in almost 10 years."

He was right, I hadn't. I was just surprised that he kept it.

"So I'm going to be in Detroit for a work thing next week and I was wondering if maybe you wanted to meet up. I'm staying at the casino downtown."

"Oh yeah, sure," I said, caught a little off-guard. I thought he hated me. Guess not. I agreed to meet up with him on Monday night. That should be interesting.

December 15

I have to say that tonight was not at all what I expected. I showed up at the casino, which was actually more just like a hotel and convention center with a few low-stakes roulette tables. I contemplated parking in valet, but found a clutch street spot instead. Just saved $15.

I texted him to let him know that I was in the lobby. Within a minute, he appeared. He still looked as sexy as ever- his jet black hair was cropped close to his head and his muscled bulged through his shirt. I hadn't gotten a good look at him the other night when he was shining his stupid flashlight in my eyes.

We went to eat in the restaurant in the hotel. We both ordered Long Islands. They were strong. After about an hour of small talk, he asked me the most brutally personal question that anyone could ask in my opinion.

"So are you happy Olivia?"

"What?" I asked, practically spitting out my drink. "Of course I am! I've got a good job, a great fiancé, a nice car-"

"You looked down when you said that."

"What's that supposed to mean?" I asked defensively.

"You're lying."

"Oh, so you're a *shrink* now?"

"Actually about to take my detective's exam. They teach us signs of deception in the first week of the course."

I rolled my eyes and motioned for the waitress to us another drink.

"Whatever," I mumbled, shaking the ice in my glass. "If you're so happy, why do you care how I am?"

"I didn't say I was happy."

I looked at him, not even caring if his crappy CSI training would register my shock. "Why not? You've got it all- I mean, a wife, kids, probably a house."

He shrugged. "I did what everyone else wanted me to do. And let me tell you, you spend your life living other people's dreams and it doesn't make you happy."

"Well duh," I said as the waitress dropped off our drinks. "My parents can go screw themselves. You remember how much I used to want to please them, right?"

He laughed. "Yeah, I remember when I first met you- you were 14 and told me about your mom's life plans for you. You were so determined not to let her down."

I snickered and took a long sip through the straw, giving myself brain freeze in the process.

"Oww," I said, putting my hand to my forehead. As if that demonstrated my position in life, I continued. "Look at me. I'm 27, drinking well drinks at a casino where I'm one of the only people not on an oxygen tank. I write stories that no one reads and pray that someone either steals or totals my car because I don't want to have to pay to get the radiator fixed. I'm not exactly the shining definition of success. Everyone expected a lot more from me. I was supposed to be a doctor- or at the very least, try to startup my own Internet company."

He looked at me, smiling and shaking his head, looking away.

"Ha! You looked away! You're lying to me. Can *I* take the detectives exam? I'll be Benson and you can be Stabler."

He mumbled something in reply but I couldn't make it out. I threw a piece of ice at him.

"Speak up or I'll show you my interrogation techniques. I know they have toothpicks around here. Olivia Mizra, much like Olivia Benson, does *not* mess around."

"It's just that...you are perfect," he said. "You grew up to be this perfect, amazing person. You're smart, you're funny, you're beautiful- and you can *challenge* me."

"You mean to like a duel?" I asked, chomping down on a piece of ice.

"No, you know what I mean. You can challenge me on an intellectual level."

"No one wants that," I scoffed.

"Yes they do," he replied. "I wish I had that."

Normally I'd have more tact, but the crappy vodka took away my inhibitions. "What's wrong with your wife?"

"Nothing. She's sweet, kind, a good mother- but she's just a doormat. Every day with her is the same."

I snickered. "*You* broke up with me. You thought you were going to go out and find this chupacabra- some magical unicorn that was a Victoria's Secret supermodel who performed brain surgery for charity and did standup comedy on the side. I wasn't good enough for you."

"That's not the reason."

"Really?" I narrowed my eyes into slits. "Then what is?"

"Your insecurities drove me fucking crazy!" he almost shouted. "You worried so much about impressing other people- including me- that I couldn't handle it anymore. It wasn't sexy. I told you so. I loved you since you were 14, but you refused to acknowledge that. If me caring for you wasn't good enough, then I was going to spend a *very* long time trying to please you."

I rolled my eyes. "Save the psychobabble for your wife's self-help magazines. You think that I'm just one of the dumb girls you used to charm? I know who I am, okay? I know that I'm not exactly anyone's first round draft pick." I shoved my straw into the ice, angrily.

"Olivia, I'm trying to talk to you," he said as he reached across the table and took my hand and slid closer to me in the booth. I could smell his cologne- he smelled good. I tried not to think about it.

"I don't need your advice," I said.

I expected a quip from him, but he just leaned back and smiled. "Look at you- you're really something else. You're exactly the same, but so different."

"I'm totally different," I said. "Before we even started the absolute disaster that was our short-lived relationship, you told me that there was no such thing as love- you said everyone was going to screw you over, so why not get there first? You taught me almost everything I know- every coping mechanism, every strategy I needed to prevent myself from getting hurt again." I sipped the rest of my drink. "If anything, *you made me*. I'm your fucked up creation. I'm your sexy Frankenstein."

I crossed my arms and stared at him.

He looked down and shook his head. "It was a long time ago." The waitress came and this time he paid her, mumbling something about needing to go outside and smoke.

"Oh really, was it? You were 25. I'm 27 now. I'm not much older than you were when you told me all this. I *am* you. Now how does that make you feel?"

He shook his head as we got up from the table and put on our coats. As we walked towards the back exit door that overlooked the river, we passed the casino.

"You gamble?" he asked.

"Sure, roulette mostly. I always quit when I'm ahead though- something else you taught me."

I could tell by his facial expression that the comment smarted.

"Well why don't we give it a few spins?" he asked.
I rolled my eyes. "Dollar stakes? Seriously? I ought to be playing my grandma for oyster crackers."

We walked in and headed to the first table. It was a Monday night, so the crowd was sparse. He put down two twenty-dollar bills and she handed us the stacks of chips. He gave me half his stack. I looked at the board and put five dollars on black, one on the number five, one on the corner of the five through nine spot, one on 16, one on the corner of 26-29, and one on the corner of 20-24. Jeremy placed one of his on the 5 on top of mine and kept the rest in the lower numbers. She spun the wheel. It landed on 20. I clapped and collected my winnings. This went on for a while. I already was up $10 and getting bored. I needed to go to the restroom too. I put five on number five, and scattered the remaining

480

five around the board. Jeremy gingerly placed two chips on top of my five. She spun the wheel. It landed on five. We jumped up and shrieked, hugging each other and collecting our chips.

I tweeted and Instagrammed a picture of my chips.

Five on the five FTW.

By the time we got outside, I was fairly sober, but not ready to go home yet. Plus, Ashley wasn't there, so there was no rush. We sat outside on a bench and looked at the Christmas lights from Windsor sparkling on the water.

"Do you go out downtown a lot?" he asked.

"Yeah, usually- I like this new place- the Avalon."

"In a noisy bar in Avalon I tried to call you. But on a midnight watch I realized Why twice you ran away," he said.

"Huh?" I asked.

"It's a song- Southern Cross. Listen to it. You'll like it."

"Is it another 80's reference?" I asked, rolling my eyes.

"Yes," he laughed. "But good music never dies."

"So why did you always bet on five?" he asked me.

"Why did you?" I retorted.

"I asked first."

I shrugged. "Lucky number I guess. You?"

"Cinco de Mayo," he responded.

"Because you're Mexican?" I asked. "Not being racist, but why?"

"It's the night that I realized I loved you. You had those margaritas and you wore that white dress with the pink belt."

"You remember what I wore?"

"Everything," he said. "Your phone was that stupid ringtone- that Pussycat Dolls song. I wanted to smash it against the wall every time I heard it."

I giggled. "But I'd just keep singing along. *Don't ya wish your girlfriend was hot like me?*"

I wrapped my arms around me, shivering. He took off his coat and put it across my shoulders.

"I'm not taking your coat," I said.

"Yes you are."

I didn't argue.

"Olivia, I thought about what you said back there. You're all grown up, but you're still the same."

I started to interrupt him, but he silenced me. "It's not a bad thing. You've got the best parts of me, but the worst too. Now maybe you're done trying to please your parents, but you're still trying to please everyone else."

"Look, you don't under-"

"Not now. I'm talking."

I closed my mouth and let him continue.

"You always say that you want to be a writer, but why haven't you even sent out your book to anyone?"

"How do you *know* I've written a book?"

"Ha, because you've been writing since you were 14 and journaling in your Backstreet Boys notebook."

I shrugged. He was right. On both counts.

"So stop fucking worrying about everyone and just start doing what you want!" he yelled, temporarily startling me. "Fuck all this stupid superficial bullshit. Who cares that you hang out with Paul Jacobi? I know you had it rough growing up, but Jesus, you totally overcompensated- and that's not good either. You tried to become what you thought I wanted- what your friends wanted, and now probably what your fiancé

483

wants. It's too late for me, but it isn't for me. This is your life. Not anyone else's."

I bit my lip, but the tears rolled out the corner of my eye.

"Oh damn, I didn't mean to make you cry," he said, wrapping his arms around me as I leaned into his chest and started sobbing.

"It's not too late," he said as he stroked my hair.

December 16

I don't know what is going on with Ashley. He barely
talks to me anymore. He's pissed off at everything.
Tonight was a prime example of that.

I pulled up to the house, my nerves tightening in my
stomach. Over the last few weeks, I've developed a
horrible anxiety about coming home. I don't know if I'm
going to get yelled at or get the silent treatment. At least
when I get yelled at, I know what I did wrong. Part of
me wonders if he has another girl on the side, but part
of me doesn't care. Maybe he needs to get it out of his
system before he gets married. I just can't fathom who it
would be. There's not a single flight attendant who I'd
stress about. Maybe there's a new one? Maybe she's
skinnier and prettier than me. I don't know.

All he does is yell at me. I showed him the green dress I
was going to wear to the party and he just yelled at me
and called me a gold-digging whore. The dress only cost
$45! When I questioned him for specifics, he said all
women were gold-digging whores and nobody listens to
him. What does that even mean? He went in the other
room, slammed the door, and that was that. I want to
kill myself right now. I can't even fathom a reason to live
without Ashley. Without him, I'm nothing- a middle age
failure at life.

Other than that, things at work are going well. I'm
writing mostly about holiday fairs, Christmas lights, hair
shows, and other such frivolous matters. Tyler enjoys
making snide remarks about my newfound friendship

with Paul Jacobi and company, but secretly relishes hearing about Paul's receding hairline.

Our stories are full of sunshine, happiness, and non-controversial. Mr. Broussard is pleased.

Part III: As it Seems

Well I lost my innocence when in I let him dive
But the way that he looked at me
Made me feel alive
And now I know
Nothin' at all
But the release that comes when you're
In mid fall...

In mid fall
In mid fall
In mid fall

Cause in this life you must find something to live for
Cause when the darkness comes a callin'
You'll go back to where you were before
Cause this life is as
Fragile as a dream, and
Nothing's ever really
As it seems...

-Lily Kershaw, As it Seems

Electronic Journal of Tiffany Harris

File Name: Tiff's Life: 2014 edition

December 16, 11:48 p.m.

Our last assignment for class asks us to write about what has influenced us and made us into the person we are and where we look for inspiration to keep growing. It's supposed to be a sort of final reflection. I sigh and try to think of something to say.

My influences come from a variety of places- from my family to my friends. All of my life I've been told that I wasn't good enough and I let it beat me down. It wore me down into nothingness. The constant bullying, snide remarks, put-downs- they've all degraded me until I feel that I am absolutely nothing. I used to think that people were right about me until I met someone special and he showed me that I was amazing. He is truly an amazing man and I couldn't imagine life without him.

I have done some horrible things in the past. I have a cabinet full of pain medicines that I used to use to self-medicate when things go too tough. If I had one person who told me that I was OK the way I was (and didn't have ulterior motives for doing so), my life might have ended up differently. But this is me. This is who I am. I hope that it's not too late to turn it around.

December 17

I legitimately do not have time for some stupid hippie B.S. assignment. The last question literally asks:

What influences have developed you both personally and professionally? What experiences have "made" you- either good or bad? What do you think you can learn from these experiences in the future?

Ugh. I'd rather stab my eyes out with hot pokers. I walked into the kitchen and poured myself a glass of lemonade before lying down on the bed to start typing. I cannot wait until Christmas break when I have a little free time.

In my short life, I've had more negative influences and experiences than positive. From a rough childhood to a mediocre adulthood, I've failed more times than I've been successful. This failure has probably been my biggest influence. While some people who experience the same failures and struggles that I have turn to drugs, alcohol, or self-destructive behavior, my coping mechanism became hard work.

Very few people have ever given me positive feedback. It's gotten to the point where I don't know what to do when I get positive feedback- when someone pays me a compliment. I assume they usually want something- and rightfully so. Most times they do.

I've taken everything negative and internalized it in such a manner that my reaction to the negative has manifested itself in my personality. Every single barb, jab, or insult has made me into who I am.

I took a sip of lemonade, tapped my fingers on the side of the keyboard and thought about what to say next. My phone buzzed and I looked down. It was Carmine.

8:13 p.m.

Carmine: Have you talked to Tony recently???

8:19 p.m.
Olivia: Not for a few days. Why?

8:23 p.m.

Carmine: Can't find him. No worries. Just wondering.

I tossed my phone on my bed. I had way more important things to do than wonder what Tony, the ultimate douche canoe, was doing.

I thought that if I pleased other people that I'd be whole. I've come to realize that you can't please everyone. I'm not sure really who I am anymore. I don't know what kinds of hobbies I'd have, what kinds of music I'd like, or even what career path I'd have taken if I hadn't tried to impress someone else.

I always say that I'm not a victim. I say this because I've never dealt with depression or any of the common clichés of victimhood- depression, feelings of helplessness, whatever. But maybe I'm a victim of my own beliefs and actions. I've driven myself to the point of madness in an effort to be what everyone else wants me to be. Nobody forced me to get on that treadmill and run for two hours. Nobody shoved a finger down my throat.

A wise person once said, "I'll always defend you from your worst enemies- even when that enemy is yourself." At the time it just seemed like a really sweet comment, but now I see that I've always been my own worst enemy.

I've taken my insecurities out on more people than I care to remember. I've hurt a lot of people in my life. I can't take back the things I've said or done, but I can be a better person- a better daughter, friend, and eventually, a wife.

I just hope it's not too late.

December 17, 10:02 p.m.

I don't know what to do. Today is probably officially the worst day of my life. I've never been so broke down, devastated, rejected in my entire life. Who the hell did I think that I was? I'm nobody. I'll never be anybody. I was so stupid to think otherwise.

I had delusions of grandeur, or I guess I should say disillusions. What did I think was going to happen? That we were going to get married, move to Novi, and live happily ever after??? Now I'm in a worse bind than ever before.

I'm pregnant.

Ashley of course, wants nothing to do with it. He questions whether or not it's even his (which it is obviously) and told me he'd give me whatever money I needed to "take care of the problem."

Doesn't he see that I don't want to take care of any problems? I just want his love- the kind of love that I know we could have if his stupid bitch fiancé wasn't in the way. Who the fuck does she think she is anyways? Fucking cunt. She doesn't even appreciate him the way I do.

I'm going to find out who she is. Ashley doesn't have a Facebook (or so he says- I haven't been able to find one). Then I'm going to tell her the truth. She'll leave him, so he won't have to feel the guilt. Oh sure, he'll probably be mad at me, but he'll forgive me soon

enough. He told me what she's wearing to this party-
dark green dress with low neckline and silver trim.
Sounds like a slutty Christmas tree.

I'm ecstatic and want to announce my big news to the
world, but I'm heartbroken and filled with rage all at the
same time.

I don't know what I'm gonna do if he rejects me. I look
at my collection of pills- sleeping pills, antidepressants,
muscle relaxers. I think of going into the garage and
turning the car on. Just going to sleep. I can't imagine
life without Ashley.

I won't imagine life without him.

December 18, 2 p.m.

Wow, just wow. That's all I can say. I woke up this morning to more frantic calls looking for Tony. I don't know why anyone would think that he called me since we're not all that tight. I suggested to Carmine that he might have lost his phone, but they said they went by his house and no one was there. No one had seen him for three days I guess. And he's not exactly the kind of person who goes off on a wilderness adventure a la Bear Grylls.

It was about ten in the morning and Tyler and I were scouring emails sent in by readers showcasing their best holiday light displays. I got a call from Carmine on my phone.

'That's weird,' I thought to myself. *'He never calls me during the day, plus I think he's on a 12 hour shift at the firehouse. He probably pocket dialed me.'*

I hit the ignore button and set my phone off to the side. It vibrated a second later showing that Carmine had left a message.

"Ooh, looks like *someone* has a call from the great Carmine Vincent," Tyler mocked. "You sure you don't want to answer that? Don't you guys have someone to mock or do you wait until lunchtime to do that?" he asked.

I rolled my eyes. I was getting kind of sick of Tyler's sarcasm. Sure, Paul Jacobi was an asshole to Tyler back in high school, but Carmine wasn't involved. Tyler's chip on his shoulder was seriously working my last nerve.

It buzzed again, this time showing a text message from Carmine.

Call me. Now.

Tyler leaned in, reading it. "Ooh, he used capitalization. Shit must be getting real. I know someone *didn't* wear sweats to school. Those fatties!"

I picked it up to call Carmine, but first looked at Tyler.

"Why don't you go get a coffee?" I asked as I handed him a dollar.

"I'm good," he said, patting his stomach. "Maybe if I get a six-pack by the summer, I can come on Paul's *fabulous* boat on Lake St. Clair this summer."

"Seriously. Five minutes. Please?" I asked.

"Fine," he huffed. "I guess I need to go through fraternity initiation to be privy to these conversations. Sigh. I'll go find a paddle and a goat." With that, he got up and stomped out of the office.

I dialed the phone.

"*What?*" I hissed before Carmine had a chance to say hello.

"Hello to you too," he responded shortly. I could hear the din of the firehouse in the background.

"What do you *want*? I'm at work."

"We found Tony. In one of his dad's storage units. He parked his car in there and turned on the ignition. The night security guard smelled something burning and called 911. By the time they broke in and found him, he was barely conscious and strung out on drugs."

"*What?*" I screamed before lowering my voice and cupping my hand over the receiver. "*Are you serious?*"

"Yeah. He's on his way to Brighton now I guess."

(Brighton is commonly referred to the large rehab facility located in Brighton, Michigan.)

"Jesus. Did you know about this?"

"I knew he was bummed out," Carmine replied, pausing to yell at someone to load something on a truck.

"About what?" I asked, not even bothering with tact.

"You know he lost that big entertainment lawyer job out in L.A., right? He lost a lot of money and was super depressed about having to work for his dad. I guess he owed some bookie in Windsor a lot of money too."

 In the background, I heard a loud bang. "Hey, I gotta go," he said. "Don't tell anyone, OK?"

"I won't," I replied. "Tony's gonna be okay, though, right?"

"Yeah I think so. I gotta go."

With that, he hung up and I sat there in a state of shock. How could this have happened to *Tony Muscarella*? He had everything- money, looks, friends-

My thoughts were interrupted by Tyler, who came in and set half of a Twix bar on my desk.

"Thanks," I mumbled, picking it up.

"Trouble in paradise?" he asked, opening another email, this one containing a photo of Christmas lights arranged in the Lions logo. "Did mommy and daddy forget to put money in Tony's account?"

"How do you know I was talking about Tony?"

"I caught the tail end. So what happened? You're an insider now- you know all the juicy details. Did they screw up the custom paint job on his Range Rover? When will poor people *ever* learn to do a job right? Hashtag rich boy problems. The struggle is real."

"Shut up," I mumbled. "You don't know anything. Let's just get back to work, okay?" I pointed to the screen. "I like that one. Let's save it."

"My, my, Olivia, look at *you*. How your loyalties have changed. It seems you forget what those people did to you."

"It was a long time ago. Let's just drop it," I responded, defensive as I crossed my arms in front of my chest and tugged on my sleeves.

I guess he knew enough to back off because he did. It didn't matter. By lunchtime, everyone knew what happened- it was all over Facebook and Twitter.

Someone had even created a hash tag - #richguyproblems, lamenting the so-called tribulations that led to Tony's demise. Tyler relished reading them out loud, which I guess he should.

He wrote half of them.

December 18, 4 p.m.

And I wonder if this is what rock bottom feels like. I haven't stopped crying for 14 hours. I didn't know it was possible to cry this long. How is it possible for one person to hurt another so badly? It's not how long I knew him- hell, I barely knew him at all. But I thought he cared about me. I thought he cared about who I was- not for some arbitrary, physical reason. I thought he was that one person whose friendship was unconditional. I guess I was wrong. Who am I to think that someone could possibly care about me without having their own angle? I know I'll never be anything more than a pawn in some fucked up game. He's right. I'm not naturally pretty. In fact, I'm horribly ugly. Did I really think that plastic surgery would make this better?

Everyone says that his wife is so fucking beautiful. If she was, why did he sleep with me? We're going to have a *child* together. That's a bond that he and her will never have. He said that I *listened* to him! That he just wanted to be loved. Well, I *did* love him. Even though I only knew him a short while, I loved him with all my heart and soul. I can't afford another child and I know that if I have this baby, I won't be able to fly, so I'll lose pay. I can't afford that, but I can't bear the thought of getting an abortion. He's offered to pay the cost, plus an additional $500. I could really use the money, but my morals tell me it's wrong.

I'm not the only person with problems- just today, Tony Muscarella, the golden boy of Grosse Pointe, tried to kill himself. No one has it easy.

I think I know what I have to do. I have to tell his wife
the truth. There's a huge Christmas party on Friday. I'll
tell her then. Maybe she'll leave him and we'll be able to
be together- he doesn't really love her anyways. Now
that I've talked myself through it, this is a dream come
true. I knew that I'd find true love eventually- all the
years of torment and anguish- look at me- I'm going to
marry a pilot!

December 19

Ugh, I do not want to go to this stupid party tomorrow night.
Ever since I voluntarily ostracized myself from his friend's
wives, I haven't had the urge to go back. Judge-y bitches. Who
needs them? At least Christine is going to the party. Her dad
is one of the senior pilots.

I keep thinking about what Jeremy said to me. Was he right?
Did I just become this manifestation of what everyone else
wanted me to be? If that was right, then what's real and
what's fake about me?

I needed to find something to go with the dress for the party.
I walked over to my dresser and began running my thumb
over a wooden bracelet. I got that because Cody liked it. I
opened my mini heart-shaped box with sorority letters
emblazoned on it and rolled my eyes at the cheesiness of it
all. Why did I ever want to join a sorority anyways? I wasn't
really friends with anyone in it. You don't buy your friends
when you join the Greek system- you buy the illusion of
friendship. The stupid matching shirts, pins, necklaces- it was
all just some sort of façade designed to give the appearance
of love, caring, and kindness. As fucked up as it sounds, even
as an 18-year-old girl, I didn't learn true friendship from girls
who dressed the same as me- I learned it from Jeremy, a self-
described "fucked in the head," tattooed guy who was almost
five years my senior and actually had a Facebook group
whose members were dedicated to talking about what an
asshole he was.

I untangled two necklaces- one was my Russian stacking doll
necklace. My mom had gotten my sister and I each one. I had
the big one and she had the smaller one. I doubt she even
still has hers.

In a perfect world, I'd be best friends with my sister, go to brunch with my sorority girlfriends and then come home to my perfect husband and kids. I'd occasionally meet new age-appropriate friends with similar interests and intellectual capabilities at book clubs and we'd have dinner parties with them.

But life isn't perfect. My best friends aren't the people who I should aspire to be like. My best friends are the most flawed group of individuals you could possibly imagine. My little band of merry misfits apparently includes ex-boyfriends, the guys who used to taunt me in high school, a girl who isn't aware that there used to be an East and West Germany, an insecure ex-cheerleader, snarky gay guys- the list goes on.

I picked up the box with the sorority letters and dumped out the contents. Amongst it was a simple silver necklace with a cross and an own charm on it. Jeremy bought it for me before we even started dating. He called me the "wise owl" because I used to hustle for extra cash writing term papers. It probably wasn't worth more than $20, but for some reason I wanted to wear it. I texted Christine.

Olivia: Can I swap dresses we were going to wear to that party? You can wear my green one, but I want to wear your black one with the high neckline.

Christine: Sure, but why?

Olivia: I have some accessories I think would look good with it.

Christine: Fine, suit yourself.

DETROIT POLICE DEPARTMENT INTERVIEW
#07013091
Case 07013091

Case Number

07013091

Item Number

317

Pouch Number

5 of 81

Evidence Room Location # 19C

Description of Evidence

Cell phone records of Tiffany Harris

	Date Recovered
Detroit Police Department	21 December

10:04 p.m.

Tiffany: Why didn't you tell her about us?

Ashley: I told you- I'm NOT leaving her!

Tiffany: We're going to have a baby!

Ashley: No WE are not. If it even is mine, you won't see more than $700 a month in child support.

504

Tiffany: I thought you cared about me!

10:07 p.m.

Ashley: Please stop texting me. I have to smooth things over with Olivia.

10:34 p.m.

Ashley: Did you know her?

Case Number

07013091

||||||||||||||||||||||||||||||||||

Item Number

314

|||||||||||||||||||||||

Pouch Number

5 of 81

Evidence Room Location # 19C

Description of Evidence

Social media records of Tiffany Harris, retrieved from cell phone

	Date Recovered
Detroit Police Department	21 December

Tiffany Harris's Facebook post:

"A penny for my thoughts, oh no, I'll sell them for a dollar. They're worth so much more after I'm a goner. And maybe you'll hear- the words I've been saying. Funny when you're dead how people start listening."

3 likes

Comments:
Jenelle Houston: Are u ok? Call me!

Angie DeMateo: I luuuuuvvvv that jam! Merry Christmas biotch!

Gina Stephonophelous: Why r u sad? Holla at me girl!

Case Number

07013091

||| |||||| ||| ||||| ||| ||||||| |||

Item Number

317

||| |||||| ||||| ||||| |||

Pouch Number

5 of 81

Evidence Room Location # 19C

Description of Evidence

Cell phone records of Tiffany Harris

	Date Recovered
Detroit Police Department	21 December

10:37 p.m.

Ashley: Did you know Olivia???

10:39 p.m.

Ashley: Seriously- this isn't fucking funny. How the fuck do you know my wife? I only caught part of a message- she was screaming about you screwing her over twice

10:43 p.m.

Ashley: This is not a fucking joke. You need to answer my goddamn calls.

10:47 p.m.

Ashley: Where the FUCK are you? If you think that you can just stir some shit up and then peace out, you have another thing coming.

10:50 p.m.

Ashley: Answer your goddamn phone.

10:55 p.m.

Ashley: I can't find Olivia. My gun is gone. If she kills herself, her blood is on YOUR hands.

10:57 p.m.

Ashley: I just called the police and put an APB out for her car. It has OnStar, so goddamn it, she better be found alive.

11:00 p.m.

Ashley: If you made my wife kill herself, I swear to God, I'll ruin you, you miserable bitch.

DETROIT POLICE DEPARTMENT INTERVIEW WITH
CHRISTINE JORDAN

Case 07013091

Interview December 21, 0245 EST

Detective Polizzi: Please state your name for the record.

CJ: Christine Sophia Jordan

DP: Please state your address.

CJ: [Redacted]

DP: Tell me what happened tonight.

CJ: Olivia and I-

DP: Ms. Mizra, I assume?

CJ: Um, yeah...well we were at this thing. My dad
        works for the airlines and so does her fiancé so we
        were at this party and some crazy lady- like a flight
        attendant or ticket counter lady- comes up to me
        and says she has to talk to me. But I've never seen

her before. So I said I would, but wanted Olivia to come with me.

DP: Why did you ask Olivia?

CJ: I don't know- in case she was crazy. My dad had a stalker once.

DP: Okay, so you find Ms. Mizra and the two of you found a quiet area with Ms. Harris?

CJ: Yeah, and it was weird- Olivia shows up and she looks at this woman and she asks her what her name is. The chick says it's Tiffany and Olivia kind of snorts and makes some snotty comment about what an epic failure this chick's become. So I don't know the back story, but I let Olivia get a few jabs in before I stop her.

DP: What did she say?

CJ: I don't remember…something about the poster child for welfare dependency and the obesity epidemic…it was weird….Olivia usually doesn't just lay into people, but then I realize they must have gone to high school together.

DP: What happened next?

CJ: This woman- this Tiffany- she says something to the nature of "I have to talk to you. It's about your fiancé." But I tell her that I don't even have a boyfriend.

DP: Then what happened?

CJ: Olivia called her a moron and we started to walk away, but she stopped us and said "I'm pregnant."

DP: What did Ms. Mizra do?

CJ: She kind of snorted and said something like "color me shocked" and asked if Tiffany knew who the father was. She said, "not now Oda. This is important." I don't even know what an Oda is. Maybe it's whatever language Olivia speaks, but she says, "It's your fiancé- Ashley. I saw your picture in his wallet and he told me what you'd be wearing. I'm sorry, but we're in love."

DP: What did Olivia say?

CJ: She was like…super shocked. She looked like she'd been punched, but she didn't yell. It was scary how calm she was. So she said something like, "No, he doesn't love you. He doesn't love anyone but himself. You're just a fat, white trash piece of ass- nothing more than a seven minute regret. That's all you'll ever be." So then Tiffany is totally crying, but still not sure why Olivia is involved. She said-

DP: Who said? Tiffany?

CJ: Yeah, she said that maybe she (Tiffany) made mistakes and maybe she whored herself out, but Olivia sold herself out and look where that got her.

DP: And this is where Ms. Mizra struck her?

CJ: Yeah- Tiffany thought that I was Ashley's wife and was still looking at me and so she was blindsided by Olivia. She hit hard- I definitely heard a crack, but I don't know if it was from Olivia's hand or Tiffany's face. Then Olivia literally turned and ran. I couldn't catch her.

513

DETROIT POLICE DEPARTMENT INTERVIEW

#07013091

Case 07013091

DETROIT POLICE DEPARTMENT INTERVIEW WITH JEREMY MONTOYA
Case 07013091

Interview December 21, 0256 EST

Detective Polizzi: Officer Montoya, I'm sorry to have to bring you in like this, but you know that it's just procedure.

JM: Yeah, man, I know. I don't have to call my union rep, right?

DP: No man, just want to know what happened. I understand Ms. Mizra called you, upset apparently.

JM: Yeah, I mean, I hadn't talked to her in a while, but we sort of reconnected- just as friends you know. She called me and I kind of got the gist of what went down. I told her to pull over, that it wasn't safe to drive in that part of town or as upset as she was. She said she had her fiancé's weapon. I mean, she has a permit, but I didn't want her alone.

DP: Do you think she was in her right mind?

514

JM: She wasn't crazy or drunk or delusional if that's what you're asking. She was upset- and understandably so. I kept trying to talk her through it and ask where she was going. I could tell she was in a car. She said she was just driving. I told her to meet me. She said she didn't want me to see her like that. So I suggested that she call this Tiffany person and try to talk things through.

DP: What did Ms. Mizra say to that?

CJ: She said she didn't have the whore's number, but then just said, "wait a second" or something and hung up on me. She didn't answer any more of my calls.

DETROIT POLICE DEPARTMENT INTERVIEW WITH CARMINE VINCENT, JR.

Case 07013091

Interview December 21, 0317 EST

Detective Polizzi: So, let me get this straight: Ms. Mizra called you before calling 911? Am I correct?

CV: Yeah, I guess. I told her to call 911.

DP: What did she say?

CV: I don't remember...she was freaking out...said Tiffany was dead...something about the bet, a curse... I didn't even know who Tiffany was at first.

DP: But you went to high school with Ms. Harris, right? Is that my understanding? That you all somehow, uh, knew each other?

CV: I mean, I guess. I kinda remember her now, but...[inaudible]. Fuck, I had no idea what Olivia was doing there down in the ghetto.

DP: Have you ever seen Ms. Mizra use a weapon?

CV: No. [Suspect shakes head.] She said she had a gun and knew how to use it, but just had it cuz [sic] of all the break-ins...she didn't shoot anyone, right? Her ex-boyfriend just said you tested her hands for gunshot residue and it was negative. She's innocent, right?

DP: I can't comment on an ongoing investigation, but I'm just trying to piece together what happened tonight. So far I have that she went to a party, got upset, placed a five minute call to you, then didn't answer another call for an hour until she called you, again, for a minute, then called 911.

CV: I guess.

DP: How did you get that black eye?

CV: Let's just say that two of your detectives had to pull her ex-fiancé and I apart in the lobby.

DP: [Inaudible sigh] So were you and Ms. Mizra romantically involved?

CV: No, it wasn't like that. But she deserved better than
        that asshole. She-

[Interrupted by knocking]

-Interview ended-

DETROIT POLICE DEPARTMENT INTERVIEW WITH
LYNDSAY SMYTH
Case 07013091

Interview December 21, 0431 EST

Detective Polizzi: Ms. Smith…am I saying it right?

LS: Yes. [crying]

DP: What happened?

LS: Tiffany was pregnant with that pilot- Ashley's- child.
        She was going to confront his fiancé at the
        Christmas party.

DP: So she followed her into the bathroom?

LS: Yea- so she walks up to her and-

DP: Her? Olivia?

LS: No, the blonde one. She thought that was his
        fiancé. They go into a corner and I can't hear much,
        but Tiffany she starts to say something and it's
        obvious that Olivia and her friend are drunk and

Tiffany's like...in shock...she didn't realize she knew her. They were friends I guess in high school- so Tiffany tells Olivia who she is and Olivia goes into full on super bitch mode, right?

DP: Can you explain what that means?

LS: She just sorta starts cackling, right? And then she called Tiffany something like a white trash single mom cliché and advises her to stop chasing pilots. I saw Olivia knock her out. Then her friend- the blonde one- says something about Tiffany being better off dead and they just leave.

DP: Did you see Tiffany talk to her later?

LS: She went to go follow her, but then I don't know. She called me but it went to voicemail. She was crying saying something about how Ashley said she would be worth more to her kids dead.

DP: Do you all have life insurance?

LS: Uh-huh, we get it automatically when we get hired. Like a hundred thousand.

521

TIME Magazine
March 17, 2015

Detroit, MI- A fire at an abandoned warehouse has claimed the lives of at least 13 victims including three Detroit firemen, two Detroit police officers, and one off-duty Indiana state trooper. At least 20 more people are listed in critical condition.

The fire, which began at a manufacturing plant located off of Ecorse Road, quickly spread to nearby facilities. The manufacturing facility was known as a place where homeless individuals "squatted." None of the facilities had been in operation since the late 1990s. Detroit Fire Marshall James Broadwell issued the following statement:

The abandoned structures, combined with an unseasonably dry winter, were both contributing factors in last night's tragic fire. A preliminary investigation has led us to believe that this is the work of an arsonist. Our thoughts and prayers are with the victims' families.

The victims so far include Frank Jernigan, 24, Carmine Vincent, 28, William Sutton, 36, Latrell Mack, 22, Leticia Hernandez, 27, Jeremy Montoya, 32, Mamie Shephard, 54, and George Willard, 68. The rest of the names will be released pending notification of the next of kin.

Anyone with information regarding the suspected arson should call the Detroit Police Department immediately.

This week's cover story is by breakout writer Octavia Marin, whose take on childhood and adult bullying has caused quite a controversy amongst experts everywhere. She will appear on the Today Show on Wednesday, March 18. Her weekly column appears in the Salt Lake City Daily newspaper.

There are No Bullies, Just People: Why we should stop putting labels on childhood (and adult) bullies

-By Octavia Marin

"You eat like a bird? Yeah, maybe a pterodactyl."

"She's so pathetic. It's like *The Devil Wears JC Penney* every day at work."

"It must be hard walking to the welfare office in those heels."

"Aren't you past your expiration date?"

"Feminist liberal hag."

"What did your tattoo used to be before you gained the freshman 50?"

"Have you considered Botox?"

"You're going to die alone."

"You should probably just kill yourself."

If these comments sound familiar to me, it's because half of them have been said to me....and I've said the other half.

Before you begin to start writing your hate mail, I implore you to read on, as my story is one that serves as the inspiration for people who may be going through what I went through- and as a cautionary tale for some who might be on the verge of making the same mistakes as I have. Bullying isn't a clear-cut epidemic between the bully and the victim. As my story shows, the line can become blurred. It's my hope that this essay will speak to those on both sides of the line.

Bullying has been with us since the beginning of mankind, long before Columbine, the event that largely brought "bullying" to light or the bizarre NFL drama that drew attention to "workplace bullying." It has been with us this long and it is not going anywhere, despite the efforts of school-implemented programs, workplace sensitivity trainings, or any other government regulation. That's right, I said that.

But that's not necessarily bad news.

My story started with moving to the United States and ended on the front page of the *Detroit Recorder*. People like to say that I am the kind of person who has gone from a childhood "victim" to an adult "bully." While I agree to a certain extent, it is naïve to place that sort of dichotomy or label on anyone.

My first experience with bullying occurred the day I moved to the United States. I was eight years old, sitting in front of my third grade class in Michigan, trying to whisper so that I wouldn't be mocked for my speech impediment or accent, which ended up being a fruitless endeavor as the kids found plenty of other things to mock me about.

"Where did you get your hair cut? Did your mom put a bowl over it?"

I spent my formative years as the brunt of other children's cruel jokes. Nothing was off-limits: my hair, clothes, speech. I faked sick so that I could go to the nurse's office as to avoid getting mocked at recess.

By the time I started high school, things had marginally improved for me until the one day when a boy who was "out of my league" offered me a ride home. I accepted, not knowing the consequences that it would have on my life. By the next day, I was a slut (despite never even kissing this boy, or any other). I was called fat, lazy, a whore. One girl called my house and left a threatening message on my parent's machine (this was before Facebook).

I recall crying and feeling hopeless, helpless, and depressed. There were days when I wished I wouldn't wake up. At times the only thing that kept me from contemplating suicide was knowing that I had a goal. For me, it was writing. I'd write blogs for my friends, stories that I dreamed would one day get published.

Although college was somewhat better, bullying was still prevalent. By the time I was accepted into the allegedly "Tier Two" sorority, I had been torn apart as a person by women who didn't even know me. Suddenly,

I was no longer Octavia, but "the obese rushee with a unibrow."

By the time I graduated, I had lost the weight and unibrow, but had acquired a huge chip on my shoulder. I felt that I had so much to prove that it became an obsession. I figured since the majority of people that I knew growing up only hurt and mocked me, then everyone must feel that way. I became bitter, antagonistic, and hateful. While I had learned to stand up for myself, I had crossed the line. Every interaction with people was a power struggle. I mercilessly mocked those who I perceived even maligned me in just the slightest. I went from retaliatory anger to complete passive-aggressive bullying. I used my gift of language to craft razor-sharp insults that cut to the core of people. I felt that the world was against me so why shouldn't I be against it?

I knew all about workplace bullying. At one of my jobs, four of us were likened to the starring characters in the *Mean Girls* movie. If one of us felt threatened by someone new, we adopted a pack mentality and made her life miserable until she quit.

Unfortunately, that wasn't what people saw when they looked at me. They saw not a victim, but a girl who enjoyed hurting people for her personal pleasure. Their perception was their reality, and in reality, I was a horrible bully.

The catalyst for change didn't come until about two months ago when I began writing a weekly opinion piece for a Utah newspaper.

Within a few hours of publication of my first writing, I was called selfish, immature, materialistic, and many names that can't be repeated in polite company.

People asked if I regret writing the articles.

Honestly, no. I know that any attempt to fight these anonymous cyber-bullies and their comments is be futile. Bullying isn't a 21st century phenomenon of bored millenials with too much time and too many gadgets. It's been going on since the beginning of mankind. If social scientists define bullying as repeated physical abuse or verbal intimidation by a bigger or stronger person towards a smaller or weaker one, then Cain slaying Abel was the first example of bullying in Biblical literature. The women of the Salem witch trials were all victims of bullies, as were the countless civil and human rights activists of the next century. On a smaller scale, most of us can recall our mothers and grandmothers gossiping about other women and struggling to exist within a power imbalance that unfortunately, often defines the feminine experience.

The epidemic isn't just limited to females. Recently a male friend, who I was somewhat close to, tried to end his life. There is no immunity from the hateful words of others. The only shield we have is our own belief system in ourselves.

 As for the article, the comments on the article were nothing new- they were just an electronic manifestation of what I, like many others, have dealt with my entire life.

Some people are always going to need to belittle others
to feel superior. Bullying doesn't stop once one turns 18.
It doesn't matter if it's in the schoolyard, in the locker
room, or an anonymous Internet forum. My 60-year-old
tenant gets bullied by other blue-haired ladies just as
much as a young girl in high school.

People assume that my articles are just about me. That's
not true. The articles are also about drawing a line in
the sand and learning to defy the clichés that others
have placed upon us. Everyday, people are criticized for
their weight, physical appearance, marital status,
income bracket, gender, race, and lifestyle choices.
People have bought into the idea that if we don't live up
to some abstract standard of perfection that we are
failures. Unfortunately, some of my peers have been
pushed to the ultimate brink and decided that it was
better to take their own lives than to continue on as a
"failure."

I'll never forget those first few hours as my columns
gained momentum and were reblogged in Utah, then
throughout the U.S. and Canada, and then abroad. As I
watched my childhood dream of writing for a major
media outlet unfold before my eyes, I also relived the
barbs, insults, and stings of the last 20 years. However, I
received hundreds of messages from supporters.

One memorable one read:

*"Thank you for giving us a voice. You said exactly what I
feel. I can relate. I thought I was alone, but I'm not."*

TIME Magazine
March 17, 2015

Mark Twain said, "the two most important days in your life are the day you are born and the day you find out why."

On that day, I found out why. I had been given this amazing opportunity to influence millions with my words.

I was able to blow off the more negative comments, but I'd be lying if I said that some didn't sting. However, on the flip side, the truth of the matter was that I'd said things way worse to people in my life, and I didn't even hide behind the anonymity of the Internet.

As I said previously, bullying isn't going to ever completely end. The government and schools can throw all of the money at it that they want. We can't ever control the actions of others. The only things that we can control are our own actions.

To those young people going through hard times, I won't lie and say that it gets better when you graduate. It is this: you have to have something to live for- a goal. Focus on that and don't ever let the words of others come between you and your goal.

If I could end this article on a positive note, it would be to send messages of hope to all readers:

No matter who you are, you are not a bully or a victim. You are an individual who has great things to offer this world. Whatever mistakes you've made or wrongs that you've endured are behind you now. It's never too late to change.

As for those who know that they are guilty of hurting others, think twice before using words or force against others. That person that you're bullying? That girl or guy that you're calling a cliché? You don't know their story. It could be your words that push someone over the edge. Ask yourself: Is temporarily gratifying your own self-indulgent mini-power trip is worth the life of another human being?

We all have the capacity for greatness or horrendous evil. I've learned that you can't control the other things that people say, and the only way to survive is to stop letting external entities- a co-worker, teammate, or an anonymous Internet blogger determine your self-worth.

A wise man once told me to stop living my life for other people. To do that is a cliché of the worst kind- for those are the actions of a coward who is too afraid to step into the light for fear of getting burned.

So many people close to me have died in the last few months. They gave the ultimate sacrifice in the battle of good vs. evil. Yet, their legacies live on in the lessons that they taught me.

Everyone has a gift. Find yours and use it for good. Mine is the gift of writing. I'm nobody, yet I'm everybody. My writing has allowed me to speak for Tiffany, Carmine, Jeremy, and the others who left us before their time.

I've thought a lot about what they would say if they were still here.

They would say that enough is enough. They would say that whoever you are, you're more than a cliché. They would tell you to be proud of who you are. It's never too late to change and to choose a more positive path.

I have chosen to take this path and rather to seek out means of selfish gratification to look for ways to help others. And most importantly, I will never turn my eyes away again.

www.ingramcontent.com/pod-product-compliance
Lightning Source LLC
Chambersburg PA
CBHW052347020726
47503CB00001B/143